Donald Stone

THE WORLD'S CLASSICS

578

THE LONGEST JOURNEY

Oxford University Press, Amen House, London E.C.4

GLASGOW   NEW YORK   TORONTO   MELBOURNE   WELLINGTON
BOMBAY   CALCUTTA   MADRAS   KARACHI   KUALA LUMPUR
CAPE TOWN   IBADAN   NAIROBI   ACCRA

E. M. FORSTER

THE LONGEST JOURNEY

*With an Introduction
by the author*

LONDON
OXFORD UNIVERSITY PRESS
1960

EDWARD MORGAN FORSTER

Born: 6 Melcombe Place, London, N.W., 1 January 1879

The Longest Journey, *first published in* 1907, *was
included in* The World's Classics *in* 1960

PRINTED IN GREAT BRITAIN

FRATRIBUS

CONTENTS

INTRODUCTION

The Longest Journey is the least popular of my five novels but the one I am most glad to have written. For in it I have managed to get nearer than elsewhere towards what was in my mind—or rather towards that junction of mind with heart where the creative impulse sparks. Thoughts and emotions collided if they did not always co-operate. I can remember writing it and how excited I was and how absorbed, and how sometimes I went wrong deliberately, as if the spirit of anti-literature had jogged my elbow. For all its faults, it is the only one of my books that has come upon me without my knowledge. Elsewhere I have had to look into the lumber-room of my past, and have found in it things that were useful to be sure; still I found them, they didn't find me, and the magic sense of being visited and of even returning the visit was absent.

So I am glad that the editor of the World's Classics should include it in the series, and should ask me to pen an introduction.

Where is my pen?

In an old diary, under the date of 18 July, 1904, it wrote as follows: 'An idea for another novel—that of a man who discovers that he has an illegitimate brother—took place since last Saturday.'

That is how the novel originated—and how frigidly! But it was not published until 1907, and during the interval several other ideas intervened to confuse or enrich the original theme. There was the metaphysical idea of Reality ('the cow is there'): there was the ethical idea that reality must be faced (Rickie won't face Stephen); there was the idea, or ideal, of the British Public School; there was the title, exhorting us in the words of Shelley not to love one person only; there was Cambridge, there was Wiltshire. I did not list the above notions consciously, but they were whirling around me as I wrote, and may well have impaired my sense of direction.

Let me try to isolate Wiltshire.

The 1904 diary records that on 12 September 'I walked out again to Figsbury Rings'. Much lies behind this entry. It recalls an emotional thrill which set my pen going. Figsbury Rings are about five miles east of Salisbury, and are just visible from the train as it runs down towards the city. As an antiquity they are unobtrusive. There is an outer circle of embankment and an inner circle, and in the centre is one small tree. The embankments are grassed, the rest of the area is planted with rotation of crops. I was then twenty-five years old, and had begun to warm to the Wiltshire downlands which I had hitherto condemned as bare and dull, and I caught fire up on the Rings. A similar experience had already befallen me in Italy and had produced my first short story. This time it wasn't just looking at a view, it was breathing the air and smelling the fields, and there was human reinforcement from the shepherds who grazed up there. They and I talked about nothing—still one of my favourite subjects; I offered a tip of sixpence which was declined, I was offered a pull at a pipe and had to decline. The whole experience was trivial in itself but vital to the novel, for it fructified my meagre conception of the half-brothers, and gave Stephen Wonham, the bastard, his home. Figsbury Rings became Cadbury Rings. The valley of the

Winterbourne below them turned into the Cad, a level crossing clanged, and that part of *The Longest Journey* was born. In a curious way it also gave birth. There was reciprocation—such as I discern in Matthew Arnold's poem of 'The Scholar Gipsy'. I received, I created, I restored, and for many years the Wiltshire landscape remained haunted by my fictional ghosts. Once I even tested the magic by staying with Lytton Strachey not very far from the Rings—an urbane and delightful host but not one to countenance fanciful transferences. He failed. The Rings survived, the Tree, the Tree remained, as it did for Matthew Arnold, though it was by no means his sort of tree.

Cambridge is the home of Rickie, the elder brother, the legitimate, his only true home: the Cambridge of G. E. Moore which I knew at the beginning of the century: the fearless uninfluential Cambridge that sought for reality and cared for truth. Ansell is the undergraduate high-priest of that local shrine, Agnes Pembroke is its deadly debunker. Captured by her and by Sawston, Rickie goes to pieces, and cannot even be rescued when Ansell joins up with Stephen and strikes. The Cambridge chapters are still romantic and crucial for me, and I still endorse Ansell's denunciation of the Great World.

There is no great world at all, only a little earth, for ever isolated from the rest of the little solar system. This little earth is full of tiny societies and Cambridge is one of them. All the societies are narrow, but some are good and some are bad—just as one house is beautiful inside and another is ugly. Observe the metaphor of the houses: I am coming back to it. The good societies say, 'I tell you to do this because I am Cambridge.' The bad ones say, 'I tell you to do that because I am the great world.' They lie. And fools like you listen to them, and believe that they are a thing which does not exist and never has existed, and confuse 'great', which has no meaning whatever, with 'good', which means salvation. Now for the other metaphor. To compare the world to Cambridge is like comparing the outsides of houses with the inside of a house. No intellectual effort is needed, no moral result is attained. You only have to say, 'Oh, what a difference! Oh, what a difference!' and then go indoors again and exhibit your broadened mind.

Sawston, which poses as the great world in miniature, need not detain us. It is the eternal home of Herbert and Agnes Pembroke, and owes something to my own public school. I was neither very happy nor very unhappy there—a Vardon who never got his ears pulled. The best of life began when I left it, and I am always puzzled when other elderly men reminisce over their respective public schools so excitedly, and compare them as if they were works of art: it sounds as if they must have had a dullish time since.

There were changes in the book as it proceeded, as is natural in a work so dispersedly conceived. Stephen was at one time called Harold and at another Siegfried, and there was a long fantasy-chapter about him, which I cancelled and will now epitomize. (It occurs near Chapter XII in the book.) He has made the unsuccessful expedition towards Salisbury and is riding back to Cadover alone. He comes to a pleasant place where the river is crossed by a railway bridge, dismounts, and bathes. An engine which is shunting stops on the bridge, and the engine-driver leans out and abuses him in the filthiest language for wearing no costume. The same thing once happened to my friend Lowes Dickinson in Herefordshire. Dickinson did not retaliate. Stephen does. Rushing up the embankment he storms the engine and spreads devastation with his fists. The fireman collapses, the engine moves on, and in a confused struggle he is thrown out on to the line. He is not hurt but is far from his clothes and his horse, thinks he knows a short cut home through the woods, loses his way, terrifies a picnic party, is terrified by a flock of sheep, panics, and cracks his head against a beech tree. When he comes to himself he is no longer himself but daft, fey, part of the woods, and the animals recognize him. He returns to his old life when he leaves the woods and sees Cadbury Rings and Rickie moving anxiously towards him, his arms piled high with honourable garments. (How Rickie knew he wanted them I forget.)

Only the flock of sheep survive out of this fantasy. Its work is more economically done by letting the boy fall asleep on the roof of Cadover, with the wind and the sun on him, murmuring 'good oh good . . .' and unable to read a short story about getting into touch with nature.

The Longest Journey dates, and poignantly. For the England that Stephen thought so good and seemed destined to inherit is done for. The growth of the population and the applications of science have destroyed her between them. There was a freshness and an out-of-door wildness in those days which the present generation cannot imagine. I am glad to have known our countryside before its roads were too dangerous to walk on and its rivers too dirty to bathe in, before its butterflies and wild flowers were decimated by arsenical spray, before Shakespeare's Avon frothed with detergents and the fish floated belly-up in the Cam.

As for the reviews. They were encouraging. One

of the reviewers—he was Will Beveridge I think—pleasantly calculated that the percentage of sudden deaths (infants excluded) amounted to over 44 per cent. of the adult population. But the book did not sell, and an uncle of mine, a meddlesome tease of a man, bought a number of remainders at sixpence each and sent them to those of my relations whom they were most likely to upset. It was this same uncle who, though sedulously masculine, gave me hints for the character of Mrs. Failing and whose house up in Northumberland provided the architecture and the atmosphere for Cadover.

E. M. FORSTER

PART ONE

CAMBRIDGE

———————◆———————

I

'The cow is there,' said Ansell, lighting a match
and holding it out over the carpet. No one spoke.
He waited till the end of the match fell off. Then he
said again, 'She is there, the cow. There, now.'

'You have not proved it,' said a voice.

'I have proved it to myself.'

'I have proved to myself that she isn't,' said the
voice. 'The cow is *not* there.' Ansell frowned and
lit another match.

'She's there for me,' he declared. 'I don't care
whether she's there for you or not. Whether I'm in
Cambridge or Iceland or dead, the cow will be
there.'

It was philosophy. They were discussing the
existence of objects. Do they exist only when there
is some one to look at them? or have they a real
existence of their own? It is all very interesting,
but at the same time it is difficult. Hence the cow.
She seemed to make things easier. She was so
familiar, so solid, that surely the truths that she
illustrated would in time become familiar and solid
also. Is the cow there or not? This was better than
deciding between objectivity and subjectivity. So

at Oxford, just at the same time, one was asking, 'What do our rooms look like in the vac.?'

'Look here, Ansell. I'm there—in the meadow— the cow's there. You're there—the cow's there. Do you agree so far?'

'Well?'

'Well, if you go, the cow stops; but if I go, the cow goes. Then what will happen if you stop and I go?'

Several voices cried out that this was quibbling.

'I know it is,' said the speaker brightly, and silence descended again, while they tried honestly to think the matter out.

Rickie, on whose carpet the matches were being dropped, did not like to join in the discussion. It was too difficult for him. He could not even quibble. If he spoke, he should simply make himself a fool. He preferred to listen, and to watch the tobacco-smoke stealing out past the window-seat into the tranquil October air. He could see the court too, and the college cat teasing the college tortoise, and the kitchen-men with supper-trays upon their heads. Hot food for one—that must be for the geographical don, who never came in for Hall; cold food for three, apparently at half a crown a head, for some one he did not know; hot food, *à la carte*—obviously for the ladies haunting the next staircase; cold food for two, at two shillings—going to Ansell's rooms for himself and Ansell, and as it passed under the lamp he saw that it was meringues again. Then the bedmakers began to arrive, chatting to each other pleasantly, and he could hear Ansell's bedmaker say, 'Oh dang!' when she found she had to lay Ansell's tablecloth; for there was not a breath stirring. The great elms were motionless, and seemed still in the glory of midsummer, for the darkness hid the yellow blotches on their leaves, and their outlines were still rounded against the tender sky. Those elms were Dryads—so Rickie believed or pretended, and the line between the two is subtler than we admit. At all events they were lady trees, and had for generations fooled the college statutes by their residence in the haunts of youth.

But what about the cow? He returned to her with a start, for this would never do. He also would try to think the matter out. Was she there or not? The cow. There or not. He strained his eyes into the night.

Either way it was attractive. If she was there, other cows were there too. The darkness of Europe was dotted with them, and in the far East their flanks were shining in the rising sun. Great herds of them stood browsing in pastures where no man came nor need ever come, or plashed knee-deep by the brink of impassable rivers. And this, moreover, was the view of Ansell. Yet Tilliard's view had a good deal in it. One might do worse than follow Tilliard, and suppose the cow not to be there unless oneself was there to see her. A cowless world, then, stretched round him on every side. Yet he had only to peep into a field, and, click! it would at once become radiant with bovine life.

Suddenly he realized that this, again, would never do. As usual, he had missed the whole point, and was overlaying philosophy with gross and senseless details. For if the cow was not there, the world and the fields were not there either. And what would Ansell care about sunlit flanks or impassable streams? Rickie rebuked his own grovelling soul, and turned his eyes away from the night, which had led him to such absurd conclusions.

The fire was dancing, and the shadow of Ansell, who stood close up to it, seemed to dominate the little room. He was still talking, or rather jerking, and he was still lighting matches and dropping their ends upon the carpet. Now and then he would make a motion with his feet as if he were running quickly backward upstairs, and would tread on the edge of the fender, so that the fire-irons went flying and the buttered-bun dishes crashed against each other in the hearth. The other philosophers were crouched in odd shapes on the sofa and table and chairs, and one, who was a little bored, had crawled to the piano and was timidly trying the Prelude to Rheingold with his knee upon the soft pedal. The air was heavy with good tobacco-smoke and the pleasant warmth of tea, and as Rickie became more sleepy the events of the day seemed to float one by one before his acquiescent eyes. In the morning he had read Theocritus, whom he believed to be the greatest of Greek poets; he had lunched with a merry don and had tasted Zwieback biscuits; then he had walked with people he liked, and had walked just long enough; and now his room was full of other people whom he liked, and when they left he would go and have supper with Ansell, whom he liked as well as any one. A year ago he had known none of these joys. He had crept cold and friendless and ignorant out of a great public school, preparing for a silent and solitary journey, and praying as a highest favour that he might be left alone. Cambridge had not answered his prayer. She had taken and soothed him, and warmed him, and had laughed at him a little, saying that he must not be so tragic yet awhile, for his boyhood had been but a dusty corridor that led to the spacious halls of youth. In one year he had made many friends and learnt much, and he might learn even more if he could but concentrate his attention on that cow.

The fire had died down, and in the gloom the man by the piano ventured to ask what would happen if an objective cow had a subjective calf. Ansell gave an angry sigh, and at that moment there was a tap on the door.

'Come in!' said Rickie.

The door opened. A tall young woman stood framed in the light that fell from the passage.

'Ladies!' whispered every one in great agitation.

'Yes?' he said nervously, limping towards the door (he was rather lame). 'Yes? Please come in. Can I be any good——'

'Wicked boy!' exclaimed the young lady, advancing a gloved finger into the room. 'Wicked, wicked boy!'

He clasped his head with his hands.

'Agnes! Oh how perfectly awful!'

'Wicked, intolerable boy!' She turned on the electric light. The philosophers were revealed with unpleasing suddenness. 'My goodness, a tea-party! Oh really, Rickie, you are too bad! I say again: wicked, abominable, intolerable boy! I'll have you horsewhipped. If you please'—she turned to the symposium, which had now risen to its feet—'If you please, he asks me and my brother for the week-end. We accept. At the station, no Rickie. We drive to where his old lodgings were—Trumpery Road or some such name—and he's left them. I'm furious, and before I can stop my brother, he's paid off the cab and there we are stranded. I've walked—walked for miles. Pray can you tell me what is to be done with Rickie?'

'He must indeed be horsewhipped,' said Tilliard pleasantly. Then he made a bolt for the door.

'Tilliard—do stop—let me introduce Miss Pembroke—don't all go!' For his friends were flying from his visitor like mists before the sun. 'Oh, Agnes, I am so sorry; I've nothing to say. I simply forgot you were coming, and everything about you.'

'Thank you, thank you! And how soon will you remember to ask where Herbert is?'

'Where is he, then?'

'I shall not tell you.'

'But didn't he walk with you?'

'I shall not tell, Rickie. It's part of your punishment. You are not really sorry yet. I shall punish you again later.'

She was quite right. Rickie was not as much upset as he ought to have been. He was sorry that he had forgotten, and that he had caused his visitors inconvenience. But he did not feel profoundly degraded, as a young man should who has acted discourteously to a young lady. Had he acted discourteously to his bedmaker or his gyp, he would have minded just as much, which was not polite of him.

'First, I'll go and get food. Do sit down and rest. Oh, let me introduce——'

Ansell was now the sole remnant of the discussion party. He still stood on the hearthrug with a burnt match in his hand. Miss Pembroke's arrival had never disturbed him.

'Let me introduce Mr. Ansell—Miss Pembroke.'

There came an awful moment—a moment when he almost regretted that he had a clever friend. Ansell remained absolutely motionless, moving neither hand nor head. Such behaviour is so unknown that Miss Pembroke did not realize what had happened, and kept her own hand stretched out longer than is maidenly.

'Coming to supper?' asked Ansell in low, grave tones.

'I don't think so,' said Rickie helplessly.

Ansell departed without another word.

'Don't mind us,' said Miss Pembroke pleasantly. 'Why shouldn't you keep your engagement with your friend? Herbert's finding lodgings,—that's why he's not here,—and they're sure to be able to give us some dinner. What jolly rooms you've got!'

'Oh no—not a bit. I say, I am sorry. I am sorry. I am most awfully sorry.'

'What about?'

'Ansell——' Then he burst forth. 'Ansell isn't a gentleman. His father's a draper. His uncles are farmers. He's here because he's so clever—just on account of his brains. Now, sit down. He isn't a gentleman at all.' And he hurried off to order some dinner.

'What a snob the boy is getting!' thought Agnes, a good deal mollified. It never struck her that those could be the words of affection—that Rickie would never have spoken them about a person whom he disliked. Nor did it strike her that Ansell's humble birth scarcely explained the quality of his rudeness. She was willing to find life full of trivialities. Six months ago and she might have minded; but now—she cared not what men might do unto her, for she had her own splendid lover, who could have knocked all these unhealthy undergraduates into a cocked-hat. She dared not tell Gerald a word of what had happened: he might have come up from wherever he was and half killed Ansell. And she determined not to tell her brother either, for her nature was kindly, and it pleased her to pass things over.

She took off her gloves, and then she took off her ear-rings and began to admire them. These ear-rings were a freak of hers—her only freak. She had always wanted some, and the day Gerald asked her to marry him she went to a shop and had her ears pierced. In some wonderful way she knew that it was right. And he had given her the rings—little gold knobs, copied, the jeweller told them, from something prehistoric—and he had kissed the spots of blood on her handkerchief. Herbert, as usual, had been shocked.

'I can't help it,' she cried, springing up. 'I'm not like other girls.' She began to pace about Rickie's room, for she hated to keep quiet. There was nothing much to see in it. The pictures were not attractive, nor did they attract her—school groups, Watts' 'Sir Percival,' a dog running after a rabbit, a man running after a maid, a cheap brown Madonna in a cheap green frame,—in short, a collection where one mediocrity was generally cancelled by another. Over the door there hung a long photograph of a city with waterways, which Agnes, who had never been to Venice, took to be Venice, but which people who had been to Stockholm knew to be Stockholm. Rickie's mother, looking rather sweet, was standing on the mantelpiece. Some more pictures had just arrived from the framers and were leaning with their faces to the wall, but she did not bother to turn them round. On the table were dirty teacups, a flat chocolate cake, and Omar Khayyám, with an Oswego biscuit between his pages. Also a vase filled with the crimson leaves of autumn. This made her smile.

Then she saw her host's shoes: he had left them lying on the sofa. Rickie was slightly deformed, and so the shoes were not the same size, and one of them had a thick heel to help him towards an even walk. 'Ugh!' she exclaimed, and removed them gingerly to the bedroom. There she saw other shoes and boots and pumps, a whole row of them, all deformed. 'Ugh! Poor boy! It is too bad. Why shouldn't he be like other people? This hereditary business is too awful.' She shut the door with a sigh. Then she recalled the perfect form of Gerald, his athletic walk, the poise of his shoulders, his arms stretched forward to receive her. Gradually she was comforted.

'I beg your pardon, miss, but might I ask how many to lay?' It was the bedmaker, Mrs. Aberdeen.

'Three, I think,' said Agnes, smiling pleasantly. 'Mr. Elliot 'll be back in a minute. He has gone to order dinner.'

'Thank you, miss.'

'Plenty of teacups to wash up!'

'But teacups is easy washing, particularly Mr. Elliot's.'

'Why are his so easy?'

'Because no nasty corners in them to hold the dirt. Mr. Anderson—he's below—has crinkly noctagons, and one wouldn't believe the difference. It was I bought these for Mr. Elliot. His one thought is to save one trouble. I never seed such a thoughtful gentleman. The world, I say, will be the better for him.' She took the teacups into the gyp room, and then returned with the tablecloth, and added, 'if he's spared.'

'I'm afraid he isn't strong,' said Agnes.

'Oh, miss, his nose! I don't know what he'd say if he knew I mentioned his nose, but really I must speak to some one, and he has neither father nor mother. His nose! It poured twice with blood in the Long.'

'Yes?'

'It's a thing that ought to be known. I assure you, that little room! . . . And in any case, Mr. Elliot's a gentleman that can ill afford to lose it. Luckily his friends were up; and I always say they're more like brothers than anything else.'

'Nice for him. He has no real brothers.'

'Oh, Mr. Hornblower, he is a merry gentleman, and Mr. Tilliard too! And Mr. Elliot himself likes his romp at times. Why, it's the merriest staircase in the buildings! Last night the bedmaker from W said to me, "What are you doing to my gentlemen? Here's Mr. Ansell come back 'ot with his collar flopping." I said, "And a good thing." Some bedders keep their gentlemen just so; but surely, miss, the world being what it is the longer one is able to laugh in it the better.'

Bedmakers have to be comic and dishonest. It is expected of them. In a picture of university life it is their only function. So when we meet one who has the face of a lady, and feelings of which a lady might be proud, we pass her by.

'Yes?' said Miss Pembroke, and then their talk was stopped by the arrival of her brother.

'It is too bad!' he exlaimed. 'It is really too bad.'

'Now, Bertie boy, Bertie boy! I'll have no peevishness.'

'I am not peevish, Agnes, but I have a full right to be. Pray, why did he not meet us? Why did he not provide rooms? And pray, why did you leave me to do all the settling? All the lodgings I knew are full, and our bedrooms look into a mews. I cannot help it. And then—look here! It really is too bad.' He held up his foot like a wounded dog. It was dripping with water.

'Oho! This explains the peevishness. Off with it at once. It'll be another of your colds.'

'I really think I had better.' He sat down by the fire and daintily unlaced his boot. 'I notice a great change in university tone. I can never remember swaggering three abreast along the pavement and charging inoffensive visitors into a gutter when I was an undergraduate. One of the men, too, wore an Eton tie. But the others, I should say, came from very queer schools, if they came from any schools at all.'

Mr. Pembroke was nearly twenty years older than his sister, and had never been as handsome. But he was not at all the person to knock into a gutter, for though not in orders, he had the air of being on the verge of them, and his features, as well as his clothes, had the clerical cut. In his presence conversation became pure and colourless and full of understatements, and—just as if he was a real clergyman—neither men nor boys ever forgot that he was there. He had observed this, and it pleased him very much. His conscience permitted him to enter the Church whenever his profession, which was the scholastic, should demand it.

'No gutter in the world's as wet as this,' said Agnes, who had peeled off her brother's sock, and was now toasting it at the embers on a pair of tongs.

'Surely you know the running water by the edge of the Trumpington Road? It's turned on occasionally to clear away the refuse—a most primitive idea. When I was up we had a joke about it, and called it the "Pem."'

'How complimentary!'

'You foolish girl,—not after me, of course. We called it the "Pem" because it is close to Pembroke College. I remember——' He smiled a little, and twiddled his toes. Then he remembered the bedmaker, and said, 'My sock is now dry. My sock, please.'

'Your sock is sopping. No, you don't!' She twitched the tongs away from him. Mrs. Aberdeen, without speaking, fetched a pair of Rickie's socks and a pair of Rickie's shoes.

'Thank you; ah, thank you. I am sure Mr. Elliot would allow it.' Then he said in French to his sister, 'Has there been the slightest sign of Frederick?'

'Now, do call him Rickie, and talk English. I found him here. He had forgotten about us, and was very sorry. Now he's gone to get some dinner, and I can't think why he isn't back.'

Mrs. Aberdeen left them.

'He wants pulling up sharply. There is nothing original in absent-mindedness. True originality lies elsewhere. Really, the lower classes have no *nous*. However can I wear such deformities?' For he had been madly trying to cram a right-hand foot into a left-hand shoe.

'Don't!' said Agnes hastily. 'Don't touch the poor fellow's things.' The sight of the smart, stubby patent leather made her almost feel faint. She had known Rickie for many years, but it seemed so dreadful and so different now that he was a man. It was her first great contact with the abnormal, and unknown fibres of her being rose in revolt against it. She frowned when she heard his uneven tread upon the stairs.

'Agnes—before he arrives—you ought never to have left me and gone to his rooms alone.

A most elementary transgression. Imagine the un-pleasantness if you had found him with friends. If Gerald——'

Rickie by now had got into a fluster. At the kitchens he had lost his head, and when his turn came—he had had to wait—he had yielded his place to those behind, saying that he didn't matter. And he had wasted more precious time buying bananas, though he knew that the Pembrokes were not partial to fruit. Amid much tardy and chaotic hospitality the meal got under way. All the spoons and forks were anyhow, for Mrs. Aberdeen's virtues were not practical. The fish seemed never to have been alive, the meat had no kick, and the cork of the college claret slid forth silently, as if ashamed of the contents. Agnes was particularly pleasant. But her brother could not recover himself. He still remembered their desolate arrival, and he could feel the waters of the Pem eating into his instep.

'Rickie,' cried the lady, 'are you aware that you haven't congratulated me on my engagement?'

Rickie laughed nervously, and said, 'Why no! No more I have.'

'Say something pretty, then.'

'I hope you'll be very happy,' he mumbled. 'But I don't know anything about marriage.'

'Oh, you awful boy! Herbert, isn't he just the same? But you do know something about Gerald, so don't be so chilly and cautious. I've just realized, looking at those groups, that you must have been at school together. Did you come much across him?'

'Very little,' he answered, and sounded shy. He got up hastily, and began to muddle with the coffee.

'But he was in the same house. Surely that's a house group?'

'He was a prefect.' He made his coffee on the simple system. One had a brown pot, into which the boiling stuff was poured. Just before serving one put in a drop of cold water, and the idea was that the grounds fell to the bottom.

'Wasn't he a kind of athletic marvel? Couldn't he knock any boy or master down?'

'Yes.'

'If he had wanted to,' said Mr. Pembroke, who had not spoken for some time.

'If he had wanted to,' echoed Rickie. 'I do hope, Agnes, you'll be most awfully happy. I don't know anything about the army, but I should think it must be most awfully interesting.'

Mr. Pembroke laughed faintly.

'Yes, Rickie. The army is a most interesting profession—the profession of Wellington and Marlborough and Lord Roberts; a most interesting profession, as you observe. A profession that may mean death—death, rather than dishonour.'

'That's nice,' said Rickie, speaking to himself. 'Any profession may mean dishonour, but one isn't allowed to die instead. The army's different. If a soldier makes a mess, it's thought rather decent of him, isn't it, if he blows out his brains? In the other professions it somehow seems cowardly.'

'I am not competent to pronounce,' said Mr. Pembroke, who was not accustomed to have his schoolroom satire commented on. 'I merely know that the army is the finest profession in the world. Which reminds me, Rickie—have you been thinking about yours?'

'No.'

'Not at all?'

'No.'

'Now, Herbert, don't bother him. Have another meringue.'

'But, Rickie, my dear boy, you're twenty. It's time you thought. The Tripos is the beginning of life, not the end. In less than two years you will have got your B.A. What are you going to do with it?'

'I don't know.'

'You're M.A., aren't you?' asked Agnes; but her brother proceeded—

'I have seen so many promising, brilliant lives wrecked simply on account of this—*not settling soon enough.* My dear boy, you must think. Consult your tastes if possible—but think. You have not a moment to lose. The Bar, like your father?'

'Oh, I wouldn't like that at all.'

'I don't mention the Church.'

'Oh, Rickie, do be a clergyman!' said Miss Pembroke. 'You'd be simply killing in a wide-awake.'

He looked at his guests hopelessly. Their kindness and competence overwhelmed him. 'I wish I could talk to them as I talk to myself,' he thought. 'I'm not such an ass when I talk to myself. I don't believe, for instance, that quite all I thought about the cow was rot.' Aloud he said, 'I've sometimes wondered about writing.'

'Writing?' said Mr. Pembroke, with the tone of one who gives everything its trial. 'Well, what about writing? What kind of writing?'

'I rather like'—he suppressed something in his throat,—'I rather like trying to write little stories.'

'Why, I made sure it was poetry!' said Agnes, 'You're just the boy for poetry.'

'I had no idea you wrote. Would you let me see something? Then I could judge.'

The author shook his head. 'I don't show it to any one. It isn't anything. I just try because it amuses me.'

'What is it about?'

'Silly nonsense.'

'Are you ever going to show it to any one?'

'I don't think so.'

Mr. Pembroke did not reply, firstly, because the meringue he was eating was, after all, Rickie's; secondly, because it was gluey and stuck his jaws together. Agnes observed that the writing was really a very good idea: there was Rickie's aunt,— she could push him.

'Aunt Emily never pushes any one; she says they always rebound and crush her.'

'I only had the pleasure of seeing your aunt once. I should have thought her a quite uncrushable person. But she would be sure to help you.'

'I couldn't show her anything. She'd think them even sillier than they are.'

'Always running yourself down! There speaks the artist!'

'I'm not modest,' he said anxiously. 'I just know they're bad.'

Mr. Pembroke's teeth were clear of meringue, and he could refrain no longer. 'My dear Rickie, your father and mother are dead, and you often say your aunt takes no interest in you. Therefore your life depends on yourself. Think it over carefully, but settle, and having once settled, stick. If you think that this writing is practicable, and that you could make your living by it—that you could, if needs be, support a wife—then by all means write. But you must work. Work and drudge. Begin at the bottom of the ladder and work upwards.'

Rickie's head drooped. Any metaphor silenced

him. He never thought of replying that art is not a ladder—with a curate, as it were, on the first rung, a rector on the second, and a bishop, still nearer heaven, at the top. He never retorted that the artist is not a bricklayer at all, but a horseman, whose business it is to catch Pegasus at once, not to practise for him by mounting tamer colts. This is hard, hot, and generally ungraceful work, but it is not drudgery. For drudgery is not art, and cannot lead to it.

'Of course I don't really think about writing,' he said, as he poured the cold water into the coffee. 'Even if my things ever were decent, I don't think the magazines would take them, and the magazines are one's only chance. I read somewhere, too, that Marie Corelli's about the only person who makes a thing out of literature. I'm certain it wouldn't pay me.'

'I never mentioned the word "pay,"' said Mr. Pembroke uneasily. 'You must not consider money. There are ideals too.'

'I have no ideals.'

'Rickie!' she exclaimed. 'Horrible boy!'

'No, Agnes, I have no ideals.' Then he got very red, for it was a phrase he had caught from Ansell, and he could not remember what came next.

'The person who has no ideals,' she exclaimed, 'is to be pitied.'

'I think so too,' said Mr. Pembroke, sipping his coffee. 'Life without an ideal would be like the sky without the sun.'

Rickie looked towards the night, wherein there now twinkled innumerable stars—gods and heroes, virgins and brides, to whom the Greeks have given their names.

'Life without an ideal——' repeated Mr. Pembroke,

and then stopped, for his mouth was full of coffee grounds. The same affliction had overtaken Agnes. After a little jocose laughter they departed to their lodgings, and Rickie, having seen them as far as the porter's lodge, hurried, singing as he went, to Ansell's room, burst open the door, and said, 'Look here! Whatever do you mean by it?'

'By what?' Ansell was sitting alone with a piece of paper in front of him. On it was a diagram— a circle inside a square, inside which was again a square.

'By being so rude. You're no gentleman, and I told her so.' He slammed him on the head with a sofa-cushion. 'I'm certain one ought to be polite, even to people who aren't saved.' ('Not saved' was a phrase they applied just then to those whom they did not like or intimately know.) 'And I believe she is saved. I never knew any one so always good-tempered and kind. She's been kind to me ever since I knew her. I wish you'd heard her trying to stop her brother: you'd have certainly come round. Not but what he was only being nice as well. But she is really nice. And I thought she came into the room so beautifully. Do you know—oh, of course, you despise music—but Anderson was playing Wagner, and he'd just got to the part where they sing

Rheingold!
Rheingold!

and the sun strikes into the waters, and the music, which up to then has so often been in E flat——'

'Goes into D sharp. I have not understood a single word, because you talk as if your mouth was full of plums, partly because I don't know whom you're talking about.'

'Miss Pembroke—whom you saw.'

'I saw no one.'

'Who came in?'

'No one came in.'

'You're an ass!' shrieked Rickie. 'She came in. You saw her come in. She and her brother have been to dinner.'

'You only think so. They were not really there.'

'But they stop till Monday.'

'You only think that they are stopping.'

'But—oh, look here, shut up! The girl like an empress——'

'I saw no empress, nor any girl, nor have you seen them.'

'Ansell, don't rag.'

'Elliot, I never rag, and you know it. She was not really there.'

There was a moment's silence. Then Rickie exclaimed, 'I've got you. You say—or was it Tilliard? —no, *you* say that the cow's there. Well—there these people are, then. Got you. Yah!'

'Did it never strike you that phenomena may be of two kinds: *one*, those which have a real existence, such as the cow; *two*, those which are the subjective product of a diseased imagination, and which, to our destruction, we invest with the semblance of reality? If this never struck you, let it strike you now.'

Rickie spoke again, but received no answer. He paced a little up and down the sombre room. Then he sat on the edge of the table and watched his clever friend draw within the square a circle, and within the circle a square, and inside that another circle, and inside that another square.

'Why will you do that?'

No answer.

'Are they real?'

'The inside one is—the one in the middle of everything, that there's never room enough to draw.'

II

A little this side of Madingley, to the left of the road, there is a secluded dell, paved with grass and planted with fir-trees. It could not have been worth a visit twenty years ago, for then it was only a scar of chalk, and it is not worth a visit at the present day, for the trees have grown too thick and choked it. But when Rickie was up, it chanced to be the brief season of its romance, a season as brief for a chalk-pit as a man—its divine interval between the bareness of boyhood and the stuffiness of age. Rickie had discovered it in his second term, when the January snows had melted and left fiords and lagoons of clearest water between the inequalities of the floor. The place looked as big as Switzerland or Norway—as indeed for the moment it was—and he came upon it at a time when his life too was beginning to expand. Accordingly the dell became for him a kind of church—a church where indeed you could do anything you liked, but where anything you did would be transfigured. Like the ancient Greeks, he could even laugh at his holy place and leave it no less holy. He chatted gaily about it, and about the pleasant thoughts with which it inspired him; he took his friends there; he even took people whom he did not like. '*Procul este, profani!*' exclaimed a delighted æsthete on being introduced to it. But this was never to be the attitude of Rickie. He did not love the vulgar herd, but he knew that his own vulgarity would be greater if he forbade it ingress, and that it was not by preciosity that he would attain to the intimate spirit of the dell. Indeed, if he had agreed with the æsthete, he would possibly not have introduced him. If the dell was to bear any inscription, he would have liked it to be 'This way to Heaven,' painted on a sign-post by the high-road, and he did not realize till later years that the number of visitors would not thereby have sensibly increased.

On the blessed Monday that the Pembrokes left, he walked out here with three friends. It was a day when the sky seemed enormous. One cloud, as large as a continent, was voyaging near the sun, whilst other clouds seemed anchored to the horizon, too lazy or too happy to move. The sky itself was of the palest blue, paling to white where it approached the earth; and the earth, brown, wet and odorous, was engaged beneath it on its yearly duty of decay. Rickie was open to the complexities of autumn; he felt extremely tiny—extremely tiny and extremely important; and perhaps the combination is as fair as any that exists. He hoped that all his life he would never be peevish or unkind.

'Elliot is in a dangerous state,' said Ansell. They had reached the dell, and had stood for some time in silence, each leaning against a tree. It was too wet to sit down.

'How's that?' asked Rickie, who had not known he was in any state at all. He shut up Keats, whom he thought he had been reading, and slipped him back into his coat-pocket. Scarcely ever was he without a book.

'He's trying to like people.'

'Then he's done for,' said Widdrington. 'He's dead.'

'He's trying to like Hornblower.'

The others gave shrill agonized cries.

'He wants to bind the college together. He wants to link us to the beefy set.'

'I do like Hornblower,' he protested. 'I don't try.'

'And Hornblower tries to like you.'

'That part doesn't matter.'

'But he does try to like you. He tries not to despise you. It is altogether a most public-spirited affair.'

'Tilliard started them,' said Widdrington. 'Tilliard thinks it such a pity the college should be split into sets.'

'Oh, Tilliard!' said Ansell, with much irritation. 'But what can you expect from a person who's eternally beautiful? The other night we had been discussing a long time, and suddenly the light was turned on. Every one else looked a sight, as they ought. But there was Tilliard sitting neatly on a little chair, like an undersized god, with not a curl crooked. I should say he will get into the Foreign Office.'

'Why are most of us so ugly?' laughed Rickie.

'It's merely a sign of our salvation—merely another sign that the college is split.'

'The college isn't split,' cried Rickie, who got excited on this subject with unfailing regularity. 'The college is, and has been, and always will be, one. What you call the beefy set aren't a set at all. They're just the rowing people, and naturally they chiefly see each other; but they're always nice to me or to any one. Of course, they think us rather asses, but it's quite in a pleasant way.'

'That's my whole objection,' said Ansell. 'What right have they to think us asses in a pleasant way? Why don't they hate us? What right has

Hornblower to smack me on the back when I've been rude to him?'

'Well, what right have you to be rude to him?'

'Because I hate him. You think it is so splendid to hate no one. I tell you it is a crime. You want to love every one equally, and that's worse than impossible—it's wrong. When you denounce sets, you're really trying to destroy friendship.'

'I maintain,' said Rickie—it was a verb he clung to, in the hope that it would lend stability to what followed—'I maintain that one can like many more people than one supposes.'

'And I maintain that you hate many more people than you pretend.'

'I hate no one,' he exclaimed with extraordinary vehemence, and the dell re-echoed that it hated no one.

'We are obliged to believe you,' said Widdrington, smiling a little; 'but we are sorry about it.'

'Not even your father?' asked Ansell.

Rickie was silent.

'Not even your father?'

The cloud above extended a great promontory across the sun. It only lay there for a moment, yet that was enough to summon the lurking coldness from the earth.

'Does he hate his father?' said Widdrington, who had not known. 'Oh, good!'

'But his father's dead. He will say it doesn't count.'

'Still, it's something. Do you hate yours?'

Ansell did not reply. Rickie said: 'I say, I wonder whether one ought to talk like this?'

'About hating dead people?'

'Yes——'

'Did you hate your mother?' asked Widdrington.

Rickie turned crimson.

'I don't see Hornblower's such a rotter,' remarked the other man, whose name was James.

'James, you are diplomatic,' said Ansell. 'You are trying to tide over an awkward moment. You can go.'

Widdrington was crimson too. In his wish to be sprightly he had used words without thinking of their meanings. Suddenly he realized that 'father' and 'mother' really meant father and mother—people whom he had himself at home. He was very uncomfortable, and thought Rickie had been rather queer. He too tried to revert to Hornblower, but Ansell would not let him. The sun came out, and struck on the white ramparts of the dell. Rickie looked straight at it. Then he said abruptly—

'I think I want to talk.'

'I think you do,' replied Ansell.

'Shouldn't I be rather a fool if I went through Cambridge without talking? It's said never to come so easy again. All the people are dead too. I can't see why I shouldn't tell you most things about my birth and parentage and education.'

'Talk away. If you bore us, we have books.'

With this invitation Rickie began to relate his history. The reader who has no book will be obliged to listen to it.

.   .   .   .   .

Some people spend their lives in a suburb, and not for any urgent reason. This had been the fate of Rickie. He had opened his eyes to filmy heavens, and taken his first walk on asphalt. He had seen civilization as a row of semi-detached villas, and society as a state in which men do not know the men who live next door. He had

himself become part of the grey monotony that sur-
rounds all cities. There was no necessity for this—
it was only rather convenient to his father.

Mr. Elliot was a barrister. In appearance he resembled his son, being weakly and lame, with hollow little cheeks, a broad white band of forehead,
and stiff impoverished hair. His voice, which he
did not transmit, was very suave, with a fine com-
mand of cynical intonation. By altering it ever so
little he could make people wince, especially if
they were simple or poor. Nor did he transmit his
eyes. Their peculiar flatness, as if the soul looked
through dirty window-panes, the unkindness of
them, the cowardice, the fear in them, were to
trouble the world no longer.

He married a girl whose voice was beautiful.
There was no caress in it, yet all who heard it were
soothed, as though the world held some unexpected
blessing. She called to her dogs one night over
invisible waters, and he, a tourist up on the bridge,
thought 'that is extraordinarily adequate.' In time
he discovered that her figure, face, and thoughts
were adequate also, and as she was not impossible
socially, he married her. 'I have taken a plunge,' he
told his family, The family, hostile at first, had not
a word to say when the woman was introduced to
them; and his sister declared that the plunge had
been taken from the opposite bank.

Things only went right for a little time. Though
beautiful without and within, Mrs. Elliot had not
the gift of making her home beautiful; and one
day, when she bought a carpet for the dining-room
that clashed, he laughed gently, said he 'really
couldn't,' and departed. Departure is perhaps too
strong a word. In Mrs. Elliot's mouth it became,
'My husband has to sleep more in town.' He often

came down to see them, nearly always unex-
pectedly, and occasionally they went to see him.
'Father's house,' as Rickie called it, only had three
rooms, but these were full of books and pictures
and flowers; and the flowers, instead of being
squashed down into the vases as they were in
mummy's house, rose gracefully from frames of
lead which lay coiled at the bottom, as doubtless
the sea serpent has to lie, coiled at the bottom of
the sea. Once he was let to lift a frame out—only
once, for he dropped some water on a creton. 'I
think he's going to have taste,' said Mr. Elliot
languidly. 'It is quite possible,' his wife replied.
She had not taken off her hat and gloves, nor even
pulled up her veil. Mr. Elliot laughed, and soon
afterwards another lady came in, and they went
away.

'Why does father always laugh?' asked Rickie
in the evening when he and his mother were sitting
in the nursery.

'It is a way of your father's.'

'Why does he always laugh at me? Am I so
funny?' Then after a pause, 'You have no sense of
humour, have you, mummy?'

Mrs. Elliot, who was raising a thread of cotton
to her lips, held it suspended in amazement.

'You told him so this afternoon. But I have seen
you laugh,' He nodded wisely. 'I have seen you
laugh ever so often. One day you were laughing
alone all down in the sweet peas.'

'Was I?'

'Yes. Were you laughing at me?'

'I was not thinking about you. Cotton, please—
a reel of number fifty white from my chest of
drawers. Left-hand drawer. Now which is your left
hand?'

'The side my pocket is.'

'And if you had no pocket?'

'The side my bad foot is.'

'I meant you to say, "the side my heart is,"' said Mrs. Elliot, holding up the duster between them. 'Most of us—I mean all of us—can feel on one side a little watch, that never stops ticking. So even if you had no bad foot you would still know which is the left. Number fifty white, please. No; I'll get it myself.' For she had remembered that the dark passage frightened him.

These were the outlines. Rickie filled them in with the slowness and the accuracy of a child. He was never told anything, but he discovered for himself that his father and mother did not love each other, and that his mother was lovable. He discovered that Mr. Elliot had dubbed him Rickie because he was rickety, that he took pleasure in alluding to his son's deformity, and was sorry that it was not more serious than his own. Mr. Elliot had not one scrap of genius. He gathered the pictures and the books and the flower-supports mechanically, not in any impulse of love. He passed for a cultured man because he knew how to select, and he passed for an unconventional man because he did not select quite like other people. In reality he never did or said or thought one single thing that had the slightest beauty or value. And in time Rickie discovered this as well.

The boy grew up in great loneliness. He worshipped his mother, and she was fond of him. But she was dignified and reticent, and pathos, like tattle, was disgusting to her. She was afraid of intimacy, in case it led to confidences and tears, and so all her life she held her son at a little distance. Her kindness and unselfishness knew no limits, but if he tried to be dramatic and thank her, she told him not to be a little goose. And so the only person he came to know at all was himself. He would play Halma against himself. He would conduct solitary conversations, in which one part of him asked and another part answered. It was an exciting game, and concluded with the formula: 'Good-bye. Thank you. I am glad to have met you. I hope before long we shall enjoy another chat.' And then perhaps he would sob for loneliness, for he would see real people—real brothers, real friends—doing in warm life the things he had pretended. 'Shall I ever have a friend?' he demanded at the age of twelve. 'I don't see how. They walk too fast. And a brother I shall never have.'

('No loss,' interrupted Widdrington.

'But I shall never have one, and so I quite want one, even now.')

When he was thirteen Mr. Elliot entered on his illness. The pretty rooms in town would not do for an invalid, and so he came back to his home. One of the first consequences was that Rickie was sent to a public school. Mrs. Elliot did what she could, but she had no hold whatever over her husband.

'He worries me,' he declared. 'He's a joke of which I have got tired.'

'Would it be possible to send him to a private tutor's?'

'No,' said Mr. Elliot, who had all the money. 'Coddling.'

'I agree that boys ought to rough it; but when a boy is lame and very delicate, he roughs it sufficiently if he leaves home. Rickie can't play games. He doesn't make friends. He isn't brilliant. Thinking it over, I feel that as it's like this, we can't ever hope to give him the ordinary education. Perhaps you could think it over too.'

'No.'

'I am sure that things are best for him as they are. The day-school knocks quite as many corners off him as he can stand. He hates it, but it is good for him. A public school will not be good for him. It is too rough. Instead of getting manly and hard, he will——'

'My head, please.'

Rickie departed in a state of bewildered misery, which was scarcely ever to grow clearer.

Each holiday he found his father more irritable, and a little weaker. Mrs. Elliot was quickly growing old. She had to manage the servants, to hush the neighbouring children, to answer the correspondence, to paper and re-paper the rooms—and all for the sake of a man whom she did not like, and who did not conceal his dislike for her. One day she found Rickie tearful, and said rather crossly, 'Well, what is it this time?'

He replied, 'Oh, mummy, I've seen your wrinkles —your grey hair—I'm unhappy.'

Sudden tenderness overcame her, and she cried, 'My darling, what does it matter? Whatever does it matter now?'

He had never known her so emotional. Yet even better did he remember another incident. Hearing high voices from his father's room, he went upstairs in the hope that the sound of his tread might stop them. Mrs. Elliot burst open the door, and seeing him, exclaimed, 'My dear! If you please, he's hit me.' She tried to laugh it off, but a few hours later he saw the bruise which the stick of the invalid had raised upon his mother's hand.

God alone knows how far we are in the grip of

our bodies. He alone can judge how far the cruelty of Mr. Elliot was the outcome of extenuating circumstances. But Mrs. Elliot could accurately judge of its extent.

At last he died. Rickie was now fifteen, and got off a whole week's school for the funeral. His mother was rather strange. She was much happier, she looked younger, and her mourning was as unobtrusive as convention permitted. All this he had expected. But she seemed to be watching him, and to be extremely anxious for his opinion on any subject—more especially on his father. Why? At last he saw that she was trying to establish confidence between them. But confidence cannot be established in a moment. They were both shy. The habit of years was upon them, and they alluded to the death of Mr. Elliot as an irreparable loss.

'Now that your father has gone, things will be very different.'

'Shall we be poorer, mother?'

'No.'

'Oh!'

'But naturally things will be very different.'

'Yes, naturally.'

'For instance, your poor father liked being near London, but I almost think we might move. Would you like that?'

'Of course, mummy.' He looked down at the ground. He was not accustomed to being consulted, and it bewildered him.

'Perhaps you might like quite a different life better?'

He giggled.

'It's a little difficult for me,' said Mrs. Elliot, pacing vigorously up and down the room, and more and more did her black dress seem a mockery. 'In some ways you ought to be consulted: nearly all the money is left to you, as you must hear some time or other. But in other ways you're only a boy. What am I to do?'

'I don't know,' he replied, appearing more helpless and unhelpful than he really was.

'For instance, would you like me to arrange things exactly as I like?'

'Oh do!' he exclaimed, thinking this a most brilliant suggestion. 'The very nicest thing of all.' And he added, in his half-pedantic, half-pleasing way, 'I shall be as wax in your hands, mamma.'

She smiled. 'Very well, darling. You shall be.' And she pressed him lovingly, as though she would mould him into something beautiful.

For the next few days great preparations were in the air. She went to see his father's sister, the gifted and vivacious Aunt Emily. They were to live in the country—somewhere right in the country, with grass and trees up to the door, and birds singing everywhere, and a tutor. For he was not to go back to school. Unbelievable! He was never to go back to school, and the headmaster had written saying that he regretted the step, but that possibly it was a wise one.

It was raw weather, and Mrs. Elliot watched over him with ceaseless tenderness. It seemed as if she could not do too much to shield him and to draw him nearer to her.

'Put on your greatcoat, dearest,' she said to him.

'I don't think I want it,' answered Rickie, remembering that he was now fifteen.

'The wind is bitter. You ought to put it on.'

'But it's so heavy.'

'Do put it on, dear.'

He was not very often irritable or rude, but he

answered, 'Oh, I shan't catch cold. I do wish you wouldn't keep on bothering.'

He did not catch cold, but while he was out his mother died. She only survived her husband eleven days, a coincidence which was recorded on their tombstone.

.   .   .   .   .

Such, in substance, was the story which Rickie told his friends as they stood together in the shelter of the dell. The green bank at the entrance hid the road and the world, and now, as in spring, they could see nothing but snow-white ramparts and the evergreen foliage of the firs. Only from time to time would a beech leaf flutter in from the woods above, to comment on the waning year, and the warmth and radiance of the sun would vanish behind a passing cloud.

About the greatcoat he did not tell them, for he could not have spoken of it without tears.

III

Mr. Ansell, a provincial draper of moderate prosperity, ought by rights to have been classed not with the cow, but with those phenomena that are not really there. But his son, with pardonable illogicality, excepted him. He never suspected that his father might be the subjective product of a diseased imagination. From his earliest years he had taken him for granted, as a most undeniable and lovable fact. To be born one thing and grow up another—Ansell had accomplished this without weakening one of the ties that bound him to his home. The rooms above the shop still seemed as comfortable, the garden behind it as gracious, as they had seemed fifteen years before, when he would sit behind Miss Appleblossom's central throne, and she, like some allegorical figure, would send the change and receipted bills spinning away from her in little boxwood balls. At first the young man had attributed these happy relations to his own tact. But in time he perceived that the tact was all on the side of his father. Mr. Ansell was not merely a man of some education; he had what no education can bring—the power of detecting what is important. Like many fathers, he had spared no expense over his boy,—he had borrowed money to start him at a rapacious and fashionable private school; he had sent him to tutors; he had sent him to Cambridge. But he knew that all this was not the important thing. The important thing was freedom. The boy must use his education as he chose, and if he paid his father back it would certainly not be in his own coin. So when Stewart said, 'At Cambridge, can I read for the Moral Science Tripos?' Mr. Ansell had only replied, 'This philosophy—do you say that it lies behind everything?'

'Yes, I think so. It tries to discover what is good and true.'

'Then, my boy, you had better read as much of it as you can.'

And a year later: 'I'd like to take up this philosophy seriously, but I don't feel justified.'

'Why not?'

'Because it brings in no return. I think I'm a great philosopher, but then all philosophers think that, though they don't dare to say so. But, however great I am, I shan't earn money. Perhaps I shan't ever be able to keep myself. I shan't even get a good social position. You've only to say one word, and I'll work for the Civil Service. I'm good enough to get in high.'

Mr. Ansell liked money and social position. But he knew that there is a more important thing, and replied, 'You must take up this philosophy seriously, I think.'

'Another thing—there are the girls.'

'There is enough money now to get Mary and Maud as good husbands as they deserve.' And Mary and Maud took the same view.

It was in this plebeian household that Rickie spent part of the Christmas vacation. His own home, such as it was, was with the Silts, needy cousins of his father's, and combined to a peculiar degree the restrictions of hospitality with the discomforts of a boarding-house. Such pleasure as he had outside Cambridge was in the homes of his friends, and it was a particular joy and honour to visit Ansell, who, though as free from social snobbishness as most of us will ever manage to be, was rather careful whom he drove up to the façade of his shop.

'I like our new lettering,' he said thoughtfully. The words 'Stewart Ansell' were repeated again and again along the High Street—curly gold letters that seemed to float in tanks of glazed chocolate.

'Rather!' said Rickie. But he wondered whether one of the bonds that kept the Ansell family united might not be their complete absence of taste—a surer bond by far than the identity of it. And he wondered this again when he sat at tea opposite a long row of crayons—Stewart as a baby, Stewart as a small boy with large feet, Stewart as a larger boy with smaller feet, Mary reading a book whose leaves were as thick as eider-downs. And yet again did he wonder it when he woke with a gasp in the night to find a harp in luminous paint throbbing and glowering at him from the adjacent wall. 'Watch and pray' was written on the harp, and until Rickie hung a towel over it the exhortation was partially successful.

It was a very happy visit. Miss Appleblossom—who now acted as housekeeper—had met him before, during her never-forgotten expedition to Cambridge, and her admiration of University life was as shrill and as genuine now as it had been then. The girls at first were a little aggressive, for on his arrival he had been tired, and Maud had taken it for haughtiness, and said he was looking down on them. But this passed. They did not fall in love with him, nor he with them, but a morning was spent very pleasantly in snowballing in the back garden. Ansell was rather different to what he was in Cambridge, but to Rickie not less attractive. And there was a curious charm in the hum of the shop, which swelled into a roar if one opened the partition door on a market-day.

'Listen to your money!' said Rickie. 'I wish I could hear mine. I wish my money was alive.'

'I don't understand.'

'Mine's dead money. It's come to me through about six dead people—silently.'

'Getting a little smaller and a little more respectable each time, on account of the death-duties.'

'It needed to get respectable.'

'Why? Did your people, too, once keep a shop?'

'Oh, not as bad as that! They only swindled. About a hundred years ago an Elliot did something shady and founded the fortunes of our house.'

'I never knew any one so relentless to his ancestors. You make up for your soapiness towards the living.'

'You'd be relentless if you'd heard the Silts, as I have, talk about "a fortune, small perhaps, but unsoiled by trade!" Of course Aunt Emily is rather different. Oh, goodness me! I've forgotten my aunt. She lives not so far. I shall have to call on her.'

Accordingly he wrote to Mrs. Failing, and said he should like to pay his respects. He told her about the Ansells, and so worded the letter that she might reasonably have sent an invitation to his friend.

She replied that she was looking forward to their *tête-à-tête*.

'You mustn't go round by the trains,' said Mr. Ansell. 'It means changing at Salisbury. By the road it's no great way. Stewart shall drive you over Salisbury Plain, and fetch you too.'

'There's too much snow,' said Ansell.

'Then the girls shall take you in their sledge.'

'That I will,' said Maud, who was not unwilling to see the inside of Cadover. But Rickie went round by the trains.

'We have all missed you,' said Ansell, when he returned. 'There is a general feeling that you are no nuisance, and had better stop till the end of the vac.'

This he could not do. He was bound for Christmas to the Silts—'as a *real* guest,' Mrs. Silt had written, underlining the word 'real' twice. And after Christmas he must go to the Pembrokes.

'These are no reasons. The only real reason for doing a thing is because you want to do it. I think the talk about "engagements" is cant.'

'I think perhaps it is,' said Rickie. But he went. Never had the turkey been so athletic, or the plum-

pudding tied into its cloth so tightly. Yet he knew
that both these symbols of hilarity had cost money,
and it went to his heart when Mr. Silt said in a
hungry voice. 'Have you thought at all of what you
want to be? No? Well, why should you? You have
no need to be anything.' And at dessert: 'I wonder
who Cadover goes to? I expect money will follow
money. It always does.' It was with a guilty feeling
of relief that he left for the Pembrokes.

The Pembrokes lived in an adjacent suburb, or
rather 'sububurb,'—the tract called Sawston, cele-
brated for its public school. Their style of life,
however, was not particularly suburban. Their
house was small and its name was Shelthorpe, but
it had an air about it which suggested a certain
amount of money and a certain amount of taste.
There were decent water-colours in the drawing-
room. Madonnas of acknowledged merit hung upon
the stairs. A replica of the Hermes of Praxiteles—
of course only the bust—stood in the hall with a
real palm behind it. Agnes, in her slap-dash way,
was a good housekeeper, and kept the pretty things
well dusted. It was she who insisted on the strip
of brown holland that led diagonally from the front
door to the door of Herbert's study: boys' grubby
feet should not go treading on her Indian square.
It was she who always cleaned the picture-frames
and washed the bust and the leaves of the palm.
In short, if a house could speak—and sometimes
it does speak more clearly than the people who
live in it—the house of the Pembrokes would have
said, 'I am not quite like other houses, yet I am
perfectly comfortable. I contain works of art and
a microscope and books. But I do not live for any
of these things or suffer them to disarrange me. I
live for myself and for the greater houses that shall

come after me. Yet in me neither the cry of money nor the cry for money shall ever be heard.'

Mr. Pembroke was at the station. He did better as a host than as a guest, and welcomed the young man with real friendliness.

'We were all coming, but Gerald has strained his ankle slightly, and wants to keep quiet, as he is playing next week in a match. And, needless to say, that explains the absence of my sister.'

'Gerald Dawes?'

'Yes; he's with us. I'm so glad you'll meet again.'

'So am I,' said Rickie with extreme awkwardness. 'Does he remember me?'

'Vividly.'

Vivid also was Rickie's remembrance of him.

'A splendid fellow,' asserted Mr. Pembroke.

'I hope that Agnes is well.'

'Thank you, yes; she is well. And I think you're looking more like other people yourself.'

'I've been having a very good time with a friend.'

'Indeed. That's right. Who was that?'

Rickie had a young man's reticence. He generally spoke of 'a friend,' 'a person I know,' 'a place I was at.' When the book of life is opening, our readings are secret, and we are unwilling to give chapter and verse. Mr. Pembroke, who was halfway through the volume, and had skipped or forgotten the earlier pages, could not understand Rickie's hesitation, nor why with such awkwardness he should pronounce the harmless dissyllable 'Ansell.'

'Ansell? Wasn't that the pleasant fellow who asked us to lunch?'

'No. That was Anderson, who keeps below. You didn't see Ansell. The ones who came to breakfast were Tilliard and Hornblower.'

'Of course. And since then you have been with the Silts. How are they?'

'Very well, thank you. They want to be remembered to you.'

The Pembrokes had formerly lived near the Elliots, and had shown great kindness to Rickie when his parents died. They were thus rather in the position of family friends.

'Please remember us when you write.' He added, almost roguishly, 'The Silts are kindness itself. All the same, it must be just a little—dull, we thought, and we thought that you might like a change. And of course we are delighted to have you besides. That goes without saying.'

'It's very good of you,' said Rickie, who had accepted the invitation because he felt he ought to.

'Not a bit. And you mustn't expect us to be otherwise than quiet in the holidays. There is a library of a sort, as you know, and you will find Gerald a splendid fellow.'

'Will they be married soon?'

'Oh no!' whispered Mr. Pembroke, shutting his eyes, as if Rickie had made some terrible *faux pas*. 'It will be a very long engagement. He must make his way first. I have seen such endless misery result from people marrying before they have made their way.'

'Yes. That it so,' said Rickie despondently, thinking of the Silts.

'It's a sad unpalatable truth,' said Mr. Pembroke, thinking that the despondency might be personal, 'but one must accept it. My sister and Gerald, I am thankful to say, have accepted it, though naturally it has been a little pill.'

Their cab lurched round the corner as he spoke,

and the two patients came in sight. Agnes was leaning over the creosoted garden-gate, and behind her there stood a young man who had the figure of a Greek athlete and the face of an English one. He was fair and clean-shaven, and his colourless hair was cut rather short. The sun was in his eyes, and they, like his mouth, seemed scarcely more than slits in his healthy skin. Just where he began to be beautiful the clothes started. Round his neck went an up-and-down collar and a mauve-and-gold tie, and the rest of his limbs were hidden by a grey lounge suit, carefully creased in the right places.

'Lovely! lovely!' cried Agnes, banging on the gate. 'Your train must have been to the minute.'

'Hullo!' said the athlete, and vomited with the greeting a cloud of tobacco-smoke. It must have been imprisoned in his mouth some time, for no pipe was visible.

'Hullo!' returned Rickie, laughing violently. They shook hands.

'Where are you going, Rickie?' asked Agnes. 'You aren't grubby. Why don't you stop? Gerald, get the large wicker-chair. Herbert has letters, but we can sit here till lunch. It's like spring.'

The garden of Shelthorpe was nearly all in front —an unusual and pleasant arrangement. The front gate and the servants' entrance were both at the side, and in the remaining space the gardener had contrived a little lawn where one could sit concealed from the road by a fence, from the neighbour by a fence, from the house by a tree, and from the path by a bush.

'This is the lovers' bower,' observed Agnes, sitting down on the bench. Rickie stood by her till the chair arrived.

'Are you smoking before lunch?' asked Mr. Dawes.

'No, thank you. I hardly ever smoke.'

'No vices. Aren't you at Cambridge now?'

'Yes.'

'What's your college?'

Rickie told him.

'Do you know Carruthers?'

'Rather!'

'I mean A. P. Carruthers, who got his soccer blue.'

'Rather! He's secretary to the college musical society.'

'A. P. Carruthers?'

'Yes.'

Mr. Dawes seemed offended. He tapped on his teeth, and remarked that the weather had no business to be so warm in winter.

'But it was fiendish before Christmas,' said Agnes.

He frowned, and asked, 'Do you know a man called Gerrish?'

'No.'

'Ah.'

'Do you know James?'

'Never heard of him.'

'He's my year too. He got a blue for hockey his second term.'

'I know nothing about the 'Varsity.'

Rickie winced at the abbreviation ''Varsity.' It was at that time the proper thing to speak of 'the University.'

'I haven't the time,' pursued Mr. Dawes.

'No, no,' said Rickie politely.

'I had the chance of being an Undergrad. myself, and, by Jove, I'm thankful I didn't!'

'Why?' asked Agnes, for there was a pause.

'Puts you back in your profession. Men who go there first, before the Army, start hopelessly behind. The same with the Stock Exchange or Painting. I know men in both, and they've never caught up the time they lost in the 'Varsity—unless, of course, you turn parson.'

'I love Cambridge,' said she. 'All those glorious buildings, and every one so happy and running in and out of each other's rooms all day long.'

'That might make an Undergrad. happy, but I beg leave to state it wouldn't me. I haven't four years to throw away for the sake of being called a 'Varsity man and hobnobbing with lords.'

Rickie was prepared to find his old schoolfellow ungrammatical and bumptious, but he was not prepared to find him peevish. Athletes, he believed, were simple, straightforward people, cruel and brutal if you like, but never petty. They knocked you down and hurt you, and then went on their way rejoicing. For this, Rickie thought, there is something to be said: he had escaped the sin of despising the physically strong—a sin against which the physically weak must guard. But here was Dawes returning again and again to the subject of the University, full of transparent jealousy and petty spite, nagging, nagging, nagging, like a maiden lady who has not been invited to a tea-party. Rickie wondered whether, after all, Ansell and the extremists might not be right, and bodily beauty and strength be signs of the soul's damnation.

He glanced at Agnes. She was writing down some orderings for the tradespeople on a piece of paper. Her handsome face was intent on the work. The bench on which she and Gerald were sitting had no back, but she sat as straight as a dart. He, though strong enough to sit straight, did not take the trouble.

'Why don't they talk to each other?' thought Rickie.

'Gerald, give this paper to the cook.'

'I can give it to the other slavey, can't I?'

'She'll be dressing.'

'Well, there's Herbert.'

'He's busy. Oh, you know where the kitchen is. Take it to the cook.'

He disappeared slowly behind the tree.

'What do you think of him?' she immediately asked.

He murmured civilly.

'Has he changed since he was a schoolboy?'

'In a way.'

'Do tell me all about him. Why won't you?'

She might have seen a flash of horror pass over Rickie's face. The horror disappeared, for, thank God, he was now a man, whom civilization protects. But he and Gerald had met, as it were, behind the scenes, before our decorous drama opens, and there the elder boy had done things to him—absurd things, not worth chronicling separately. An apple-pie bed is nothing; pinches, kicks, boxed ears, twisted arms, pulled hair, ghosts at night, inky books, befouled photographs, amount to very little by themselves. But let them be united and continuous, and you have a hell that no grown-up devil can devise. Between Rickie and Gerald there lay a shadow that darkens life more often than we suppose. The bully and his victim never quite forget their first relations. They meet in clubs and country houses, and clap one another on the back; but in both the memory is green of a more strenuous day, when they were boys together.

He tried to say, 'He was the right kind of boy, and I was the wrong kind.' But Cambridge would not let him smooth the situation over by self-belittlement. If he had been the wrong kind of boy, Gerald had been a worse kind. He murmured, 'We are different, very,' and Miss Pembroke, perhaps suspecting something, asked no more. But she kept to the subject of Mr. Dawes, humorously depreciating her lover and discussing him without reverence. Rickie laughed, but felt uncomfortable. When people were engaged, he felt that they should be outside criticism. Yet here he was criticizing. He could not help it. He was dragged in.

'I hope his ankle is better.'

'Never was bad. He's always fussing over something.'

'He plays next week in a match, I think Herbert says.'

'I dare say he does.'

'Shall we be going?'

'Pray go if you like. I shall stop at home. I've had enough of cold feet.'

It was all very colourless and odd.

Gerald returned, saying, 'I can't stand your cook. What's she want to ask me questions for? I can't stand talking to servants. I say, "If I speak to you, well and good"—and it's another thing besides if she were pretty.'

'Well, I hope our ugly cook will have lunch ready in a minute,' said Agnes. 'We're frightfully unpunctual this morning, and I daren't say anything, because it was the same yesterday, and if I complain again they might leave. Poor Rickie must be starved.'

'Why, the Silts gave me all these sandwiches and I've never eaten them. They always stuff one.'

'And you thought you'd better, eh?' said Mr. Dawes, 'in case you weren't stuffed here.'

Miss Pembroke, who house-kept somewhat economically, looked annoyed.

The voice of Mr. Pembroke was now heard calling from the house, 'Frederick! Frederick! My dear boy, pardon me. It was an important letter about the Church Defence, otherwise—— Come in and see your room.'

He was glad to quit the little lawn. He had learnt too much there. It was dreadful: they did not love each other. More dreadful even than the case of his father and mother, for they, until they married, had got on pretty well. But this man was already rude and brutal and cold: he was still the school bully who twisted up the arms of little boys, and ran pins into them at chapel, and struck them in the stomach when they were swinging on the horizontal bar. Poor Agnes; why ever had she done it? Ought not somebody to interfere?

He had forgotten his sandwiches, and went back to get them.

Gerald and Agnes were locked in each other's arms.

He only looked for a moment, but the sight burnt into his brain. The man's grip was the stronger. He had drawn the woman on to his knee, was pressing her, with all his strength, against him. Already her hands slipped off him, and she whispered, 'Don't—you hurt——' Her face had no expression. It stared at the intruder and never saw him. Then her lover kissed it, and immediately it shone with mysterious beauty, like some star.

Rickie limped away without the sandwiches, crimson and afraid. He thought, 'Do such things actually happen?' and he seemed to be looking

down coloured valleys. Brighter they glowed, till
gods of pure flame were born in them, and then
he was looking at pinnacles of virgin snow. While
Mr. Pembroke talked, the riot of fair images increased. They invaded his being and lit lamps at
unsuspected shrines. Their orchestra commenced
in that suburban house, where he had to stand
aside for the maid to carry in the luncheon. Music
flowed past him like a river. He stood at the springs
of creation and heard the primeval monotony. Then
an obscure instrument gave out a little phrase. The
river continued unheeding. The phrase was repeated, and a listener might know it was a fragment of the Tune of tunes. Nobler instruments
accepted it, the clarionet protected, the brass encouraged, and it rose to the surface to the whisper
of violins. In full unison was Love born, flame of
the flame, flushing the dark river beneath him
and the virgin snows above. His wings were infinite, his youth eternal; the sun was a jewel on
his finger as he passed it in benediction over the
world. Creation, no longer monotonous, acclaimed
him, in widening melody, in brighter radiances.
Was Love a column of fire? Was he a torrent of
song? Was he greater than either—the touch of
a man on a woman?

It was the merest accident that Rickie had not
been disgusted. But this he could not know.

Mr. Pembroke, when he called the two dawdlers
into lunch, was aware of a hand on his arm and a
voice that murmured, 'Don't—they may be happy.'

He stared, and struck the gong. To its music
they approached, priest and high priestess.

'Rickie, can I give these sandwiches to the boot
boy?' said the one. 'He would love them.'

'The gong! Be quick! The gong!'

'Are you smoking before lunch?' said the other.

But they had got into heaven, and nothing could get them out of it. Others might think them surly or prosaic. He knew. He could remember every word they spoke. He would treasure every motion, every glance of either, and so in time to come when the gates of heaven had shut, some faint radiance, some echo of wisdom might remain with him outside.

As a matter of fact, he saw them very little during his visit. He checked himself because he was unworthy. What right had he to pry, even in the spirit, upon their bliss? It was no crime to have seen them on the lawn. It would be a crime to go to it again. He tried to keep himself and his thoughts away, not because he was ascetic, but because they would not like it if they knew. This behaviour of his suited them admirably. And when any gracious little thing occurred to them—any little thing that his sympathy had contrived and allowed—they put it down to chance or to each other.

So the lovers fall into the background. They are part of the distant sunrise, and only the mountains speak to them. Rickie talks to Mr. Pembroke, amidst the unlit valleys of our over-habitable world.

IV

Sawston School had been founded by a tradesman in the seventeenth century. It was then a tiny grammar-school in a tiny town, and the City Company who governed it had to drive half a day through the woods and heath on the occasion of their annual visit. In the twentieth century they still drove, but only from the railway station; and found themselves not in a tiny town, nor yet in a large one, but amongst innumerable residences, detached and semi-detached, which had gathered round the school. For the intentions of the founder had been altered, or at all events amplified, and instead of educating the 'poore of my home,' he now educated the upper middle classes of England. The change had taken place not so very far back. Till the nineteenth century the grammar-school was still composed of day scholars from the neighbourhood. Then two things happened. Firstly, the school's property rose in value, and it became rich. Secondly, for no obvious reason, it suddenly emitted a quantity of bishops. The bishops, like the stars from a Roman candle, were of all colours, and flew in all directions, some high, some low, some to distant colonies, one into the Church of Rome. But many a father traced their course in the papers; many a mother wondered whether her son, if properly ignited, might not burn as bright; many a family moved to the place where living and education were so cheap, where day-boys were not looked down upon, and where the orthodox and the up-to-date were said to be combined. The school doubled its numbers. It built new classrooms, laboratories, and a gymnasium. It dropped the prefix 'Grammar.' It coaxed the sons of the local tradesmen into a new foundation, the 'Commercial School,' built a couple of miles away. And it started boarding-houses. It had not the gracious antiquity of Eton or Winchester, nor, on the other hand, had it a conscious policy like Lancing, Wellington, and other purely modern foundations. Where traditions served, it clung to them. Where new departures seemed desirable, they were made. It aimed at producing the average Englishman, and, to a very great extent, it succeeded.

Here Mr. Pembroke passed his happy and industrious life. His technical position was that of master to a form low down on the Modern Side. But his work lay elsewhere. He organized. If no organization existed, he would create one. If one did exist, he would modify it. 'An organization,' he would say, 'is after all not an end in itself. It must contribute to a movement.' When one good custom seemed likely to corrupt the school, he was ready with another; he believed that without innumerable customs there was no safety, either for boys or men. Perhaps he is right, and always will be right. Perhaps each of us would go to ruin if for one short hour we acted as we thought fit, and attempted the service of perfect freedom. The school caps, with their elaborate symbolism, were his; his the many-tinted bathing-drawers, that showed how far a boy could swim; his the hierarchy of jerseys and blazers. It was he who instituted Bounds, and Call, and the two sorts of exercise-paper, and the three sorts of caning, and 'The Sawstonian,' a bi-terminal magazine. His plump finger was in every pie. The dome of his skull, mild but impressive, shone at every masters' meeting. He was generally acknowledged to be the coming man.

His last achievement had been the organization of the day-boys. They had been left too much to themselves, and were weak in *esprit de corps*; they were apt to regard home, not school, as the most important thing in their lives. Moreover, they got out of their parents' hands; they did their preparation any time and sometimes anyhow. They

C

shirked games, they were out at all hours, they ate what they should not, they smoked, they bicycled on the asphalt. Now all was over. Like the boarders, they were to be in at 7.15 p.m., and were not allowed out after unless with a written order from their parent or guardian; they, too, must work at fixed hours in the evening, and before breakfast next morning from 7 to 8. Games were compulsory. They must not go to parties in term time. They must keep to bounds. Of course the reform was not complete. It was impossible to control the dieting, though, on a printed circular, day-parents were implored to provide simple food. And it is also believed that some mothers disobeyed the rule about preparation, and allowed their sons to do all the work overnight and have a longer sleep in the morning. But the gulf between day-boys and boarders was considerably lessened, and grew still narrower when the day-boys too were organized into a House with house-master and colours of their own. 'Through the House,' said Mr. Pembroke, 'one learns patriotism for the school, just as through the school one learns patriotism for the country. Our only course, therefore, is to organize the day-boys into a House.' The headmaster agreed, as he often did, and the new community was formed. Mr. Pembroke, to avoid the tongues of malice, had refused the post of house-master for himself, saying to Mr. Jackson, who taught the sixth, 'You keep too much in the background. Here is a chance for you.' But this was a failure. Mr. Jackson, a scholar and a student, neither felt nor conveyed any enthusiasm, and when confronted with his House, would say, 'Well, I don't know what we're all here for. Now I should think you'd better go home to your mothers.' He returned to his background, and next term Mr. Pembroke was to take his place.

Such were the themes on which Mr. Pembroke discoursed to Rickie's civil ear. He showed him the school, and the library, and the subterranean hall where the day-boys might leave their coats and caps, and where, on festal occasions, they supped. He showed him Mr. Jackson's pretty house, and whispered, 'Were it not for his brilliant intellect, it would be a case of Quick-march!' He showed him the racquet-court, happily completed, and the chapel, unhappily still in need of funds. Rickie was impressed, but then he was impressed by everything. Of course a House of day-boys seemed a little shadowy after Agnes and Gerald, but he imparted some reality even to that.

'The racquet-court,' said Mr. Pembroke, 'is most gratifying. We never expected to manage it this year. But before the Easter holidays every boy received a subscription card, and was given to understand that he must collect thirty shillings. You will scarcely believe me, but they nearly all responded. Next term there was a dinner in the great school, and all who had collected, not thirty shillings, but as much as a pound, were invited to it—for naturally one was not precise for a few shillings, the response being the really valuable thing. Practically the whole school had to come.'

'They must enjoy the court tremendously.'

'Ah, it isn't used very much. Racquets, as I dare say you know, is rather an expensive game. Only the wealthier boys play—and I'm sorry to say that it is not of our wealthier boys that we are always proudest. But the point is that no public school can be called first-class until it has one. They are building them right and left.'

'And now you must finish the chapel?'

'Now we must complete the chapel.' He paused reverently, and said, 'And here is a fragment of the original building.'

Rickie at once had a rush of sympathy. He, too, looked with reverence at the morsel of Jacobean brickwork, ruddy and beautiful amidst the machine-squared stones of the modern apse. The two men, who had so little in common, were thrilled with patriotism. They rejoiced that their country was great, noble, and old.

'Thank God I'm English,' said Rickie suddenly.

'Thank Him indeed,' said Mr. Pembroke, laying a hand on his back.

'We've been nearly as great as the Greeks, I do believe. Greater, I'm sure, than the Italians, though they did get closer to beauty. Greater than the French, though we do take all their ideas. I can't help thinking that England is immense. English literature certainly.'

Mr. Pembroke removed his hand. He found such patriotism somewhat craven. Genuine patriotism comes only from the heart. It knows no parleying with reason. English ladies will declare abroad that there are no fogs in London, and Mr. Pembroke, though he would not go to this, was only restrained by the certainty of being found out. On this occasion he remarked that the Greeks lacked spiritual insight, and had a low conception of woman.

'As to women—oh! there they were dreadful,' said Rickie, leaning his hand on the chapel. 'I realize that more and more. But as to spiritual insight, I don't quite like to say; and I find Plato too difficult, but I know men who don't, and I fancy they mightn't agree with you.'

'Far be it from me to disparage Plato. And for philosophy as a whole I have the greatest respect. But it is the crown of a man's education, not the foundation. Myself, I read it with the utmost profit, but I have known endless trouble result from boys who attempted it too soon, before they were set.'

'But if those boys had died first,' cried Rickie with sudden vehemence, 'without knowing what there is to know——'

'Or isn't to know!' said Mr. Pembroke sarcastically.

'Or what there isn't to know. Exactly. That's it.'

'My dear Rickie, what do you mean? If an old friend may be frank, you are talking great rubbish.' And, with a few well-worn formulæ, he propped up the young man's orthodoxy. The props were unnecessary. Rickie had his own equilibrium. Neither the Revivalism that assails a boy at about the age of fifteen, nor the scepticism that meets him five years later, could sway him from his allegiance to the church into which he had been born. But his equilibrium was personal, and the secret of it useless to others. He desired that each man should find his own.

'What does philosophy do?' the propper continued. 'Does it make a man happier in life? Does it make him die more peacefully? I fancy that in the long-run Herbert Spencer will get no further than the rest of us. Ah, Rickie! I wish you could move among schoolboys, and see their healthy contempt for all that they cannot touch!' Here he was going too far, and had to add, 'Their spiritual capacities, of course, are another matter.' Then he remembered the Greeks, and said, 'Which proves my original statement.'

Submissive signs, as of one propped, appeared in

Rickie's face. Mr. Pembroke then questioned him about the men who found Plato not difficult. But here he kept silence, patting the school chapel gently, and presently the conversation turned to topics with which they were both more competent to deal.

'Does Agnes take much interest in the school?'

'Not as much as she did. It is the result of her engagement. If our naughty soldier had not carried her off, she might have made an ideal schoolmaster's wife. I often chaff him about it, for he a little despises the intellectual professions. Natural, perfectly natural. How can a man who faces death feel as we do towards *mensa* or *tupto*?'

'Perfectly true. Absolutely true.'

Mr. Pembroke remarked to himself that Frederick was improving.

'If a man shoots straight and hits straight and speaks straight, if his heart is in the right place, if he has the instincts of a Christian and a gentleman—then I, at all events, ask no better husband for my sister.'

'How could you get a better?' he cried. 'Do you remember the thing in "The Clouds"?' And he quoted, as well as he could, from the invitation of the Dikaios Logos, the description of the young Athenian, perfect in body, placid in mind, who neglects his work at the Bar and trains all day among the woods and meadows, with a garland on his head and a friend to set the pace; the scent of new leaves is upon them; they rejoice in the freshness of spring; over their heads the plane-tree whispers to the elm,—perhaps the most glorious invitation to the brainless life that has ever been given.

'Yes, yes,' said Mr. Pembroke, who did not want

a brother-in-law out of Aristophanes. Nor had he got one, for Mr. Dawes would not have bothered over the garland or noticed the spring, and would have complained that the friend ran too slowly or too fast.

'And as for her——!' But he could think of no classical parallel for Agnes. She slipped between examples. A kindly Medea, a Cleopatra with a sense of duty—these suggested her a little. She was not born in Greece, but came overseas to it—a dark, intelligent princess. With all her splendour, there were hints of splendour still hidden—hints of an older, richer, and more mysterious land. He smiled at the idea of her being 'not there.' Ansell, clever as he was, had made a bad blunder. She had more reality than any other woman in the world.

Mr. Pembroke looked pleased at this boyish enthusiasm. He was fond of his sister, though he knew her to be full of faults. 'Yes, I envy her,' he said. 'She has found a worthy helpmeet for life's journey, I do believe. And though they chafe at the long engagement, it is a blessing in disguise. They learn to know each other thoroughly before contracting more intimate ties.'

Rickie did not assent. The length of the engagement seemed to him unspeakably cruel. Here were two people who loved each other, and they could not marry for years because they had no beastly money. Not all Herbert's pious skill could make this out a blessing. It was bad enough being 'so rich' at the Silts; here he was more ashamed of it than ever. In a few weeks he would come of age and his money be his own. What a pity things were so crookedly arranged. He did not want money, or at all events he did not want so much.

'Suppose,' he meditated, for he became much worried over this—'suppose I had a hundred pounds a year less than I shall have. Well, I should still have enough. I don't want anything but food, lodging, clothes, and now and then a railway fare. I haven't any tastes. I don't collect anything or play games. Books are nice to have, but after all there is Mudie's, or if it comes to that, the Free Library. Oh, my profession! I forgot I shall have a profession. Well, that will leave me with more to spare than ever.' And he supposed away till he lost touch with the world and with what it permits, and committed an unpardonable sin.

It happened towards the end of his visit— another airless day of that mild January. Mr. Dawes was playing against a scratch team of cads, and had to go down to the ground in the morning to settle something. Rickie proposed to come too.

Hitherto he had been no nuisance. 'You will be frightfully bored,' said Agnes, observing the cloud on her lover's face. 'And Gerald walks like a maniac.'

'I had a little thought of the Museum this morning,' said Mr. Pembroke. 'It is very strong in flint arrow-heads.'

'Ah, that's your line, Rickie. I do envy you and Herbert the way you enjoy the past.'

'I almost think I'll go with Dawes, if he'll have me. I can walk quite fast just to the ground and back. Arrow-heads are wonderful, but I don't really enjoy them yet, though I hope I shall in time.'

Mr. Pembroke was offended, but Rickie held firm.

In a quarter of an hour he was back at the house alone, nearly crying.

'Oh, did the wretch go too fast?' called Miss Pembroke from her bedroom window.

'I went too fast for him.' He spoke quite sharply, and before he had time to say he was sorry and didn't mean exactly that, the window had shut.

'They've quarrelled,' she thought. 'Whatever about?'

She soon heard. Gerald returned in a cold stormy temper. Rickie had offered him money.

'My dear fellow, don't be so cross. The child's mad.'

'If it was, I'd forgive that. But I can't stand unhealthiness.'

'Now, Gerald, that's where I hate you. You don't know what it is to pity the weak.'

'Woman's job. So you wish I'd taken a hundred pounds a year from him. Did you ever hear such blasted cheek? Marry us—he, you, and me—a hundred pounds down and as much annual—he, of course, to pry into all we did, and we to kow-tow and eat dirt-pie to him. If that's Mr. Rickety Elliot's idea of a soldier and an Englishman, it isn't mine, and I wish I'd had a horse-whip.'

She was roaring with laughter. 'You're babies, a pair of you, and you're the worst. Why couldn't you let the little silly down gently? There he was puffing and sniffing under my window, and I thought he'd insulted you. Why didn't you accept?'

'Accept?' he thundered.

'It would have taken the nonsense out of him for ever. Why, he was only talking out of a book.'

'More fool he.'

'Well, don't be angry with a fool. He means no harm. He muddles all day with poetry and old dead people, and then tries to bring it into life. It's too funny for words.'

Gerald repeated that he could not stand un-healthiness.

'I don't call that exactly unhealthy.'

'I do. And why he could give the money's worse.

'What do you mean?'

He became shy. 'I hadn't meant to tell you. It's not quite for a lady.' For, like most men who are rather animals, he was intellectually a prude. 'He says he can't ever marry, owing to his foot. It wouldn't be fair to posterity. His grandfather was crocked, his father too, and he's as bad. He thinks that it's hereditary, and may get worse next generation. He's discussed it all over with other Undergrads. A bright lot they must be. He daren't risk having any children. Hence the hundred quid.'

She stopped laughing. 'Oh, little beast, if he said all that!'

He was encouraged to proceed. Hitherto he had not talked about their schooldays. Now he told her everything,—the 'barley-sugar,' as he called it, the pins in chapel and how one afternoon he had tied him head downward on to a tree-trunk and then ran away—of course only for a moment.

For this she scolded him well. But she had a thrill of joy when she thought of the weak boy in the clutches of the strong one.

V

Gerald died that afternoon. He was broken up in the football match. Rickie and Mr. Pembroke were on the ground when the accident took place. It was no good torturing him by a drive to the hospital, and he was merely carried to the little pavilion and laid upon the floor. A doctor came, and so did a clergyman, but it seemed better to leave him for the last few minutes with Agnes, who had ridden down on her bicycle.

It was a strange lamentable interview. The girl was so accustomed to health, that for a time she could not understand. It must be a joke that he chose to lie there in the dust, with a rug over him, and his knees bent up towards his chin. His arms were as she knew them, and their admirable muscles showed clear and clean beneath the jersey. The face, too, though a little flushed, was uninjured: it must be some curious joke.

'Gerald, what have you been doing?'

He replied, 'I can't see you. It's too dark.'

'Oh, I'll soon alter that,' she said in her old brisk way. She opened the pavilion door. The people who were standing by it moved aside. She saw a deserted meadow, steaming and grey, and beyond it slate-roofed cottages, row beside row, climbing a shapeless hill. Towards London the sky was yellow. 'There. That's better.' She sat down by him again, and drew his hand into her own. 'Now we are all right, aren't we?'

'Where are you?'

This time she could not reply.

'What is it? Where am I going?'

'Wasn't the rector here?' said she after a silence.

'He explained heaven, and thinks that I—but— I couldn't tell a parson; but I don't seem to have any use for any of the things there.'

'We are Christians,' said Agnes shyly. 'Dear love, we don't talk about these things, but we believe them. I think that you will get well and be as strong again as ever; but, in any case, there is a spiritual life, and we know that some day you and I—'

'I shan't do as a spirit,' he interrupted, sighing

pitifully. 'I want you as I am, and it cannot be managed. The rector had to say so. I want—I don't want to talk. I can't see you. Shut that door.'

She obeyed, and crept into his arms. Only this time her grasp was the stronger. Her heart beat louder and louder as the sound of his grew more faint. He was crying like a little frightened child, and her lips were wet with his tears. 'Bear it bravely,' she told him.

'I can't,' he whispered. 'It isn't to be done. I can't see you,' and passed from her trembling, with open eyes.

She rode home on her bicycle, leaving the others to follow. Some ladies who did not know what had happened bowed and smiled as she passed, and she returned their salute.

'Oh, miss, is it true?' cried the cook, her face streaming with tears.

Agnes nodded. Presumably it was true. Letters had just arrived: one was for Gerald from his mother. Life, which had given them no warning, seemed to make no comment now. The incident was outside nature, and would surely pass away like a dream. She felt slightly irritable, and the grief of the servants annoyed her.

They sobbed. 'Ah, look at his marks! Ah, little he thought—little he thought!' In the brown holland strip by the front door a heavy football boot had left its impress. They had not liked Gerald, but he was a man, they were women, he had died. Their mistress ordered them to leave her.

For many minutes she sat at the foot of the stairs, rubbing her eyes. An obscure spiritual crisis was going on. Should she weep like the servants? or should she bear up and trust in the consoler Time? Was the death of a man so terrible after all? As she invited herself to apathy there were steps on the gravel, and Rickie Elliot burst in. He was splashed with mud, his breath was gone, and his hair fell wildly over his meagre face. She thought, 'These are the people who are left alive!' From the bottom of her soul she hated him.

'I came to see what you're doing,' he cried.

'Resting.'

He knelt beside her, and she said, 'Would you please go away?'

'Yes, dear Agnes, of course; but I must see first that you mind.'

Her breath caught. Her eyes moved to the treads, going outwards, so firmly, so irretrievably.

He panted, 'It's the worst thing that can ever happen to you in all your life, and you've got to mind it—you've got to mind it. They'll come saying, "Bear up—trust to time." No, no; they're wrong. Mind it.'

Through all her misery she knew that this boy was greater than they supposed. He rose to his feet, and with intense conviction cried: 'But I know—I understand. It's your death as well as his. He's gone, Agnes, and his arms will never hold you again. In God's name, mind such a thing, and don't sit fencing with your soul. Don't stop being great; that's the one crime he'll never forgive you.'

She faltered, 'Who—who forgives?'

'Gerald.'

At the sound of his name she slid forward, and all her dishonesty left her. She acknowledged that life's meaning had vanished. Bending down, she kissed the footprint. 'How can he forgive me?' she sobbed. 'Where has he gone to? You never could dream such an awful thing. He couldn't see me though I opened the door—wide—plenty of light; and then he could not remember the things that should comfort him. He wasn't a—he wasn't ever a great reader, and he couldn't remember the things. The rector tried, and he couldn't—I came, and I couldn't——' She could not speak for tears. Rickie did not check her. He let her accuse herself, and fate, and Herbert, who had postponed their marriage. She might have been a wife six months; but Herbert had spoken of self-control and of all life before them. He let her kiss the footprints till their marks gave way to the marks of her lips. She moaned, 'He is gone—where is he?' and then he replied quite quietly, 'He is in heaven.'

She begged him not to comfort her; she could not bear it.

'I did not come to comfort you. I came to see that you mind. He is in heaven, Agnes. The greatest thing is over.'

Her hatred was lulled. She murmured, 'Dear Rickie!' and held up her hand to him. Through her tears his meagre face showed as a seraph's who spoke the truth and forbade her to juggle with her soul. 'Dear Rickie—but for the rest of my life what am I to do?'

'Anything—if you remember that the greatest thing is over.'

'I don't know you,' she said tremulously. 'You have grown up in a moment. You never talked to us, and yet you understand it all. Tell me again— I can only trust you—where is he?'

'He is in heaven.'

'You are sure?'

It puzzled her that Rickie, who could scarcely tell you the time without a saving clause, should be so certain about immortality.

VI

He did not stop for the funeral. Mr. Pembroke thought that he had a bad effect on Agnes, and prevented her from acquiescing in the tragedy as rapidly as she might have done. As he expressed it, 'one must not court sorrow,' and he hinted to the young man that they desired to be alone. Rickie went back to the Silts.

He was only there a few days. As soon as term opened he returned to Cambridge, for which he longed passionately. The journey thither was now familiar to him, and he took pleasure in each landmark. The fair valley of Tewin Water, the cutting into Hitchin where the train traverses the chalk, Baldock Church, Royston with its promise of downs, were nothing in themselves, but dear as stages in his pilgrimage towards the abode of peace. On the platform he met friends. They had all had pleasant vacations: it was a happy world. The atmosphere alters.

Cambridge, according to her custom, welcomed her sons with open drains. Pettycury was up, so was Trinity Street, and navvies peeped out of King's Parade. Here it was gas, there electric light, but everywhere something, and always a smell. It was also the day that the wheels fell off the station tram, and Rickie, who was naturally inside, was among the passengers who 'sustained no injury but a shock, and had as hearty a laugh over the mishap afterwards as any one.'

Tilliard fled into a hansom, cursing himself for having tried to do the thing cheaply. Hornblower also swept past yelling derisively, with his luggage neatly piled above his head. 'Let's get out and walk,' muttered Ansell. But Rickie was succouring a distressed female—Mrs. Aberdeen. 'Oh, Mrs. Aberdeen, I never saw you; I am so glad to see you—I am so very glad.' Mrs. Aberdeen was cold. She did not like being spoken to outside the college, and was also distrait about her basket. Hitherto no genteel eye had ever seen inside it, but in the collision its little calico veil fell off, and there was revealed—nothing. The basket was empty, and never would hold anything illegal. All the same she was distrait, and 'We shall meet later, sir, I dessy,' was all the greeting Rickie got from her.

'Now what kind of life has Mrs. Aberdeen?' he exclaimed, as he and Ansell pursued the Station Road. 'Here these bedders come and make us comfortable. We owe an enormous amount to them, their wages are absurd, and we know nothing about them. Off they go to Barnwell, and then their lives are hidden. I just know that Mrs. Aberdeen has a husband, but that's all. She never will talk about him. Now I do so want to fill in her life. I see one-half of it. What's the other half? She may have a real jolly house in good taste, with a little garden, and books, and pictures. Or, again, she mayn't. But in any case one ought to know. I know she'd dislike it, but she oughtn't to dislike. After all, bedders are to blame for the present lamentable state of things, just as much as gentlefolk. She ought to want me to come, She ought to introduce me to her husband.'

They had reached the corner of Hills Road. Ansell spoke for the first time. He said, 'Ugh!'

'Drains?'

'Yes. A spiritual cesspool.'

Rickie laughed.

'I expected it from your letter.'

'The one you never answered?'

'I answer none of your letters. You are quite hopeless by now. You can go to the bad. But I refuse to accompany you. I refuse to believe that every human being is a moving wonder of supreme interest and tragedy and beauty—which was what the letter in question amounted to. You'll find plenty who will believe it. It's a very popular view among people who are too idle to think; it saves them the trouble of detecting the beautiful from the ugly, the interesting from the dull, the tragic from the melodramatic. You had just come from Sawston, and were apparently carried away by the fact that Miss Pembroke had the usual amount of arms and legs.'

Rickie was silent. He had told his friend how he felt, but not what had happened. Ansell could discuss love and death admirably, but somehow he would not understand lovers or a dying man, and in the letter there had been scant allusion to these concrete facts. Would Cambridge understand them either? He watched some dons who were peeping into an excavation, and throwing up their hands with humorous gestures of despair. These men would lecture next week on Catiline's conspiracy, on Luther, on Evolution, on Catullus. They dealt with so much and they had experienced so little. Was it possible he would ever come to think Cambridge narrow? In his short life Rickie had known two sudden deaths, and that is enough to disarrange any placid outlook on the world. He knew once for all that we are all of us bubbles on an extremely rough sea. Into this sea humanity has built, as it were, some little breakwaters—scientific knowledge, civilized restraint—so that the bubbles do not break so frequently or so soon. But the sea has not altered, and it was only a chance that he, Ansell, Tilliard, and Mrs. Aberdeen had not all been killed in the tram.

They waited for the other tram by the Roman Catholic Church, whose florid bulk was already receding into twilight. It is the first big building that the incoming visitor sees. 'Oh, here comes the colleges!' cries the Protestant parent, and then learns that it was built by a Papist who made a fortune out of movable eyes for dolls. 'Built out of dolls' eyes to contain idols'—that at all events is the legend and the joke. It watches over the apostate city, taller by many a yard than anything within, and asserting, however wildly, that here is eternity, stability, and bubbles unbreakable upon a windless sea.

A costly hymn tune announced five o'clock, and in the distance the more lovable note of St. Mary's could be heard, speaking from the heart of the town. Then the tram arrived—the slow stuffy tram that plies every twenty minutes between the un-known and the market-place—and took them past the desecrated grounds of Downing, past Adden-brooke's Hospital, girt like any Venetian palace with a mantling canal, past the Fitzwilliam, tower-ing upon immense substructions like any Roman temple, right up to the gates of one's own college, which looked like nothing else in the world. The porters were glad to see them, but wished it had been a hansom. 'Our luggage,' explained Rickie, 'comes in the hotel omnibus, if you would kindly pay a shilling for mine.' Ansell turned aside to some large lighted windows, the abode of a hospitable don, and from other windows there floated familiar voices and the familiar mistakes in a Beethoven sonata. The college, though small, was civilized, and proud of its civilization. It was not sufficient glory to be a Blue there, nor an additional glory to get drunk. Many a maiden lady, who had read that Cambridge men were sad dogs, was surprised and perhaps a little disappointed at the reasonable life which greeted her. Miss Appleblossom in particular had had a tremendous shock. The sight of young fellows making tea and drinking water had made her wonder whether this was Cambridge College at all. 'It is so,' she exclaimed afterwards. 'It is just as I say; and what's more, I wouldn't have it otherwise. Stewart says it's as easy to get into the swim, and not at all expensive.' The direction of the swim was determined a little by the genius of the place—for places have genius, though the less we talk about it the better—and a good deal by the tutors and resident fellows, who treated with rare dexterity the products that came up yearly from the public schools. They taught the perky boy that he was not everything, and the limp boy that he might be something. They even welcomed those boys who were neither limp nor perky, but odd—those boys who had never been at a public school at all, and such do not find a welcome everywhere. And they did everything with ease—one might almost say with nonchalance,—so that the boys noticed nothing, and received education, often for the first time in their lives.

But Rickie turned to none of these friends, for just then he loved his rooms better than any person. They were all he really possessed in the world, the only place he could call his own. Over the door was his name, and through the paint, like a grey ghost, he could still read the name of his predecessor. With a sigh of joy he entered the perishable home that was his for a couple of years.

There was a beautiful fire, and the kettle boiled at once. He made tea on the hearth-rug and ate the biscuits which Mrs. Aberdeen had brought for him up from Anderson's. 'Gentlemen,' she said, 'must learn to give and take.' He sighed again and again, like one who had escaped from danger. With his head on the fender and all his limbs relaxed, he felt almost as safe as he felt once when his mother killed a ghost in the passage by carrying him through it in her arms. There was no ghost now; he was frightened at reality; he was frightened at the splendours and horrors of the world.

A letter from Miss Pembroke was on the table. He did not hurry to open it, for she, and all that she did, was overwhelming. She wrote like the Sibyl; her sorrowful face moved over the stars and shattered their harmonies; last night he saw her with the eyes of Blake, a virgin widow, tall, veiled, consecrated, with her hands stretched out against an everlasting wind. Why would she write? Her letters were not for the likes of him, nor to be read in rooms like his.

'We are not leaving Sawston,' she wrote. 'I saw how selfish it was of me to risk spoiling Herbert's career. I shall get used to any place. Now that he is gone, nothing of that sort can matter. Every one has been most kind, but you have comforted me most, though you did not mean to. I cannot think how you did it, or understood so much. I still think of you as a little boy with a lame leg,—I know you will let me say this,—and yet when it came to the point you knew more than people who have been all their lives with sorrow and death.'

Rickie burnt this letter, which he ought not to have done, for it was one of the few tributes Miss Pembroke ever paid to imagination. But he felt that it did not belong to him: words so sincere should be for Gerald alone. The smoke rushed up the chimney, and he indulged in a vision. He saw it reach the outer air and beat against the low ceiling of clouds. The clouds were too strong for it; but in them was one chink, revealing one star, and through this the smoke escaped into the light of stars innumerable. Then—but then the vision failed, and the voice of science whispered that all smoke remains on earth in the form of smuts, and is troublesome to Mrs. Aberdeen.

'I am jolly unpractical,' he mused. 'And what is the point of it when real things are so wonderful? Who wants visions in a world that has Agnes and Gerald?' He turned on the electric light and pulled open the table-drawer. There, among spoons and corks and string, he found a fragment of a little story that he had tried to write last term. It was called 'The Bay of the Fifteen Islets,' and the action took place on St. John's Eve off the coast of Sicily. A party of tourists land on one of the islands. Suddenly the boatmen become uneasy, and say that the island is not generally there. It is an extra one, and they had better have tea on one of the ordinaries. 'Pooh, volcanic!' says the leading tourist, and the ladies say how interesting. The island begins to rock, and so do the minds of its visitors. They start to quarrel and jabber. Fingers burst up through the sand—black fingers of sea devils. The island tilts. The tourists go mad. But just before the catastrophe one man, *integer vitæ scelerisque purus,* sees the truth. Here are no devils. Other muscles, other minds, are pulling the island to its subterranean home. Through the advancing wall of waters he sees no grisly faces, no ghastly medieval limbs, but—— But what nonsense! When real things are so wonderful, what is the point of pretending?

And so Rickie deflected his enthusiasms. Hitherto they had played on gods and heroes, on the infinite and the impossible, on virtue and beauty and strength. Now, with a steadier radiance, they transfigured a man who was dead and a woman who was still alive.

VII

Love, say orderly people, can be fallen into by two methods: (1) through the desires, (2) through the imagination. And if the orderly people are English, they add that (1) is the inferior method, and characteristic of the South. It is inferior. Yet those who pursue it at all events know what they want; they are not puzzling to themselves or ludicrous to others; they do not take the wings of the morning and fly into the uttermost parts of the sea before walking to the registry office; they cannot breed a tragedy quite like Rickie's.

He is, of course, absurdly young—not twenty-one—and he will be engaged to be married at twenty-three. He has no knowledge of the world; for example, he thinks that if you do not want money you can give it to friends who do. He believes in humanity because he knows a dozen decent people. He believes in women because he has loved his mother. And his friends are as young and as ignorant as himself. They are full of the wine of life. But they have not tasted the cup—let us call it the teacup—of experience, which has made men of Mr. Pembroke's type what they are. Oh, that teacup! To be taken at prayers, at

friendship, at love, till we are quite sane, quite efficient, quite experienced, and quite useless to God
or man. We must drink it, or we shall die. But we
need not drink it always. Here is our problem
and our salvation. There comes a moment—God
knows when—at which we can say, 'I will experience no longer. I will create. I will be an
experience.' But to do this we must be both acute
and heroic. For it is not easy, after accepting six
cups of tea, to throw the seventh in the face of the
hostess. And to Rickie this moment has not, as yet,
been offered.

Ansell, at the end of his third year, got a first
in the Moral Science Tripos. Being a scholar, he
kept his rooms in college, and at once began to
work for a Fellowship. Rickie got a creditable
second in the Classical Tripos, Part I, and retired
to sallow lodgings in Mill Lane, carrying with him
the degree of B.A. and a small exhibition, which
was quite as much as he deserved. For Part II he
read Greek Archæology, and got a second. All this
means that Ansell was much cleverer than Rickie.
As for the cow, she was still going strong, though
turning a little academic as the years passed over
her.

'We are bound to get narrow,' sighed Rickie.
He and his friend were lying in a meadow during
their last summer term. In his incurable love for
flowers he had plaited two garlands of buttercups
and cow-parsley, and Ansell's lean Jewish face was
framed in one of them. 'Cambridge is wonderful,
but it's so tiny. You have no idea—at least, I
think you have no idea—how the great world
looks down on it.'

'I read the letters in the papers.'

'It's a bad look-out.'

'How?'

'Cambridge has lost touch with the times.'

'Was she ever intended to touch them?'

'She satisfies,' said Rickie mysteriously, 'neither the professions, nor the public schools, nor the great thinking mass of men and women. There is a general feeling that her day is over, and naturally one feels pretty sick.'

'Do you still write short stories?'

'Why?'

'Because your English has gone to the devil. You think and talk in journalese. Define a great thinking mass.'

Rickie sat up and adjusted his floral crown.

'Estimate the worth of a general feeling.'

Silence.

'And thirdly, where is the great world?'

'Oh, that——!'

'Yes. That,' exclaimed Ansell, rising from his couch in violent excitement. 'Where is it? How do you set about finding it? How long does it take to get there? What does it think? What does it do? What does it want? Oblige me with specimens of its art and literature.' Silence. 'Till you do, my opinions will be as follows. There is no great world at all, only a little earth, for ever isolated from the rest of the little solar system. The little earth is full of tiny societies, and Cambridge is one of them. All the societies are narrow, but some are good and some are bad—just as one house is beautiful inside and another ugly. Observe the metaphor of the houses: I am coming back to it. The good societies say, "I tell you to do this because I am Cambridge." The bad ones say, "I tell you to do that because I am the great world"— not because I am "Peckham," or "Billingsgate," or

"Park Lane," but "because I am the great world." They lie. And fools like you listen to them, and believe that they are a thing which does not exist and never has existed, and confuse "great," which has no meaning whatever, with "good," which means salvation. Look at this great wreath: it'll be dead to-morrow. Look at that good flower: it'll come up again next year. Now for the other metaphor. To compare the world to Cambridge is like comparing the outsides of houses with the inside of a house. No intellectual effort is needed, no moral result is attained. You only have to say, "Oh, what a difference! Oh, what a difference!" and then come indoors again and exhibit your broadened mind.'

'I never shall come indoors again,' said Rickie. 'That's the whole point.' And his voice began to quiver. 'It's well enough for those who'll get a Fellowship, but in a few weeks I shall go down. In a few years it'll be as if I've never been up. It matters very much to me what the world is like. I can't answer your questions about it; and that's no loss to you, but so much the worse for me. And then you've got a house—not a metaphorical one, but a house with father and sisters. I haven't, and never shall have. There'll never again be a home for me like Cambridge. I shall only look at the outsides of homes. According to your metaphor, I shall live in the street, and it matters very much to me what I find there.'

'You'll live in another house right enough,' said Ansell, rather uneasily. 'Only take care you pick out a decent one. I can't think why you flop about so helplessly, like a bit of sea-weed. In four years you've taken as much root as any one.'

'Where?'

'I should say you've been fortunate in your friends.'

'Oh—that!' But he was not cynical—or cynical in a very tender way. He was thinking of the irony of friendship—so strong it is, and so fragile. We fly together, like straws in an eddy, to part in the open stream. Nature has no use for us; she has cut her stuff differently. Dutiful sons, loving husbands, responsible fathers—these are what she wants, and if we are friends it must be in our spare time. Abram and Sarai were sorrowful, yet their seed became as sand of the sea, and distracts the politics of Europe at this moment. But a few verses of poetry is all that survives of David and Jonathan.

'I wish we were labelled,' said Rickie. He wished that all the confidence and mutual knowledge that is born in such a place as Cambridge could be organized. People went down into the world saying, 'We know and like each other; we shan't forget.' But they did forget, for man is so made that he cannot remember long without a symbol; he wished there was a society, a kind of friendship office, where the marriage of true minds could be registered.

'Why labels?'

'To know each other again.'

'I have taught you pessimism splendidly.' He looked at his watch.

'What time?'

'Not twelve.'

Rickie got up.

'Why go?' He stretched out his hand and caught hold of Rickie's ankle.

'I've got that Miss Pembroke to lunch—that girl whom you say never's there.'

'Then why go? All this week you have pre-

tended Miss Pembroke awaited you. Wednesday—
Miss Pembroke to lunch. Thursday—Miss Pembroke to tea. Now again—and you didn't even
invite her.'

'To Cambridge, no. But the Hall man they're
stopping with has so many engagements that she
and her friend can often come to me, I'm glad to
say. I don't think I ever told you much, but over
two years ago the man she was going to marry
was killed at football. She nearly died of grief. This
visit to Cambridge is almost the first amusement
she has felt up to taking. Oh, they go back to-
morrow! Give me breakfast to-morrow.'

'All right.'

'But I shall see you this evening. I shall be round
at your paper on Schopenhauer. Lemme go.'

'Don't go,' he said idly. 'It's much better for
you to talk to me.'

'Lemme go, Stewart.'

'It's amusing that you're so feeble. You—simply
—can't—get—away. I wish I wanted to bully you.'

Rickie laughed, and suddenly overbalanced into
the grass. Ansell, with unusual playfulness, held
him prisoner. They lay there for a few minutes,
talking and ragging aimlessly. Then Rickie seized
his opportunity and jerked away.

'Go, go!' yawned the other. But he was a little
vexed, for he was a young man with great capacity
for pleasure, and it pleased him that morning to
be with his friend. The thought of two ladies waiting lunch did not deter him; stupid women, why
shouldn't they wait? Why should they interfere
with their betters? With his ear on the ground he
listened to Rickie's departing steps, and thought,
'He wastes a lot of time keeping engagements.
Why will he be pleasant to fools?' And then he

thought, 'Why has he turned so unhappy? It isn't as if he's a philosopher, or tries to solve the riddle of existence. And he's got money of his own.' Thus thinking, he fell asleep.

Meanwhile Rickie hurried away from him, and slackened and stopped, and hurried again. He was due at the Union in ten minutes, but he could not bring himself there. He dared not meet Miss Pembroke: he loved her.

The devil must have planned it. They had started so gloriously; she had been a goddess both in joy and sorrow. She was a goddess still. But he had dethroned the god whom once he had glorified equally. Slowly, slowly, the image of Gerald had faded. That was the first step. Rickie had thought, 'No matter. He will be bright again. Just now all the radiance chances to be in her.' And on her he had fixed his eyes. He thought of her awake. He entertained her willingly in dreams. He found her in poetry and music and in the sunset. She made him kind and strong. She made him clever. Through her he kept Cambridge in its proper place, and lived as a citizen of the great world. But one night he dreamt that she lay in his arms. This displeased him. He determined to think a little about Gerald instead. Then the fabric collapsed.

It was hard on Rickie thus to meet the devil. He did not deserve it, for he was comparatively civilized, and knew that there was nothing shameful in love. But to love this woman! If only it had been any one else! Love in return—that he could expect from no one, being too ugly and too unattractive. But the love he offered would not then have been vile. The insult to Miss Pembroke, who was consecrated, and whom he had consecrated, who could still see Gerald, and always would see him, shining on his everlasting throne—this was the crime from the devil, the crime that no penance would ever purge. She knew nothing. She never would know. But the crime was registered in heaven.

He had been tempted to confide in Ansell. But to what purpose? He would say, 'I love Miss Pembroke,' and Stewart would reply, 'You ass.' And then, 'I'm never going to tell her.' 'You ass,' again. After all, it was not a practical question; Agnes would never hear of his fall. If his friend had been, as he expressed it, 'labelled'; if he had been a father, or still better a brother, one might tell him of the discreditable passion. But why irritate him for no reason? Thinking 'I am always angling for sympathy; I must stop myself,' he hurried onward to the Union.

He found his guests half-way up the stairs, reading the advertisements of coaches for the Long Vacation. He heard Mrs. Lewin say, 'I wonder what he'll end by doing.' A little over-acting his part, he apologized nonchalantly for his lateness.

'It's always the same,' cried Agnes. 'Last time he forgot I was coming altogether.' She wore a flowered muslin—something indescribably liquid and cool. It reminded him a little of those swift piercing streams, neither blue nor green, that gush out of the Dolomites. Her face was clear and brown, like the face of a mountaineer; her hair was so plentiful that it seemed banked up above it; and her little toque, though it answered the note of the dress, was almost ludicrous, poised on so much natural glory. When she moved, the sunlight flashed on her ear-rings.

He led them up to the luncheon-room. By now he was conscious of his limitations as a host, and never attempted to entertain ladies in his lodgings. Moreover, the Union seemed less intimate. It had a faint flavour of a London club; it marked the undergraduate's nearest approach to the great world. Amid its waiters and serviettes one felt impersonal, and able to conceal the private emotions. Rickie felt that if Miss Pembroke knew one thing about him, she knew everything. During this visit he took her to no place that he greatly loved.

'Sit down, ladies. Fall to. I'm sorry. I was out towards Coton with a dreadful friend.'

Mrs. Lewin pushed up her veil. She was a typical May-term chaperon, always pleasant, always hungry, and always tired. Year after year she came up to Cambridge in a tight silk dress, and year after year she nearly died of it. Her feet hurt, her limbs were cramped in a canoe, black spots danced before her eyes from eating too much mayonnaise. But still she came, if not as a mother as an aunt, if not as an aunt as a friend. Still she ascended the roof of King's, still she counted the balls of Clare, still she was on the point of grasping the organization of the May races. 'And who is your friend?' she asked.

'His name is Ansell.'

'Well, now, did I see him two years ago—as a bedmaker in something they did at the Foot Lights? Oh, how I roared.'

'You didn't see Mr. Ansell at the Foot Lights,' said Agnes, smiling.

'How do you know?' asked Rickie.

'He'd scarcely be so frivolous.'

'Do you remember seeing him?'

'For a moment.'

What a memory she had! And how splendidly during that moment she had behaved!

'Isn't he marvellously clever?'

'I believe so.'

'Oh, give me clever people!' cried Mrs. Lewin. 'They are kindness itself at the Hall, but I assure you I am depressed at times. One cannot talk bump-rowing for ever.'

'I never hear about him, Rickie; but isn't he really your greatest friend?'

'I don't go in for greatest friends.'

'Do you mean you like us all equally?'

'All differently, those of you I like.'

'Ah, you've caught it!' cried Mrs. Lewin. 'Mr. Elliot gave it you there well.'

Agnes laughed, and, her elbows on the table, regarded them both through her fingers—a habit of hers. Then she said, 'Can't we see the great Mr. Ansell?'

'Oh, let's. Or would he frighten me?'

'He would frighten you,' said Rickie. 'He's a trifle weird.'

'My good Rickie, if you knew the deathly dullness of Sawston—every one saying the proper thing at the proper time. I so proper, Herbert so proper! Why, weirdness is the one thing I long for! Do arrange something.'

'I'm afraid there's no opportunity. Ansell goes some vast bicycle ride this afternoon; this evening you're tied up at the Hall; and to-morrow you go.'

'But there's breakfast to-morrow,' said Agnes. 'Look here, Rickie, bring Mr. Ansell to breakfast with us at Buol's.'

Mrs. Lewin seconded the invitation.

'Bad luck again,' said Rickie boldly; 'I'm already fixed up for breakfast. I'll tell him of your very kind intention.'

'Let's have him alone,' murmured Agnes.

'My dear girl, I should die through the floor! Oh, it'll be all right about breakfast. I rather think we shall get asked this evening by that shy man who has the pretty rooms in Trinity.'

'Oh, very well. Where is it you breakfast, Rickie?'

He faltered. 'To Ansell's, it is——' It seemed as if he was making some great admission. So self-conscious was he, that he thought the two women exchanged glances. Had Agnes already explored that part of him that did not belong to her? Would another chance step reveal the part that did? He asked them abruptly what they would like to do after lunch.

'Anything,' said Mrs. Lewin,—'anything in the world.'

A walk? A boat? Ely? A drive? Some objection was raised to each. 'To tell the truth,' she said at last, 'I do feel a wee bit tired, and what occurs to me is this. You and Agnes shall leave me here and have no more bother. I shall be perfectly happy snoozling in one of these delightful drawing-room chairs. Do what you like, and then pick me up after it.'

'Alas! it's against regulations,' said Rickie. 'The Union won't trust lady visitors on its premises alone.'

'But who's to know I'm alone? With a lot of men in the drawing-room, how's each to know that I'm not with the others?'

'That would shock Rickie,' said Agnes, laughing. 'He's frightfully high-principled.'

'No, I'm not,' said Rickie, thinking of his recent shiftiness over breakfast.

'Then come for a walk with me. I want exercise. Some connection of ours was once rector of Madingley. I shall walk out and see the church.'

Mrs. Lewin was accordingly left in the Union.

'This is jolly!' Agnes exclaimed as she strode along the somewhat depressing road that leads out of Cambridge past the observatory. 'Do I go too fast?'

'No, thank you. I get stronger every year. If it wasn't for the look of the thing, I should be quite happy.'

'But you don't care for the look of the thing. It's only ignorant people who do that, surely.'

'Perhaps. I care. I like people who are well-made and beautiful. They are of some use in the world. I understand why they are there. I cannot understand why the ugly and crippled are there, however healthy they may feel inside. Don't you know how Turner spoils his pictures by introducing a man like a bolster in the foreground? Well, in actual life every landscape is spoilt by men of worse shapes still.'

'You sound like a bolster with the stuffing out.' They laughed. She always blew his cobwebs away like this, with a puff of humorous mountain air. Just now—the associations he attached to her were various—she reminded him of a heroine of Meredith's—but a heroine at the end of the book. All had been written about her. She had played her mighty part, and knew that it was over. He and he alone was not content, and wrote for her daily a trivial and impossible sequel.

Last time they had talked about Gerald. But that was some six months ago, when things felt easier. To-day Gerald was the faintest blur. Fortunately the conversation turned to Mr. Pembroke and to education. Did women lose a lot by not knowing Greek? 'A heap,' said Rickie, roughly. But modern languages? Thus they got to Germany, which he had visited last Easter with Ansell; and thence to the German Emperor, and what a to-do he made; and from him to our own king (still Prince of Wales), who had lived while an undergraduate at Madingley Hall. Here it was. And all the time he thought, 'It is hard on her. She has no right to be walking with me. She would be ill with disgust if she knew. It is hard on her to be loved.'

They looked at the Hall, and went inside the pretty little church. Some Arundel prints hung upon the pillars, and Agnes expressed the opinion that pictures inside a place of worship were a pity. Rickie did not agree with this. He said again that nothing beautiful was ever to be regretted.

'You're cracked on beauty,' she whispered—they were still inside the church. 'Do hurry up and write something.'

'Something beautiful?'

'I believe you can. I'm going to lecture you seriously all the way home. Take care that you don't waste your life.'

They continued the conversation outside. 'But I've got to hate my own writing. I believe that most people come to that stage—not so early though. What I write is too silly. It can't happen. For instance, a stupid vulgar man is engaged to a lovely young lady. He wants her to live in the towns, but she only cares for woods. She shocks him this way and that, but gradually he tames her, and makes her nearly as dull as he is. One day she has a last explosion—over the snobby wedding-presents—

and flies out of the drawing-room window, shouting, "Freedom and truth!" Near the house is a little dell full of fir-trees, and she runs into it. He comes there the next moment. But she's gone.'

'Awfully exciting. Where?'

'Oh Lord, she's a Dryad!' cried Rickie, in great disgust. 'She's turned into a tree.'

'Rickie, it's very good indeed. That kind of thing has something in it. Of course you get it all through Greek and Latin. How upset the man must be when he sees the girl turn.'

'He doesn't see her. He never gueses. Such a man could never see a Dryad.'

'So you describe how she turns just before he comes up?'

'No. Indeed I don't ever say that she does turn. I don't use the word "Dryad" once.'

'I think you ought to put that part plainly. Otherwise, with such an original story, people might miss the point. Have you had any luck with it?'

'Magazines? I haven't tried. I know what the stuff's worth. You see, a year or two ago I had a great idea of getting into touch with Nature, just as the Greeks were in touch; and seeing England so beautiful, I used to pretend that her trees and coppices and summer fields of parsley were alive. It's funny enough now, but it wasn't funny then, for I got in such at state that I believed, actually believed, that Fauns lived in a certain double hedgerow near the Gog Magogs, and one evening I walked round a mile sooner than go through it alone.'

'Good gracious!' She laid her hand on his shoulder.

He moved to the other side of the road. 'It's all right now. I've changed those follies for others.

But while I had them I began to write, and even now I keep on writing, though I know better. I've got quite a pile of little stories, all harping on this ridiculous idea of getting into touch with Nature.'

'I wish you weren't so modest. It's simply splendid as an idea. Though—but tell me about the Dryad who was engaged to be married. What was she like?'

'I can show you the dell in which the young person disappeared. We pass it on the right in a moment.'

'It does seem a pity that you don't make something of your talents. It seems such a waste to write little stories and never publish them. You must have enough for a book. Life is so full in our days that short stories are the very thing; they get read by people who'd never tackle a novel. For example, at our Dorcas we tried to read out a long affair by Henry James—Herbert saw it recommended in *The Times*. There was no doubt it was very good, but one simply couldn't remember from one week to another what had happened. So now our aim is to get something that just lasts the hour. I take you seriously, Rickie, and that is why I am so offensive. You are too modest. People who think they can do nothing so often do nothing. I want you to plunge.'

It thrilled him like a trumpet-blast. She took him seriously. Could he but thank her for her divine affability! But the words would stick in his throat, or worse still, would bring other words along with them. His breath came quickly, for he seldom spoke of his writing, and no one, not even Ansell, had advised him to plunge.

'But do you really think that I could take up literature?'

'Why not? You can try. Even if you fail, you can
try. Of course we think you tremendously clever;
and I met one of your dons at tea, and he said that
your degree was not in the least a proof of your
abilities: he said that you knocked up and got
flurried in examinations. Oh!'—her cheek flushed,
—'I wish I was a man. The whole world lies before them. They can do anything. They aren't
cooped up with servants and tea-parties and
twaddle. But where's this dell where the Dryad
disappeared?'

'We've passed it.' He had meant to pass it. It
was too beautiful. All he had read, all he had
hoped, all he had loved, seemed to quiver in its
enchanted air. It was perilous. He dared not enter
it with such a woman.

'How long ago?' She turned back. 'I don't want
to miss the dell. Here it must be,' she added after
a few moments, and sprang up the green bank
that hid the entrance from the road. 'Oh, what a
jolly place!'

'Go right in if you want to see it,' said Rickie,
and did not offer to go with her. She stood for a
moment looking at the view, for a few steps will
increase a view in Cambridgeshire. The wind blew
her dress against her. Then, like a cataract again,
she vanished pure and cool into the dell.

The young man thought of her feelings no
longer. His heart throbbed louder and louder, and
seemed to shake him to pieces.

'Rickie!'

She was calling from the dell, For an answer he
sat down where he was, on the dust-bespattered
margin. She could call as loud as she liked. The
devil had done much, but he should not take him
to her.

'Rickie!'—and it came with the tones of an angel. He drove his fingers into his ears, and invoked the name of Gerald. But there was no sign, neither angry motion in the air nor hint of January mist. June—fields of June, sky of June, songs of June. Grass of June beneath him, grass of June over the tragedy he had deemed immortal. A bird called out of the dell: 'Rickie!'

A bird flew into the dell.

.　　.　　.　　.　　.

'Did you take me for the Dryad?' she asked. She was sitting down with his head on her lap. He had laid it there for a moment before he went out to die, and she had not let him take it away.

'I prayed you might not be a woman,' he whispered.

'Darling, I am very much a woman. I do not vanish into groves and trees. I thought you would never come to me.'

'Did you expect——?'

'I hoped. I called hoping.'

Inside the dell it was neither June nor January. The chalk walls barred out the seasons, and the fir-trees did not seem to feel their passage. Only from time to time the odours of summer slipped in from the wood above, to comment on the waxing year. She bent down to touch him with her lips.

He started, and cried passionately, 'Never forget that your greatest thing is over. I have forgotten: I am too weak. You shall never forget. What I said to you then is greater than what I say to you now. What he gave you then is greater than anything you will get from me.'

She was frightened. Again she had the sense of something abnormal. Then she said, 'What is all this nonsense?' and folded him in her arms.

VIII

Ansell stood looking at his breakfast-table, which was laid for four instead of for two. His bedmaker, equally peevish, explained how it had happened. Last night, at one in the morning, the porter had been awoke with a note for the kitchens, and in that note Mr. Elliot said that all these things were to be sent to Mr. Ansell's.

'The fools have sent the original order as well. Here's the lemon-sole for two. I can't move for food.'

'The note being ambigerous, the Kitchens judged best to send it all.' She spoke of the kitchens in a half-respectful, half-pitying way, much as one speaks of Parliament.

'Who's to pay for it?' He peeped into the new dishes. Kidneys entombed in an omelette, hot roast chicken in watery gravy, a glazed but pallid pie.

'And who's to wash it up?' said the bedmaker to her help outside.

Ansell had disputed late last night concerning Schopenhauer, and was a little cross and tired. He bounced over to Tilliard, who kept opposite. Tilliard was eating gooseberry jam.

'Did Elliot ask you to breakfast with me?'

'No,' said Tilliard mildly.

'Well, you'd better come, and bring every one you know.'

So Tilliard came, bearing himself a little formally,

for he was not very intimate with his neighbour.
Out of the window they called to Widdrington.
But he laid his hand on his stomach, thus indicating
it was too late.

'Who's to pay for it?' repeated Ansell, as a man
appeared from the Buttery carrying coffee on a
bright tin tray.

'College coffee! How nice!' remarked Tilliard,
who was cutting the pie. 'But before term ends
you must come and try my new machine. My
sister gave it me. There is a bulb at the top, and as
the water boils——'

'He might have counter-ordered the lemon-sole.
That's Rickie all over. Violently economical, and
then loses his head, and all the things go bad.'

'Give them to the bedder while they're hot.'
This was done. She accepted them dispassionately,
with the air of one who lives without nourishment.
Tilliard continued to describe his sister's coffee
machine.

'What's that?' They could hear panting and
rustling on the stairs.

'It sounds like a lady,' said Tilliard fearfully. He
slipped the piece of pie back. It fell into position
like a brick.

'Is it here? Am I right? Is it here?' The door
opened and in came Mrs. Lewin. 'Oh horrors! I've
made a mistake.'

'That's all right,' said Ansell awkwardly.

'I wanted Mr. Elliot. Where are they?'

'We expect Mr. Elliot every moment,' said
Tilliard.

'Don't tell me I'm right,' cried Mrs. Lewin, 'and
that you're the terrifying Mr. Ansell.' And, with
obvious relief, she wrung Tilliard warmly by the
hand.

'I'm Ansell,' said Ansell, looking very uncouth and grim.

'How stupid of me not to know it,' she gasped, and would have gone on to I know not what, but the door opened again. It was Rickie.

'Here's Miss Pembroke,' he said. 'I am going to marry her.'

There was a profound silence.

'We oughtn't to have done things like this,' said Agnes, turning to Mrs. Lewin. 'We have no right to take Mr. Ansell by surprise. It is Rickie's fault. He was that obstinate. He would bring us. He ought to be horsewhipped.'

'He ought indeed,' said Tilliard pleasantly, and bolted. Not till he gained his room did he realize that he had been less apt than usual. As for Ansell, the first thing he said was, 'Why didn't you counter-order the lemon-sole?'

In such a situation Mrs. Lewin was of priceless value. She led the way to the table, observing, 'I quite agree with Miss Pembroke. I loathe surprises. Never shall I forget my horror when the knife-boy painted the dove's cage with the dove inside. He did it as a surprise. Poor Parsival nearly died. His feathers were bright green!'

'Well, give me the lemon-soles,' said Rickie. 'I like them.'

'The bedder's got them.'

'Well, there you are! What's there to be annoyed about?'

'And while the cage was drying we put him among the bantams. They had been the greatest allies. But I suppose they took him for a parrot or a hawk, or something that bantams hate; for while his cage was drying they picked out his feathers, and *picked* out his feathers, and *Picked* out his feathers, till he was perfectly bald. "Hugo, look," said I. "This is the end of Parsival. Let me have no more surprises." He burst into tears.'

Thus did Mrs. Lewin create an atmosphere. At first it seemed unreal, but gradually they got used to it, and breathed scarcely anything else throughout the meal. In such an atmosphere everything seemed of small and equal value, and the engagement of Rickie and Agnes, like the feathers of Parsival, fluttered lightly to the ground. Ansell was generally silent. He was no match for these two quiet clever women. Only once was there a hitch.

They had been talking gaily enough about the betrothal when Ansell suddenly interrupted with, 'When is the marriage?'

'Mr. Ansell,' said Agnes, blushing, 'I wish you hadn't asked that. That part's dreadful. Not for years, as far as we can see.'

But Rickie had not seen as far. He had not talked to her of this at all. Last night they had spoken only of love. He exclaimed, 'Oh, Agnes— don't!' Mrs. Lewin laughed roguishly.

'Why this delay?' asked Ansell.

Agnes looked at Rickie, who replied, 'I must get money, worse luck.'

'I thought you'd got money.'

He hesitated, and then said, 'I must get my foot on the ladder, then.'

Ansell began with, 'On what ladder?' but Mrs. Lewin, using the privilege of her sex, exclaimed, 'Not another word. If there's a thing I abominate, it is plans. My head goes whirling at once.' What she really abominated was questions, and she saw that Ansell was turning serious. To appease him, she put on her clever manner and asked him about Germany. How had it impressed him? Were we so totally unfitted to repel invasion? Was not German scholarship overestimated? He replied discourteously, but he did reply; and if she could have stopped him thinking, her triumph would have been complete.

When they rose to go, Agnes held Ansell's hand for a moment in her own.

'Good-bye,' she said. 'It was very unconventional of us to come as we did, but I don't think any of us are conventional people.'

He only replied, 'Good-bye.' The ladies started off. Rickie lingered behind to whisper, 'I would have it so. I would have you begin square together. I can't talk yet—I've loved her for years—I can't think what she's done it for. I'm going to write short stories. I shall start this afternoon. She declares there may be something in me.'

As soon as he had left, Tilliard burst in, white with agitation, and crying, 'Did you see my awful *faux pas*—about the horsewhip? What shall I do? I must call on Elliot. Or had I better write?'

'Miss Pembroke will not mind,' said Ansell gravely. 'She is unconventional.' He knelt in an arm-chair and hid his face in the back.

'It was like a bomb,' said Tilliard.

'It was meant to be.'

'I do feel a fool. What must she think?'

'Never mind, Tilliard. You've not been as big a fool as myself. At all events, you told her he must be horsewhipped.'

Tilliard hummed a little tune. He hated anything nasty, and there was nastiness in Ansell. 'What did *you* tell her?' he asked.

'Nothing.'

'What do you think of it?'

'I think: Damn those women.'

'Ah, yes. One hates one's friends to get engaged. It makes one feel so old: I think that is one of the reasons. The brother just above me has lately married, and my sister was quite sick about it, though the thing was suitable in every way.'

'Damn *these* women, then,' said Ansell, bouncing round in the chair. 'Damn these particular women.'

'They looked and spoke like ladies.'

'Exactly. Their diplomacy was ladylike. Their lies were ladylike. They've caught Elliot in a most ladylike way. I saw it all during the one moment we were natural. Generally we were clattering after the married one, whom—like a fool—I took for a fool. But for one moment we were natural, and during that moment Miss Pembroke told a lie, and made Rickie believe it was the truth.'

'What did she say?'

'She said "we see" instead of "I see."'

Tilliard burst into laughter. This jaundiced young philosopher, with his kinky view of life, was too much for him.

'She said "we see,"' repeated Ansell, 'instead of "I see," and she made him believe that it was the truth. She caught him and makes him believe that he caught her. She came to see me and makes him think that it is his idea. That is what I mean when I say that she is a lady.'

'You are too subtle for me. My dull eyes could only see two happy people.'

'I never said they weren't happy.'

'Then, my dear Ansell, why are you so cut up? It's beastly when a friend marries,—and I grant he's rather young,—but I should say it's the best thing for him. A decent woman—and you have proved not one thing against her—a decent woman will keep him up to the mark and stop him getting slack. She'll make him responsible and manly, for much as I like Rickie, I always think him a little effeminate. And, really,'—his voice grew sharper, for he was irritated by Ansell's conceit,—'and, really, you talk as if you were mixed up in the affair. They pay a civil visit to your rooms, and you see nothing but dark plots and challenges to war.'

'War!' cried Ansell, crashing his fists together. 'It's war, then!'

'Oh, what a lot of tommy-rot,' said Tilliard. 'Can't a man and woman get engaged? My dear boy—excuse me talking like this—what on earth is it to do with us? We're his friends, and I hope we always shall be, but we shan't keep his friendship by fighting. We're bound to fall into the background. Wife first, friends some way after. You may resent the order, but it is ordained by nature.'

'The point is, not what's ordained by nature or any other fool, but what's right.'

'You are hopelessly unpractical,' said Tilliard, turning away. 'And let me remind you that you've already given away your case by acknowledging that they're happy.'

'She is happy because she has conquered; he is happy because he has at last hung all the world's beauty on to a single peg. He was always trying to do it. He used to call the peg humanity. Will either of these happinesses last? His can't. Hers only for a time. I fight this woman not only because she fights me, but because I foresee the most appalling catastrophe. She wants Rickie, partly to replace another man whom she lost two years ago, partly to make something out of him. He is to write. In time she will get sick of this. He won't get famous. She will only see how thin he is and how lame.

She will long for a jollier husband, and I don't blame her. And, having made him thoroughly miserable and degraded, she will bolt—if she can do it like a lady.'

Such were the opinions of Stewart Ansell.

IX

Seven letters written in June:

CAMBRIDGE.

DEAR RICKIE,

I would rather write, and you can guess what kind of letter this is when I say it is a fair copy: I have been making rough drafts all the morning. When I talk I get angry, and also at times try to be clever—two reasons why I fail to get attention paid to me. This is a letter of the prudent sort. If it makes you break off the engagement, its work is done. You are not a person who ought to marry at all. You are unfitted in body: that we once discussed. You are also unfitted in soul: you want and you need to like many people, and a man of that sort ought not to marry. 'You never were attached to that great sect' who can like one person only, and if you try to enter it you will find destruction. I have read in books—and I cannot afford to despise books, they are all that I have to go by—that men and women desire different things. Man wants to love mankind; woman wants to love one man. When she has him her work is over. She is the emissary of Nature, and Nature's bidding has been fulfilled. But man does not care a damn for Nature —or at least only a very little damn. He cares for a hundred things besides, and the more civilized he is the more he will care for these other hundred things, and demand not only a wife and children, but also friends, and work, and spiritual freedom.

I believe you to be extraordinarily civilized.

Yours ever,

S. A.

SHELTHORPE, 9 SAWSTON PARK ROAD,
SAWSTON.

DEAR ANSELL,

But I'm in love—a detail you've forgotten. I can't listen to English Essays. The wretched Agnes may be an 'emissary of Nature,' but I only grinned when I read it. I may be extraordinarily civilized, but I don't feel so; I'm in love, and I've found a woman to love me, and I mean to have the hundred other things as well. She wants me to have them —friends, and work, and spiritual freedom, and everything. You and your books miss this, because your books are too sedate. Read poetry—not only Shelley. Understand Beatrice, and Clara Middleton, and Brunhilde in the first scene of Götterdämmerung. Understand Goethe when he says 'the eternal feminine leads us on,' and don't write another English essay.

Yours ever affectionately,

R. E.

CAMBRIDGE.

DEAR RICKIE,

What am I to say? 'Understand Xanthippe and Mrs. Bennett, and Elsa in the question scene of Lohengrin'? 'Understand Euripides when he says the eternal feminine leads us a pretty dance'? I shall say nothing of the sort. The allusions in this English Essay shall not be literary. My personal objections to Miss Pembroke are as follows:—

(1) She is not serious.
(2) She is not truthful.

SHELTHORPE, 9 SAWSTON PARK ROAD,
SAWSTON.

MY DEAR STEWART,

You couldn't know. I didn't know for a moment. But this letter of yours is the most wonderful thing that has ever happened to me yet—more wonderful (I don't exaggerate) than the moment when Agnes promised to marry me. I always knew you liked me, but I never knew how much until this letter. Up to now I think we have been too much like the strong heroes in books who feel so much and say so little, and feel all the more for saying so little. Now that's over and we shall never be that kind of an ass again. We've hit—by accident— upon something permanent. You've written to me, 'I hate the woman who will be your wife,' and I write back, 'Hate her. Can't I love you both?' She will never come between us, Stewart (she wouldn't wish to, but that's by the way), because our friendship has now passed beyond intervention. No third person could break it. We couldn't ourselves, I fancy. We may quarrel and argue till one of us dies, but the thing is registered. I only wish, dear man, you could be happier. For me, it's as if a light was suddenly held behind the world.

R. E.

SHELTHORPE, 9 SAWSTON PARK ROAD,
SAWSTON.

DEAR MRS. LEWIN,

The time goes flying, but I am getting to learn my wonderful boy. We speak a great deal about his work. He has just finished a curious thing called 'Nemi'—about a Roman ship that is actually sunk in some lake. I cannot think how he describes the things, when he has never seen them. If, as I hope, he goes to Italy next year, he should turn out something really good. Meanwhile we are hunting for a publisher. Herbert believes that a collection of short stories is hard to get published. It is, after all, better to write one long one.

But you must not think we only talk books. What we say on other topics cannot so easily be repeated! Oh, Mrs. Lewin, he is a dear, and dearer than ever now that we have him at Sawston. Herbert, in a quiet way, has been making inquiries about those Cambridge friends of his. Nothing against them, but they seem to be terribly eccentric. None of them are good at games, and they spend all their spare time thinking and discussing. They discuss what one knows and what one never will know and what one had much better not know. Herbert says it is because they have not got enough to do.

Ever your grateful and affectionate friend,

AGNES PEMBROKE.

SHELTHORPE, 9 SAWSTON PARK ROAD,
SAWSTON.

DEAR MR. SILT,

Thank you for the congratulations, which I have handed over to the delighted Rickie.[1] I am sorry

---

[1] The congratulations were really addressed to Agnes —a social blunder which Mr. Pembroke deftly corrects.

that the rumour reached you that I was not pleased. Anything pleases me that promises my sister's happiness, and I have known your cousin nearly as long as you have. It will be a very long engagement, for he must make his way first. The dear boy is not nearly as wealthy as he supposed; having no tastes, and hardly any expenses, he used to talk as if he was a millionaire. He must at least double his income before they can dream of more intimate ties. This has been a bitter pill, but I am glad to say that they have accepted it bravely.

Hoping that you and Mrs. Silt will profit by your week at Margate.

I remain, yours very sincerely,
HERBERT PEMBROKE.

CADOVER, WILTS.

DEAR { MISS PEMBROKE,
       AGNES,

I hear that you are going to marry my nephew. I have no idea what he is like, and wonder whether you would bring him that I may find out. Isn't September rather a nice month? You might have to go to Stone Henge, but with that exception would be left unmolested. I do hope you will manage the visit. We met once at Mrs. Lewin's, and I have a very clear recollection of you.

Believe me,
Yours sincerely,
EMILY FAILING.

X

The rain tilted a little from the south-west. For the most part it fell from a grey cloud silently, but now and then the tilt increased, and a kind of sigh passed over the country as the drops lashed the walls, trees, shepherds, and other motionless objects that stood in their slanting career. At times the cloud would descend and visibly embrace the earth, to which it had only sent messages; and the earth itself would bring forth clouds—clouds of a whiter breed —which formed in the shallow valleys and followed the courses of the streams. It seemed the beginning of life. Again God said, 'Shall we divide the waters from the land or not? Was not the firmament labour and glory sufficient?' At all events it was the beginning of life pastoral, behind which imagination cannot travel.

Yet complicated people were getting wet—not only the shepherds. For instance, the piano-tuner was sopping. So was the vicar's wife. So were the lieutenant and the peevish damsels in his Battleston car. Gallantry, charity, and art pursued their various missions, perspiring and muddy, while out on the slopes beyond them stood the eternal man and the eternal dog, guarding eternal sheep until the world is vegetarian.

Inside an arbour—which faced east, and thus avoided the bad weather—there sat a complicated person who was dry. She looked at the drenched world with a pleased expression, and would smile when a cloud lay down on the village, or when the rain sighed louder than usual against her solid shelter. Ink, paper-clips, and foolscap paper were on a table before her, and she could also reach an umbrella, a waterproof, a walking-stick, and an electric bell. Her age was between elderly and old, and her forehead was wrinkled with an expression of slight but perpetual pain. But the lines round her mouth indicated that she had laughed a great deal during her life, just as the clean tight skin round her eyes perhaps indicated that she had not often cried. She was dressed in brown silk. A brown silk shawl lay most becomingly over her beautiful hair.

After long thought she wrote on the paper in front of her, 'The subject of this memoir first saw the light at Wolverhampton on May the 14th, 1842.' She laid down her pen and said 'Ugh!' A robin hopped in and she welcomed him. A sparrow followed and she stamped her foot. She watched some thick white water which was sliding like a snake down the gutter of the gravel path. It had just appeared. It must have escaped from a hollow in the chalk up behind. The earth could absorb no longer. The lady did not think of all this, for she hated questions of whence and wherefore, and the ways of the earth ('our dull stepmother') bored her unspeakably. But the water, just the snake of water was amusing, and she flung her golosh at it to dam it up. Then she wrote feverishly, 'The subject of this memoir first saw the light in the middle of the night. It was twenty to eleven. His pa was a parson, but he was not his pa's son, and never went to heaven.' There was the sound of a train, and presently white smoke appeared, rising laboriously through the heavy air. It distracted her, and for about a quarter of an hour she sat perfectly still, doing nothing. At last she pushed the spoilt paper aside, took a fresh piece, and was beginning to write, 'On May the 14th, 1842,' when there was a crunch on the gravel, and a furious voice said, 'I am sorry for Flea Thompson.'

'I dare say I am sorry for him too,' said the lady: her voice was languid and pleasant. 'Who is he?'

'Flea's a liar, and next time we meet he'll be a football.' Off slipped a sodden ulster. He hung it up angrily upon a peg: the arbour provided several.

'But who is he, and why has he that disastrous name?'

'Flea? Fleance. All the Thompsons are named out of Shakespeare. He grazes the Rings.'

'Ah, I see. A pet lamb.'

'Lamb! Shepherd!'

'One of my shepherds?'

'The last time I go with his sheep. But not the last time he sees me. I am sorry for him. He dodged me to-day.'

'Do you mean to say'—she became animated—'that you have been out in the wet keeping the sheep of Flea Thompson?'

'I had to.' He blew on his fingers and took off his cap. Water trickled over his unshaven cheeks. His hair was so wet that it seemed worked upon his scalp in bronze.

'Get away, bad dog!' screamed the lady, for he had given himself a shake and spattered her dress with water. He was a powerful boy of twenty, admirably muscular, but rather too broad for his height. People called him 'Podge' until they were dissuaded. Then they called him 'Stephen' or 'Mr. Wonham.' Then he said, 'You can call me Podge if you like.'

'As for Flea——!' he began tempestuously. He sat down by her, and with much heavy breathing told the story,—'Flea has a girl at Wintersbridge, and

I had to go with his sheep while he went to see her. Two hours. We agreed. Half an hour to go, an hour to kiss his girl, and half an hour back—and he had my bike. Four hours! Four hours and seven minutes I was on the Rings, with a fool of a dog, and sheep doing all they knew to get the turnips.'

'My farm is a mystery to me,' said the lady, stroking her fingers. 'Some day you must really take me to see it. It must be like a Gilbert and Sullivan opera, with a chorus of agitated employers. How is it that I have escaped? Why have I never been summoned to milk the cows, or flay the pigs, or drive the young bullocks to the pasture?'

He looked at her with astonishingly blue eyes— the only dry things he had about him. He could not see into her: she would have puzzled an older and a cleverer man. He may have seen round her.

'A thing of beauty you are not. But I sometimes think you are a joy for ever.'

'I beg your pardon?'

'Oh, you understand right enough,' she exclaimed irritably, and then smiled, for he was conceited, and did not like being told that he was not a thing of beauty. 'Large and steady feet,' she continued, 'have this disadvantage—you can knock down a man, but you will never knock down a woman.'

'I don't know what you mean. I'm not likely——'

'Oh, never mind—never, never mind. I was being funny. I repent. Tell me about the sheep. Why did you go with them?'

'I did tell you. I had to.'

'But why?'

'He had to see his girl.'

'But why?'

His eyes shot past her again. It was so obvious

that the man had to see his girl. For two hours
though—not for four hours seven minutes.

'Did you have any lunch?'

'I don't hold with regular meals.'

'Did you have a book?'

'I don't hold with books in the open. None of the
older men read.'

'Did you commune with yourself, or don't you
hold with that?'

'Oh Lord, don't ask me!'

'You distress me. You rob the Pastoral of its lin-
gering romance. Is there no poetry and no thought
in England? Is there no one, in all these downs,
who warbles with eager thought the Doric lay?'

'Chaps sing to themselves at times, if you mean
that.'

'I dream of Arcady. I open my eyes: Wiltshire.
Of Amaryllis: Flea Thompson's girl. Of the pensive
shepherd, twitching his mantle blue: you in an
ulster. Aren't you sorry for me?'

'May I put in a pipe?'

'By all means put a pipe in. In return, tell me of
what you were thinking for the four hours and the
seven minutes.'

He laughed shyly. 'You do ask a man such questions.'

'Did you simply waste the time?'

'I suppose so.'

'I thought that Colonel Robert Ingersoll says you
must be strenuous.'

At the sound of this name he whisked open a
little cupboard, and declaring, 'I haven't a moment
to spare,' took out of it a pile of 'Clarion' and other
reprints, adorned as to their covers with bald or
bearded apostles of humanity. Selecting a bald one,
he began at once to read, occasionally exclaiming,

'That's got them,' 'That's knocked Genesis,' with similar ejaculations of an aspiring mind. She glanced at the pile. Renan, minus the style. Darwin, minus the modesty. A comic edition of the book of Job, by 'Excelsior,' Pittsburg, Pa. 'The Beginning of Life,' with diagrams. 'Angel or Ape?' by Mrs. Julia P. Chunk. She was amused, and wondered idly what was passing within his narrow but not uninteresting brain. Did he suppose that he was going to 'find out'? She had tried once herself, but had since subsided into a sprightly orthodoxy. Why didn't he read poetry, instead of wasting his time between books like these and country like that?

The cloud parted, and the increase of light made her look up. Over the valley she saw a grave sullen down, and on its flanks a little brown smudge—her sheep, together with her shepherd, Fleance Thompson, returned to his duties at last. A trickle of water came through the arbour roof. She shrieked in dismay.

'That's all right,' said her companion, moving her chair, but still keeping his place in his book.

She dried up the spot on the manuscript. Then she wrote: 'Anthony Eustace Failing, the subject of this memoir, was born at Wolverhampton.' But she wrote no more. She was fidgety. Another drop fell from the roof. Likewise an earwig. She wished she had not been so playful in flinging her golosh into the path. The boy who was overthrowing religion breathed somewhat heavily as he did so. Another earwig. She touched the electric bell.

'I'm going in,' she observed. 'It's far too wet. Again the cloud parted and caused her to add, 'Weren't you rather kind to Flea?' But he was deep in the book. He read like a poor person, with lips apart and a finger that followed the print. At times

he scratched his ear, or ran his tongue along a
straggling blonde moustache. His face had after all
a certain beauty: at all events the colouring was
regal—a steady crimson from throat to forehead:
the sun and the winds had worked on him daily
ever since he was born. 'The face of a strong man,'
thought the lady. 'Let him thank his stars he isn't
a silent strong man, or I'd turn him into the gutter.'
Suddenly it struck her that he was like an Irish
terrier. He worried infinity as if it was a bone.
Gnashing his teeth, he tried to carry the eternal
subtleties by violence. As a man he often bored
her, for he was always saying and doing the same
things. But as a philosopher he really was a joy for
ever, an inexhaustible buffoon. Taking up her pen,
she began to caricature him. She drew a rabbit-
warren where rabbits were at play in four dimen-
sions. Before she had introduced the principal
figure, she was interrupted by the footman. He had
come up from the house to answer the bell. On
seeing her he uttered a respectful cry.

'Madam! Are you here? I am very sorry. I looked
for you everywhere. Mrs. Elliot and Miss Pembroke
arrived nearly an hour ago.'

'Oh dear, oh dear!' exclaimed Mrs. Failing.
'Take these papers. Where's the umbrella? Mr.
Stephen will hold it over me. You hurry back and
apologize. Are they happy?'

'Miss Pembroke inquired after you, madam.'

'Have they had tea?'

'Yes, madam.'

'Leighton!'

'Yes, sir.'

'I believe you knew she was here all the time.
You didn't want to wet your pretty skin.'

'You must not call me "she" to the servants,' said

Mrs. Failing as they walked away, she limping with a stick, he holding a great umbrella over her. 'I will not have it.' Then more pleasantly, 'And don't tell him he lies. We all lie. I knew quite well they were coming by the four-six train. I saw it pass.'

'That reminds me. Another child run over at the Roman crossing. Whish—bang—dead.'

'Oh my foot! Oh my foot, my foot!' said Mrs. Failing, and paused to take breath.

'Bad?' he asked callously.

Leighton, with bowed head, passed them with the manuscript and disappeared among the laurels. The twinge of pain, which had been slight, passed away, and they proceeded, descending a green air-less corridor which opened into the gravel drive.

'Isn't it odd,' said Mrs. Failing, 'that the Greeks should be enthusiastic about laurels—that Apollo should pursue any one who could possibly turn into such a frightful plant? What do you make of Rickie?'

'Oh, I don't know.'

'Shall I lend you his story to read?'

He made no reply.

'Don't you think, Stephen, that a person in your precarious position ought to be civil to my relatives?'

'Sorry, Mrs. Failing. I meant to be civil. I only hadn't anything to say.'

She laughed. 'Are you a dear boy? I sometimes wonder; or are you a brute?'

Again he had nothing to say. Then she laughed more mischievously, and said—

'How can you be either, when you are a philosopher? Would you mind telling me—I am so anxious to learn—what happens to people when they die?'

'Don't ask *me*.' He knew by bitter experience that she was making fun of him.

'Oh, but I do ask you. Those paper books of yours are so up-to-date. For instance, what has happened to the child you say was killed on the line?'

The rain increased. The drops pattered hard on the leaves, and outside the corridor men and women were struggling, however stupidly, with the facts of life. Inside it they wrangled. She teased the boy, and laughed at his theories, and proved that no man can be an agnostic who has a sense of humour. Suddenly she stopped, not through any skill of his, but because she had remembered some words of Bacon: 'The true atheist is he whose hands are cauterized by holy things.' She thought of her distant youth. The world was not so humorous then, but it had been more important. For a moment she respected her companion, and determined to vex him no more.

They left the shelter of the laurels, crossed the broad drive, and were inside the house at last. She had got quite wet, for the weather would not let her play the simple life with impunity. As for him, he seemed a piece of the wet.

'Look here,' she cried, as he hurried up to his attic, 'don't shave!'

He was delighted with the permission.

'I have an idea that Miss Pembroke is of the type that pretends to be unconventional and really isn't. I want to see how she takes it. Don't shave.'

In the drawing-room she could hear the guests conversing in the subdued tones of those who have not been welcomed. Having changed her dress and glanced at the poems of Milton, she went to them, with uplifted hands of apology and horror.

'But I must have tea,' she announced, when they

had assured her that they understood. 'Otherwise
I shall start by being cross. Agnes, stop me. Give
me tea.'

Agnes, looking pleased, moved to the table and
served her hostess. Rickie followed with a pagoda
of sandwiches and little cakes.

'I feel twenty-seven years younger. Rickie, you
are so like your father. I feel it is twenty-seven
years ago, and that he is bringing your mother to
see me for the first time. It is curious—almost terrible—to see history repeating itself.'

The remark was not tactful.

'I remember that visit well,' she continued
thoughtfully. 'I suppose it was a wonderful visit,
though we none of us knew it at the time. We all
fell in love with your mother. I wish she would
have fallen in love with us. She couldn't bear me,
could she?'

'I never heard her say so, Aunt Emily.'

'No; she wouldn't. I am sure your father said so,
though. My dear boy, don't look so shocked. Your
father and I hated each other. He said so, I said so,
I say so; say so too. Then we shall start fair.—Just
a cocoanut cake.—Agnes, don't you agree that it's
always best to speak out?'

'Oh, rather, Mrs. Failing. But I'm shockingly
straightforward.'

'So am I,' said the lady. 'I like to get down to
the bed-rock.—Hullo! Slippers? Slippers in the
drawing-room?'

A young man had come in silently. Agnes observed with a feeling of regret that he had not
shaved. Rickie, after a moment's hesitation, remembered who it was, and shook hands with him.

'You've grown since I saw you last.'

He showed his teeth amiably.

'How long ago was that?' asked Mrs. Failing.

'Three years, wasn't it? Came over from the Ansells—friends.'

'How disgraceful, Rickie! Why don't you come and see me oftener?'

He could not retort that she never asked him.

'Agnes will make you come. Oh, let me introduce—Mr. Wonham—Miss Pembroke.'

'I am deputy hostess,' said Agnes. 'May I give you some tea?'

'Thank you, but I have had a little beer.'

'It is one of the shepherds,' said Mrs. Failing, in low tones. Agnes smiled rather wildly. Mrs. Lewin had warned her that Cadover was an extraordinary place, and that one must never be astonished at anything. A shepherd in the drawing-room! No harm. Still one ought to know whether it was a shepherd or not. At all events he was in gentleman's clothing. She was anxious not to start with a blunder, and therefore did not talk to the young fellow, but tried to gather what he was from the demeanour of Rickie.

'I am sure, Mrs. Failing, that you need not talk of "making" people come to Cadover. There will be no difficulty, I should say.'

'Thank you, my dear. Do you know who once said those exact words to me?'

'Who?'

'Rickie's mother.'

'Did she really?'

'My sister-in-law was a dear. You will have heard Rickie's praises, but now you must hear mine. I never knew a woman who was so unselfish and yet had such capacities for life.'

'Does one generally exclude the other?' asked Rickie.

'Unselfish people, as a rule, are deathly dull. They have no colour. They think of other people because it is easier. They give money because they are too stupid or too idle to spend it properly on themselves. That was the beauty of your mother—she gave away, but she also spent on herself, or tried to.'

The light faded out of the drawing-room, in spite of it being September and only half-past six. From her low chair Agnes could see the trees by the drive, black against a blackening sky. That drive was half a mile long, and she was praising its gravelled surface when Rickie called in a voice of alarm, 'I say, when did our train arrive?'

'Four-six.'

'I said so.'

'It arrived at four-six on the time-table,' said Mr. Wonham. 'I want to know when it got to the station?'

'I tell you again it was punctual. I tell you I looked at my watch. I can do no more.'

Agnes was amazed. Was Rickie mad? A minute ago and they were boring each other over dogs. What had happened?

'Now, now! Quarrelling already?' asked Mrs. Failing. The footman, bringing a lamp, lit up two angry faces.

'He says——'

'He says——'

'He says we ran over a child.'

'So you did. You ran over a child in the village at four-seven by my watch. Your train was late. You couldn't have got to the station till four-ten.'

'I don't believe it. We had passed the village by four-seven. Agnes, hadn't we passed the village?

It must have been an express that ran over the child.'

'Now is it likely,'—he appealed to the practical world—'is it likely that the company would run a stopping train and then an express three minutes after it?'

'A child——' said Rickie. 'I can't believe that the train killed a child.' He thought of their journey. They were alone in the carriage. As the train slackened speed he had caught her for a moment in his arms. The rain beat on the windows, but they were in heaven.

'You've got to believe it,' said the other, and proceeded to 'rub it in.' His healthy, irritable face drew close to Rickie's. 'Two children were kicking and screaming on the Roman crossing. Your train, being late, came down on them. One of them was pulled off the line, but the other was caught. How will you get out of that?'

'And how will you get out of it?' cried Mrs. Failing, turning the tables on him. 'Where's the child now? What has happened to its soul? You must know, Agnes, that this young gentleman is a philosopher.'

'Oh, drop all that,' said Mr. Wonham, suddenly collapsing.

'Drop it? Where? On my nice carpet?'

'I hate philosophy,' remarked Agnes, trying to turn the subject, for she saw that it made Rickie unhappy.

'So do I. But I daren't say so before Stephen. He despises us women.'

'No, I don't,' said the victim, swaying to and fro on the window-sill, whither he had retreated.

'Yes, he does. He won't even trouble to answer

us. Stephen! Podge! Answer me. What has happened to the child's soul?'

He flung open the window and leant from them
into the dusk. They heard him mutter something
about a bridge.

'What did I tell you? He won't answer my question.' The delightful moment was approaching
when the boy would lose his temper: she knew it
by a certain tremor in his heels.

'There wants a bridge,' he exploded. 'A bridge
instead of all this rotten talk and the level-crossing.
It wouldn't break you to build a two-arch bridge.
Then the child's soul, as you call it—well, nothing
would have happened to the child at all.'

A gust of night air entered, accompanied by rain.
The flowers in the vases rustled, and the flame of
the lamp shot up and smoked the glass. Slightly
irritated, she ordered him to close the window.

XI

Cadover was not a large house. But it is the largest
house with which this story has dealings, and must
always be thought of with a respect. It was built
about the year 1800, and favoured the architecture
of ancient Rome—chiefly by means of five lank
pilasters, which stretched from the top of it to the
bottom. Between the pilasters was the glass front
door, to the right of them the drawing-room windows, to the left of them the windows of the
dining-room, above them a triangular area, which
the better-class servants knew as a 'pendiment', and
which had in its middle a small round hole, according to the usage of Palladio. The classical note was
also sustained by eight grey steps which led from
the building down into the drive, and by an attempt

at a formal garden on the adjoining lawn. The lawn
ended in a Ha-ha ('Ha! ha! who shall regard it?'),
and thence the bare land sloped down into the village. The main garden (walled) was to the left as
one faced the house, while to the right was that
laurel avenue, leading up to Mrs. Failing's arbour.

It was a comfortable but not very attractive
place, and, to a certain type of mind, its situation
was not attractive either. From the distance it
showed as a grey box, huddled against evergreens.
There was no mystery about it. You saw it for
miles. Its hill had none of the beetling romance of
Devonshire, none of the subtle contours that prelude a cottage in Kent, but proffered its burden
crudely, on a huge bare palm. 'There's Cadover,'
visitors would say. 'How small it still looks. We
shall be late for lunch.' And the view from the
windows, though extensive, would have not been
accepted by the Royal Academy. A valley, contain-
ing a stream, a road, a railway; over the valley
fields of barley and wurzel, divided by no pretty
hedges, and passing into a great and formless down
—this was the outlook, desolate at all times, and
almost terrifying beneath a cloudy sky. The down
was called 'Cadbury Rings' ('Cocoa Squares' if you
were young and funny), because high upon it—one
cannot say 'on the top,' there being scarcely any
tops in Wiltshire—because high upon it there stood
a double circle of entrenchments. A bank of grass
enclosed a ring of turnips, which enclosed a second
bank of grass, which enclosed more turnips, and
in the middle of the pattern grew one small tree.
British? Roman? Saxon? Danish? The competent
reader will decide. The Thompson family knew it
to be far older than the Franco-German war. It was
the property of Government. It was full of gold and

dead soldiers who had fought with the soldiers on Castle Rings and been beaten. The road to Londinium, having forded the stream and crossed the valley road and the railway, passed up by these entrenchments. The road to London lay half a mile to the right of them.

To complete this survey one must mention the church and the farm, both of which lay over the stream, in Cadford. Between them they ruled the village, one claiming the souls of the labourers, the other their bodies. If a man desired other religion or other employment he must leave. The church lay up by the railway, the farm was down by the water meadows. The vicar, a gentle charitable man, scarcely realized his power, and never tried to abuse it. Mr. Wilbraham, the agent, was of another mould. He knew his place, and kept others to theirs: all society seemed spread before him like a map. The line between the county and the local, the line between the labourer and the artisan—he knew them all, and strengthened them with no uncertain touch. Everything with him was graduated —carefully graduated civility towards his superiors, towards his inferiors carefully graduated incivility. So—for he was a thoughtful person—so alone, declared he, could things be kept together.

Perhaps the Comic Muse, to whom so much is now attributed, had caused this estate to be left to Mr. Failing. Mr. Failing was the author of some brilliant books on socialism,—that was why his wife married him,—and for twenty-five years he reigned up at Cadover and tried to put his theories into practice. He believed that things could be kept together by accenting the similarities, not the differences of men. 'We are all much more alike than we confess,' was one of his favourite speeches. As a speech it sounded very well, and his wife had applauded; but when it resulted in hard work, evenings in the reading-room, mixed parties, and long unobtrusive talks with dull people, she got bored. In her piquant way she declared that she was not going to love her husband, and succeeded. He took it quietly, but his brilliancy decreased. His health grew worse, and he knew that when he died there was no one to carry on his work. He felt, besides, that he had done very little. Toil as he would, he had not a practical mind, and could never dispense with Mr. Wilbraham. For all his tact, he would often stretch out the hand of brother-hood too soon, or withhold it when it would have been accepted. Most people misunderstood him, or only understood him when he was dead. In after years his reign became a golden age; but he counted a few disciples in his lifetime, a few young labourers and tenant farmers, who swore tempestu-ously that he was not really a fool. This, he told himself, was as much as he deserved.

Cadover was inherited by his widow. She tried to sell it; she tried to let it; but she asked too much, and as it was neither a pretty place nor fertile, it was left on her hands. With many a groan she settled down to banishment. Wiltshire people, she declared, were the stupidest in England. She told them so to their faces, which made them no brighter. And their county was worthy of them: no distinction in it—no style—simply land.

But her wrath passed, or remained only as a graceful fretfulness. She made the house comfort-able, and abandoned the farm to Mr. Wilbraham. With a good deal of care she selected a small circle of acquaintances, and had them to stop in the summer months. In the winter she would go to town and frequent the *salons* of the literary. As her lameness increased she moved about less, and at the time of her nephew's visit seldom left the place that had been forced upon her as a home. Just now she was busy. A prominent politician had quoted her husband. The young generation asked, 'Who is this Mr. Failing?' and the publishers wrote, 'Now is the time.' She was collecting some essays and penning an introductory memoir.

Rickie admired his aunt, but did not care for her. She reminded him too much of his father. She had the same affliction, the same heartlessness, the same habit of taking life with a laugh—as if life is a pill! He also felt that she had neglected him. He would not have asked much: as for 'prospects', they never entered his head; but she was his only near relative, and a little kindness and hospitality during the lonely years would have made incalculable difference. Now that he was happier and could bring her Agnes, she had asked him to stop at once. The sun as it rose next morning spoke to him of a new life. He too had a purpose and a value in the world at last. Leaning out of the window, he gazed at the earth washed clean and heard through the pure air the distant noises of the farm.

But that day nothing was to remain divine but the weather. His aunt, for reasons of her own, decreed that he should go for a ride with the Wonham boy. They were to look at Old Sarum, proceed thence to Salisbury, lunch there, see the sights, call on a certain canon for tea, and return to Cadover in the evening. The arrangement suited no one. He did not want to ride, but to be with Agnes; nor did Agnes want to be parted from him, nor Stephen to go with him. But the clearer the wishes of her guests became, the more determined was Mrs. Failing to

disregard them. She smoothed away every difficulty, she converted every objection into a reason,
and she ordered the horses for half-past nine.

'It is a bore,' he grumbled as he sat in their little
private sitting-room, breaking his finger-nails upon
the coachman's gaiters. 'I can't ride. I shall fall off.
We should have been so happy here. It's just like
Aunt Emily. Can't you imagine her saying afterwards, "Lovers are absurd. I made a point of keeping them apart," and then everybody laughing.'

With a pretty foretaste of the future, Agnes knelt
before him and did the gaiters up. 'Who is this Mr.
Wonham, by the bye?'

'I don't know. Some connection of Mr. Failing's,
I think.'

'Does he live here?'

'He used to be at school or something. He seems
to have grown into a tiresome person.'

'I suppose that Mrs. Failing has adopted him?'

'I suppose so. I believe that she has been quite
kind. I do hope that she'll be kind to you this
morning. I hate leaving you with her.'

'Why, you say she likes me.'

'Yes, but that wouldn't prevent—you see she
doesn't mind what she says or what she repeats if it
amuses her. If she thought it really funny, for instance, to break off our engagement, she'd try.'

'Dear boy, what a frightful remark! But it would
be funnier for us to see her trying. Whatever could
she do?'

He kissed the hands that were still busy with the
fastenings. 'Nothing. I can't see one thing. We
simply lie open to each other, you and I. There
isn't one new corner in either of us that she could
reveal. It's only that I always have in this house the
most awful feeling of insecurity.'

'Why?'

'If any one says or does a foolish thing it's always here. All the family breezes have started here. It's a kind of focus for aimed and aimless scandal. You know, when my father and mother had their special quarrel, my aunt was mixed up in it,—I never knew how or how much—but you may be sure that she didn't calm things down, unless she found things more entertaining calm.'

'Rickie! Rickie!' cried the lady from the garden, 'your riding-master's impatient.'

'We really oughtn't to talk of her like this here,' whispered Agnes. 'It's a horrible habit.'

'The habit of the country, Agnes. Ugh, this gossip!' Suddenly he flung his arms over her. 'Dear —dear—let's beware of I don't know what—of nothing at all perhaps.'

'Oh, buck up!' yelled the irritable Stephen. 'Which am I to shorten—left stirrup or right?'

'Left!' shouted Agnes.

'How many holes?'

They hurried down. On the way she said: 'I'm glad of the warning. Now I'm prepared. Your aunt will get nothing out of me.'

Her betrothed tried to mount with the wrong foot, according to his invariable custom. She also had to pick up his whip. At last they started, the boy showing off pretty consistently, and she was left alone with her hostess.

'Dido is quiet as a lamb,' said Mrs. Fielding, 'and Stephen is a good fielder. What a blessing it is to have cleared out the men. What shall you and I do this heavenly morning?'

'I'm game for anything.'

'Have you quite unpacked?'

'Yes.'

'Any letters to write?'

'No.'

'Then let's go to my arbour. No, we won't. It gets the morning sun, and it'll be too hot to-day.' Already she regretted clearing out the men. On such a morning she would have liked to drive, but her third animal had gone lame. She feared, too, that Miss Pembroke was going to bore her. However, they did go to the arbour. In languid tones she pointed out the various objects of interest.

'There's the Cad, which goes into the something, which goes into the Avon. Cadbury Rings opposite, Cadchurch to the extreme left: you can't see it. You were there last night. It is famous for the drunken parson and the railway-station. Then Cad Dauntsey. Then Cadford, that side of the stream, connected with Cadover, this. Observe the fertility of the Wiltshire mind.'

'A terrible lot of Cads,' said Agnes brightly.

Mrs. Failing divided her guests into those who made this joke and those who did not. The latter class was very small.

'The vicar of Cadford—not the nice drunkard— declares the name is really "Chadford", and he worried on till I put up a window to St. Chad in our church. His wife pronounces it "Hyadford". I could smack them both. How do you like Podge? Ah! you jump; I meant you to. How do you like Podge Wonham?'

'Very nice,' said Agnes, laughing.

'Nice! He is a hero.'

There was a long interval of silence. Each lady looked, without much interest, at the view. Mrs. Failing's attitude towards Nature was severely æsthetic—an attitude more sterile than the severely practical. She applied the test of beauty to shadow and odour and sound; they never filled her with reverence or excitement; she never knew them as a resistless trinity that may intoxicate the worshipper with joy. If she liked a ploughed field, it was only as a spot of colour—not also as a hint of the endless strength of the earth. And to-day she could approve of one cloud, but object to its fellow. As for Miss Pembroke, she was not approving or objecting at all. 'A hero?' she questioned, when the interval had passed. Her voice was indifferent, as if she had been thinking of other things.

'A hero? Yes. Didn't you notice how heroic he was?'

'I don't think I did.'

'Not at dinner? Ah, Agnes, always look out for heroism at dinner. It is their great time. They live up to the stiffness of their shirt fronts. Do you mean to say that you never noticed how he set down Rickie?'

'Oh, that about poetry!' said Agnes, laughing. 'Rickie would not mind it for a moment. But why do you single out that as heroic?'

'To snub people! to set them down! to be rude to them! to make them feel small! Surely that's the life-work of a hero?'

'I shouldn't have said that. And as a matter of fact Mr. Wonham was wrong over the poetry. I made Rickie look it up afterwards.'

'But of course. A hero always is wrong.'

'To me,' she persisted, rather gently, 'a hero has always been a strong wonderful being, who champions——'

'Ah, wait till you are the dragon! I have been a dragon most of my life, I think. A dragon that wants nothing but a peaceful cave. Then in comes the strong, wonderful, delighted being, and gains a princess by piercing my hide. No, seriously, my dear Agnes, the chief characteristics of a hero are infinite disregard for the feelings of others, plus general inability to understand them.'

'But surely Mr. Wonham——'

'Yes; aren't we being unkind to the poor boy. Ought we to go on talking?'

Agnes waited, remembering the warnings of Rickie, and thinking that anything she said might perhaps be repeated.

'Though even if he was here he wouldn't understand what we are saying.'

'Wouldn't understand?'

Mrs. Failing gave the least flicker of an eye towards her companion. 'Did you take him for clever?'

'I don't think I took him for anything.' She smiled. 'I have been thinking of other things, and of another boy.'

'But do think for a moment of Stephen. I will describe how he spent yesterday. He rose at eight. From eight to eleven he sang. The song was called, "Father's boots will soon fit Willie." He stopped once to say to the footman, "She'll never finish her book. She idles." "She" being I. At eleven he went out, and stood in the rain till four, but had the luck to see a child run over at the level-crossing. By half-past four he had knocked the bottom out of Christianity.'

Agnes looked bewildered.

'Aren't you impressed? I was. I told him that he was on no account to unsettle the vicar. Open that cupboard. One of those sixpenny books tells Podge that he's made of hard little black things, another that he's made of brown things, larger and squashy. There seems a discrepancy, but anything is better for a thoughtful youth than to be made in the Garden of Eden. Let us eliminate the poetic, at whatever cost to the probable.' Then for a moment she spoke more gravely. 'Here he is at twenty, with nothing to hold on by. I don't know what's to be done. I suppose it's my fault. But I've never had any bother over the Church of England; have you?'

'Of course I go with my Church,' said Miss Pembroke, who hated this style of conversation. 'I don't know, I'm sure. I think you should consult a man.'

'Would Rickie help me?'

'Rickie would do anything he can.' And Mrs. Failing noted the half official way in which she vouched for her lover. 'But of course Rickie is a little—complicated. I doubt whether Mr. Wonham would understand him. He wants—doesn't he?— some one who's a little more assertive and more accustomed to boys. Some one more like my brother.'

'Agnes!' she seized her by the arm. 'Do you suppose that Mr. Pembroke would undertake my Podge?'

She shook her head. 'His time is so filled up. He gets a boarding-house next term. Besides—after all I don't know what Herbert would do.'

'Morality. He would teach him morality. The Thirty-Nine Articles may come of themselves, but if you have no morals you come to grief. Morality is all I demand from Mr. Herbert Pembroke. He shall be excused the use of the globes. You know, of course, that Stephen was expelled from a public school? He stole.'

The school was not a public one, and the expulsion, or rather request for removal, had taken place when Stephen was fourteen. A violent spasm of dishonesty—such as often heralds the approach of manhood—had overcome him. He stole everything, especially what was difficult to steal, and hid the plunder beneath a loose plank in the passage. He was betrayed by the inclusion of a ham. This was the crisis of his career. His benefactress was just then rather bored with him. He had stopped being a pretty boy, and she rather doubted whether she would see him through. But she was so enraged with the letters of the schoolmaster, and so delighted with those of the criminal, that she had him back and gave him a prize.

'No,' said Agnes, 'I didn't know. I should be happy to speak to Herbert, but, as I said, his time will be very full. But I know he has friends who make a speciality of weakly or—or unusual boys.'

'My dear, I've tried it. Stephen kicked the weakly boys and robbed apples with the unusual ones. He was expelled again.'

Agnes began to find Mrs. Failing rather tiresome. Wherever you trod on her, she seemed to slip away from beneath your feet. Agnes liked to know where she was and where other people were as well. She said: 'My brother thinks a great deal of home life. I dare say he'd think that Mr. Wonham is best where he is—with you. You have been so kind to him. You'—she paused—'have been to him both father and mother.'

'I'm too hot,' was Mrs. Failing's reply. It seemed that Miss Pembroke had at last touched a topic on which she was reticent. She rang the electric bell, —it was only to tell the footman to take the reprints to Mr. Wonham's room,—and then murmuring something about work, proceeded herself to the house.

'Mrs. Failing——' said Agnes, who had not expected such a speedy end to their chat.

'Call me Aunt Emily. My dear?'

'Aunt Emily, what did you think of that story Rickie sent you?'

'It is bad,' said Mrs. Failing. 'But. But. But.' Then she escaped, having told the truth, and yet leaving a pleasurable impression behind her.

XII

The excursion to Salisbury was but a poor business —in fact, Rickie never got there. They were not out of the drive before Mr. Wonham began doing acrobatics. He showed Rickie how very quickly he could turn round in his saddle and sit with his face to Æneas's tail. 'I see,' said Rickie coldly, and became almost cross when they arrived in this condition at the gate behind the house, for he had to open it, and was afraid of falling. As usual, he anchored just beyond the fastenings, and then had to turn Dido, who seemed as long as a battleship. To his relief a man came forward and murmuring, 'Worst gate in the parish,' pushed it wide and held it respectfully. 'Thank you,' cried Rickie; 'many thanks.' But Stephen, who was riding into the world back first, said majestically, 'No, no; it doesn't count. You needn't think it. You make it worse by touching your hat. Four hours and seven minutes! You'll see me again.' The man answered nothing.

'Eh, but I'll hurt him,' he chanted, as he swung into position. 'That was Flea. Eh, but he's forgotten my fists; eh, but I'll hurt him.'

'Why?' ventured Rickie. Last night, over cigarettes, he had been bored to death by the story of Flea. The boy had a little reminded him of Gerald —the Gerald of history, not the Gerald of romance. He was more genial, but there was the same brutality, the same peevish insistence on the pound of flesh.

'Hurt him till he learns.'

'Learns what?'

'Learns, of course,' retorted Stephen. Neither of them was very civil. They did not dislike each other, but they each wanted to be somewhere else —exactly the situation that Mrs. Failing had expected.

'He behaved badly,' said Rickie, 'because he is poorer than we are, and more ignorant. Less money has been spent on teaching him to behave.'

'Well, I'll teach him for nothing.'

'Perhaps his fists are stronger than yours!'

'They aren't. I looked.'

After this conversation flagged. Rickie glanced back at Cadover, and thought of the insipid day that lay before him. Generally he was attracted by fresh people, and Stephen was almost fresh: they had been to him symbols of the unknown, and all that they did was interesting. But now he cared for the unknown no longer. He knew.

Mr. Wilbraham passed them in his dog-cart, and lifted his hat to his employer's nephew. Stephen he ignored: he could not find him on the map.

'Good morning,' said Rickie. 'What a lovely morning!'

'I say,' called the other, 'another child dead!' Mr. Wilbraham, who had seemed inclined to chat, whipped up his horse and left them.

'There goes an out and outer,' said Stephen; and then, as if introducing an entirely new subject— 'Don't you think Flea Thompson treated me disgracefully?'

'I suppose he did. But I'm scarcely the person to sympathize.' The allusion fell flat, and he had to explain it. 'I should have done the same myself,—promised to be away two hours, and stopped four.'

'Stopped—oh—oh, I understand. You being in love, you mean?'

He smiled and nodded.

'Oh, I've no objection to Flea loving. He says he can't help it. But as long as my fists are stronger, he's got to keep it in line.'

'In line?'

'A man like that, when he's got a girl, thinks the rest can go to the devil. He goes cutting his work and breaking his word. Wilbraham ought to sack him. I promise you when I've a girl I'll keep her in line, and if she turns nasty, I'll get another.'

Rickie smiled and said no more. But he was sorry that any one should start life with such a creed—all the more sorry because the creed caricatured his own. He too believed that life should be in a line—a line of enormous length, full of countless interests and countless figures, all well beloved. But woman was not to be 'kept' to this line. Rather did she advance it continually, like some triumphant general, making each unit still more interesting, still more lovable, than it had been before. He loved Agnes, not only for herself, but because she was lighting up the human world. But he could scarcely explain this to an inexperienced animal, nor did he make the attempt.

For a long time they proceeded in silence. The hill behind Cadover was in harvest, and the horses moved regretfully between the sheaves. Stephen had picked a grass leaf, and was blowing cat-calls upon it. He blew very well, and this morning all his soul went into the wail. For he was ill. He was tortured with the feeling that he could not get away and do—do something, instead of being civil to this anæmic prig. Four hours in the rain was better than this: he had not wanted to fidget in the rain. But now the air was like wine, and the stubble was smelling of wet, and over his head white clouds trundled more slowly and more seldom through broadening tracts of blue. There never had been such a morning, and he shut up his eyes and called to it. And whenever he called, Rickie shut up his eyes and winced.

At last the blade broke. 'We don't go quick, do we?' he remarked, and looked on the weedy track for another.

'I wish you wouldn't let me keep you. If you were alone you would be galloping or something of that sort.'

'I was told I must go your pace,' he said mournfully. 'And you promised Miss Pembroke not to hurry.'

'Well, I'll disobey.' But he could not rise above a gentle trot, and even that nearly jerked him out of the saddle.

'Sit like *this*,' said Stephen. 'Can't you see—like *this*?' Rickie lurched forward, and broke his thumbnail on the horse's neck. It bled a little, and had to be bound up.

'Thank you—awfully kind—no tighter, please —I'm simply spoiling your day.'

'I can't think how a man can help riding. You've only to leave it to the horse so!—so!—just as you leave it to the water in swimming.'

Rickie left it to Dido, who stopped immediately.

'I said *leave* it.' His voice rose irritably. 'I didn't say "die". Of course she stops if you die. First you sit her as if you're Sandow exercising, and then you sit like a corpse. Can't you tell her you're alive? That's all she wants.'

In trying to convey the information, Rickie dropped his whip. Stephen picked it up and rammed it into the belt of his own Norfolk jacket. He was scarcely a fashionable horseman. He was not even graceful. But he rode as a living man, though Rickie was too much bored to notice it. Not a muscle in him was idle, not a muscle working hard. When he returned from a gallop his limbs were still unsatisfied and his manners still irritable. He did not know that he was ill: he knew nothing about himself at all.

'Like a howdah in the Zoo,' he grumbled. 'Mother Failing will buy elephants.' And he proceeded to criticize his benefactress. Rickie, keenly alive to bad taste, tried to stop him, and gained instead a criticism of religion. Stephen overthrew the Mosaic cosmogony. He pointed out the discrepancies in the Gospels. He levelled his wit against the most beautiful spire in the world, now rising against the southern sky. Between whiles he went for a gallop. After a time Rickie stopped listening, and simply went his way. For Dido was a perfect mount, and as indifferent to the motions of Æneas as if she was strolling in the Elysian fields. He had had a bad night, and the strong air made him sleepy. The wind blew from the Plain. Cadover and its valley had disappeared, and though they had not climbed much and could not see far, there was a sense of infinite space. The fields were enormous, like fields on the Continent, and the brilliant sun showed up their colours well. The green of the turnips, the gold of the harvest, and the brown of the newly turned clods, were each contrasted with morsels of grey down. But the general effect was pale, or rather silvery, for Wiltshire is not a county of heavy tints. Beneath these colours lurked the unconquer-

able chalk, and wherever the soil was poor it
emerged. The grassy track, so gay with scabious
and bed-straw, was snow-white at the bottom of
its ruts. A dazzling amphitheatre gleamed in the
flank of a distant hill, cut for some Olympian
audience. And here and there, whatever the surface crop, the earth broke into little embankments,
little ditches, little mounds: there had been no lack
of drama to solace the gods.

In Cadover, the perilous house, Agnes had already parted from Mrs. Failing. His thoughts returned to her. Was she, the soul of truth, in safety?
Was her purity vexed by the lies and selfishness?
Would she elude the caprice which had, he vaguely
knew, caused suffering before? Ah, the frailty of
joy! Ah, the myriads of longings that pass without
fruition, and the turf grows over them! Better men,
women as noble—they had died up here and their
dust had been mingled, but only their dust. These
are morbid thoughts, but who dare contradict
them? There is much good luck in the world, but
it is luck. We are none of us safe. We are children,
playing or quarrelling on the line, and some of us
have Rickie's temperament, or his experiences, and
admit it.

So he mused, that anxious little speck, and all
the land seemed to comment on his fears and on
his love.

Their path lay upward, over a great bald skull,
half grass, half stubble. It seemed each moment
there would be a splendid view. The view never
came, for none of the inclines were sharp enough,
and they moved over the skull for many minutes,
scarcely shifting a landmark or altering the blue
fringe of the distance. The spire of Salisbury did
alter, but very slightly, rising and falling like the

mercury in a thermometer. At the most it would be half hidden; at the least the tip would show behind the swelling barrier of earth. They passed two elder-trees—a great event. The bare patch, said Stephen, was owing to the gallows. Rickie nodded. He had lost all sense of incident. In this great solitude—more solitary than any Alpine range—he and Agnes were floating alone and for ever, between the shapeless earth and the shapeless clouds. An immense silence seemed to move towards them. A lark stopped singing, and they were glad of it. They were approaching the Throne of God. The silence touched them; the earth and all danger dissolved, but ere they quite vanished Rickie heard himself saying, 'Is it exactly what we intended?'

'Yes,' said a man's voice; 'it's the old plan.' They were in another valley. Its sides were thick with trees. Down it ran another stream and another road: it, too, sheltered a string of villages. But all was richer, larger, and more beautiful—the valley of the Avon below Amesbury.

'I've been asleep!' said Rickie, in awestruck tones.

'Never!' said the other facetiously. 'Pleasant dreams?'

'Perhaps—I'm really tired of apologizing to you. How long have you been holding me on?'

'All in the day's work.' He gave him back the reins.

'Where's that round hill?'

'Gone where the good niggers go. I want a drink.

This is Nature's joke in Wiltshire—her one joke. You toil on windy slopes, and feel very primeval. You are miles from your fellows, and lo! a little valley full of elms and cottages. Before Rickie had waked up to it, they had stopped by a thatched public-house, and Stephen was yelling like a maniac for beer.

There was no occasion to yell. He was not very thirsty, and they were quite ready to serve him. Nor need he have drunk in the saddle, with the air of a warrior who carries important despatches and has not the time to dismount. A real soldier, bound on a similar errand, rode up to the inn, and Stephen at first feared that he would yell louder, and was hostile. But they made friends and treated each other, and slanged the proprietor and ragged the pretty girls; while Rickie, as each wave of vulgarity burst over him, sunk his head lower and lower and wished that the earth would swallow him up. He was only used to Cambridge, and to a very small corner of that. He and his friends there believed in free speech. But they spoke freely about generalities. They were scientific and philosophic. They would have shrunk from the empirical freedom that results from a little beer.

That was what annoyed him as he rode down the new valley with two chattering companions. He was more skilled than they were in the principles of human existence, but he was not so indecently familiar with the examples. A sordid village scandal —such as Stephen described as a huge joke— sprang from certain defects in human nature, with which he was theoretically acquainted. But the example! He blushed at it like a maiden lady, in spite of its having a parallel in a beautiful idyll of Theocritus. Was experience going to be such a splendid thing after all? Were the outside of houses so very beautiful?

'That's spicy!' the soldier was saying. 'Got any more like that?'

'I'se got a pome,' said Stephen, and drew a piece of paper from his pocket. The valley had broadened. Old Sarum rose before them, ugly and majestic.

'Write this yourself?' he asked, chuckling.

'Rather,' said Stephen, lowering his head and kissing Æneas between the ears.

'But who's old Em'ly?' Rickie winced and frowned.

'Now you're asking.

> Old Em'ly she limps,
> And as——

'I am so tired,' said Rickie. Why should he stand it any longer? He would go home to the woman he loved. 'Do you mind if I give up Salisbury?'

'But we've seen nothing!' cried Stephen.

'I shouldn't enjoy anything, I am so absurdly tired.'

'Left turn, then—all in the day's work.' He bit at his moustache angrily.

'Good gracious me, man!—of course I'm going back alone. I'm not going to spoil your day. How could you think it of me?'

Stephen gave a loud sigh of relief. 'If you do want to go home, here's your whip. Don't fall off. Say to *her* you wanted it, or there might be ructions.'

'Certainly. Thank you for your kind care of me.'

> Old Em'ly she limps,
> And as——

Soon he was out of earshot. Soon they were lost to view. Soon they were out of his thoughts. He forgot the coarseness and the drinking and the ingratitude. A few months ago he would not have

forgotten so quickly, and he might also have de-
tected something else. But a lover is dogmatic. To
him the world shall be beautiful and pure. When it
is not, he ignores it.

'He's not tired,' said Stephen to the soldier; 'he
wants his girl.' And they winked at each other, and
cracked jokes over the eternal comedy of love.
They asked each other if they'd let a girl spoil a
morning's ride. They both exhibited a profound
cynicism. Stephen, who was quite without ballast,
described the household at Cadover: he should say
that Rickie would find Miss Pembroke kissing the
footman.

'I say the footman's kissing old Em'ly.'

'Jolly day,' said Stephen. His voice was suddenly
constrained. He was not sure whether he liked the
soldier after all, nor whether he had been wise in
showing him his compositions.

> Old Em'ly she limps,
> And as I——

'All right, Thomas. That'll do.'

> Old Em'ly——

'I wish you'd dry up, like a good fellow. This is
the lady's horse, you know, hang it, after all.'

'In-deed!'

'Don't you see—when a fellow's on a horse, he
can't let another fellow—kind of—don't you know?'

The man did know. 'There's sense in that,' he
said approvingly. Peace was restored, and they
would have reached Salisbury if they had not had
some more beer. It unloosed the soldier's fancies,
and again he spoke of old Em'ly and recited the
poem, with Aristophanic variations.

'Jolly day,' repeated Stephen, with a straighten-
ing of the eyebrows and a quick glance at the

other's body. He then warned him against the variations. In consequence he was accused of being a member of the Y.M.C.A. His blood boiled at this. He refuted the charge, and became great friends with the soldier, for the third time.

'Any objection to "Sorcy Mr. and Mrs. Tackleton"?'

'Rather not.'

The soldier sang 'Saucy Mr. and Mrs. Tackleton.' It is really a work for two voices, most of the sauciness disappearing when taken as a solo. Nor is Mrs. Tacketon's name Em'ly.

'I call it a jolly rotten song,' said Stephen crossly. 'I won't stand being got at.'

'P'r'aps y'like therold songs. Lishen.

> Of all the gulls that arsshmart,
>   There's none like pretty—Em'ly;
> For she's the darling of merart——

'Now, that's wrong.' He rode up close to the singer.

'Shright.'

''Tisn't.'

'It's as my mother taught me.'

'I don't care.'

'I'll not alter from mother's way.'

Stephen was baffled. Then he said, 'How does your mother make it rhyme?'

'Wot?'

'Squat. You're an ass, and I'm not. Poems want rhymes. "Alley" comes next line.'

He said 'alley' was —— welcome to come if it liked.

'It can't. You want Sally. Sally—alley. Em'ly—alley doesn't do.'

'Emily—femily!' cried the soldier, with an inspiration that was not his when sober. 'My mother taught me femily.

> For she's the darling of merart,
> And she lives in my femily.

'Well, you'd best be careful, Thomas, and your mother too.'

'*Your* mother's no better than she should be,' said Thomas vaguely.

'Do you think I haven't heard that before?' retorted the boy.

The other concluded he might now say anything. So he might—the name of old Emily excepted. Stephen cared little about his benefactress's honour, but a great deal about his own. He had made Mrs. Failing into a test. For the moment he would die for her, as a knight would die for a glove. He is not to be distinguished from a hero.

Old Sarum was passed. They approached the most beautiful spire in the world. 'Lord! another of these large churches!' said the soldier. Unfriendly to Gothic, he lifted both hands to his nose, and declared that old Em'ly was buried there. He lay in the mud. His horse trotted back towards Amesbury. Stephen had twisted him out of the saddle.

'I've done him!' he yelled, though no one was there to hear. He rose up in his stirrups and shouted with joy. He flung his hands round Æneas's neck. The elderly horse understood, capered, and bolted. It was a centaur that dashed into Salisbury and scattered the people. In the stable he would not dismount. 'I've done him!' he yelled to the ostlers —apathetic men. Stretching upwards, he clung to a beam. Æneas moved on and he was left hanging. Greatly did he incommode them by his exercises.

He pulled up, he circled, he kicked the other customers. At last he fell to the earth, deliciously fatigued. His body worried him no longer.

He went, like the baby he was, to buy a white linen hat. There were soldiers about, and he thought it would disguise him. Then he had a little lunch to steady the beer. This day had turned out admirably. All the money that should have fed Rickie he could spend on himself. Instead of toiling over the Cathedral and seeing the stuffed penguins, he could stop the whole time in the cattle market. There he met and made some friends. He watched the cheap-jacks, and saw how necessary it was to have a confident manner. He spoke confidently himself about lambs, and people listened. He spoke confidently about pigs, and they roared with laughter. He must learn more about pigs. He witnessed a performance—not too namby-pamby—of Punch and Judy. 'Hullo, Podge!' cried a naughty little girl. He tried to catch her, and failed. She was one of the Cadford children. For Salisbury on market day, though it is not picturesque, is certainly representative, and you read the names of half the Wiltshire villages upon the carriers' carts. He found, in Penny Farthing Street, the cart from Wintersbridge. It would not start for several hours, but the passengers always used it as a club, and sat in it every now and then during the day. No less than three ladies were there now, staring at the shafts. One of them was Flea Thompson's girl. He asked her, quite politely, why her lover had broken faith with him in the rain. She was silent. He warned her of approaching vengeance. She was still silent, but another woman hoped that a gentleman would not be hard on a poor person. Something in this annoyed him; it wasn't a question of gentility and

poverty—it was a question of two men. He determined to go back by Cadbury Rings, where the
shepherd would now be.

He did. But this part must be treated lightly. He
rode up to the culprit with the air of a Saint George,
spoke a few stern words from the saddle, tethered
his steed to a hurdle, and took off his coat. 'Are you
ready?' he asked.

'Yes, sir,' said Flea, and flung him on his back.

'That's not fair,' he protested.

The other did not reply, but flung him on his
head.

'How on earth did you learn that?'

'By trying often,' said Flea.

Stephen sat on the ground, picking mud out of
his forehead. 'I meant it to be fists,' he said gloomily.

'I know, sir.'

'It's jolly smart though, and—and I beg your
pardon all round.' It cost him a great deal to say
this, but he was sure that it was the right thing to
say. He must acknowledge the better man. Whereas
most people, if they provoke a fight and are flung,
say, 'You cannot rob me of my moral victory.'

There was nothing further to be done. He
mounted again, not exactly depressed, but feeling
that this delightful world is extraordinarily un-
reliable. He had never expected to fling the soldier
or to be flung by Flea. 'One nips or is nipped,' he
thought, 'and never knows beforehand. I should
not be surprised if many people had more in them
than I suppose, while others were just the other
way round. I haven't seen that sort of thing in
Ingersoll, but it's quite important.' Then his
thoughts turned to a curious incident of long ago,
when he had been 'nipped'—as a little boy. He was
trespassing in those woods, when he met in a

narrow glade a flock of sheep. They had neither dog nor shepherd, and advanced towards him silently. He was accustomed to sheep, but had never happened to meet them in a wood before, and disliked it. He retired, slowly at first, then fast; and the flock, in a dense mass, pressed after him. His terror increased. He turned and screamed at their long white faces; and still they came on, all stuck together, like some horrible jelly. If once he got into them! Bellowing and screeching, he rushed into the undergrowth, tore himself all over, and reached home in convulsions. Mr. Failing, his only grown-up friend, was sympathetic, but quite stupid. 'Pan ovium custos,' he remarked as he pulled out the thorns. 'Why not?' 'Pan ovium custos.' Stephen learnt the meaning of the phrase at school, 'A pan of eggs for custard.' He still remembered how the other boys looked as he peeped at them between his legs, awaiting the descending cane.

So he returned, full of pleasant disconnected thoughts. He had had a rare good time. He liked every one—even that poor little Elliot—and yet no one mattered. They were all out. On the landing he saw the new housemaid. He felt skittish and irresistible. Should he slip his arm round her waist? Perhaps better not; she might box his ears. And he wanted to smoke on the roof before dinner. So he only said, 'Please will you stop the boy blacking my brown boots,' and she, with downcast eyes, answered, 'Yes, sir; I will indeed.'

His room was in the pediment. Classical architecture, like all things in this world that attempt serenity, is bound to have its lapses into the undignified, and Cadover lapsed hopelessly when it came to Stephen's room. It gave him one round window, to see through which he must lie upon his stomach, one trap-door opening upon the leads, three iron girders, three beams, six buttresses, no ceiling, unless you count the walls, no walls unless you count the ceiling, and in its embarrassment presented him with the gurgly cistern that supplied the bath water. Here he lived, absolutely happy, and unaware that Mrs. Failing had poked him up here on purpose, to prevent him from growing too bumptious. Here he worked and sang and practised on the ocharoon. Here, in the crannies, he had constructed shelves and cupboards and useless little drawers. He had only one picture—the Demeter of Cnidus—and she hung straight from the roof like a joint of meat. Once she was in the drawing-room; but Mrs. Failing had got tired of her, and decreed her removal and this degradation. Now she faced the sunrise; and when the moon rose its light also fell on her, and trembled, like light upon the sea. For she was never still, and if the draught increased she would twist on her string, and would sway and tap upon the rafters until Stephen woke up and said what he thought of her. 'Want your nose?' he would murmur. 'Don't you wish you may get it.' Then he drew the clothes over his ears, while above him, in the wind and the darkness, the goddess continued her motions.

To-day, as he entered, he trod on the pile of six-penny reprints. Leighton had brought them up. He looked at the portraits on their covers, and began to think that these people were not everything. What a fate, to look like Colonel Ingersoll, or to marry Mrs. Julia P. Chunk! The Demeter turned towards him as he bathed, and in the cold water he sang—

They aren't beautiful, they aren't modest;
I'd just as soon follow an old stone goddess,—

and sprang upward through the skylight on to the roof.

Years ago, when a nurse was washing him, he had slipped from her soapy hands and got up here. She implored him to remember that he was a little gentleman; but he forgot the fact—if it was a fact —and not even the butler could get him down. Mr. Failing, who was sitting alone in the garden too ill to read, heard a shout, 'Am I an acro-terium?' He looked up and saw a naked child poised on the summit of Cadover. 'Yes,' he replied; 'but they are unfashionable. Go in,' and the vision had remained with him as something peculiarly gracious. He felt that nonsense and beauty have close connections, —closer connections than Art will allow,—and that both would remain when his own heaviness and his own ugliness had perished. Mrs. Failing found in his remains a sentence that puzzled her. 'I see the respectable mansion. I see the smug fortress of culture. The doors are shut. The windows are shut. But on the roof the children go dancing for ever.'

Stephen was a child no longer. He never stood on the pediment now, except for a bet. He never, or scarcely ever, poured water down the chimneys. When he caught the cat, he seldom dropped her into the housekeeper's bedroom. But still, when the weather was fair, he liked to come up after bathing, and get dry in the sun. To-day he brought with him a towel, a pipe of tobacco, and Rickie's story. He must get it done some time, and he was tired of the sixpenny reprints. The sloping gable was warm, and he lay back on it with closed eyes, gasping for pleasure. Starlings criticized him, soots fell on his clean body, and over him a little cloud was tinged with the colours of evening. 'Good! good!' he

whispered. 'Good, oh good!' and opened the manuscript reluctantly.

What a production! Who was this girl! Where
did she go to? Why so much talk about trees? 'I
take it he wrote it when feeling bad,' he murmured,
and let it fall into the gutter. It fell face downwards,
and on the back he saw a neat little *résumé* in Miss
Pembroke's handwriting, intended for such as him.
'Allegory. Man = modern civilization (in bad
sense). Girl = getting into touch with Nature.'

In touch with Nature! The girl was a tree! He
lit his pipe and gazed at the radiant earth. The foreground was hidden, but there was the village with
its elms, and the Roman Road, and Cadbury Rings.
There, too, were those woods, and little beech
copses, crowning a waste of down. Not to mention
the air, or the sun, or water. Good, oh good!

In touch with Nature! What cant would the
books think of next? His eyes closed. He was sleepy.
Good, oh good! Sighing into his pipe, he fell asleep.

XIII

Glad as Agnes was when her lover returned for
lunch, she was at the same time rather dismayed:
she knew that Mrs. Failing would not like her plans
altered. And her dismay was justified. Their hostess
was a little stiff, and asked whether Stephen had
been obnoxious.

'Indeed he hasn't. He spent the whole time looking after me.'

'From which I conclude he was more obnoxious
than usual.'

Rickie praised him diligently. But his candid
nature showed everything through. His aunt soon
saw that they had not got on. She had expected this

—almost planned it. Nevertheless she resented it, and her resentment was to fall on him.

The storm gathered slowly, and many other things went to swell it. Weakly people, if they are not careful, hate one another, and when the weakness is hereditary the temptation increases. Elliots had never got on among themselves. They talked of 'The Family', but they always turned outwards to the health and beauty that lie so promiscuously about the world. Rickie's father had turned, for a time at all events, to his mother. Rickie himself was turning to Agnes. And Mrs. Failing now was irritable, and unfair to the nephew who was lame like her horrible brother and like herself. She thought him invertebrate and conventional. She was envious of his happiness. She did not trouble to understand his art. She longed to shatter him, but knowing as she did that the human thunderbolt often rebounds and strikes the wielder, she held her hand.

Agnes watched the approaching clouds. Rickie had warned her; now she began to warn him. As the visit wore away she urged him to be pleasant to his aunt, and so convert it into a success.

He replied, 'Why need it be a success?'—a reply in the manner of Ansell.

She laughed. 'Oh, that's so like you men—all theory! What about your great theory of hating no one? As soon as it comes in useful you drop it.'

'I don't hate Aunt Emily. Honestly. But certainly I don't want to be near her or think about her. Don't you think there are two great things in life that we ought to aim at—truth and kindness? Let's have both if we can, but let's be sure of having one or the other. My aunt gives up both for the sake of being funny.'

'And Stephen Wonham,' pursued Agnes. 'There's another person you hate—or don't think about, if you prefer it put like that.'

'The truth is, I'm changing. I'm beginning to see that the world has many people in it who don't matter. I had time for them once. Not now.' There was only one gate to the kingdom of heaven now.

Agnes surprised him by saying, 'But the Wonham boy is evidently a part of your aunt's life. She laughs at him, but she is fond of him.'

'What's that to do with it?'

'You ought to be pleasant to him on account of it.'

'Why on earth?'

She flushed a little. 'I'm old-fashioned. One ought to consider one's hostess, and fall in with her life. After we leave it's another thing. But while we take her hospitality I think it's our duty.'

Her good sense triumphed. Henceforth he tried to fall in with Aunt Emily's life. Aunt Emily watched him trying. The storm broke, as storms sometimes do, on Sunday.

Sunday church was a function at Cadover, though a strange one. The pompous landau rolled up to the house at a quarter to eleven. Then Mrs. Failing said, 'Why am I being hurried?' and after an interval descended the steps in her ordinary clothes. She regarded the church as a sort of sitting-room, and refused even to wear a bonnet there. The village was shocked, but at the same time a little proud; it would point out the carriage to strangers and gossip about the pale smiling lady who sat in it, always alone, always late, her hair always draped in an expensive shawl.

This Sunday, though late as usual, she was not alone. Miss Pembroke, *en grande toilette*, sat by

her side. Rickie, looking plain and devout, perched
opposite. And Stephen actually came too, murmuring that it would be the Benedicite, which he had
never minded. There was also the Litany, which
drove him into the air again, much to Mrs. Failing's
delight. She enjoyed this sort of thing. It amused
her when her *protégé* left the pew, looking bored,
athletic, and dishevelled, and groping most obviously for his pipe. She liked to keep a thorough-
bred pagan to shock people. 'He's gone to worship
Nature,' she whispered. Rickie did not look up.
'Don't you think he's charming?' He made no
reply. 'Charming,' whispered Agnes over his head.

During the sermon she analysed her guests. Miss
Pembroke—undistinguished, unimaginative, tolerable. Rickie—intolerable. 'And how pedantic!' she
mused. 'He smells of the University library. If he
was stupid in the right way he would be a don.' She
looked round the tiny church; at the whitewashed
pillars, the humble pavement, the window full of
magenta saints. There was the vicar's wife. And
Mrs. Wilbraham's bonnet. Ugh! The rest of the
congregation were poor women, with flat, hopeless
faces—she saw them Sunday after Sunday, but did
not know their names—diversified with a few reluctant ploughboys, and the vile little school children,
row upon row. 'Ugh! what a hole,' thought Mrs.
Failing, whose Christianity was of the type best
described as 'cathedral'. 'What a hole for a cultured
woman! I don't think it has blunted my sensations,
though; I still see its squalor as clearly as ever. And
my nephew pretends he is worshipping. Pah! the
hypocrite.' Above her the vicar spoke of the danger
of hurrying from one dissipation to another. She
treasured his words, and continued: 'I cannot stand
smugness. It is the one, the unpardonable sin.

Fresh air! The fresh air that has made Stephen Wonham fresh and companionable and strong. Even if it kills, I will let in the fresh air.'

Thus reasoned Mrs. Failing, in the facile vein of Ibsenism. She imagined herself to be a cold-eyed Scandinavian heroine. Really she was an English old lady, who did not mind giving other people a chill provided it was not infectious.

Agnes, on the way back, noted that her hostess was a little snappish. But one is so hungry after morning service, and either so hot or so cold, that he would be a saint indeed who becomes a saint at once. Mrs. Failing, after asserting vindictively that it was impossible to make a living out of litera-ture, was courteously left alone. Roast-beef and moselle might yet work miracles, and Agnes still hoped for the introductions—the introductions to certain editors and publishers—on which her whole diplomacy was bent. Rickie would not push him-self. It was his besetting sin. Well for him that he would have a wife, and a loving wife, who knew the value of enterprise.

Unfortunately lunch was a quarter of an hour late, and during that quarter of an hour the aunt and the nephew quarrelled. She had been inveigh-ing against the morning service, and he quietly and deliberately replied, 'If organized religion is any-thing—and it is something to me—it will not be wrecked by a harmonium and a dull sermon.'

Mrs. Failing frowned. 'I envy you. It is a great thing to have no sense of beauty.'

'I think I have a sense of beauty, which leads me astray if I am not careful.'

'But this is a great relief to me. I thought the present-day young man was an agnostic! Isn't agnosticism all the thing at Cambridge?'

F

'Nothing is the "thing" at Cambridge. If a few men are agnostic there, it is for some grave reason, not because they are irritated with the way the parson says his vowels.'

Agnes intervened. 'Well, I side with Aunt Emily. I believe in ritual.'

'Don't, my dear, side with me. He will only say you have no sense of religion either.'

'Excuse me,' said Rickie,—perhaps he too was a little hungry,—'I never suggested such a thing. I never would suggest such a thing. Why cannot you understand my position? I almost feel it is that you won't.'

'I try to understand your position night and day, dear—what you mean, what you like, why you came to Cadover, and why you stop here when my presence is so obviously unpleasing to you.'

'Luncheon is served,' said Leighton, but he said it too late. They discussed the beef and the moselle in silence. The air was heavy and ominous. Even the Wonham boy was affected by it, shivered at times, choked once, and hastened anew into the sun. He could not understand clever people.

Agnes, in a brief anxious interview, advised the culprit to take a solitary walk. She would stop near Aunt Emily, and pave the way for an apology.

'Don't worry too much. It doesn't really matter.'

'I suppose not, dear. But it seems a pity, considering we are so near the end of our visit.'

'Rudeness and crossness matter, and I've shown both, and already I'm sorry, and hope she'll let me apologize. But from the selfish point of view it doesn't matter a straw. She's no more to us than the Wonham boy or the boot boy.'

'Which way will you walk?'

'I think to that entrenchment. Look at it.' They

were sitting on the steps. He stretched out his
hand to Cadbury Rings, and then let it rest for a
moment on her shoulder. 'You're changing me,' he
said gently. 'God bless you for it.'

He enjoyed his walk. Cadford was a charming
village, and for a time he hung over the bridge by
the mill. So clear was the stream that it seemed not
water at all, but some invisible quintessence in
which the happy minnows and the weeds were
vibrating. And he paused again at the Roman crossing, and thought for a moment of the unknown
child. The line curved suddenly: certainly it was
dangerous. Then he lifted his eyes to the down.
The entrenchment showed like the rim of a saucer,
and over its narrow line peeped the summit of the
central tree. It looked interesting. He hurried forward, with the wind behind him.

The Rings were curious rather than impressive.
Neither embankment was over twelve feet high,
and the grass on them had not the exquisite green
of Old Sarum, but was grey and wiry. But Nature
(if she arranges anything) had arranged that from
them, at all events, there should be a view. The
whole system of the country lay spread before
Rickie, and he gained an idea of it that he never
got in his elaborate ride. He saw how all the water
converges at Salisbury; how Salisbury lies in a
shallow basin, just at the change of the soil. He
saw to the north the Plain, and the stream of the
Cad flowing down from it, with a tributary that
broke out suddenly, as the chalk streams do: one
village had clustered round the source and clothed
itself with trees. He saw Old Sarum, and hints of
the Avon valley, and the land above Stonehenge.
And behind him he saw the great wood beginning
unobtrusively, as if the down too needed shaving;

and into it the road to London slipped, covering the bushes with white dust. Chalk made the dust white, chalk made the water clear, chalk made the clean rolling outlines of the land, and favoured the grass and the distant coronals of trees. Here is the heart of our island: the Chilterns, the North Downs, the South Downs radiate hence. The fibres of England unite in Wiltshire, and did we condescend to worship her, here we should erect our national shrine.

People at that time were trying to think imperially. Rickie wondered how they did it, for he could not imagine a place larger than England. And other people talked of Italy, the spiritual fatherland of us all. Perhaps Italy would prove marvellous. But at present he conceived it as something exotic, to be admired and reverenced, but not to be loved like these unostentatious fields. He drew out a book,—it was natural for him to read when he was happy, and to read out loud,—and for a little time his voice disturbed the silence of that glorious afternoon. The book was Shelley, and it opened at a passage that he had cherished greatly two years before, and marked as 'very good'.

> I never was attached to that great sect
> Whose doctrine is that each one should select
> Out of the world a mistress or a friend,
> And all the rest, though fair and wise, commend
> To cold oblivion,—though it is the code
> Of modern morals, and the beaten road
> Which those poor slaves with weary footsteps tread
> Who travel to their home among the dead
> By the broad highway of the world,—and so
> With one sad friend, perhaps a jealous foe,
> The dreariest and the longest journey go.

It was 'very good'—fine poetry, and, in a sense,

true. Yet he was surprised that he had ever selected it so vehemently. This afternoon it seemed a little inhuman. Half a mile off two lovers were keeping company where all the villagers could see them. They cared for no one else; they felt only the pressure of each other, and so progressed, silent and oblivious, across the land. He felt them to be nearer the truth than Shelley. Even if they suffered or quarrelled, they would have been nearer the truth. He wondered whether they were Henry Adams and Jessica Thompson, both of this parish, whose banns had been asked, for the second time, in the church this morning. Why could he not marry on fifteen shillings a-week? And he looked at them with respect, and wished that he was not a cumbersome gentleman.

Presently he saw something less pleasant—his aunt's pony carriage. It had crossed the railway, and was advancing up the Roman road along by the straw stacks. His impulse was to retreat, but some one waved to him. It was Agnes. She waved continually, as much as to say, 'Wait for us.' Mrs. Failing herself raised the whip in a nonchalant way. Stephen Wonham was following on foot, some way behind. He put the Shelley back into his pocket and waited for them. When the carriage stopped by some hurdles he went down from the embankment and helped them to dismount. He felt rather nervous.

His aunt gave him one of her disquieting smiles, but said pleasantly enough, 'Aren't the Rings a little immense? Agnes and I came here because we wanted an antidote to the morning service.'

'Pang!' said the church bell suddenly; 'pang! pang!' It sounded petty and ludicrous. They all laughed. Rickie blushed, and Agnes, with a glance that said 'apologize', darted away to the entrenchment, as though unable to restrain her curiosity.

'The pony won't move,' said Mrs. Failing. 'Leave him for Stephen to tie up. Will you walk me to the tree in the middle? Booh! I'm tired. Give me your arm—unless you're tired as well.'

'No. I came out partly in the hope of helping you.'

'How sweet of you.' She contrasted his blatant unselfishness with the hardness of Stephen. Stephen never came out to help you. But if you got hold of him he was some good. He didn't wobble and bend at the critical moment. Her fancy compared Rickie to the cracked church bell sending forth its message of 'Pang! pang!' to the countryside, and Stephen to the young pagans who were said to lie under this field guarding their pagan gold.

'This place is full of ghosties,' she remarked; 'have you seen any yet?'

'I've kept on the outer rim so far.'

'Let's go to the tree in the centre.'

'Here's the path.' The bank of grass where he had sat was broken by a gap, through which chariots had entered, and farm carts entered now. The track, following the ancient track, led straight through turnips to a similar gap in the second circle and thence continued, through more turnips, to the central tree.

'Pang!' said the bell, as they paused at the entrance.

'You needn't unharness,' shouted Mrs. Failing, for Stephen was approaching the carriage.

'Yes, I will,' he retorted.

'You will, will you?' she murmured with a smile. 'I wish your brother wasn't quite so uppish. Let's get on. Doesn't that church distract you?'

'It's so faint here,' said Rickie. And it sounded fainter inside, though the earthwork was neither thick nor tall; and the view, though not hidden, was greatly diminished. He was reminded for a moment of that chalk pit near Madingley, whose ramparts excluded the familiar world. Agnes was here, as she had once been there. She stood on the farther barrier, waiting to receive them when they had traversed the heart of the camp.

'Admire my mangel-wurzels,' said Mrs. Failing. 'They are said to grow so splendidly on account of the dead soldiers. Isn't it a sweet thought? Need I say it is your brother's?'

'Wonham's——?' he suggested. It was the second time that she had made the little slip. She nodded, and he asked her what kind of ghosties haunted this curious field.

'The D.,' was her prompt reply. 'He leans against the tree in the middle, especially on Sunday afternoons, and all his worshippers rise through the turnips and dance round him.'

'Oh, these were decent people,' he replied, looking downwards—'soldiers and shepherds. They have no ghosts. They worshipped Mars or Pan—Erda perhaps; not the devil.'

'Pang!' went the church, and was silent, for the afternoon service had begun. They entered the second entrenchment, which was in height, breadth, and composition similar to the first, and excluded still more of the view. His aunt continued friendly. Agnes stood watching them.

'Soldiers may seem decent in the past,' she continued, 'but wait till they turn into Tommies from Bulford Camp, who rob the chickens.'

'I don't mind Bulford Camp,' said Rickie, looking, though in vain, for signs of its snowy tents.

'The men there are the sons of the men here, and have come back to the old country. War's horrible, yet one loves all continuity. And no one could mind a shepherd.'

'Indeed! What about your brother—a shepherd if ever there was? Look how he bores you! Don't be so sentimental.'

'But—oh, you mean——'

'Your brother Stephen.'

He glanced at her nervously. He had never known her so queer before. Perhaps it was some literary allusion that he had not caught; but her face did not at that moment suggest literature. In the deferential tones that one uses to an old and infirm person he said, 'Stephen Wonham isn't my brother, Aunt Emily.'

'My dear, you're that precise. One can't say "half-brother" every time.'

They approached the central tree.

'How you do puzzle me,' he said, dropping her arm and beginning to laugh. 'How could I have a half-brother?'

She made no answer.

Then a horror leapt straight at him, and he beat it back and said, 'I will not be frightened.' The tree in the centre revolved, the tree disappeared, and he saw a room—the room where his father had lived in town. 'Gently,' he told himself, 'gently.'

Still laughing, he said, 'I, with a brother—younger—it's not possible.' The horror leapt again, and he exclaimed, 'It's a foul lie!'

'My dear, my dear!'

'It's a foul lie! He wasn't—I won't stand——'

'My dear, before you say several noble things remember that it's worse for him than for you—

worse for your brother, for your half-brother, for your younger brother.'

But he heard her no longer. He was gazing at the past, which he had praised so recently, which gaped ever wider, like an unhallowed grave. Turn where he would, it encircled him. It took visible form: it was this double entrenchment of the Rings. His mouth went cold, and he knew that he was going to faint among the dead. He started running, missed the exit, stumbled on the inner barrier, fell into darkness——

'Get his head down,' said a voice. 'Get the blood back into him. That's all he wants. Leave him to me. Elliot!'—the blood was returning—'Elliot, wake up!'

He woke up. The earth he had dreaded lay close to his eyes, and seemed beautiful. He saw the structure of the clods. A tiny beetle swung on the grass blade. On his own neck a human hand pressed, guiding the blood back to his brain.

There broke from him a cry, not of horror, but of acceptance. For one short moment he understood. 'Stephen——' he began, and then he heard his own name called: 'Rickie! Rickie!' Agnes had hurried from her post on the margin, and, as if understanding also, caught him to her breast.

Stephen offered to help them further, but finding that he made things worse, he stepped aside to let them pass and then sauntered inwards. The whole field, with its concentric circles, was visible, and the broad leaves of the turnips rustled in the gathering wind. Miss Pembroke and Elliot were moving towards the Cadover entrance. Mrs. Failing stood watching in her turn on the opposite bank. He was not an inquisitive boy; but as he leant against the tree he wondered what it was all about, and whether he would ever know.

XIV

On the way back—at that very level-crossing where he had paused on his upward route—Rickie stopped suddenly and told the girl why he had fainted. Hitherto she had asked him in vain. His tone had gone from him, and he told her harshly and brutally, so that she started away with a horrified cry. Then his manner altered, and he exclaimed: 'Will you mind? Are you going to mind?'

'Of course I mind,' she whispered. She turned from him, and saw up on the sky-line two figures that seemed to be of enormous size.

'They're watching us. They stand on the edge watching us. This country's so open—you—you can't—they watch us wherever we go. Of course you mind.'

They heard the rumble of the train, and she pulled herself together. 'Come, dearest, we shall be run over next. We're saying things that have no sense.' But on the way back he repeated: 'They can still see us. They can see every inch of this road. They watch us for ever.' And when they arrived at the steps, there, sure enough, were still the two figures gazing from the outer circle of the Rings.

She made him go to his room at once: he was almost hysterical. Leighton brought out some tea for her, and she sat drinking it on the little terrace. Of course she minded. Again she was menaced by the abnormal. All had seemed so fair and so simple, so in accordance with her ideas; and then, like a corpse, this horror rose up to the surface. She saw the two figures descend and pause while one of them harnessed the pony; she saw them drive downward, and knew that before long she must

face them and the world. She glanced at her engagement ring.

When the carriage drove up Mrs. Failing dis-
mounted, but did not speak. It was Stephen who
inquired after Rickie. She, scarcely knowing the
sound of her own voice, replied that he was a little
tired.

'Go and put up the pony,' said Mrs. Failing
rather sharply. 'Agnes, give me some tea.'

'It is rather strong,' said Agnes as the carriage
drove off and left them alone. Then she noticed that
Mrs. Failing herself was agitated. Her lips were
trembling, and she saw the boy depart with mani-
fest relief.

'Do you know,' she said hurriedly, as if talking
against time—'do you know what upset Rickie?'

'I do indeed know.'

'Has he told any one else?'

'I believe not.'

'Agnes—have I been a fool?'

'You have been very unkind,' said the girl, and
her eyes filled with tears.

For a moment Mrs. Failing was annoyed. 'Unkind? I do not see that at all. I believe in looking
facts in the face. Rickie must know his ghosts in
time. Why not this afternoon?'

She rose with quiet dignity, but her tears came
faster. 'That is not so. You told him to hurt him. I
cannot think what you did it for. I suppose because
he was rude to you after church. It is a mean,
cowardly revenge.'

'What—what if it's a lie?'

'Then, Mrs. Failing, it is sickening of you. There
is no other word. Sickening. I am sorry—a nobody
like myself—to speak like this. How *could* you,
oh, how could you demean yourself? Why, not even

a poor person——' Her indignation was fine and genuine. But her tears fell no longer. Nothing menaced her if they were not really brothers.

'It is not a lie, my dear; sit down. I will swear so much solemnly. It is not a lie, but——'

Agnes waited.

'——we can call it a lie if we choose.'

'I am not so childish. You have said it, and we must all suffer. You have had your fun: I conclude you did it for fun. You cannot go back. He——' She pointed towards the stables, and could not finish her sentence.

'I have not been a fool twice.'

Agnes did not understand.

'My dense lady, can't you follow? I have not told Stephen one single word, neither before nor now.'

There was a long silence.

Indeed, Mrs. Failing was in an awkward position. Rickie had irritated her, and, in her desire to shock him, she had imperilled her own peace. She had felt so unconventional upon the hillside, when she loosed the horror against him; but now it was darting at her as well. Suppose the scandal out. Stephen, who was absolutely without delicacy, would tell it to people as soon as tell them the time. His paganism would be too assertive; it might even be in bad taste. After all, she had a prominent position in the neighbourhood; she was talked about, respected, looked up to. After all, she was growing old. And therefore, though she had no true regard for Rickie, nor for Agnes, nor for Stephen, nor for Stephen's parents, in whose tragedy she had assisted, yet she did feel that if the scandal revived it would disturb the harmony of Cadover, and therefore tried to retrace her steps. It is easy to say

shocking things: it is so different to be connected
with anything shocking. Life and death were not
involved, but comfort and discomfort were.

The silence was broken by the sound of feet on
the gravel. Agnes said hastily, 'Is that really true—
that he knows nothing?'

'You, Rickie, and I are the only people alive that
know. He realizes what he is—with a precision that
is sometimes alarming. Who he is, he doesn't know
and doesn't care. I suppose he would know when
I'm dead. There are papers.'

'Aunt Emily, before he comes, may I say to you
I'm sorry I was so rude?'

Mrs. Failing had not disliked her courage. 'My
dear, you may. We're all off our hinges this Sunday. Sit down by me again.'

Agnes obeyed, and they awaited the arrival of
Stephen. They were clever enough to understand
each other. The thing must be hushed up. The
matron must repair the consequences of her petu-
lance. The girl must hide the stain in her future
husband's family. Why not? Who was injured?
What does a grown-up man want with a grown-up
brother? Rickie upstairs, how grateful he would be
to them for saving him.

'Stephen!'

'Yes.'

'I'm tired of you. Go and bathe in the sea.'

'All right.'

And the whole thing was settled. She liked no
fuss, and so did he. He sat down on the steps to
tighten his boot-laces. Then he would be ready.
Mrs. Failing laid two or three sovereigns on the
step above him. Agnes tried to make conversation,
and said, with averted eyes, that the sea was a long
way off.

'The sea's downhill. That's all I know about it.' He swept up the money with a word of pleasure: he was kept like a baby in such things. Then he started off, but slowly, for he meant to walk till the morning.

'He will be gone days,' said Mrs. Failing. 'The comedy is finished. Let us come in.'

She went to her room. The storm that she had raised had shattered her. Yet, because it was stilled for a moment, she resumed her old emancipated manner, and spoke of it as a comedy.

As for Miss Pembroke, she pretended to be emancipated no longer. People like 'Stephen Wonham' were social thunderbolts, to be shunned at all costs, or at almost all costs. Her joy was now unfeigned, and she hurried upstairs to impart it to Rickie.

'I don't think we are rewarded if we do right, but we are punished if we lie. It's the fashion to laugh at poetic justice, but I do believe in half of it. Cast bitter bread upon the waters, and after many days it really will come back to you.' These were the words of Mr. Failing. They were also the opinions of Stewart Ansell, another unpractical person. Rickie was trying to write to him when she entered with the good news.

'Dear, we're saved! He doesn't know, and he never is to know. I can't tell you how glad I am. All the time we saw them standing together up there, she wasn't telling him at all. She was keeping him out of the way, in case you let it out. Oh, I like her! She may be unwise, but she is nice, really. She said, "I've been a fool, but I haven't been a fool twice." You must forgive her, Rickie. I've forgiven her, and she me; for at first I was so angry with her. Oh, my darling boy, I am so glad!'

He was shivering all over, and could not reply. At last he said, 'Why hasn't she told him?'

'Because she has come to her senses.'

'But she can't behave to people like that. She must tell him.'

'Why?'

'Because he must be told such a real thing.'

'Such a real thing?' the girl echoed, screwing up her forehead. 'But—but you don't mean you're glad about it?'

His head bowed over the letter. 'My God—no! But it's a real thing. She must tell him. I nearly told him myself—up there—when he made me look at the ground, but you happened to prevent me.'

How Providence had watched over them!

'She won't tell him. I know that much.'

'Then, Agnes, darling'—he drew her to the table —'we must talk together a little. If she won't, then we ought to.'

'*We* tell him?' cried the girl, white with horror. 'Tell him now, when everything has been comfortably arranged?'

'You see, darling'—he took hold of her hand— 'what one must do is to think the thing out and settle what's right. I'm still all trembling and stupid. I see it mixed up with other things. I want you to help me. It seems to me that here and there in life we meet with a person or incident that is symbolical. It's nothing in itself, yet for the moment it stands for some eternal principle. We accept it, at whatever cost, and we have accepted life. But if we are frightened and reject it, the moment, so to speak, passes; the symbol is never offered again. Is this nonsense? Once before a symbol was offered to me—I shall not tell you how; but I did accept it, and cherished it through much anxiety, and repulsion. And in the end I am rewarded. There will be no reward this time, I think, from such a man—the son of such a man. But I want to do what is right.'

'Because doing right is its own reward,' said Agnes anxiously.

'I do not think that. I have seen few examples of it. Doing right is simply doing right.'

'I think that all you say is wonderfully clever; but since you ask me, it *is* nonsense, dear Rickie, absolutely.'

'Thank you,' he said humbly, and began to stroke her hand. 'But all my disgust; my indignation with my father, my love for——' He broke off; he could not bear to mention the name of his mother. 'I was trying to say, I oughtn't to follow these impulses too much. There are other things. Truth. Our duty to acknowledge each man accurately, however vile he is. And apart from ideals' (here she had won the battle),—'and leaving ideals aside, I couldn't meet him and keep silent. It isn't in me. I should blurt it out.'

'But you won't meet him!' she cried. 'It's all been arranged. We've sent him to the sea. Isn't it splendid? He's gone. My own boy won't be fantastic, will he?' Then she fought the fantasy on its own ground. 'And, by the bye, what you call the "symbolic moment" is over. You had it up by the Rings. You tried to tell him. I interrupted you. It's not your fault. You did all you could.'

She thought this excellent logic, and was surprised that he looked so gloomy. 'So he's gone to the sea. For the present that does settle it. Has Aunt Emily talked about him yet?'

'No. Ask her to-morrow if you wish to know. Ask her kindly. It would be so dreadful if you did not part friends, and——'

'What's that?'

It was Stephen calling up from the drive. He had come back. Agnes threw out her hand in despair.

'Elliot!' the voice called.

They were facing each other, silent and motionless. Then Rickie advanced to the window. The girl darted in front of him. He thought he had never seen her so beautiful. She was stopping his advance quite frankly with widespread arms.

'Elliot!'

He moved forward—into what? He pretended to himself he would rather see his brother before he answered; that it was easier to acknowledge him thus. But at the back of his soul he knew that the woman had conquered, and that he was moving forward to acknowledge her. 'If he calls me again——' he thought.

'Elliot!'

'Well, if he calls me once again, I will answer him, vile as he is.'

He did not call again.

Stephen had really come back for some tobacco, but as he passed under the windows he thought of the poor fellow who had been 'nipped' (nothing serious, said Mrs. Failing), and determined to shout good-bye to him. And once or twice, as he followed the river into darkness, he wondered what it was like to be so weak,—not to ride, not to swim, not to care for anything but books and a girl.

They embraced passionately. The danger had brought them very near to each other. They both needed a home to confront the menacing tumultuous world. And what weary years of work, of waiting, lay between them and that home! Still holding her fast, he said, 'I was writing to Ansell when you came in.'

'Do you owe him a letter?'

'No.' He paused. 'I was writing to tell him about this. He would help us. He always picks out the important point.'

'Darling, I don't like to say anything, and I know that Mr. Ansell would keep a secret, but haven't we picked out the important point for ourselves?'

He released her and tore the letter up.

XV

The sense of purity is a puzzling, and at times a fearful thing. It seems so noble, and it starts at one with morality. But it is a dangerous guide, and can lead us away not only from what is gracious, but also from what is good. Agnes, in this tangle, had followed it blindly, partly because she was a woman, and it meant more to her than it can ever mean to a man; partly because, though dangerous, it is also obvious, and makes no demand upon the intellect. She could not feel that Stephen had full human rights. He was illicit, abnormal, worse than a man diseased. And Rickie, remembering whose son he was, gradually adopted her opinion. He, too, came to be glad that his brother had passed from him untried, that the symbolic moment had been rejected. Stephen was the fruit of sin; therefore he was sinful. He, too, became a sexual snob.

And now he must hear the unsavoury details. That evening they sat in the walled garden. Agnes, according to arrangement, left him alone with his aunt. He asked her, and was not answered.

'You are shocked,' she said in a hard, mocking voice. 'It is very nice of you to be shocked, and I do not wish to grieve you further. We will not allude to it again. Let us all go on just as we are. The comedy is finished.'

He could not tolerate this. His nerves were shattered, and all that was good in him revolted as well. To the horror of Agnes, who was within earshot, he replied, 'You used to puzzle me, Aunt Emily, but I understand you at last. You have forgotten what other people are like. Continual selfishness leads to that. I am sure of it. I see now how you look at the world. "Nice of me to be shocked!" I want to go to-morrow, if I may.'

'Certainly, dear. The morning trains are the best.' And so the disastrous visit ended.

As he walked back to the house he met a certain poor woman, whose child Stephen had rescued at the level-crossing, and who had decided, after some delay, that she must thank the kind gentleman in person. 'He has got some brute courage,' thought Rickie, 'and it was decent of him not to boast about it.' But he had labelled the boy as 'Bad', and it was convenient to revert to his good qualities as seldom as possible. He preferred to brood over his coarseness, his caddish ingratitude, his irreligion. Out of these he constructed a repulsive figure, forgetting how slovenly his own perceptions had been during the past week, how dogmatic and intolerant his attitude to all that was not Love.

During the packing he was obliged to go up to the attic to find the Dryad manuscript, which had never been returned. Leighton came too, and for about half an hour they hunted in the flickering light of a candle. It was a strange ghostly place, and Rickie was quite startled when a picture swung towards him, and he saw the Demeter of Cnidus, shimmering and grey. Leighton suggested the roof: Mr. Stephen sometimes left things on the roof. So they climbed out of the skylight—the night was perfectly still—and continued the search among the gables. Enormous stars hung overhead, and the roof was bounded by chasms, impenetrable and black. 'It doesn't matter,' said Rickie, suddenly convinced of the futility of all that he did. 'Oh, let us look properly,' said Leighton, a kindly, pliable man, who had tried to shirk coming, but who was genuinely sympathetic now that he had come. They were rewarded: the manuscript lay in a gutter, charred and smudged.

The rest of the year was spent by Rickie partly in bed,—he had a curious breakdown,—partly in the attempt to get his little stories published. He had written eight or nine, and hoped they would make up a book, and that the book might be called 'Pan Pipes'. He was very energetic over this; he liked to work, for some imperceptible bloom had passed from the world, and he no longer found such acute pleasure in people. Mr. Failing's old publishers, to whom the book was submitted, replied that, greatly as they found themselves interested, they did not see their way to making an offer at present. They were very polite, and singled out for special praise 'Andante Pastorale', which Rickie had thought too sentimental, but which Agnes had persuaded him to include. The stories were sent to another publisher, who considered them for six weeks, and then returned them. A fragment of red cotton, placed by Agnes between the leaves, had not shifted in position.

'Can't you try something longer, Rickie?' she said; 'I believe we're on the wrong track. Try an out-and-out love-story.'

'My notion just now,' he replied, 'is to leave the passions on the fringe.' She nodded, and tapped for the waiter: they had met in a London restaurant. 'I can't soar; I can only indicate. That's where the musicians have the pull, for music has wings, and when she says "Tristan" and he says "Isolde", you are on the heights at once. What do people mean when they call love music artificial?'

'I know what they mean, though I can't exactly explain. Or couldn't you make your stories more obvious? I don't see any harm in that. Uncle Willie floundered hopelessly. He doesn't read much, and he got muddled. I had to explain, and then he was delighted. Of course, to write down to the public would be quite another thing and horrible. You have certain ideas, and you must express them. But couldn't you express them more clearly?'

'You see——' He got no further than 'you see.'

'The soul and the body. The soul's what matters,' said Agnes, and tapped for the waiter again. He looked at her admiringly, but felt that she was not a perfect critic. Perhaps she was too perfect to be a critic. Actual life might seem to her so real that she could not detect the union of shadow and adamant that men call poetry. He would even go further and acknowledge that she was not as clever as himself—and he was stupid enough! She did not like discussing anything or reading solid books, and she was a little angry with such women as did. It pleased him to make these concessions, for they touched nothing in her that he valued. He looked round the restaurant, which was in Soho, and decided that she was incomparable.

'At half-past two I call on the editor of the "Holborn". He's got a stray story to look at, and he's written about it.'

'Oh, Rickie! Rickie! Why didn't you put on a boiled shirt!'

He laughed, and teased her. 'The soul's what matters. We literary people don't care about dress.'

'Well, you ought to care. And I believe you do. Can't you change?'

'Too far.' He had rooms in South Kensington. 'And I've forgot my card-case. There's for you!'

She shook her head. 'Naughty, naughty boy! Whatever will you do?'

'Send in my name, or ask for a bit of paper and write it. Hullo! that's Tilliard!'

Tilliard blushed, partly on account of the *faux pas* he had made last June, partly on account of the restaurant. He explained how he came to be pigging in Soho: it was so frightfully convenient and so frightfully cheap.

'Just why Rickie brings me,' said Miss Pembroke.

'And I suppose you're here to study life?' said Tilliard, sitting down.

'I don't know,' said Rickie, gazing round at the waiters and the guests.

'Doesn't one want to see a good deal of life for writing? There's life of a sort in Soho,—*Un peu de faisan, s'il vous plaît.*'

Agnes also grabbed at the waiter, and paid. She always did the paying, Rickie muddled so with his purse.

'I'm cramming,' pursued Tilliard, 'and so naturally I come into contact with very little at present. But later on I hope to see things.' He blushed a little, for he was talking for Rickie's edification. 'It is most frightfully important not to get a narrow or academic outlook, don't you think? A person like Ansell, who goes from Cambridge, home—home, Cambridge—it must tell on him in time.'

'But Mr. Ansell is a philosopher.'

'A very kinky one,' said Tilliard abruptly. 'Not

my idea of a philosopher. How goes his dissertation?'

'He never answers my letters,' replied Rickie. 'He never would. I've heard nothing since June.'

'It's a pity he sends in this year. There are so many good people in. He'd have a far better chance if he waited.'

'So I said, but he wouldn't wait. He's so keen about this particular subject.'

'What is it?' asked Agnes.

'About things being real, wasn't it, Tilliard?'

'That's near enough.'

'Well, good luck to him!' said the girl. 'And good luck to you, Mr. Tilliard! Later on, I hope, we'll meet again.'

They parted. Tilliard liked her, though he did not feel that she was quite in his *couche sociale*. His sister, for instance, would never have been lured into a Soho restaurant—except for the experience of the thing. Tilliard's *couche sociale* permitted experiences. Provided his heart did not go out to the poor and the unorthodox, he might stare at them as much as he liked. It was seeing life.

Agnes put her lover safely into an omnibus at Cambridge Circus. She shouted after him that his tie was rising over his collar, but he did not hear her. For a moment she felt depressed, and pictured quite accurately the effect that his appearance would have on the editor. The editor was a tall neat man of forty, slow of speech, slow of soul, and extraordinarily kind. He and Rickie sat over a fire, with an enormous table behind them, whereon stood many books waiting to be reviewed.

'I'm sorry,' he said, and paused.

Rickie smiled feebly.

'Your story does not convince.' He tapped it. 'I

have read it—with very great pleasure. It convinces in parts, but it does not convince as a whole; and stories, don't you think, ought to convince as a whole?'

'They ought indeed,' said Rickie, and plunged into self-depreciation. But the editor checked him.

'No—no. Please don't talk like that. I can't bear to hear any one talk against imagination. There are countless openings for imagination,—for the mysterious, for the supernatural, for all the things you are trying to do, and which, I hope, you will succeed in doing. I'm not *objecting* to imagination; on the contrary, I'd advise you to cultivate it, to accent it. Write a really good ghost story and we'd take it at once. Or'—he suggested it as an alternative to imagination—'or you might get inside life. It's worth doing.'

'Life?' echoed Rickie anxiously. He looked round the pleasant room, as if life might be fluttering there, like an imprisoned bird. Then he looked at the editor; perhaps he was sitting inside life at this very moment.

'See life, Mr. Elliot, and then send us another story.' He held out his hand. 'I am sorry I have had to say "No, thank you"; it's so much nicer to say, "Yes, please."' He laid his hand on the young man's sleeve, and added, 'Well, the interview's not been so alarming after all, has it?'

'I don't think that either of us is a very alarming person,' was not Rickie's reply. It was what he thought out afterwards in the omnibus. His reply was 'Ow,' delivered with a slight giggle.

As he rumbled westward, his face was drawn, and his eyes moved quickly to the right and left, as if he would discover something in the squalid fashionable streets—some bird on the wing, some radiant archway, the face of some god beneath a beaver hat. He loved, he was loved, he had seen death and other things; but the heart of all things was hidden. There was a password and he could not learn it, nor could the kind editor of the 'Holborn' teach him. He sighed, and then sighed more piteously. For had he not known the password once —known it and forgotten it already?

But at this point his fortunes become intimately connected with those of Mr. Pembroke.

PART TWO

SAWSTON

◆

XVI

In three years Mr. Pembroke had done much to solidify the day-boys at Sawston School. If they were not solid, they were at all events curdling, and his activities might reasonably turn elsewhere. He had served the school for many years, and it was really time he should be entrusted with a boarding-house. The headmaster, an impulsive man who darted about like a minnow and gave his mother a great deal of trouble, agreed with him, and also agreed with Mrs. Jackson when she said that Mr. Jackson had served the school for many years and that it was really time he should be entrusted with a boarding-house. Consequently, when Dunwood House fell vacant, the headmaster found himself in rather a difficult position.

Dunwood House was the largest and most lucrative of the boarding-houses. It stood almost opposite the school buildings. Originally it had been a villa residence—a red-brick villa, covered with creepers and crowned with terra-cotta dragons. Mr. Annison, founder of its glory, had lived here, and had had one or two boys to live with him. Times changed. The fame of the bishops blazed brighter, the school increased, the one or two boys became a dozen, and an addition was made to Dunwood

House that more than doubled its size. A huge new building, replete with every convenience, was stuck on to its right flank. Dormitories, cubicles, studies, a preparation-room, a dining-room, parquet floors, hot-air pipes—no expense was spared, and the twelve boys roamed over it like princes. Baize doors communicated on every floor with Mr. Annison's part, and he, an anxious gentle man, would stroll backwards and forwards, a little depressed at the hygienic splendours, and conscious of some vanished intimacy. Somehow he had known his boys better when they had all muddled together as one family, and algebras lay strewn upon the drawing-room chairs. As the house filled, his interest in it decreased. When he retired—which he did the same summer that Rickie left Cambridge—it had already passed the summit of excellence and was beginning to decline. Its numbers were still satisfactory, and for a little time it would subsist on its past reputation. But that mysterious asset the tone had lowered, and it was therefore of great importance that Mr. Annison's successor should be a first-class man. Mr. Coates, who came next in seniority, was passed over, and rightly. The choice lay between Mr. Pembroke and Mr. Jackson, the one an organizer, the other a humanist. Mr. Jackson was master of the Sixth, and—with the exception of the headmaster, who was too busy to impart knowledge—the only first-class intellect in the school. But he could not, or rather would not, keep order. He told his form that if it chose to listen to him it would learn; if it didn't, it wouldn't. One half listened. The other half made paper frogs, and bored holes in the raised map of Italy with their penknives. When the penknives gritted he punished them with undue severity, and then forgot to make them show the punishments up. Yet out of this chaos two facts emerged. Half the boys got scholarships at the University, and some of them—including several of the paper-frog sort—remained friends with him throughout their lives. Moreover, he was rich, and had a competent wife. His claim to Dunwood House was stronger than one would have supposed.

The qualifications of Mr. Pembroke have already been indicated. They prevailed—but under conditions. If things went wrong, he must promise to resign.

'In the first place,' said the headmaster, 'you are doing so splendidly with the day-boys. Your attitude towards the parents is magnificent. I don't know how to replace you there. Whereas, of course, the parents of a boarder——'

'Of course,' said Mr. Pembroke.

The parent of a boarder, who only had to remove his son if he was discontented with the school, was naturally in a more independent position than the parent who had brought all his goods and chattels to Sawston, and was renting a house there.

'Now the parents of boarders—this is my second point—practically demand that the house-master should have a wife.'

'A most unreasonable demand,' said Mr. Pembroke.

'To my mind also a bright motherly matron is quite sufficient. But that is what they demand. And that is why—do you see?—we *have* to regard your appointment as experimental. Possibly Miss Pembroke will be able to help you. Or I don't know whether if ever——' He left the sentence unfinished. Two days later Mr. Pembroke proposed to Mrs. Orr.

He had always intended to marry when he could

afford it; and once he had been in love, violently in
love, but had laid the passion aside, and told it to
wait till a more convenient season. This was, of
course, the proper thing to do, and prudence should
have been rewarded. But when, after the lapse of
fifteen years, he went, as it were, to his spiritual
larder and took down Love from the top shelf to
offer him to Mrs. Orr, he was rather dismayed.
Something had happened. Perhaps the god had
flown; perhaps he had been eaten by the rats. At
all events, he was not there.

Mr. Pembroke was conscientious and romantic,
and knew that marriage without love is intolerable.
On the other hand, he could not admit that love
had vanished from him. To admit this would argue
that he had deteriorated. Whereas he knew for a
fact that he improved, year by year. Each year he
grew more moral, more efficient, more learned,
more genial. So how could he fail to be more loving? He did not speak to himself as follows, because
he never spoke to himself; but the following notions
moved in the recesses of his mind: 'It is not the fire
of youth. But I am not sure that I approve of the
fire of youth. Look at my sister! Once she has suffered, twice she has been most imprudent, and put
me to great inconvenience besides, for if she was
stopping with me she would have done the house-
keeping. I rather suspect that it is a nobler, riper
emotion that I am laying at the feet of Mrs. Orr.'
It never took him long to get muddled, or to reverse
cause and effect. In a short time he believed that he
had been pining for years, and only waiting for this
good fortune to ask the lady to share it with him.

Mrs. Orr was quiet, clever, kindly, capable, and
amusing, and they were old acquaintances. Altogether it was not surprising that he should ask

her to be his wife, nor very surprising that she should refuse. But she refused with a violence that alarmed them both. He left her house declaring that he had been insulted, and she, as soon as he left, passed from disgust into tears.

He was much annoyed. There was a certain Miss Herriton who, though far inferior to Mrs. Orr, would have done instead of her. But now it was impossible. He could not go offering himself about Sawston. Having engaged a matron who had a reputation for being bright and motherly, he moved into Dunwood House and opened the Michaelmas term. Everything went wrong. The cook left: the boys had a disease called roseola; Agnes, who was still drunk with her engagement, was of no assistance, but kept flying up to London to push Rickie's fortunes; and, to crown everything, the matron was too bright and not motherly enough: she neglected the little boys and was over-attentive to the big ones. She left abruptly, and the voice of Mrs. Jackson arose, prophesying disaster.

Should he avert it by taking orders? Parents do not demand that a house-master should be a clergyman, yet it reassures them when he is. And he would have to take orders some time, if he hoped for a school of his own. His religious convictions were ready to hand, but he spent several uncomfortable days hunting up his religious enthusiasms. It was not unlike his attempt to marry Mrs. Orr. But his piety was more genuine, and this time he never came to the point. His sense of decency forbade him hurrying into a Church that he reverenced. Moreover, he thought of another solution: Agnes must marry Rickie in the Christmas holidays, and they must come, both of them, to Sawston, she as housekeeper, he as assistant-master. The girl was a good worker when once she was settled down; and as for Rickie, he could easily be fitted in somewhere in the school. He was not a good classic, but good enough to take the Lower Fifth. He was no athlete, but boys might profitably note that he was a perfect gentleman all the same. He had no experience, but he would gain it. He had no decision, but he could simulate it. 'Above all,' thought Mr. Pembroke, 'it will be something regular for him to do.' Of course this was not 'above all'. Dunwood House held that position. But Mr. Pembroke soon came to think that it was, and believed that he was planning for Rickie, just as he had believed that he was pining for Mrs. Orr.

Agnes, when she got back from the lunch in Soho, was told of the plan. She refused to give any opinion until she had seen her lover. A telegram was sent to him, and next morning he arrived. He was very susceptible to the weather, and perhaps it was unfortunate that the morning was foggy. His train had been stopped outside Sawston Station, and there he had sat for half an hour, listening to the unreal noises that came from the line, and watching the shadowy figures that worked there. The gas was alight in the great drawing-room, and in its depressing rays he and Agnes greeted each other, and discussed the most momentous question of their lives. They wanted to be married: there was no doubt of that. They wanted it, both of them, dreadfully. But should they marry on these terms?

'I'd never thought of such a thing, you see. When the scholastic agencies sent me circulars after the Tripos, I tore them up at once.'

'There are the holidays,' said Agnes. 'You would have three months in the year to yourself and could do your writing then.'

'But who'll read what I've written?' and he told her about the editor of the 'Holborn'.

She became extremely grave. At the bottom of her heart she had always mistrusted the little stories, and now people who knew agreed with her. How could Rickie, or any one, make a living by pretending that Greek gods were alive, or that young ladies could vanish into trees? A sparkling society tale, full of verve and pathos, would have been another thing, and the editor might have been convinced by it.

'But what does he *mean*?' Rickie was saying. 'What does he *mean* by life?'

"I know what he means, but I can't exactly explain. You ought to see life, Rickie. I think he's right there. And Mr. Tilliard was right when he said one oughtn't to be academic.'

He stood in the twilight that fell from the window, she in the twilight from the gas. 'I wonder what Ansell would say,' he murmured.

'Oh, poor Mr. Ansell!'

He was somewhat surprised. Why was Ansell poor? It was the first time the epithet had been applied to him.

'But to change the conversation,' said Agnes. 'If we did marry, we might get to Italy at Easter and escape this horrible fog.'

'Yes. Perhaps there——' Perhaps life would be there. He thought of Renan, who declares that on the Acropolis at Athens beauty and wisdom do exist, really exist, as external powers. He did not aspire to beauty or wisdom, but he prayed to be delivered from the shadow of unreality that had begun to darken the world. For it was as if some power had pronounced against him—as if, by some heedless action, he had offended an Olympian god.

Like many another, he wondered whether the god might be appeased by work—hard uncongenial work. Perhaps he had not worked hard enough, or had enjoyed his work too much, and for that reason the shadow was falling.

'—And above all, a schoolmaster has wonderful opportunities of doing good; one mustn't forget that.'

To do good! For what other reason are we here? Let us give up our refined sensations, and our comforts, and our art, if thereby we can make other people happier and better. The woman he loved had urged him to do good! With a vehemence that surprised her, he exclaimed, 'I'll do it.'

'Think it over,' she cautioned, though she was greatly pleased.

'No; I think over things too much.'

The room grew brighter. A boy's laughter floated in, and it seemed to him that people were as important and vivid as they had been six months before. Then he was at Cambridge, idling in the parsley meadows, and weaving perishable garlands out of flowers. Now he was at Sawston, preparing to work a beneficent machine. No man works for nothing, and Rickie trusted that to him also benefits might accrue; that his wound might heal as he laboured, and his eyes recapture the Holy Grail.

XVII

In practical matters Mr. Pembroke was often a generous man. He offered Rickie a good salary, and insisted on paying Agnes as well. And as he housed them for nothing, and as Rickie would also have a salary from the school, the money question disappeared—if not for ever, at all events for the present.

'I can work you in,' he said. 'Leave all that to me, and in a few days you shall hear from the head-master. He shall create a vacancy. And once in, we stand or fall together. I am resolved on that.'

Rickie did not like the idea of being 'worked in', but he was determined to raise no difficulties. It is so easy to be refined and high-minded when we have nothing to do. But the active, useful man cannot be equally particular. Rickie's programme involved a change in values as well as a change of occupation.

'Adopt a frankly intellectual attitude,' Mr. Pembroke continued. 'I do not advise you at present even to profess any interest in athletics or organization. When the headmaster writes, he will probably ask whether you are an all-round man. Boldly say no. A bold "no" is at times the best. Take your stand upon classics and general culture.'

Classics! A second in the Tripos. General culture! A smattering of English Literature, and less than a smattering of French.

'That is how we begin. Then we get you a little post—say that of librarian. And so on, until you are indispensable.'

Rickie laughed; the headmaster wrote, the reply was satisfactory, and in due course the new life began.

Sawston was already familiar to him. But he knew it as an amateur, and under an official gaze it grouped itself afresh. The school, a bland Gothic building, now showed as a fortress of learning, whose outworks were the boarding-houses. Those straggling roads were full of the houses of the parents of the day-boys. These shops were in

bounds, those out. How often had he passed Dunwood House! He had once confused it with its rival,
Cedar View. Now he was to live there—perhaps
for many years. On the left of the entrance a large
saffron drawing-room, full of cosy corners and
dumpy chairs: here the parents would be received.
On the right of the entrance a study, which he
shared with Herbert: here the boys would be caned
—he hoped not often. In the hall a framed certificate praising the drains, the bust of Hermes, and a
carved teak monkey holding out a salver. Some of
the furniture had come from Shelthorpe, some had
been bought from Mr. Annison, some of it was new.
But throughout he recognized a certain decision of
arrangement. Nothing in the house was accidental,
or there merely for its own sake. He contrasted it
with his room at Cambridge, which had been a
jumble of things that he loved dearly and of things
that he did not love at all. Now these also had come
to Dunwood House, and had been distributed
where each was seemly—Sir Percival to the drawing-room, the photograph of Stockholm to the passage, his chair, his inkpot, and the portrait of his
mother to the study. And then he contrasted it with
the Ansells' house, to which their resolute ill-taste
had given unity. He was extremely sensitive to the
inside of a house, holding it an organism that expressed the thoughts, conscious and subconscious,
of its inmates. He was equally sensitive to places.
He would compare Cambridge with Sawston, and
either with a third type of existence, to which, for
want of a better name, he gave the name of 'Wiltshire'.

It must not be thought that he is going to waste
his time. These contrasts and comparisons never
took him long, and he never indulged in them until

the serious business of the day was over. And, as time passed, he never indulged in them at all.

The school returned at the end of January, before he had been settled in a week. His health had improved, but not greatly, and he was nervous at the prospect of confronting the assembled house. All day long cabs had been driving up, full of boys in bowler hats too big for them; and Agnes had been superintending the numbering of the said hats, and the placing of them in cupboards, since they would not be wanted till the end of the term. Each boy had, or should have had, a bag so that he need not unpack his box till the morrow. One boy had only a brown-paper parcel, tied with hairy string, and Rickie heard the firm pleasant voice say, 'But you'll bring a bag next term,' and the submissive, 'Yes, Mrs. Elliot,' of the reply. In the passage he ran against the head boy, who was alarmingly like an undergraduate. They looked at each other suspiciously, and parted. Two minutes later he ran into another boy, and then into another, and began to wonder whether they were doing it on purpose, and if so, whether he ought to mind. As the day wore on, the noises grew louder—trampings of feet, breakdowns, jolly little squawks—and the cubicles were assigned, and the bags unpacked, and the bathing arrangements posted up, and Herbert kept on saying, 'All this is informal—all this is informal. We shall meet the house at eight-fifteen.'

And so, at eight-ten, Rickie put on his cap and gown,—hitherto symbols of pupilage, now to be symbols of dignity,—the very cap and gown that Widdrington had so recently hung upon the college fountain. Herbert, similarly attired, was waiting for him in their private dining-room, where also sat Agnes, ravenously devouring scrambled eggs. 'But you'll wear your hoods,' she cried. Herbert considered, and then said she was quite right. He fetched his white silk, Rickie the fragment of rabbits' wool that marks the degree of B.A. Thus attired, they proceeded through the baize door. They were a little late, and the boys, who were marshalled in the preparation-room, were getting uproarious. One, forgetting how far his voice carried, shouted, 'Cave! Here comes the Whelk.' And another young devil yelled, 'The Whelk's brought a limpet with him!'

'You mustn't mind,' said Herbert kindly. 'We masters make a point of never minding nicknames —unless, of course, they are applied openly, in which case a thousand lines is not too much.' Rickie assented, and they entered the preparation-room just as the prefects had established order.

Here Herbert took his seat on a high-legged chair, while Rickie, like a queen-consort, sat near him on a chair with somewhat shorter legs. Each chair had a desk attached to it, and Herbert flung up the lid of his, and then looked round the preparation-room with a quick frown, as if the contents had surprised him. So impressed was Rickie that he peeped sideways, but could only see a little blotting-paper in the desk. Then he noticed that the boys were impressed too. Their chatter ceased. They attended.

The room was almost full. The prefects, instead of lolling disdainfully in the back row, were ranged like councillors beneath the central throne. This was an innovation of Mr. Pembroke's. Carruthers, the head boy, sat in the middle, with his arm round Lloyd. It was Lloyd who had made the matron too bright: he nearly lost his colours in consequence. These two were very grown up. Beside them sat Tewson, a saintly child in spectacles, who had risen to this height by reason of his immense learning. He, like the others, was a school prefect. The house prefects, an inferior brand, were beyond, and behind came the indistinguishable many. The faces all looked alike as yet— except the face of one boy, who was inclined to cry.

'School,' said Mr. Pembroke, slowly closing the lid of the desk,—'school is the world in miniature.' Then he paused, as a man well may who has made such a remark. It is not, however, the intention of this work to quote an opening address. Rickie, at all events, refused to be critical: Herbert's experience was far greater than his, and he must take his tone from him. Nor could any one criticize the exhortations to be patriotic, athletic, learned, and religious, that flowed like a four-part fugue from Mr. Pembroke's mouth. He was a practised speaker—that is to say, he held his audience's attention. He told them that this term, the second of his reign, was *the* term for Dunwood House; that it behoved every boy to labour during it for his house's honour, and, through the house, for the honour of the school. Taking a wider range, he spoke of England, or rather of Great Britain, and of her continental foes. Portraits of empire builders hung on the wall, and he pointed to them. He quoted imperial poets. He showed how patriotism has broadened since the days of Shakespeare, who, for all his genius, could only write of his country as—

This fortress built by Nature for herself
Against infection and the hand of war;
This happy breed of men, this little world;
This precious stone set in the silver sea.

And it seemed that only a short ladder lay

between the preparation-room and the Anglo-Saxon hegemony of the globe. Then he paused, and in the silence came 'sob, sob, sob', from a little boy, who was regretting a villa in Guildford and his mother's half acre of garden.

The proceeding terminated with the broader patriotism of the school anthem, recently composed by the organist. Words and tune were still a matter for taste, and it was Mr. Pembroke (and he only because he had the music) who gave the right intonation to

> Perish each laggard! Let it not be said
> That Sawston such within her walls hath bred.

'Come, come,' he said pleasantly, as they ended with harmonies in the style of Richard Strauss. 'This will never do. We must grapple with the anthem this term. You're as tuneful as—as day-boys!' Hearty laughter, and then the whole house filed past them and shook hands.

'But how did it impress you?' Herbert asked, as soon as they were back in their own part. Agnes had provided them with a tray of food: the meals were still anyhow, and she had to fly at once to see after the boys.

'I liked the look of them.'

'I meant rather, how did the house impress you as a house?'

'I don't think I thought,' said Rickie rather nervously. 'It is not easy to catch the spirit of a thing at once. I only saw a room full of boys.'

'My dear Rickie, don't be so diffident. You are perfectly right. You only did see a roomful of boys. As yet there's nothing else to see. The house, like the school, lacks tradition. Look at Winchester. Look at the traditional rivalry between Eton and

Harrow. Tradition is of incalculable importance, if a school is to have any status. Why should Sawston be without?'

'Yes. Tradition is of incalculable value. And I envy those schools that have a natural connection with the past. Of course Sawston has a past, though not of the kind that you quite want. The sons of poor tradesmen went to it at first. So wouldn't its traditions be more likely to linger in the Commercial School?' he concluded nervously.

'You have a great deal to learn—a very great deal. Listen to me. Why has Sawston no traditions?' His round, rather foolish, face assumed the expression of a conspirator. Bending over the mutton, he whispered, 'I can tell you why. Owing to the day-boys. How can traditions flourish in such soil? Picture the day-boy's life—at home for meals, at home for preparation, at home for sleep, running home with every fancied wrong. There are day-boys in your class, and, mark my words, they will give you ten times as much trouble as the boarders, —late, slovenly, stopping away at the slightest pretext. And then the letters from the parents! "Why has my boy not been moved this term?" "Why has my boy been moved this term?" "I am a dissenter, and do not wish my boy to subscribe to the school mission." "Can you let my boy off early to water the garden?" Remember that I have been a day-boy house-master, and tried to infuse some *esprit de corps* into them. It is practically impossible. They come as units, and units they remain. Worse. They infect the boarders. Their pestilential, critical, discontented attitude is spreading over the school. If I had my own way——'

He stopped somewhat abruptly.

'Was that why you laughed at their singing?'

'Not at all. Not at all. It is not my habit to set one section of the school against the other.'

After a little they went the rounds. The boys were in bed now. 'Good night!' called Herbert, standing in the corridor of the cubicles, and from behind each of the green curtains came the sound of a voice replying, 'Good night, sir!' 'Good night,' he observed into each dormitory. Then he went to the switch in the passage and plunged the whole house into darkness. Rickie lingered behind him, strangely impressed. In the morning those boys had been scattered over England, leading their own lives. Now, for three months, they must change everything—see new faces, accept new ideals. They, like himself, must enter a beneficent machine, and learn the value of *esprit de corps*. Good luck attend them—good luck and a happy release. For his heart would have them not in these cubicles and dormitories, but each in his own dear home, amongst faces and things that he knew.

Next morning, after chapel, he made the acquaintance of his class. Towards that he felt very differently. *Esprit de corps* was not expected of it. It was simply two dozen boys who were gathered together for the purpose of learning Latin. His duties and difficulties would not lie here. He was not required to provide it with an atmosphere. The scheme of work was already mapped out, and he started gaily upon familiar words—

Pan ovium custos, tua si tibi Maenala curae,
Adsis, O Tegaee, favens.

'Do you think that beautiful?' he asked, and received the honest answer, 'No, sir; I don't think I do.' He met Herbert in high spirits in the quadrangle during the interval. But Herbert thought his enthusiasm rather amateurish, and cautioned him.

'You must take care they don't get out of hand. I approve of a lively teacher, but discipline must be established first.'

'I felt myself a learner, not a teacher. If I'm wrong over a point, or don't know, I mean to tell them at once.'

Herbert shook his head.

'It's different if I was really a scholar. But I can't pose as one, can I? I know much more than the boys, but I know very little. Surely the honest thing is to be myself to them. Let them accept or refuse me as that. That's the only attitude we shall any of us profit by in the end.'

Mr. Pembroke was silent. Then he observed, 'There is, as you say, a higher attitude and a lower attitude. Yet here, as so often, cannot we find a golden mean between them?'

'What's that?' said a dreamy voice. They turned and saw a tall, spectacled man, who greeted the newcomer kindly, and took hold of his arm. 'What's that about the golden mean?'

'Mr. Jackson—Mr. Elliot: Mr. Elliot—Mr. Jackson,' said Herbert, who did not seem quite pleased. 'Rickie, have you a moment to spare me?'

But the humanist spoke to the young man about the golden mean and the pinchbeck mean, adding, 'You know the Greeks aren't broad church clergymen. They really aren't, in spite of much conflicting evidence. Boys will regard Sophocles as a kind of enlightened bishop, and something tells me that they are wrong.'

'Mr. Jackson is a classical enthusiast,' said Herbert. 'He makes the past live. I want to talk to you about the humdrum present.'

'And I am warning him against the humdrum past. That's another point, Mr. Elliot. Impress on your class that many Greeks and most Romans were frightfully stupid, and if they disbelieve you, read Ctesiphon with them, or Valerius Flaccus. Whatever is that noise?'

'It comes from your class-room, I think,' snapped the other master.

'So it does. Ah, yes. I expect they are putting your little Tewson into the waste-paper basket.'

'I always lock my class-room in the interval——'

'Yes?'

'——and carry the key in my pocket.'

'Ah. But, Mr. Elliot, I am a cousin of Widdrington's. He wrote to me about you. I am so glad. Will you, first of all, come to supper next Sunday?'

'I am afraid,' put in Herbert, 'that we poor house-masters must deny ourselves festivities in term time.'

'But mayn't he come once, just once?'

'May, my dear Jackson! My brother-in-law is not a baby. He decides for himself.'

Rickie naturally refused. As soon as they were out of hearing, Herbert said, 'This is a little unfortunate. Who is Mr. Widdrington?'

'I knew him at Cambridge.'

'Let me explain how we stand,' he continued, after a pause. 'Jackson is the worst of the reactionaries here, while I—why should I conceal it?—have thrown in my lot with the party of progress. You will see how we suffer from him at the masters' meetings. He has no talent for organization, and yet he is always inflicting his ideas on others. It was like his impertinence to dictate to you what authors you should read, and meanwhile the sixth-form room like a bear-garden, and a school prefect being put into the waste-paper basket. My good Rickie, there's nothing to smile at. How is the school to go on with a man like that? It would be a case of "quick march", if it was not for his brilliant intellect. That's why I say it's a little unfortunate. You will have very little in common, you and he.'

Rickie did not answer. He was very fond of Widdrington, who was a quaint, sensitive person. And he could not help being attracted to Mr. Jackson, whose welcome contrasted pleasantly with the official breeziness of his other colleagues. He wondered, too, whether it is so very reactionary to contemplate the antique.

'It is true that I vote Conservative,' pursued Mr. Pembroke, apparently confronting some objector. 'But why? Because the Conservatives, rather than the Liberals, stand for progress. One must not be misled by catchwords.'

'Didn't you want to ask me something?'

'Ah, yes. You found a boy in your form called Varden?'

'Varden? Yes; there is.'

'Drop on him heavily. He has broken the statutes of the school. He is attending as a day-boy. The statutes provide that a boy must reside with his parents or guardians. He does neither. It must be stopped. You must tell the headmaster.'

'Where does the boy live?'

'At a certain Mrs. Orr's, who has no connection with the school of any kind. It must be stopped. He must either enter a boarding-house or go.'

'But why should I tell?' said Rickie. He remembered the boy, an unattractive person with protruding ears. 'It is the business of his house-master.'

'House-master—exactly. Here we come back again. Who is now the day-boy's house-master?

Jackson once again—as if anything was Jackson's business! I handed the house back last term in a flourishing condition. It has already gone to rack and ruin for the second time. To return to Varden. I have unearthed a put-up job. Mrs. Jackson and Mrs. Orr are friends. Do you see? It all works round.'

'I see. It does—or might.'

'The headmaster will never sanction it when it's put to him plainly.'

'But why should I put it?' said Rickie, twisting the ribbons of his gown round his fingers.

'Because you're the boy's form-master.'

'Is that a reason?'

'Of course it is.'

'I only wondered whether——' He did not like to say that he wondered whether he need do it his first morning.

'By some means or other you must find out—of course you know already, but you must find out from the boy. I know—I have it! Where's his health certificate?'

'He had forgotten it.'

'Just like them. Well, when he brings it, it will be signed by Mrs. Orr, and you must look at it and say, "Orr—Orr—Mrs. Orr?" or something to that effect, and then the whole thing will come naturally out.'

The bell rang, and they went in for the hour of school that concluded the morning. Varden brought his health certificate—a pompous document asserting that he had not suffered from roseola or kindred ailments in the holidays—and for a long time Rickie sat with it before him, spread open upon his desk. He did not quite like the job. It suggested intrigue, and he had come to Sawston not to in-

trigue but to labour. Doubtless Herbert was right,
and Mr. Jackson and Mrs. Orr were wrong. But why
could they not have it out among themselves? Then
he thought, 'I am a coward, and that's why I'm
raising these objections,' called the boy up to him,
and it did all come out naturally, more or less.
Hitherto Varden had lived with his mother; but she
had left Sawston at Christmas, and now he would
live with Mrs. Orr. 'Mr. Jackson, sir, said it would
be all right.'

'Yes, yes,' said Rickie; 'quite so.' He remembered
Herbert's dictum: 'Masters must present a united
front. If they do not—the deluge.' He sent the boy
back to his seat, and after school took the com-
promising health certificate to the headmaster.
The headmaster was at that time easily excited by
a breach of the constitution. 'Parents or guardians,'
he repeated—'parents or guardians,' and flew with
those words on his lips to Mr. Jackson.

To say that Rickie was a cat's-paw is to put it too
strongly. Herbert was strictly honourable, and never
pushed him into an illegal or really dangerous position; but there is no doubt that on this and on
many other occasions he had to do things that he
would not otherwise have done. There was always
some diplomatic corner that had to be turned, always something that he had to say or not to say. As
the term wore on he lost his independence—almost
without knowing it. He had much to learn about
boys, and he learnt not by direct observation—for
which he believed he was unfitted—but by sedu-
lous imitation of the more experienced masters.
Originally he had intended to be friends with his
pupils, and Mr. Pembroke commended the intention highly; but you cannot be friends either with
boy or man unless you give yourself away in the

process, and Mr. Pembroke did not commend this. He, for 'personal intercourse', substituted the safer 'personal influence', and gave his junior hints on the setting of kindly traps, in which the boy does give himself away and reveals his shy delicate thoughts, while the master, intact, commends or corrects them. Originally Rickie had meant to help boys in the anxieties that they undergo when changing into men: at Cambridge he had numbered this among life's duties. But here is a subject in which we must inevitably speak as one human being to another, not as one who has authority or the shadow of authority, and for this reason the elder schoolmaster could suggest nothing but a few formulæ. Formulæ, like kindly traps, were not in Rickie's line, so he abandoned these subjects altogether and confined himself to work hard at what was easy. In the house he did as Herbert did, and referred all doubtful subjects to him. In his form, oddly enough, he became a martinet. It is so much simpler to be severe. He grasped the school regulations, and insisted on prompt obedience to them. He adopted the doctrine of collective responsibility. When one boy was late, he punished the whole form. 'I can't help it,' he would say, as if he was a power of nature. As a teacher he was rather dull. He curbed his own enthusiasms, finding that they distracted his attention, and that while he throbbed to the music of Virgil the boys in the back row were getting unruly. But on the whole he liked his form work: he knew why he was there, and Herbert did not overshadow him so completely.

What was amiss with Herbert? He had known that something was amiss, and had entered into partnership with open eyes. The man was kind and unselfish; more than that, he was truly charitable,

and it was a real pleasure to him to give pleasure
to others. Certainly he might talk too much about it
afterwards; but it was the doing, not the talking,
that he really valued, and benefactors of this sort
are not too common. He was, moreover, diligent
and conscientious: his heart was in his work, and
his adherence to the Church of England no mere
matter of form. He was capable of affection: he was
usually courteous and tolerant. Then what was
amiss? Why, in spite of all these qualities, should
Rickie feel that there was something wrong with
him—nay, that he was wrong as a whole, and that
if the Spirit of Humanity should ever hold a judg-
ment he would assuredly be classed among the
goats? The answer at first sight appeared a grace-
less one—it was that Herbert was stupid. Not
stupid in the ordinary sense—he had a business-
like brain, and acquired knowledge easily—but
stupid in the important sense: his whole life was
coloured by a contempt of the intellect. That he
had a tolerable intellect of his own was not the
point: it is in what we value, not in what we have,
that the test of us resides. Now, Rickie's intellect
was not remarkable. He came to his worthier results rather by imagination and instinct than by
logic. An argument confused him, and he could
with difficulty follow it even on paper. But he saw
in this no reason for satisfaction, and tried to make
such use of his brain as he could, just as a weak
athlete might lovingly exercise his body. Like a
weak athlete, too, he loved to watch the exploits, or
rather the efforts, of others—their efforts not so
much to acquire knowledge as to dispel a little of
the darkness by which we and all our acquisitions
are surrounded. Cambridge had taught him this,
and he knew, if for no other reason, that his time

there had not been vain. And Herbert's contempt for such efforts revolted him. He saw that for all his fine talk about a spiritual life he had but one test for things—success: success for the body in this life or for the soul in the life to come. And for this reason Humanity, and perhaps such other tribunals as there may be, would assuredly reject him.

XVIII

Meanwhile he was a husband. Perhaps his union should have been emphasized before. The crown of life had been attained, the vague yearnings, the misread impulses, had found accomplishment at last. Never again must he feel lonely, or as one who stands out of the broad highway of the world and fears, like poor Shelley, to undertake the longest journey. So he reasoned, and at first took the accomplishment for granted. But as the term passed he knew that behind the yearning there remained a yearning, behind the drawn veil a veil that he could not draw. His wedding had been no mighty landmark: he would often wonder whether such and such a speech or incident came after it or before. Since that meeting in the Soho restaurant there had been so much to do—clothes to buy, presents to thank for, a brief visit to a Training College, a honeymoon as brief. In such a bustle, what spiritual union could take place? Surely the dust would settle soon: in Italy, at Easter, he might perceive the infinities of love. But love had shown him its infinities already. Neither by marriage nor by any other device can men insure themselves a vision; and Rickie's had been granted him three years before, when he had seen his wife and a dead man clasped in each other's arms. She was never to be so real to him again.

She ran about the house looking handsomer than ever. Her cheerful voice gave orders to the servants. As he sat in the study correcting compositions, she would dart in and give him a kiss. 'Dear girl——' he would murmur, with a glance at the rings on her hand. The tone of their marriage life was soon set. It was to be a frank good-fellowship, and before long he found it difficult to speak in a deeper key.

One evening he made the effort. There had been more beauty than was usual at Sawston. The air was pure and quiet. To-morrow the fog might be here, but to-day one said, 'It is like the country.' Arm in arm they strolled in the side-garden, stopping at times to notice the crocuses, or to wonder when the daffodils would flower. Suddenly he tightened his pressure, and said, 'Darling, why don't you still wear ear-rings?'

'Ear-rings?' She laughed. 'My taste has improved, perhaps.'

So after all they never mentioned Gerald's name. But he hoped it was still dear to her. He did not want her to forget the greatest moment in her life. His love desired not ownership but confidence, and to a love so pure it does not seem terrible to come second.

He valued emotion—not for itself, but because it is the only final path to intimacy. She, ever robust and practical, always discouraged him. She was not cold; she would willingly embrace him. But she hated being upset, and would laugh or thrust him off when his voice grew serious. In this she reminded him of his mother. But his mother—he had never concealed it from himself—had glories to

which his wife would never attain; glories that had
unfolded against a life of horror—a life even more
horrible than he had guessed. He thought of her
often during these earlier months. Did she bless
his union, so different to her own? Did she love his
wife? He tried to speak of her to Agnes, but again
she was reluctant. And perhaps it was this aversion
to acknowledge the dead, whose images alone have
immortality, that made her own image somewhat
transient, so that when he left her no mystic influence remained, and only by an effort could he
realize that God had united them for ever.

They conversed and differed healthily upon
other topics. A rifle corps was to be formed: she
hoped that the boys would have proper uniforms,
instead of shooting in their old clothes, as Mr. Jackson had suggested. There was Tewson; could
nothing be done about him? He would slink away
from the other prefects and go with boys of his own
age. There was Lloyd: he would not learn the
school anthem, saying that it hurt his throat. And
above all there was Varden, who, to Rickie's bewilderment, was now a member of Dunwood House.

'He had to go somewhere,' said Agnes. 'Lucky
for his mother that we had a vacancy.'

'Yes—but when I meet Mrs. Orr—I can't help
feeling ashamed.'

'Oh, Mrs. Orr! Who cares for her? Her teeth are
drawn. If she chooses to insinuate that we planned
it, let her. Hers was rank dishonesty. She attempted
to set up a boarding-house.'

Mrs. Orr, who was quite rich, had attempted no
such thing. She had taken the boy out of charity,
and without a thought of being unconstitutional.
But in had come this officious 'Limpet' and upset
the headmaster, and she was scolded, and Mrs.

Varden was scolded, and Mr. Jackson was scolded,
and the boy was scolded and placed with Mr.
Pembroke, whom she revered less than any man
in the world. Naturally enough, she considered it a
further attempt of the authorities to snub the day-
boys, for whose advantage the school had been
founded. She and Mrs. Jackson discussed the subject at their tea-parties, and the latter lady was sure
that no good, no good of any kind, would come to
Dunwood House from such ill-gotten plunder.

'We say, "Let them talk,"' persisted Rickie, 'but
I never did like letting people talk. We are right
and they are wrong, but I wish the thing could
have been done more quietly. The headmaster does
get so excited. He has given a gang of foolish people
their opportunity. I don't like being branded as the
"day-boy's foe", when I think how much I would
have given to be a day-boy myself. My father
found me a nuisance, and put me through the mill,
and I can never forget it—particularly the evenings.'

'There's very little bullying here,' said Agnes.

'There was very little bullying at my school.
There was simply the atmosphere of unkindness,
which no discipline can dispel. It's not what people
do to you, but what they mean, that hurts.'

'I don't understand.'

'Physical pain doesn't hurt—at least not what I
call hurt—if a man hits you by accident or in play.
But just a little tap, when you know it comes from
hatred, is too terrible. Boys do hate each other: I
remember it, and see it again. They can make
strong isolated friendships, but of general good-
fellowship they haven't a notion.'

'All I know is there's very little bullying here.'

'You see, the notion of good-fellowship develops

late: you can just see its beginning here among the prefects: up at Cambridge it flourishes amazingly. That's why I pity people who don't go up to Cambridge: not because a University is smart, but because those are the magic years, and—with luck— you see up there what you couldn't see before and mayn't ever see again.'

'Aren't these the magic years?' the lady demanded.

He laughed and hit at her. 'I'm getting somewhat involved. But hear me, O Agnes, for I am practical. I approve of our public schools. Long may they flourish. But I do not approve of the boarding-house system. It isn't an inevitable adjunct——'

'Good gracious me!' she shrieked. 'Have you gone mad?'

'Silence, madam. Don't betray me to Herbert, or he'll give us the sack. But seriously, what is the good of throwing boys so much together? Isn't it building their lives on a wrong basis? They don't understand each other. I wish they did, but they don't. They don't realize that human beings are simply marvellous. When they do, the whole of life changes, and you get the true thing. But don't pretend you've got it before you have. Patriotism and *esprit de corps* are all very well, but masters a little forget that they must grow from a sentiment. They cannot create one. Cannot—cannot—cannot. I never cared a straw for England until I cared for Englishmen, and boys can't love the school when they hate each other. Ladies and gentlemen, I will now conclude my address. And most of it is copied out of Mr. Ansell.'

The truth is, he was suddenly ashamed. He had been carried away on a flood of his old emotions.

Cambridge and all that it meant had stood before him passionately clear, and beside it stood his mother and the sweet family life which nurses up a boy until he can salute his equals. He was ashamed, for he remembered his new resolution—to work without criticizing, to throw himself vigorously into the machine, not to mind if he was pinched now and then by the elaborate wheels.

'Mr. Ansell!' cried his wife, laughing somewhat shrilly. 'Aha! Now I understand. It's just the kind of thing poor Mr. Ansell would say. Well, I'm brutal. I believe it *does* Varden *good* to have his ears pulled now and then, and I don't care whether they pull them in play or not. Boys ought to rough it, or they never grow up into men, and your mother would have agreed with me. Oh yes; and you're all wrong about patriotism. It can, can, can create a sentiment.'

She was unusually precise, and had followed his thoughts with an attention that was also unusual. He wondered whether she was not right, and regretted that she proceeded to say, 'My dear boy, you mustn't talk these heresies inside Dunwood House! You sound just like one of that reactionary Jackson set, who want to fling the school back a hundred years and have nothing but day-boys all dressed anyhow.'

'The Jackson set have their points.'

'You'd better join it.'

'The Dunwood House set has its points.' For Rickie suffered from the Primal Curse, which is not —as the Authorized Version suggests—the knowledge of good and evil, but the knowledge of good-and-evil.

'Then stick to the Dunwood House set.'

'I do, and shall.' Again he was ashamed. Why

would he see the other side of things? He rebuked
his soul, not unsuccessfully, and then they returned
to the subject of Varden.

'I'm certain he suffers,' said he, for she would do
nothing but laugh. 'Each boy who passes pulls his
ears—very funny, no doubt; but every day they
stick out more and get redder, and this afternoon,
when he didn't know he was being watched, he
was holding his head and moaning. I hate the look
about his eyes.'

'I hate the whole boy. Nasty weedy thing.'

'Well, I'm a nasty weedy thing, if it comes to
that.'

'No, you aren't,' she cried, kissing him. But he
led her back to the subject. Could nothing be suggested? He drew up some new rules—alterations
in the times of going to bed, and so on—the effect
of which would be to provide few opportunities for
the pulling of Varden's ears. The rules were submitted to Herbert, who sympathized with weakli-
ness more than did his sister, and gave them his
careful consideration. But unfortunately they collided with other rules, and on a closer examination
he found that they also ran contrary to the funda-
mentals on which the government of Dunwood
House was based. So nothing was done. Agnes was
rather pleased, and took to teasing her husband
about Varden. At last he asked her to stop. He felt
uneasy about the boy—almost superstitious. His
first morning's work had brought sixty pounds a
year to their hotel.

XIX

They did not get to Italy at Easter. Herbert had the
offer of some private pupils, and needed Rickie's

help. It seemed unreasonable to leave England
when money was to be made in it, so they went to
Ilfracombe instead. They spent three weeks among
the natural advantages and unnatural disadvan-
tages of that resort. It was out of the season, and
they encamped in a huge hotel, which took them at
a reduction. By a disastrous chance the Jacksons
were down there too, and a good deal of constrained
civility had to pass between the two families. Constrained it was not in Mr. Jackson's case. At all
times he was ready to talk, and as long as they kept
off the school it was pleasant enough. But he was
very indiscreet and feminine tact had often to inter-
vene. 'Go away, dear ladies,' he would then observe.
'You think you see life because you see the chasms
in it. Yet all the chasms are full of female skeletons.'
The ladies smiled anxiously. To Rickie he was
friendly and even intimate. They had long talks on
the deserted Capstone, while their wives sat reading in the Winter Garden and Mr. Pembroke kept
an eye upon the tutored youths. 'Once I had
tutored youths,' said Mr. Jackson, 'but I lost them
all by letting them paddle with my nieces. It is
so impossible to remember what is proper.' And
sooner or later their talk gravitated towards his
central passion—the Fragments of Sophocles. Some
day ('never,' said Herbert) he would edit them. At
present they were merely in his blood. With the
zeal of a scholar and the imagination of a poet he
reconstructed lost dramas—Niobe, Phædra, Philoc-
tetes against Troy, whose names, but for an accident, would have thrilled the world. 'Is it worth it?'
he cried. 'Had we better be planting potatoes?'
And then: 'We had; but this is the second best.'

Agnes did not approve of these colloquies. Mr.
Jackson was not a buffoon, but he behaved like one,

which is what matters; and from the Winter Garden she could see people laughing at him, and at her husband, who got excited too. She hinted once or twice, but no notice was taken, and at last she said rather sharply. 'Now, you're not to, Rickie. I won't have it.'

'He's a type that suits me. He knows people I know, or would like to have known. He was a friend of Tony Failing's. It is so hard to realize that a man connected with one was great. Uncle Tony seems to have been. He loved poetry and music and pictures, and everything tempted him to live in a kind of cultured paradise, with the door shut upon squalor. But to have more decent people in the world—he sacrificed everything to that. He would have "smashed the whole beauty-shop" if it would help him. I really couldn't go as far as that. I don't think one need go as far—pictures might have to be smashed, but not music or poetry; surely they help—and Jackson doesn't think so either.'

'Well, I won't have it, and that's enough.' She laughed, for her voice had a little been that of the professional scold. 'You see we must hang together. He's in the reactionary camp.'

'He doesn't know it. He doesn't know that he is in any camp at all.'

'His wife is, which comes to the same.'

'Still, it's the holidays——' He and Mr. Jackson had drifted apart in the term, chiefly owing to the affair of Varden. 'We were to have the holidays to ourselves, you know.' And following some line of thought, he continued, 'He cheers one up. He does believe in poetry. Smart, sentimental books do seem absolutely absurd to him, and gods and fairies far nearer to reality. He tries to express all modern

life in the terms of Greek mythology, because the
Greeks looked very straight at things, and Demeter
or Aphrodite are thinner veils than "The survival
of the fittest", or "A marriage has been arranged",
and other draperies of modern journalese.'

'And do you know what that means?'

'It means that poetry, not prose, lies at the core.'

'No. I can tell you what it means—balderdash.'

His mouth fell. She was sweeping away the cobwebs with a vengeance. 'I hope you're wrong,' he
replied, 'for those are the lines on which I've been
writing, however badly, for the last two years.'

'But you write stories, not poems.'

He looked at his watch. 'Lessons again. One
never has a moment's peace.'

'Poor Rickie! You shall have a real holiday in the
summer.' And she called after him to say, 'Remember, dear, about Mr. Jackson. Don't go talking so
much to him.'

Rather arbitrary. Her tone had been a little
arbitrary of late. But what did it matter? Mr. Jackson was not a friend, and he must risk the chance of
offending Widdrington. After the lesson he wrote to
Ansell, whom he had not seen since June, asking
him to come down to Ilfracombe, if only for a day.
On reading the letter over, its tone displeased him.
It was quite pathetic: it sounded like a cry from
prison. 'I can't send him such nonsense,' he thought,
and wrote again. But phrase it as he would, the
letter always suggested that he was unhappy.
'What's wrong?' he wondered. 'I could write anything I wanted to him once.' So he scrawled 'Come!'
on a post-card. But even this seemed too serious.
The post-card followed the letters, and Agnes
found them all in the waste-paper basket.

Then she said, 'I've been thinking—oughtn't you

to ask Mr. Ansell over? A breath of sea air would
do the poor thing good.'

There was no difficulty now. He wrote at once,
'My dear Stewart,—We both so much wish you
could come over.' But the invitation was refused.
A little uneasy, he wrote again, using the dialect of
their past intimacy. The effect of this letter was
not pathetic but jaunty, and he felt a keen regret
as soon as it slipped into the box. It was a relief to
receive no reply.

He brooded a good deal over this painful yet
intangible episode. Was the pain all of his own
creating? or had it been produced by something external? And he got the answer that brooding always
gives—it was both. He was morbid, and had been
so since his visit to Cadover—quicker to register
discomfort than joy. But, none the less, Ansell was
definitely brutal, and Agnes definitely jealous.
Brutality he could understand, alien as it was to
himself. Jealousy, equally alien, was a harder
matter. Let husband and wife be as sun and moon,
or as moon and sun. Shall they therefore not give
greeting to the stars? He was willing to grant that
the love that inspired her might be higher than his
own. Yet did it not exclude them both from much
that is gracious? That dream of his when he rode
on the Wiltshire expanses—a curious dream: the
lark silent, the earth dissolving. And he awoke from
it into a valley full of men.

She was jealous in many ways—sometimes in an
open humorous fashion, sometimes more subtly,
never content till 'we' had extended our patronage
and, if possible, our pity. She began to patronize
and pity Ansell, and most sincerely trusted that he
would get his fellowship. Otherwise what was the
poor fellow to do? Ridiculous as it may seem, she

was even jealous of Nature. One day her husband escaped from Ilfracombe to Morthoe, and came back ecstatic over its fangs of slate, piercing an oily sea. 'Sounds like an hippopotamus,' she said peevishly. And when they returned to Sawston through the Virgilian counties, she disliked him looking out of the window, for all the world as if Nature was some dangerous woman.

He resumed his duties with a feeling that he had never left them. Again he confronted the assembled house. This term was again *the* term; school still the world in miniature. The music of the four-part fugue entered into him more deeply, and he began to hum its little phrases. The same routine, the same diplomacies, the same old sense of only half knowing boys or men—he returned to it all; and all that changed was the cloud of unreality, which ever brooded a little more densely than before. He spoke to his wife about this,—he spoke to her about everything,—and she was alarmed, and wanted him to see a doctor. But he explained that it was nothing of any practical importance, nothing that interfered with his work or his appetite, nothing more than a feeling that the cow was not really there. She laughed, and 'How is the cow to-day?' soon passed into a domestic joke.

XX

Ansell was in his favourite haunt—the reading-room of the British Museum. In that book-encircled space he always could find peace. He loved to see the volumes rising tier above tier into the misty dome. He loved the chairs that glide so noiselessly, and the radiating desks, and the central area, where the catalogue shelves curve round the superintendent's throne. There he knew that his life was not ignoble. It was worth while to grow old and dusty seeking for truth though truth is unattainable, re-stating questions that have been stated at the be-ginning of the world. Failure would await him, but not disillusionment. It was worth while reading books, and writing a book or two which few would read, and no one, perhaps, endorse. He was not a hero, and he knew it. His father and sisters, by their steady goodness, had made this life possible. But, all the same, it was not the life of a spoilt child.

In the next chair to him sat Widdrington, en-gaged in his historical research. His desk was edged with enormous volumes, and every few moments an assistant brought him more. They rose like a wall against Ansell. Towards the end of the morning a gap was made, and through it they held the following conversation.

'I've been stopping with my cousin at Sawston.'

'M'm.'

'It was quite exciting. The air rang with battle. About two-thirds of the masters have lost their heads, and are trying to produce a gimcrack copy of Eton. Last term, you know, with a great deal of puffing and blowing, they fixed the numbers of the school. This term they want to create a new boarding-house.'

'They are very welcome.'

'But the more boarding-houses they create, the less room they leave for day-boys. The local mothers are frantic, and so is my queer cousin. I never knew him so excited over sub-Hellenic things. There was an indignation meeting at his house. He is supposed to look after the day-boys' interests, but no one thought he would—least of all the people who gave him the post. The speeches were most eloquent. They argued that the school was founded for day-boys, and that it's intolerable to handicap them. One poor lady cried, "Here's my Harold in the school, and my Toddie coming on. As likely as not I shall be told there is no vacancy for him. Then what am I to do? If I go, what's to become of Harold; and if I stop, what's to become of Toddie?" I must say I was touched. Family life is more real than national life—at least I've ordered all these books to prove it is—and I fancy that the bust of Euripides agreed with me, and was sorry for the hot-faced mothers. Jackson will do what he can. He didn't quite like to state the naked truth—which is, that boarding-houses pay. He explained it to me afterwards: they are the only future open to a stupid master. It's easy enough to be a beak when you're young and athletic, and can offer the latest University smattering. The difficulty is to keep your place when you get old and stiff, and younger smatterers are pushing up behind you. Crawl into a boarding-house and you're safe. A master's life is frightfully tragic. Jackson's fairly right himself, because he has got a first-class intellect. But I met a poor brute who was hired as an athlete. He has missed his shot at a boarding-house, and there's nothing in the world for him to do but to trundle down the hill.'

Ansell yawned.

'I saw Rickie too. Once I dined there.'

Another yawn.

'My cousin thinks Mrs. Elliot one of the most horrible women he has ever seen. He calls her "Medusa in Arcady". She's so pleasant, too. But certainly it was a very stony meal.'

'What kind of stoniness?'

'No one stopped talking for a moment.'

'That's the real kind,' said Ansell moodily. 'The only kind.'

'Well, I,' he continued, 'am inclined to compare her to an electric light. Click! she's on. Click! she's off. No waste. No flicker.'

'I wish she'd fuse.'

'She'll never fuse—unless anything was to happen at the main.'

'What do you mean by the main?' said Ansell, who always pursued a metaphor relentlessly.

Widdrington did not know what he meant, and suggested that Ansell should visit Sawston to see whether one could know.

'It is no good me going. I should not find Mrs. Elliot: she has no real existence.'

'Rickie has.'

'I very much doubt it. I had two letters from Ilfracombe last April, and I very much doubt that the man who wrote them can exist.' Bending downwards, he began to adorn the manuscript of his dissertation with a square, and inside that a circle, and inside that another square. It was his second dissertation: the first had failed.

'I think he exists: he is so unhappy.'

Ansell nodded. 'How did you know he was unhappy?'

'Because he was always talking.' After a pause he added. 'What clever young men we are!'

'Aren't we? I expect we shall get asked in marriage soon. I say, Widdrington, shall we——?'

'Accept? Of course. It is not young-manly to say no.'

'I meant shall we ever do a more tremendous thing,—fuse Mrs. Elliot.'

'No,' said Widdrington promptly. 'We shall never

do that all our lives.' He added, 'I think you might
go down to Sawston, though.'

'I have already refused or ignored three invita-
tions.'

'So I gathered.'

'What's the good of it?' said Ansell, through his
teeth. 'I will not put up with little things. I would
rather be rude than listen to twaddle from a man
I've known.'

'You might go down to Sawston, just for a night,
to see him.'

'I saw him last month—at least, so Tilliard in-
forms me. He says that we all three lunched together, that Rickie paid, and that the conversation
was most interesting.'

'Well, I contend that he does exist, and that if
you go—oh, I can't be clever any longer. You really
must go, man. I'm certain he's miserable and lonely.
Dunwood House reeks of commerce and snobbery
and all the things he hated most. He doesn't do any
writing. He doesn't make any friends. He is so odd,
too. In this day-boy row that has just started he's
gone for my cousin. Would you believe it? Quite
spitefully. It made quite a difficulty when I wanted
to dine. It isn't like him—either the sentiments or
the behaviour. I'm sure he's not himself. Pembroke
used to look after the day-boys, and so he can't very
well take the lead against them, and perhaps
Rickie's doing his dirty work—and has overdone it,
as decent people generally do. He's even altering
to talk to. Yet he's not been married a year. Pembroke and that wife simply run him. I don't see
why they should, and no more do you; and that's
why I want you to go to Sawston, if only for one
night.'

Ansell shook his head, and looked up at the

dome as other men look at the sky. In it the great
arc lamps spluttered and flared, for the month was
again November. Then he lowered his eyes from
the cold violet radiance to the books.

'No, Widdrington; no. We don't go to see people
because they are happy or unhappy. We go when
we can talk to them. I cannot talk to Rickie, therefore I will not waste my time at Sawston.'

'I think you're right,' said Widdrington softly.
'But we are bloodless brutes. I wonder whether—if
we were different people—something might be
done to save him. That is the curse of being a little
intellectual. You and our sort have always seen too
clearly. We stand aside—and meanwhile he turns
into stone. Two philosophic youths repining in the
British Museum! What have we done? What shall
we ever do? Just drift and criticize, while people
who know what they want snatch it away from us
and laugh.'

'Perhaps you are that sort. I'm not. When the
moment comes I shall hit out like any ploughboy.
Don't believe those lies about intellectual people.
They're only written to soothe the majority. Do
you suppose, with the world as it is, that it's an
easy matter to keep quiet? Do you suppose that I
didn't want to rescue him from that ghastly woman?
Action! Nothing's easier than action; as fools tes-
tify. But I want to act rightly.'

'The superintendent is looking at us. I must get
back to my work.'

'You think this all nonsense,' said Ansell, detain-
ing him. 'Please remember that if I do act, you are
bound to help me.'

Widdrington looked a little grave. He was no
anarchist. A few plaintive cries against Mrs. Elliot
were all that he was prepared to emit.

'There's no mystery,' continued Ansell. 'I haven't the shadow of a plan in my head. I know not only Rickie but the whole of his history: you remember the day near Madingley. Nothing in either helps me: I'm just watching.'

'But what for?'

'For the Spirit of Life.'

Widdrington was surprised. It was a phrase unknown to their philosophy. They had trespassed into poetry.

'You can't fight Medusa with anything else. If you ask me what the Spirit of Life is, or to what it is attached, I can't tell you. I only tell you, watch for it. Myself I've found it in books. Some people find it out of doors or in each other. Never mind. It's the same spirit, and I trust myself to know it anywhere, and to use it rightly.'

But at this point the superintendent sent a message.

Widdrington then suggested a stroll in the galleries. It was foggy: they needed fresh air. He loved and admired his friend, but to-day he could not grasp him. The world as Ansell saw it seemed such a fantastic place, governed by brand-new laws. What more could one do than to see Rickie as often as possible, to invite his confidence, to offer him spiritual support? And Mrs. Elliot—what power could 'fuse' a respectable woman?

Ansell consented to the stroll, but, as usual, only breathed depression. The comfort of books deserted him among those marble goddesses and gods. The eye of an artist finds pleasure in texture and poise, but he could only think of the vanished incense and deserted temples beside an unfurrowed sea.

'Let us go,' he said. 'I do not like carved stones.'

'You are too particular,' said Widdrington. 'You

are always expecting to meet living people. One
never does. I am content with the Parthenon frieze.'
And he moved along a few yards of it, while Ansell
followed, conscious only of its pathos.

'There's Tilliard,' he observed. 'Shall we kill
him?'

'Please,' said Widdrington, and as he spoke Tilliard joined them. He brought them news. That
morning he had heard from Rickie: Mrs. Elliot was
expecting a child.

'A child?' said Ansell, suddenly bewildered.

'Oh, I forgot,' interposed Widdrington. 'My
cousin did tell me.'

'You forgot! Well, after all, I forgot that it might
be. We are indeed young men.' He leant against
the pedestal of Ilissus and remembered their talk
about the Spirit of Life. In his ignorance of what
a child means, he wondered whether the opportunity he sought lay here.

'I am very glad,' said Tilliard, not without intention. 'A child will draw them even closer together.
I like to see young people wrapped up in their
child.'

'I suppose I must be getting back to my dissertation,' said Ansell. He left the Parthenon to pass
by the monuments of our more reticent beliefs—the
temple of the Ephesian Artemis, the statue of the
Cnidian Demeter. Honest, he knew that here were
powers he could not cope with, nor, as yet, understand.

XXI

The mists that had gathered round Rickie seemed
to be breaking. He had found light neither in work
for which he was unfitted nor in a woman who had

ceased to respect him, and whom he was ceasing
to love. Though he called himself fickle and took all
the blame of their marriage on his own shoulders,
there remained in Agnes certain terrible faults of
heart and head, and no self-reproach would diminish them. The glamour of wedlock had faded; indeed, he saw now that it had faded even before
wedlock, and that during the final months he had
shut his eyes and pretended it was still there. But
now the mists were breaking.

That November the supreme event approached.
He saw it with Nature's eyes. It dawned on him, as
on Ansell, that personal love and marriage only
cover one side of the shield, and that on the other
is graven the epic of birth. In the midst of lessons
he would grow dreamy, as one who spies a new
symbol for the universe, a fresh circle within the
square. Within the square shall be a circle, within
the circle another square, until the visual eye is
baffled. Here is meaning of a kind. His mother had
forgotten herself in him. He would forget himself
in his son.

He was at his duties when the news arrived—
taking preparation. Boys are marvellous creatures.
Perhaps they will sink below the brutes; perhaps
they will attain to a woman's tenderness. Though
they despised Rickie, and had suffered under
Agnes's meanness, their one thought this term was
to be gentle and to give no trouble.

'Rickie—one moment——'

His face grew ashen. He followed Herbert into
the passage, closing the door of the preparation-
room behind him. 'Oh, is she safe?' he whispered.

'Yes, yes,' said Herbert; but there sounded in his
answer a sombre hostile note.

'Our boy?'

'Girl—a girl, dear Rickie; a little daughter. She —she is in many ways a healthy child. She will live —oh yes.' A flash of horror passed over his face. He hurried into the preparation-room, lifted the lid of his desk, glanced mechanically at the boys, and came out again.

Mrs. Lewin appeared through the door that led into their own part of the house.

'Both going on well!' she cried; but her voice also was grave, exasperated.

'What is it?' he gasped. 'It's something you daren't tell me.'

'Only this——' stuttered Herbert. 'You mustn't mind when you see—she's lame.'

Mrs. Lewin disappeared.

'Lame! but not as lame as I am?'

'Oh, my dear boy, worse. Don't—oh, be a man in this. Come away from the preparation-room. Remember she'll live—in many ways healthy— only just this one defect.'

The horror of that week never passed away from him. To the end of his life he remembered the excuses—the consolations that the child would live; suffered very little, if at all; would walk with crutches; would certainly live. God was more merciful. A window was opened too wide on a draughty day. After a short, painless illness his daughter died. But the lesson he had learnt so glibly at Cambridge should be heeded now; no child should ever be born to him again.

XXII

That same term there took place at Dunwood House another event. With their private tragedy it seemed to have no connexion; but in time Rickie

perceived it as a bitter comment. Its developments
were unforeseen and lasting. It was perhaps the
most terrible thing he had to bear.

Varden had now been a boarder for ten months.
His health had broken in the previous term,—
partly, it is to be feared, as the result of the indifferent food,—and during the summer holidays he
was attacked by a series of agonizing earaches. His
mother, a feeble person, wished to keep him at
home, but Herbert dissuaded her. Soon after the
death of the child there arose at Dunwood House
one of those waves of hostility of which no boy
knows the origin nor any master can calculate the
course. Varden had never been popular—there was
no reason why he should be—but he had never
been seriously bullied hitherto. One evening
nearly the whole house set on him. The prefects
absented themselves, the bigger boys stood round,
and the lesser boys, to whom power was delegated,
flung him down, and rubbed his face under the
desks, and wrenched at his ears. The noise penetrated the baize doors, and Herbert swept through
and punished the whole house, including Varden,
whom it would not do to leave out. The poor man
was horrified. He approved of a little healthy rough-
ness, but this was pure brutality. What had come
over his boys? Were they not gentlemen's sons? He
would not admit that if you herd together human
beings before they can understand each other the
great god Pan is angry, and will in the end evade
your regulations and drive them mad. That night
the victim was screaming with pain, and the doctor
next day spoke of an operation. The suspense lasted
a whole week. Comment was made in the local
papers, and the reputation not only of the house
but of the school was imperilled. 'If only I had

known,' repeated Herbert—'if only I had known I would have arranged it all differently. He should have had a cubicle.' The boy did not die, but he left Sawston, never to return.

The day before his departure Rickie sat with him some time, and tried to talk in a way that was not pedantic. In his own sorrow, which he could share with no one, least of all with his wife, he was still alive to the sorrows of others. He still fought against apathy, though he was losing the battle.

'Don't lose heart,' he told him. 'The world isn't all going to be like this. There are temptations and trials, of course, but nothing at all of the kind you have had here.'

'But school is the world in miniature, is it not, sir?' asked the boy, hoping to please one master by echoing what had been told him by another. He was always on the look-out for sympathy: it was one of the things that had contributed to his downfall.

'I never noticed that myself. I was unhappy at school, and in the world people can be very happy.'

Varden sighed and rolled about his eyes. 'Are the fellows sorry for what they did to me?' he asked in an affected voice,. 'I am sure I forgive them from the bottom of my heart. We ought to forgive our enemies, oughtn't we, sir?'

'But they aren't your enemies. If you meet in five years' time you may find each other splendid fellows.'

The boy would not admit this. He had been reading some revivalistic literature. 'We ought to forgive our enemies,' he repeated; 'and however wicked they are, we ought not to wish them evil. When I was ill, and death seemed nearest, I had many kind letters on this subject.'

Rickie knew about these 'many kind letters'.

Varden had induced the silly nurse to write to
people—people of all sorts, people that he scarcely
knew or did not know at all—detailing his misfor-
tune, and asking for spiritual aid and sympathy.

'I am sorry for them,' he pursued. 'I would not
like to be like them.'

Rickie sighed. He saw that a year at Dunwood
House had produced a sanctimonious prig. 'Don't
think about them, Varden. Think about anything
beautiful—say, music. You like music. Be happy.
It's your duty. You can't be good until you've had
a little happiness. Then perhaps you will think less
about forgiving people and more about loving
them.'

'I love them already, sir.' And Rickie, in despera-
tion, asked if he might look at the many kind letters.

Permission was gladly given. A neat bundle was
produced, and for about twenty minutes the master
perused it, while the invalid kept watch on his
face. Rooks cawed out in the playing-fields, and
close under the window there was the sound of
delightful, good-tempered laughter. A boy is no
devil, whatever boys may be. The letters were
chilly productions, somewhat clerical in tone, by
whomsoever written. Varden, because he was ill at
the time, had been taken seriously. The writers
declared that his illness was fulfilling some mysterious purpose: suffering engendered spiritual
growth: he was showing signs of this already. They
consented to pray for him, some majestically, others
shyly. But they all consented with one exception,
who worded his refusal as follows:

Dear A. C. Varden,

I ought to say that I never remember seeing you.
I am sorry that you are ill, and hope you are wrong

about it. Why did you not write before, for I could have helped you then. When they pulled your ear, you ought to have gone like this (here was a rough sketch). I could not undertake praying, but would think of you instead, if that would do. I am twenty-two in April, built rather heavy, ordinary broad face, with eyes, &c. I write all this because you have mixed me with some one else, for I am not married, and do not want to be. I cannot think of you always, but will promise a quarter of an hour daily (say 7.0–7.15 a.m.), and might come to see you when you are better—that is, if you are a kid, and you read like one. I have been otter-hunting.

Yours sincerely,

STEPHEN WONHAM.

XXIII

Rickie went straight from Varden to his wife, who lay on the sofa in her bedroom. There was now a wide gulf between them. She, like the world she had created for him, was unreal.

'Agnes, darling,' he began, stroking her hand, 'such an awkward little thing has happened.'

'What is it, dear? Just wait, till I've added up this book.'

She had got over the tragedy: she got over everything.

When she was at leisure he told her. Hitherto, they had seldom mentioned Stephen. He was classed among the unprofitable dead.

She was more sympathetic than he expected. 'Dear Rickie,' she murmured with averted eyes. 'How tiresome for you.'

'I wish that Varden had stopped with Mrs. Orr.'

'Well, he leaves us for good to-morrow.'

'Yes, yes. And I made him answer the letter and apologize. They had never met. It was some confusion with a man in the Church Army, living at a place called Codford. I asked the nurse. It is all explained.'

'There the matter ends.'

'I suppose so—if matters ever end.'

'If, by ill-luck, the person does call, I will just see him and say that the boy has gone.'

'You, or I. I have got over all nonsense by this time. He's absolutely nothing to me now.' He took up the tradesman's book and played with it idly. On its crimson cover was stamped a grotesque sheep. How stale and stupid their life had become!

'Don't talk like that, though,' she said uneasily. 'Think how disastrous it would be if you made a slip in speaking to him.'

'Would it? It would have been disastrous once. But I expect, as a matter of fact, that Aunt Emily has made the slip already.'

His wife was displeased. 'You need not talk in that cynical way. I credit Aunt Emily with better feeling. When I was there she did mention the matter, but only once. She, and I, and all who have any sense of decency, know better than to make slips, or to think of making them.'

Agnes kept up what she called 'the family connection'. She had been once alone to Cadover, and also corresponded with Mrs. Failing. She had never told Rickie anything about her visit, nor had he ever asked her. But, from this moment, the whole subject was reopened.

'Most certainly he knows nothing,' she continued. 'Why, he does not even realize that Varden lives in our house! We are perfectly safe—unless

Aunt Emily were to die. Perhaps then—but we are perfectly safe for the present.'

'When she did mention the matter, what did she say?'

'We had a long talk,' said Agnes quietly. 'She told me nothing new—nothing new about the past, I mean. But we had a long talk about the present. I think'—and her voice grew displeased again—'that you have been both wrong and foolish in refusing to make up your quarrel with Aunt Emily.'

'Wrong and wise, I should say.'

'It isn't to be expected that she—so much older and so sensitive—can make the first step. But I know she'd be glad to see you."

'As far as I can remember that final scene in the garden, I accused her of "forgetting what other people were like". She'll never pardon me for saying that.'

Agnes was silent. To her the phrase was meaningless. Yet Rickie was correct: Mrs. Failing had resented it more than anything.

'At all events,' she suggested, 'you might go and see her.'

'No, dear. Thank you, no.'

'She is, after all——' She was going to say 'your father's sister', but the expression was scarcely a happy one, and she turned it into, 'She is, after all, growing old and lonely.'

'So are we all!' he cried, with a lapse of tone that was now characteristic in him.

'She oughtn't to be so isolated from her proper relatives.'

There was a moment's silence. Still playing with the book, he remarked, 'You forget, she's got her favourite nephew.'

A bright red flush spread over her cheeks. 'What

is the matter with you this afternoon?' she asked.
'I should think you'd better go for a walk.'

'Before I go, tell me what is the matter with you.'
He also flushed. 'Why do you want me to make it
up with my aunt?'

'Because it's right and proper.'

'So? Or because she is old?'

'I don't understand,' she retorted. But her eyes
dropped. His sudden suspicion was true: she was
legacy-hunting.

'Agnes, dear Agnes,' he began with passing tenderness, 'how can you think of such things? You
behave like a poor person. We don't want any
money from Aunt Emily, or from any one else. It
isn't virtue that makes me say it; we are not tempted
in that way: we have as much as we want already.'

'For the present,' she answered, still looking
aside.

'There isn't any future,' he cried in a gust of
despair.

'Rickie, what do you mean?'

What did he mean? He meant that the relations
between them were fixed—that there would never
be an influx of interest, nor even of passion. To the
end of life they would go on beating time, and this
was enough for her. She was content with the daily
round, the common task, performed indifferently.
But he had dreamt of another helpmate, and of
other things.

'We don't want money—why, we don't even
spend any on travelling. I've invested all my salary
and more. As far as human foresight goes, we shall
never want money.' And his thoughts went out to
the tiny grave. 'You spoke of "right and proper", but
the right and proper thing for my aunt to do is to
leave every penny she's got to Stephen.'

Her lip quivered, and for one moment he thought that she was going to cry. 'What am I to do with you?' she said. 'You talk like a person in poetry.'

'I'll put it in prose. He's lived with her for twenty years, and he ought to be paid for it.'

Poor Agnes! Indeed, what was she to do? The first moment she set foot in Cadover she had thought, 'Oh, here is money. We must try and get it.' Being a lady, she never mentioned the thought to her husband, but she concluded that it would occur to him too. And now, though it had occurred to him at last, he would not even write his aunt a little note.

He was to try her yet further. While they argued this point he flashed out with, 'I ought to have told him that day when he called up to our room. There's where I went wrong first.'

'Rickie!'

'In those days I was sentimental. I minded. For two pins I'd write to him this afternoon. Why shouldn't he know he's my brother? What's all this ridiculous mystery?'

She became incoherent.

'But *why* not? A reason why he shouldn't know.'

'A reason why he *should* know,' she retorted. 'I never heard such rubbish! Give me a reason why he should know.'

'Because the lie we acted has ruined our lives.'

She looked in bewilderment at the well-appointed room.

'It's been like poison we won't acknowledge. How many times have you thought of my brother? I've thought of him every day—not in love; don't misunderstand; only as a medicine I shirked. Down in what they call the subconscious self he has been hurting me.' His voice broke. 'Oh, my darling, we acted a lie then, and this letter reminds us of it and gives us one more chance. I have to say "we" lied. I should be lying again if I took quite all the blame. Let us ask God's forgiveness together. Then let us write, as coldly as you please, to Stephen, and tell him he is my father's son.'

Her reply need not be quoted. It was the last time he attempted intimacy. And the remainder of their conversation, though long and stormy, is also best forgotten.

Thus the first effect of Varden's letter was to make them quarrel. They had not openly disagreed before. In the evening he kissed her and said, 'How absurd I was to get angry about things that happened last year. I will certainly not write to the person.' She returned the kiss. But he knew that they had destroyed the habit of reverence, and would quarrel again.

On his rounds he looked in at Varden and asked nonchalantly for the letter. He carried it off to his room. It was unwise of him, for his nerves were already unstrung, and the man he had tried to bury was stirring ominously. In the silence he examined the handwriting till he felt that a living creature was with him, whereas he, because his child had died, was dead. He perceived more clearly the cruelty of Nature, to whom our refinement and piety are but as bubbles, hurrying downwards on the turbid waters. They break, and the stream continues. His father, as a final insult, had brought into the world a man unlike all the rest of them,—a man dowered with coarse kindliness, and rustic strength, a kind of cynical ploughboy, against whom their own misery and weakness might stand more vividly relieved. 'Born an Elliot—born a gentleman.' So the vile phrase ran. But here was an Elliot whose badness was not even gentlemanly. For that Stephen was bad inherently he never doubted for a moment. And he would have children: he, not Rickie, would contribute to the stream; he, through his remote posterity, might be mingled with the unknown sea.

Thus musing he lay down to sleep, feeling diseased in body and soul. It was no wonder that the night was the most terrible he had ever known. He revisited Cambridge, and his name was a grey ghost over the door. Then there recurred the voice of a gentle shadowy woman, Mrs. Aberdeen, 'It doesn't seem hardly right.' Those had been her words, her only complaint against the mysteries of change and death. She bowed her head and laboured to make her 'gentlemen' comfortable. She was labouring still. As he lay in bed he asked God to grant him her wisdom; that he might keep sorrow within due bounds; that he might abstain from extreme hatred and envy of Stephen. It was seldom that he prayed so definitely, or ventured to obtrude his private wishes. Religion was to him a service, a mystic communion with good; not a means of getting what he wanted on the earth. But to-night, through suffering, he was humbled, and became like Mrs. Aberdeen.

Hour after hour he awaited sleep and tried to endure the faces that frothed in the gloom—his aunt's, his father's, and, worst of all, the triumphant face of his brother. Once he struck at it, and awoke, having hurt his hand on the wall. Then he prayed hysterically for pardon and rest.

Yet again did he awake, and from a more mysterious dream. He heard his mother crying. She was crying quite distinctly in the darkened room. He whispered, 'Never mind, my darling, never mind,' and a voice echoed, 'Never mind—come

away—let them die out—let them die out.' He lit
a candle, and the room was empty. Then, hurrying
to the window, he saw above mean houses the
frosty glories of Orion.

Henceforward he deteriorates. Let those who
censure him suggest what he should do. He has
lost the work that he loved, his friends, and his
child. He remained conscientious and decent, but
the spiritual part of him proceeded towards ruin.

XXIV

The coming months, though full of degradation and
anxiety, were to bring him nothing so terrible as
that night. It was the crisis of his agony. He was an
outcast and a failure. But he was not again forced
to contemplate these facts so clearly. Varden left
in the morning, carrying a fatal letter with him. The
whole house was relieved. The good angel was with
the boys again, or else (as Herbert preferred to
think) they had learnt a lesson, and were more
humane in consequence. At all events, the disastrous term concluded quietly.

In the Christmas holidays the two masters made
an abortive attempt to visit Italy, and at Easter
there was talk of a cruise in the Ægean. Herbert
actually went, and enjoyed Athens and Delphi. The
Elliots paid a few visits together in England. They
returned to Sawston about ten days before school
opened, to find that Widdrington was again stopping with the Jacksons. Intercourse was painful, for
the two families were scarcely on speaking terms;
nor did the triumphant scaffoldings of the new
boarding-house make things easier. (The party of
progress had carried the day.) Widdrington was by

nature touchy, but on this occasion he refused to take offence, and often dropped in to see them. His manner was friendly but critical. They agreed he was a nuisance. Then Agnes left, very abruptly, to see Mrs. Failing, and while she was away Rickie had a little stealthy intercourse.

Her absence, convenient as it was, puzzled him. Mrs. Silt, half goose, half stormy-petrel, had recently paid a flying visit to Cadover, and thence had flown, without an invitation, to Sawston. Generally, she was not a welcome guest. On this occasion Agnes had welcomed her, and—so Rickie thought—had made her promise not to tell him something that she knew. The ladies had talked mysteriously. 'Mr. Silt would be one with you there,' said Mrs. Silt. Could there be any connection between the two visits?

Agnes's letters told him nothing: they never did. She was too clumsy or too cautious to express herself on paper. A drive to Stonehenge; an anthem in the Cathedral; Aunt Emily's love. And when he met her at Waterloo he learnt nothing (if there was anything to learn) from her face.

'How did you enjoy yourself?'

'Thoroughly.'

'Were you and she alone?'

'Sometimes. Sometimes other people.'

'Will Uncle Tony's Essays be published?'

Here she was more communicative. The book was at last in proof. Aunt Emily had written a charming introduction; but she was so idle, she never finished things off.

They got into an omnibus for the Army and Navy Stores; she wanted to do some shopping before going down to Sawston.

'Did you read any of the Essays?'

'Every one. Delightful. Couldn't put them down. Now and then he spoilt them by statistics—but you should read his descriptions of Nature. He agrees with you: says the hills and trees are alive! Aunt Emily called you his spiritual heir, which I thought nice of her. We both so lamented that you have stopped writing.' She quoted fragments of the Essays as they went up in the Stores' lift.

'What else did you talk about?'

'I've told you all my news. Now for yours. Let's have tea first.'

They sat down in the corridor amid ladies in every stage of fatigue—haggard ladies, scarlet ladies, ladies with parcels that twisted from every finger like joints of meat. Gentlemen were scarcer, but all were of the sub-fashionable type, to which Rickie himself now belonged.

'I haven't done anything,' he said feebly. 'Ate, read, been rude to tradespeople, talked to Widdrington. Herbert arrived this morning. He has brought a most beautiful photograph of the Parthenon.'

'Mr. Widdrington?'

'Yes.'

'What did you talk about?'

She might have heard every word. It was only the feeling of pleasure that he wished to conceal. Even when we love people, we desire to keep some corner secret from them, however small: it is a human right: it is personality. She began to cross-question him, but they were interrupted. A young lady at an adjacent table suddenly rose and cried, 'Yes, it is you. I thought so from your walk.' It was Maud Ansell.

'Oh, do come and join us!' he cried. 'Let me introduce my wife.'

Maud bowed quite stiffly, but Agnes, taking it for ill-breeding, was not offended.

'That I will come!' she continued in shrill, pleasant tones, adroitly poising her tea things on either hand, and transferring them to the Elliots' table. 'Why haven't you ever come to us, pray?'

'I think you didn't ask me!'

'You weren't to be asked.' She sprawled forward with a wagging finger. But her eyes had the honesty of her brother's. 'Don't you remember the day you left us? Father said, "Now, Mr. Elliot——" Or did he call you "Elliot"? How one does forget. Anyhow, father said you weren't to wait for an invitation, and you said, "No; I won't." Ours is a fair-sized house,' —she turned somewhat haughtily to Agnes,—'and the second spare room, which we call the "harp room" on account of a harp that hangs on the wall, is always reserved for Stewart's friends.'

'How is Mr. Ansell, your brother?'

Maud's face fell. 'Hadn't you heard?' she said in awestruck tones.

'No.'

'He hasn't got his fellowship. It's the second time he's failed. That means he will never get one. He will never be a don, nor live in Cambridge and that, as we had hoped.'

'Oh, poor, poor fellow!' said Mrs. Elliot with a remorse that was sincere, though her congratulations would not have been. 'I am so very sorry.'

But Maud turned to Rickie. 'Mr. Elliot, you might know. Tell me. What is wrong with Stewart's philosophy? What ought he to put in, or to alter, so as to succeed?'

Agnes, who knew better than this, smiled.

'I don't know,' said Rickie sadly. 'They were none of them so clever, after all.'

'Hegel,' she continued vindictively. 'They say he's read too much Hegel. But they never tell him what to read instead. Their own stuffy books, I suppose. Look here—no, that's the "Windsor".' After a little groping she produced a copy of 'Mind', and handed it round as if it was a geological specimen. 'Inside that there's a paragraph written about something Stewart's written about before, and there it says he's read too much Hegel, and it seems now that that's been the trouble all along.' Her voice trembled. 'I call it most unfair, and the fellowship's gone to a man who has counted the petals on an anemone.'

Rickie had no inclination to smile.

'I wish Stewart had tried Oxford instead.'

'I don't wish it!'

'You say that,' she continued hotly, 'and then you never come to see him, though you knew you were not to wait for an invitation.'

'If it comes to that, Miss Ansell,' retorted Rickie, in the laughing tones that one adopts on such occasions, 'Stewart won't come to me, though he *has* had an invitation.'

'Yes,' chimed in Agnes, 'we ask Mr. Ansell again and again, and he will have none of us.'

Maud looked at her with a flashing eye. 'My brother is a very peculiar person, and we ladies can't understand him. But I know one thing, and that's that he has a reason all round for what he does. Look here, I must be getting on. Waiter! Wai-ai-aiter! Bill, please. Separately, of course. Call the Army and Navy cheap! I know better!'

'How does the drapery department compare?' said Agnes sweetly.

The girl gave a sharp choking sound, gathered

up her parcels, and left them. Rickie was too much disgusted with his wife to speak.

'Appalling person!' she gasped. 'It was naughty of me, but I couldn't help it. What a dreadful fate for a clever man! To fail in life completely, and then to be thrown back on a family like that!'

'Maud is a snob and a Philistine. But, in her case, something emerges.'

She glanced at him, but proceeded in her suavest tones, 'Do let us make one great united attempt to get Mr. Ansell to Sawston.'

'No.'

'What a changeable friend you are! When we were engaged you were always talking about him.'

'Would you finish your tea, and then we will buy the linoleum for the cubicles.'

But she returned to the subject again, not only on that day but throughout the term. Could nothing be done for poor Mr. Ansell? It seemed that she could not rest until all that he had once held dear was humiliated. In this she strayed outside her nature; she was unpractical. And those who stray outside their nature invite disaster. Rickie, goaded by her, wrote to his friend again. The letter was in all ways unlike his old self. Ansell did not answer it. But he did write to Mr. Jackson, with whom he was not acquainted.

DEAR MR. JACKSON,

I understand from Widdrington that you have a large house. I would like to tell you how convenient it would be for me to come and stop in it. June suits me best.

Yours truly,
STEWART ANSELL.

To which Mr. Jackson replied that not only in June but during the whole year his house was at the disposal of Mr. Ansell and of any one who resembled him.

But Agnes continued her life, cheerfully beating time. She, too, knew that her marriage was a failure, and in her spare moments regretted it. She wished that her husband was handsomer, more successful, more dictatorial. But she would think, 'No, no; one mustn't grumble. It can't be helped.' Ansell was wrong in supposing she might ever leave Rickie. Spiritual apathy prevented her. Nor would she ever be tempted by a jollier man. Here criticism would willingly alter its tone. For Agnes also has her tragedy. She belonged to the type—not necessarily an elevated one—that loves once and once only. Her love for Gerald had not been a noble passion: no imagination transfigured it. But such as it was, it sprang to embrace him, and he carried it away with him when he died. *Les amours qui suivent sont moins involontaires*: by an effort of the will she had warmed herself for Rickie.

She is not conscious of her tragedy, and therefore only the gods need weep at it. But it is fair to remember that hitherto she moves as one from whom the inner life has been withdrawn.

XXV

'I am afraid,' said Agnes, unfolding a letter that she had received in the morning, 'that things go far from satisfactory at Cadover.'

The three were alone at supper. It was the June of Rickie's second year at Sawston.

'Indeed?' said Herbert, who took a friendly interest. 'In what way?'

'Do you remember us talking of Stephen—Stephen Wonham, who by an odd coincidence——'

'Yes. Who wrote last year to that miserable failure Varden. I do.'

'It is about him.'

'I did not like the tone of his letter.'

Agnes had made her first move. She waited for her husband to reply to it. But he, though full of a painful curiosity, would not speak. She moved again.

'I don't think, Herbert, that Aunt Emily, much as I like her, is the kind of person to bring a young man up. At all events the results have been disastrous this time.'

'What has happened?'

'A tangle of things.' She lowered her voice. 'Drink.'

'Dear! Really! Was Mrs. Failing fond of him?'

'She used to be. She let him live at Cadover ever since he was a little boy. Naturally that cannot continue.'

Rickie never spoke.

'And now he has taken to be violent and rude,' she went on.

'In short, a beggar on horseback. Who is he? Has he no relatives?'

'She has always been both father and mother to him. Now it must all come to an end. I blame her—and she blames herself—for not being severe enough. He has grown up without fixed principles. He has always followed his inclinations, and one knows the result of that.'

Herbert assented. 'To me Mrs. Failing's course is perfectly plain. She has a certain responsibility. She must pay the youth's passage to one of the

colonies, start him handsomely in some business,
and then break off all communications.'

'How funny! It is exactly what she is going to do.'

'I shall then consider that she has behaved in
a thoroughly honourable manner.' He held out his
plate for gooseberries. 'His letter to Varden was
neither helpful nor sympathetic, and, if written at
all, it ought to have been both. I am not in the least
surprised to learn that he has turned out badly.
When you write next, would you tell her how sorry
I am?'

'Indeed I will. Two years ago, when she was
already a little anxious, she did so wish you could
undertake him.'

'I could not alter a grown man.' But in his heart
he thought he could, and smiled at his sister
amiably. 'Terrible, isn't it?' he remarked to Rickie.
Rickie, who was trying not to mind anything, assented. And an onlooker would have supposed
them a dispassionate trio, who were sorry both for
Mrs. Failing and for the beggar who would bestride
her horses' backs no longer. A new topic was introduced by the arrival of the evening post.

Herbert took up all the letters, as he often did.
'Jackson?' he exclaimed. 'What does the fellow
want?' He read, and his tone was mollified, '"Dear
Mr. Pembroke,—Could you, Mrs. Elliot, and Mr.
Elliot come to supper with us on Saturday next? I
should not merely be pleased, I should be grateful.
My wife is writing formally to Mrs. Elliot"—(Here,
Agnes, take your letter),—"but I venture to write as
well, and to add my more uncouth entreaties."—An
olive-branch. It is time! But (ridiculous person!)
does he think that we can leave the House deserted
and all go out pleasuring in term time?—Rickie, a
letter for you.'

'Mine's the formal invitation,' said Agnes. 'How very odd! Mr. Ansell will be there. Surely we asked him here! Did you know he knew the Jacksons?'

'This makes refusal very difficult,' said Herbert, who was anxious to accept. 'At all events, Rickie ought to go.'

'I do not want to go,' said Rickie, slowly opening his own letter. 'As Agnes says, Ansell has refused to come to us. I cannot put myself out for him.'

'Who's yours from?' she demanded.

'Mrs. Silt,' replied Herbert, who had seen the handwriting.

'I trust she does not want to pay us a visit this term, with the examinations impending and all the machinery at full pressure. Though, Rickie, you will have to accept the Jacksons' invitation.'

'I cannot possibly go. I have been too rude; with Widdrington we always meet here. I'll stop with the boys——' His voice caught suddenly. He had opened Mrs. Silt's letter.

'The Silts are not ill, I hope?'

'No. But, I say,'——he looked at his wife,——'I do think this is going too far. Really, Agnes——'

'What has happened?'

'It is going too far,' he repeated. He was nerving himself for another battle. 'I cannot stand this sort of thing. There are limits.'

He laid the letter down. It was Herbert who picked it up, and read: 'Aunt Emily has just written to us. We are so glad that her troubles are over, in spite of the expense. It never does to live apart from one's own relatives so much as she has done up to now. He goes next Saturday to Canada. What you told her about him just turned the scale. She has asked us——'

'No, it's too much,' he interrupted. 'What I told

her—told her about him—no, I will have it out at
last. Agnes!'

'Yes?' said his wife, raising her eyes from Mrs.
Jackson's formal invitation.

'It's you—it's you. I never mentioned him to her.
Why, I've never seen her or written to her since. I
accuse you.'

Then Herbert overbore him, and he collapsed.
He was asked what he meant. Why was he so excited? Of what did he accuse his wife? Each time
he spoke more feebly, and before long the brother
and sister were laughing at him. He felt bewildered,
like a boy who knows that he is right but cannot put
his case correctly. He repeated, 'I've never mentioned him to her. It's a libel. Never in my life.' And
they cried, 'My dear Rickie, what an absurd fuss!'
Then his brain cleared. His eye fell on the letter
that his wife had received from his aunt, and he
reopened the battle.

'Agnes, give me that letter if you please.'

'Mrs. Jackson's?'

'My aunt's.'

She put her hand on it, and looked at him
doubtfully. She saw that she had failed to bully
him.

'My aunt's letter,' he repeated, rising to his feet
and bending over the table towards her.

'Why, dear?'

'Yes, why indeed?' echoed Herbert. He too had
bullied Rickie, but from a purer motive: he had
tried to stamp out a dissension between husband
and wife. It was not the first time he had intervened.

'The letter. For this reason: it will show me what
you have done. I believe you have ruined Stephen.
You have worked at it for two years. You have put

words into my mouth to "turn the scale" against him. He goes to Canada—and all the world thinks it is owing to me. As I said before—I advise you to stop smiling—you have gone a little too far.'

They were all on their feet now, standing round the little table. Agnes said nothing, but the fingers of her delicate hand tightened upon the letter. When her husband snatched at it she resisted, and with the effect of a harlequinade everything went on the floor—lamb, mint sauce, gooseberries, lemonade, whisky. At once they were swamped in domesticities. She rang the bell for the servant, cries arose, dusters were brought, broken crockery (a wedding present) picked up from the carpet; while he stood wrathfully at the window, regarding the obscured sun's decline.

'I *must* see her letter,' he repeated, when the agitation was over. He was too angry to be diverted from his purpose. Only slight emotions are thwarted by an interlude of farce.

'I've had enough of this quarrelling,' she retorted. 'You know that the Silts are inaccurate. I think you might have given me the benefit of the doubt. If you will know—have you forgotten that ride you took with him?'

'I——' He was again bewildered,. 'The ride where I dreamt——'

'The ride where you turned back because you could not listen to a disgraceful poem?'

'I don't understand.'

'The poem was Aunt Emily. He read it to you and a stray soldier. Afterwards you told me. You said, "Really it is shocking, his ingratitude. She ought to know about it." She does know, and I should be glad of an apology.'

He had said something of the sort in a fit of

irritation. Mrs. Silt was right—he had helped to turn the scale.

'Whatever I said, you knew what I meant. You knew I'd sooner cut my tongue out than have it used against him. Even then.' He sighed. Had he ruined his brother? A curious tenderness came over him, and passed when he remembered his own dead child. '*We* have ruined him, then. Have you any objection to "we"? *We* have disinherited him.'

'I decide against you,' interposed Herbert. 'I have now heard both sides of this deplorable affair. You are talking most criminal nonsense. "Disinherit!" Sentimental twaddle. It's been clear to me from the first that Mrs. Failing has been imposed upon by the Wonham man, a person with no legal claim on her, and any one who exposes him performs a public duty——'

'—And gets money.'

'Money?' He was always uneasy at the word. 'Who mentioned money?'

'Just understand me, Herbert, and of what it is that I accuse my wife.' Tears came into his eyes. 'It is not that I like the Wonham man, or think that he isn't a drunkard and worse. He's too awful in every way. But he ought to have my aunt's money, because he's lived all his life with her, and is her nephew as much as I am. You see, my father went wrong.' He stopped, amazed at himself. How easy it had been to say! He was withering up: the power to care about this stupid secret had died.

When Herbert understood, his first thought was for Dunwood House. 'Why have I never been told?' was his first remark.

'We settled to tell no one,' said Agnes. 'Rickie, in his anxiety to prove me a liar, has broken his promise.'

'I ought to have been told,' said Herbert, his anger increasing. 'Had I known, I could have averted this deplorable scene.'

'Let me conclude it,' said Rickie, again collapsing and leaving the dining-room. His impulse was to go straight to Cadover and make a business-like statement of the position to Stephen. Then the man would be armed, and perhaps fight the two women successfully. But he resisted the impulse. Why should he help one power of evil against another? Let them go intertwined to destruction. To enrich his brother would be as bad as enriching himself. If their aunt's money ever did come to him, he would refuse to accept it. That was the easiest and most dignified course. He troubled himself no longer with justice or pity, and the next day he asked his wife's pardon for his behaviour.

In the dining-room the conversation continued. Agnes, without much difficulty, gained her brother as an ally. She acknowledged that she had been wrong in not telling him, and he then declared that she had been right on every other point. She slurred a little over the incident of her treachery, for Herbert was sometimes clear-sighted over details, though easily muddled in a general survey. Mrs. Failing had had plenty of direct causes for complaint, and she dwelt on these. She dwelt, too, on the very handsome way in which the young man, 'though he knew nothing, and had never asked to know,' was being treated by his aunt.

'"Handsome" is the word,' said Herbert. 'I hope not indulgently. He does not deserve indulgence.'

And she knew that he, like herself, could remember money, and that it lent an acknowledged halo to her cause.

'It is not a savoury subject,' he continued, with

sudden stiffness. 'I understand why Rickie is so
hysterical. My impulse'—he laid his hand on her
shoulder—'is to abandon it at once. But if I am to
be of any use to you, I must hear it all. There are
moments when we must look facts in the face.'

She did not shrink from the subject as much as
he thought, as much as she herself could have
wished. Two years before, it had filled her with
a physical loathing. But by now she had accustomed
herself to it.

'I am afraid, Bertie boy, there is nothing else to
hear. I have tried to find out again and again, but
Aunt Emily will not tell me. I suppose it is natural.
She wants to shield the Elliot name. She only told
us in a fit of temper; then we all agreed to keep it
to ourselves; then Rickie again mismanaged her,
and ever since she has refused to let us know any
details.'

'A most unsatisfactory position.'

'So I feel.' She sat down again with a sigh. Mrs.
Failing had been a great trial to her orderly mind.
'She is an odd woman. She is always laughing. She
actually finds it amusing that we know no more.'

'They are an odd family.'

'They are indeed.'

Herbert, with unusual sweetness, bent down and
kissed her.

She thanked him.

Their tenderness soon passed. They exchanged it
with averted eyes. It embarrassed them. There are
moments for all of us when we seem obliged to
speak in a new unprofitable tongue. One might
fancy a seraph, vexed with our normal language,
who touches the pious to blasphemy, the blasphe-
mous to piety. The seraph passes, and we proceed
unaltered—conscious, however, that we have not

been ourselves, and that we may fail in this function yet again. So Agnes and Herbert, as they proceeded to discuss the Jacksons' supper-party, had
an uneasy memory of spiritual deserts, spiritual
streams.

XXVI

Poor Mr. Ansell was actually sitting in the garden
of Dunwood House. It was Sunday morning. The
air was full of roasting beef. The sound of a manly
hymn, taken very fast, floated over the road from
the school chapel. He frowned, for he was reading
a book, the Essays of Anthony Eustace Failing.

He was here on account of this book—at least so
he told himself. It had just been published, and the
Jacksons were sure that Mr. Elliot would have a
copy. For a book one may go anywhere. It would
not have been logical to enter Dunwood House for
the purpose of seeing Rickie, when Rickie had not
come to supper yesterday to see him. He was at
Sawston to assure himself of his friend's grave.
With quiet eyes he had intended to view the
sods, with unfaltering fingers to inscribe the epi-
taph. Love remained. But in high matters he was
practical. He knew that it would be useless to
reveal it.

'Morning!' said a voice behind him.

He saw no reason to reply to this superfluous
statement, and went on with his reading.

'Morning!' said the voice again.

As for the Essays, the thought was somewhat old-
fashioned, and he picked many holes in it; nor was
he anything but bored by the prospect of the
brotherhood of man. However, Mr. Failing stuck to
his guns, such as they were, and fired from them

several good remarks. Very notable was his distinction between coarseness and vulgarity (coarseness, revealing something; vulgarity, concealing something), and his avowed preference for coarseness. Vulgarity, to him, had been the primal curse, the shoddy reticence that prevents man opening his heart to man, the power that makes against equality. From it sprang all the things that he hated—class shibboleths, ladies, lidies, the game laws, the Conservative party—all the things that accent the divergencies rather than the similarities in human nature. Whereas coarseness——But at this point Herbert Pembroke had scrawled with a blue pencil: 'Childish. One reads no further.'

'Morning!' repeated the voice.

Ansell read further, for here was the book of a man who had tried, however unsuccessfully, to practise what he preached. Mrs. Failing, in her Introduction, described with delicate irony his difficulties as a landlord; but she did not record the love in which his name was held. Nor could her irony touch him when he cried: 'Attain the practical through the unpractical. There is no other road.' Ansell was inclined to think that the unpractical is its own reward, but he respected those who attempted to journey beyond it. We must all of us go over the mountains. There is certainly no other road.

'Nice morning!' said the voice.

It was not a nice morning, so Ansell felt bound to speak. He answered: 'No. Why?' A clod of earth immediately struck him on the back. He turned round indignantly, for he hated physical rudeness. A square man of ruddy aspect was pacing the gravel path, his hands deep in his pockets. He was very angry. Then he saw that the clod of earth

I

nourished a blue lobelia, and that a wound of corresponding size appeared on the pie-shaped bed. He was not so angry. 'I expect they will mind it,' he reflected. Last night, at the Jacksons', Agnes had displayed a brisk pity that made him wish to wring her neck. Maud had not exaggerated. Mr. Pembroke had patronized through a sorrowful voice and large round eyes. Till he met these people he had never been told that his career was a failure. Apparently it was. They would never have been civil to him if it had been a success, if they or theirs had anything to fear from him.

In many ways Ansell was a conceited man; but he was never proud of being right. He had foreseen Rickie's catastrophe from the first, but derived from this no consolation. In many ways he was pedantic; but his pedantry lay close to the vineyards of life— far closer than that fetich Experience of the innumerable teacups. He had a great many facts to learn, and before he died he learnt a suitable quantity. But he never forgot that the holiness of the heart's imagination can alone classify these facts— can alone decide which is an exception, which an example. 'How unpractical it all is!' That was his comment on Dunwood House. 'How unbusinesslike! They live together without love. They work without conviction. They seek money without requiring it. They die, and nothing will have happened, either for themselves or for others.' It is a comment that the academic mind will often make when first confronted with the world.

But he was becoming illogical. The clod of earth had disturbed him. Brushing the dirt off his back, he returned to the book. What a curious affair was the essay on 'Gaps'! Solitude, star-crowned, pacing the fields of England, has a dialogue with Seclusion.

He, poor little man, lives in the choicest scenery—
among rocks, forests, emerald lawns, azure lakes.
To keep people out he has built round his domain
a high wall, on which is graven his motto—'Procul
este, profani.' But he cannot enjoy himself. His only
pleasure is in mocking the absent Profane. They
are in his mind night and day. Their blemishes and
stupidities form the subject of his great poem, 'In
the Heart of Nature'. Then Solitude tells him that
so it always will be until he makes a gap in the wall,
and permits his seclusion to be the sport of circum-
stance. He obeys. The Profane invade him; but for
short intervals they wander elsewhere, and during
those intervals the heart of Nature is revealed to
him.

This dialogue had really been suggested to Mr.
Failing by a talk with his brother-in-law. It also
touched Ansell. He looked at the man who had
thrown the clod, and was now pacing with obvious
youth and impudence upon the lawn. 'Shall I im-
prove my soul at his expense?' he thought. 'I suppose I had better.' In friendly tones he remarked,
'Were you waiting for Mr. Pembroke?'

'No,' said the young man. 'Why?'

Ansell, after a moment's admiration, flung the
Essays at him. They hit him in the back. The next
moment he lay on his own back in the lobelia pie.

'But it hurts!' he gasped, in the tones of a
puzzled civilization. 'What you do hurts!' For the
young man was nicking him over the shins with the
rim of the book cover. 'Little brute—*ee—ow!*'

'Then say Pax!'

Something revolted in Ansell. Why should he say
Pax? Freeing his hand, he caught the little brute
under the chin, and was again knocked into the
lobelias by a blow on the mouth.

'Say Pax!' he repeated, pressing the philosopher's skull into the mould; and he added, with an anxiety that was somehow not offensive, 'I do advise you. You'd really better.'

Ansell swallowed a little blood. He tried to move, and he could not. He looked carefully into the young man's eyes and into the palm of his right hand, which at present swung unclenched, and he said 'Pax!'

'Shake hands!' said the other, helping him up. There was nothing Ansell loathed so much as the hearty Britisher; but he shook hands, and they stared at each other awkwardly. With civil murmurs they picked the little blue flowers off each other's clothes. Ansell was trying to remember why they had quarrelled, and the young man was wondering why he had not guarded his chin properly. In the distance a hymn swung off—

Fight the good . Fight with . All thy . Might.

They would be across from chapel soon.

'Your book, sir?'

'Thank you, sir—yes.'

'Why!' cried the young man—'why, it's "What We Want"! At least the binding's exactly the same.'

'It's called "Essays",' said Ansell.

'Then that's it. Mrs. Failing, you see, she wouldn't call it that, because three W's, you see, in a row, she said, are vulgar, and sound like Tolstoy, if you've heard of him.'

Ansell confessed to an acquaintance, and then said, 'Do you think "What We Want" vulgar?' He was not at all interested, but he desired to escape from the atmosphere of pugilistic courtesy, more painful to him than blows themselves.

'It *is* the same book,' said the other—'same title, same binding.' He weighed it like a brick in his muddy hands.

'Open it to see if the inside corresponds,' said Ansell, swallowing a laugh and a little more blood with it.

With a liberal allowance of thumb-marks, he turned the pages over and read, "——the rural silence that is not a poet's luxury but a practical need for all men." Yes, it *is* the same book.' Smiling pleasantly over the discovery, he handed it back to the owner.

'And is it true?'

'I beg your pardon?'

'Is it true that rural silence is a practical need?'

'Don't ask me!'

'Have you ever tried it?'

'What?'

'Rural silence.'

'A field with no noise in it, I suppose you mean. I don't understand.'

Ansell smiled, but a slight fire in the man's eye checked him. After all, this was a person who could knock one down. Moreover, there was no reason why he should be teased. He had it in him to retort 'No. Why?' He was not stupid in essentials. He was irritable—in Ansell's eyes a frequent sign of grace. Sitting down on the upturned seat, he remarked, 'I like the book in many ways. I don't think "What We Want" would have been a vulgar title. But I don't intend to spoil myself on the chance of mending the world, which is what the creed amounts to. Nor am I keen on rural silences.'

'Curse!' he said thoughtfully, sucking at an empty pipe.

'Tobacco?'

'Please.'

'Rickie's is invariably filthy.'

'Who says I know Rickie?'

'Well, you know his aunt. It's a possible link. Be gentle with Rickie. Don't knock him down if he doesn't think it's a nice morning.'

The other was silent.

'Do you know him well?'

'Kind of.' He was not inclined to talk. The wish to smoke was very violent in him, and Ansell noticed how he gazed at the wreaths that ascended from bowl and stem, and how, when the stem was in his mouth, he bit it. He gave the idea of an animal with just enough soul to contemplate its own bliss. United with refinement, such a type was common in Greece. It is not common to-day, and Ansell was surprised to find it in a friend of Rickie's. Rickie, if he could even 'kind of know' such a creature, must be stirring in his grave.

'Do you know his wife too?'

'Oh, yes. In a way I know Agnes. But thank you for this tobacco. Last night I nearly died. I have no money.'

'Take the whole pouch—do.'

After a moment's hesitation he did. 'Fight the good' had scarcely ended, so quickly had their intimacy grown.

'I suppose you're a friend of Rickie's?'

Ansell was tempted to reply, 'I don't know him at all.' But it seemed no moment for the severer truths, so he said, 'I knew him well at Cambridge, but I have seen very little of him since.'

'Is it true that his baby was lame?'

'I believe so.'

His teeth closed on his pipe. Chapel was over.

The organist was prancing through the voluntary, and the first ripple of boys had already reached Dunwood House. In a few minutes the masters would be here too, and Ansell, who was becoming interested, hurried the conversation forward.

'Have you come far?'

'From Wiltshire. Do you know Wiltshire?' And for the first time there came into his face the shadow of a sentiment, the passing tribute to some mystery. 'It's a good country. I live in one of the finest valleys out of Salisbury Plain. I mean, I lived.'

'Have you been dismissed from Cadover, without a penny in your pocket?'

He was alarmed at this. Such knowledge seemed simply diabolical. Ansell explained that if his boots were chalky, if his clothes had obviously been slept in, if he knew Mrs. Failing, if he knew Wiltshire, and if he could buy no tobacco—then the deduction was possible. 'You do just attend,' he murmured.

The house was filling with boys, and Ansell saw, to his regret, the head of Agnes over the thuya hedge that separated the small front garden from the side lawn where he was sitting. After a few minutes it was followed by the heads of Rickie and Mr. Pembroke. All the heads were turned the other way. But they would find his card in the hall, and if the man had left any message they would find that too. 'What are you?' he demanded. 'Who are you—your name—I don't care about that. But it interests me to class people, and up to now I have failed with you.'

'I——' He stopped. Ansell reflected that there are worse answers. 'I really don't know what I am. Used to think I was something special, but strikes me now I feel much like other chaps. Used to look

down on the labourers. Used to take for granted
I was a gentleman, but really I don't know where
I do belong.'

'One belongs to the place one sleeps in and to the
people one eats with.'

'As often as not I sleep out of doors and eat by
myself, so that doesn't get you any further.'

A silence, akin to poetry, invaded Ansell. Was it
only a pose to like this man, or was he really wonderful? He was not romantic, for Romance is a
figure with outstretched hands, yearning for the
unattainable. Certain figures of the Greeks, to
whom we continually return, suggested him a little.
One expected nothing of him—no purity of phrase
nor swift-edged thought. Yet the conviction grew
that he had been back somewhere—back to some
table of the gods, spread in a field where there is no
noise, and that he belonged for ever to the guests
with whom he had eaten.

Meanwhile he was simple and frank, and what
he could tell he would tell to any one. He had not
the suburban reticence. Ansell asked him, 'Why did
Mrs. Failing turn you out of Cadover? I should like
to hear that too.'

'Because she was tired of me. Because, again, I
couldn't keep quiet over the farm hands. I ask you,
is it right?' He became incoherent. Ansell caught,
'And they grow old—they don't play games—it
ends they can't play.' An illustration emerged. 'Take
a kitten—if you fool about with her, she goes on
playing well into a cat.'

'But Mrs. Failing minded no mice being
caught.'

'Mice?' said the young man blankly. 'What I was
going to say is, that some one was jealous of my
being at Cadover. I'll mention no names, but I fancy

it was Mrs. Silt. I'm sorry for her if it was. Anyhow, she set Mrs. Failing against me. It came on the top of other things—and out I went.'

'What did Mrs. Silt, whose name I don't mention, say?'

He looked guilty. 'I don't know. Easy enough to find something to say. The point is that she said something. You know, Mr.—I don't know your name, mine's Wonham, but I'm more grateful than I can put it over this tobacco. I mean, you ought to know there *is* another side to this quarrel. It's wrong, but it's there.'

Ansell told him not to be uneasy: he had already guessed that there might be another side. But he could not make out why Mr. Wonham should have come straight from the aunt to the nephew. They were now sitting on the upturned seat. 'What We Want', a good deal shattered, lay between them.

'On account of above-mentioned reasons, there was a row. I don't know—you can guess the style of thing. She wanted to treat me to the colonies, and had up the parson to talk soft-sawder and make out that a boundless continent was the place for a lad like me. I said, "I can't run up to the Rings without getting tired, nor gallop a horse out of this view without tiring it, so what is the point of a boundless continent?" Then I saw that she was frightened of me, and bluffed a bit more, and in the end I was nipped. She caught me—just like her —when I had nothing on but flannels, and was coming into the house, having licked the Cadchurch team. She stood up in the doorway between those stone pilasters and said, "No! Never again!" and behind her was Wilbraham, whom I tried to turn out, and the gardener, and poor old Leighton,

who hates being hurt. She said, "There's a hundred
pounds for you at the London bank, and as much
more in December. Go!" I said, "Keep your—
money, and tell me whose son I am." I didn't care
really. I only said it on the off-chance of hurting
her. Sure enough, she caught on to the door-handle
(being lame) and said, "I can't—I promised—I
don't really want to, and Wilbraham did stare.
Then—she's very queer—she burst out laughing,
and went for the packet after all, and we heard
her laugh through the window as she got it. She
rolled it at me down the steps, and she says, "A
leaf out of the eternal comedy for you, Stephen,"
or something of that sort. I opened it as I walked
down the drive, she laughing always and catching
on to the handle of the front door. Of course it
wasn't comic at all. But down in the village there
were both cricket teams, already a little tight, and
the mad plumber shouting "Rights of Man!" They
knew I was turned out. We did have a row, and
kept it up too. They daren't touch Wilbraham's
windows, but there isn't much glass left up at
Cadover. When you start, it's worth going on, but
in the end I had to cut. They subscribed a bob
here and a bob there, and these are Flea Thompson's Sundays. I sent a line to Leighton not to forward my own things: I don't fancy them. They
aren't really mine.' He did not mention his great
symbolic act, performed, it is to be feared, when he
was rather drunk and the friendly policeman was
looking the other way. He had cast all his flannels
into the little mill-pond, and then waded himself
through the dark cold water to the new clothes on
the other side. Some one had flung his pipe and
his packet after him. The packet had fallen short.
For this reason it was wet when he handed it to

Ansell, and ink that had been dry for twenty-three years had begun to run again.

'I wonder if you're right about the hundred pounds,' said Ansell gravely. 'It is pleasant to be proud, but it is unpleasant to die in the night through not having any tobacco.'

'But I'm not proud. Look how I've taken your pouch! The hundred pounds was—well, can't you see yourself, it was quite different? It was, so to speak, *inconvenient* for me to take the hundred pounds. Or look again how I took a shilling from a boy who earns nine bob a-week! Proves pretty conclusively I'm not proud.'

Ansell saw it was useless to argue. He perceived, beneath the slatternly use of words, the man,—buttoned up in them, just as his body was buttoned up in a shoddy suit,—and he wondered more than ever that such a man should know the Elliots. He looked at the face, which was frank, proud, and beautiful, if truth is beauty. Of mercy or tact such a face knew little. It might be coarse, but it had in it nothing vulgar or wantonly cruel. 'May I read these papers?' he said.

'Of course. Oh yes; didn't I say? I'm Rickie's half-brother, come here to tell him the news. He doesn't know. There it is, put shortly for you. I was saying, though, that I bolted in the dark, slept in the rifle-butts above Salisbury,—the sheds where they keep the cardboard men, you know, never locked up as they ought to be. I turned the whole place upside down to teach them.'

'Here is your packet again,' said Ansell. 'Thank you. How interesting!' He rose from the seat and turned towards Dunwood House. He looked at the bow-windows, the cheap picturesque gables, the terra-cotta dragons clawing a dirty sky. He listened to the clink of plates and to the voice of Mr. Pembroke taking one of his innumerable roll-calls. He looked at the bed of lobelias. How interesting! What else was there to say?

'One must be the son of some one,' remarked Stephen. And that was all he had to say. To him those names on the moistened paper were mere antiquities. He was neither proud of them nor ashamed. A man must have parents, or he cannot enter the delightful world. A man, if he has a brother, may reasonably visit him, for they may have interests in common. He continued his narrative,—how in the night he had heard the clocks, how at daybreak, instead of entering the city, he had struck eastward to save money,—while Ansell still looked at the house and found that all his imagination and knowledge could lead him no farther than this: how interesting!

'—And what do you think of that for a holy horror?'

'For a what?' said Ansell, his thoughts far away.

'This man I am telling you about, who gave me a lift towards Andover, who said I was a blot on God's earth.'

One o'clock struck. It was strange that neither of them had had any summons from the house.

'He said I ought to be ashamed of myself. He said, "I'll not be the means of bringing shame to an honest gentleman and lady." I told him not to be a fool. I said I knew what I was about. Rickie and Agnes are properly educated, which leads people to look at things straight, and not go screaming about blots. A man like me, with just a little reading at odd hours—I've got so far, and Rickie has been through Cambridge.'

'And Mrs. Elliot?'

'Oh, she won't mind, and I told the man so; but he kept on saying, "I'll not be the means of bringing shame to an honest gentleman and lady," until I got out of his rotten cart.' His eye watched the man, a Nonconformist, driving away over God's earth. 'I caught the train by running. I got to Waterloo at——'

Here the parlourmaid fluttered towards them. Would Mr. Wonham come in? Mrs. Elliot would be glad to see him now.

'Mrs. Elliot?' cried Ansell. 'Not Mr. Elliot?'

'It's all the same,' said Stephen, and moved towards the house. 'You see, I only left my name. They don't know why I've come.'

'Perhaps Mr. Elliot sees me meanwhile?'

The parlourmaid looked blank. Mr. Elliot had not said so. He had been with Mrs. Elliot and Mr. Pembroke in the study. Now the gentlemen had gone upstairs.

'All right, I can wait.' After all, Rickie was treating him as he had treated Rickie, as one in the grave, to whom it is futile to make any loving motion. Gone upstairs—to brush his hair for dinner! The irony of the situation appealed to him strongly. It reminded him of the Greek Drama, where the actors know so little and the spectators so much.

'But, by the bye,' he called after Stephen, 'I think I ought to tell you—don't——'

'What is it?'

'Don't——' Then he was silent. He had been tempted to explain everything, to tell the fellow how things stood,—that he must avoid this if he wanted to attain that; that he must break the news to Rickie gently; that he must have at least one battle royal with Agnes. But it was contrary to his own spirit to coach people: he held the human soul to be a very delicate thing, which can receive eternal damage from a little patronage. Stephen must go into the house simply as himself, for thus alone would he remain there.

'I ought to knock my pipe out? Was that it?'

'By no means. Go in, your pipe and you.'

He hesitated, torn between propriety and desire. Then he followed the parlourmaid into the house smoking. As he entered the dinner-bell rang, and there was the sound of rushing feet, which died away into shuffling and silence. Through the window of the boys' dining-hall came the colourless voice of Rickie—

Benedictus benedicat.

Ansell prepared himself to witness the second act of the drama; forgetting that all this world, and not part of it, is a stage.

XXVII

The parlourmaid took Mr. Wonham to the study. He had been in the drawing-room before, but had got bored, and so had strolled out into the garden. Now he was in better spirits, as a man ought to be who has knocked down a man. As he passed through the hall he sparred at the teak monkey, and hung his cap on the bust of Hermes. And he greeted Mrs. Elliot with a pleasant clap of laughter. 'Oh, I've come with the most tremendous news!' he cried.

She bowed, but did not shake hands, which rather surprised him. But he never troubled over 'details'. He seldom watched people, and never thought that they were watching him. Nor could he guess how much it meant to her that he should enter her presence smoking. Had she not said once at Cadover, 'Oh, *please* smoke; I love the smell of a pipe'?

'Would you sit down? Exactly there, please.' She placed him at a large table, opposite an inkpot and a pad of blotting-paper. 'Will you tell your "tremendous news" to me? My brother and my husband are giving the boys their dinner.'

'Ah!' said Stephen, who had had neither time nor money for breakfast in London.

'I told them not to wait for me.'

So he came to the point at once. He trusted this handsome woman. His strength and his youth called to hers, expecting no prudish response. 'It's very odd. It is that I'm Rickie's brother. I've just found out. I've come to tell you all.'

'Yes?'

He felt in his pocket for the papers. 'Half-brother I ought to have said.'

'Yes?'

'I'm illegitimate. Legally speaking, that is, I've been turned out of Cadover. I haven't a penny. I——'

'There is no occasion to inflict the details.' Her face, which had been an even brown, began to flush slowly in the centre of the cheeks. The colour spread till all that he saw of her was suffused, and she turned away. He thought he had shocked her, and so did she. Neither knew that the body can be insincere and express not the emotions we feel but those that we should like to feel. In reality she was quite calm, and her dislike of him had nothing emotional in it as yet.

'You see——' he began. He was determined to tell the fidgety story, for the sooner it was over the sooner they would have something to eat. Delicacy he lacked, and his sympathies were limited. But such as they were, they rang true: he put no decorous phantom between him and his desires.

'I do see. I have seen for two years.' She sat down at the head of the table, where there was another inkpot. Into this she dipped a pen. 'I have seen everything, Mr. Wonham—who you are, how you have behaved at Cadover, how you must have treated Mrs. Failing yesterday; and now'—her voice became very grave—'I see why you have come here, penniless. Before you speak, we know what you will say.'

His mouth fell open, and he laughed so merrily that it might have given her a warning. But she was thinking how to follow up her first success. 'And I thought I was bringing tremendous news!' he cried. 'I only twisted it out of Mrs. Failing last night. And Rickie knows too?'

'We have known for two years.'

'But come, by the bye, if you've known for two years, how is it you didn't——' The laugh died out of his eyes. 'You aren't ashamed?' he asked, half rising from his chair. 'You aren't like the man towards Andover?'

'Please, please sit down,' said Agnes, in the even tones she used when speaking to the servants; 'let us not discuss side issues. I am a horribly direct person, Mr. Wonham. I go always straight to the point.' She opened a cheque-book. 'I am afraid I shall shock you. For how much?'

He was not attending.

'There is the paper we suggest you shall sign.' She pushed towards him a pseudo-legal document, just composed by Herbert.

'"In consideration of the sum of . . . . . ., I agree

to perpetual silence—to restrain from libellous . . .
never to molest the said Frederick Elliot by in-
truding——"'

His brain was not quick. He read the document
over twice, and he could still say, 'But what's that
cheque for?'

'It is my husband's. He signed for you as soon
as we heard you were here. We guessed you had
come to be silenced. Here is his signature. But he
has left the filling in for me. For how much? I will
cross it, shall I? You will just have started a bank-
ing account, if I understand Mrs. Failing rightly.
It is not quite accurate to say you are penniless; I
heard from her just before you returned from your
cricket. She allows you two hundred a year, I think.
But this additional sum—shall I date the cheque
Saturday or for to-morrow?'

At last he found words. Knocking his pipe out on
the table, he said slowly, 'Here's a very bad mistake.'

'It is quite possible,' retorted Agnes. She was
glad she had taken the offensive, instead of waiting
till he began his blackmailing, as had been the
advice of Rickie. Aunt Emily had said that very
spring, 'One's only hope with Stephen is to start
bullying first.' Here he was, quite bewildered,
smearing his pipe-ashes with his thumb. He asked
to read the document again. 'A stamp and all!' he
remarked.

They had anticipated that his claim would ex-
ceed two pounds.

'I see. All right. It takes a fool a minute. Never
mind. I've made a bad mistake.'

'You refuse?' she exclaimed, for he was standing
at the door. 'Then do your worst! We defy you!'

'That's all right, Mrs. Elliot,' he said roughly. 'I don't want a scene with you, nor yet with your husband. We'll say no more about it. It's all right. I meant no harm.'

'But your signature then! You must sign— you——'

He pushed past her, and said as he reached for his cap, 'There, that's all right. It's my mistake. I'm sorry.' He spoke like a farmer who had failed to sell a sheep. His manner was utterly prosaic, and up to the last she thought he had not understood her. 'But it's money we offer you,' she informed him, and then darted back to the study, believing for one terrible moment that he had picked up the blank cheque. When she returned to the hall he had gone. He was walking down the road rather quickly. At the corner he cleared his throat, spat into the gutter, and disappeared.

'There's an odd finish,' she thought. She was puzzled, and determined to recast the interview a little when she related it to Rickie. She had not succeeded, for the paper was still unsigned. But she had so cowed Stephen that he would probably rest content with his two hundred a year, and never come troubling them again. Clever management, for one knew him to be rapacious: she had heard tales of him lending to the poor and exacting repayment to the uttermost farthing. He had also stolen at school. Moderately triumphant, she hurried into the side-garden: she had just remembered Ansell: she, not Rickie, had received his card.

'Oh, Mr. Ansell!' she exclaimed, awaking him from some day-dream. 'Haven't either Rickie or Herbert been out to you? Now, do come into dinner, to show you aren't offended. You will find all of us assembled in the boys' dining-hall.'

To her annoyance he accepted.

'That is, if the Jacksons are not expecting you.'

The Jacksons did not matter. If he might brush his clothes and bathe his lip, he would like to come.

'Oh, what has happened to you? And oh, my pretty lobelias!'

He replied, 'A momentary contact with reality,' and she, who did not look for sense in his remarks, hurried away to the dining-hall to announce him.

The dining-hall was not unlike the preparation-room. There was the same parquet floor, and dado of shiny pitch-pine. On its walls also were imperial portraits, and over the harmonium to which they sang the evening hymns was spread the Union Jack. Sunday dinner, the most pompous meal of the week, was in progress. Her brother sat at the head of the high table, her husband at the head of the second. To each she gave a reassuring nod and went to her own seat, which was among the junior boys. The beef was being carried out; she stopped it. 'Mr. Ansell is coming,' she called. 'Herbert, there is more room by you; sit up straight, boys.' The boys sat up straight, and a respectful hush spread over the room.

'Here he is!' called Rickie cheerfully, taking his cue from his wife. 'Oh, this is splendid!' Ansell came in. 'I'm so glad you managed this. I couldn't leave these wretches last night!' The boys tittered suitably. The atmosphere seemed normal. Even Herbert, though longing to hear what had happened to the blackmailer, gave adequate greeting to their guest: 'Come in, Mr. Ansell; come here. Take us as you find us!'

'I understood,' said Stewart, 'that I should find you all. Mrs. Elliot told me I should. On that understanding I came.'

It was at once evident that something had gone wrong.

Ansell looked round the room carefully. Then clearing his throat and ruffling his hair, he began—

'I cannot see the man with whom I have talked, intimately, for an hour, in your garden.'

The worst of it was they were all so far from him and from each other, each at the end of a tableful of inquisitive boys. The two masters looked at Agnes for information, for her reassuring nod had not told them much. She looked hopelessly back.

'I cannot see this man,' repeated Ansell, who remained by the harmonium in the midst of astonished waitresses. 'Is he to be given no lunch?'

Herbert broke the silence by fresh greetings. Rickie knew that the contest was lost, and that his friend had sided with the enemy. It was the kind of thing he would do. One must face the catastrophe quietly and with dignity. Perhaps Ansell would have turned on his heel, and left behind him only vague suspicions, if Mrs. Elliot had not tried to talk him down. 'Man,' she cried—'what man? Oh, I know—terrible bore! Did he get hold of you?'—thus committing their first blunder, and causing Ansell to say to Rickie, 'Have you seen your brother?'

'I have not.'

'Have you been told he was here?'

Rickie's answer was inaudible.

'Have you been told you have a brother?'

'Let us continue this conversation later.'

'Continue it? My dear man, how can we until you know what I'm talking about? You must think me mad; but I tell you solemnly that you have a brother of whom you've never heard, and that he was in this house ten minutes ago.' He paused impressively. 'Your wife has happened to see him first. Being neither serious nor truthful, she is keeping you apart, telling him some lie and not telling you a word.'

There was a murmur of alarm. One of the prefects rose, and Ansell set his back to the wall, quite ready for a battle. For two years he had waited for this opportunity. He would hit out at Mrs. Elliot like any ploughboy now that it had come. Rickie said: 'There is a slight misunderstanding. I, like my wife, have known what there is to know for two years'—a dignified rebuff, but their second blunder.

'Exactly,' said Agnes. 'Now I think Mr. Ansell had better go.'

'Go?' exploded Ansell. 'I've everything to say yet. I beg your pardon, Mrs. Elliot, I am concerned with you no longer. This man'—he turned to the avenue of faces—'this man who teaches you has a brother. He has known of him two years and been ashamed. He has—oh—oh—how it fits together! Rickie, it's you, not Mrs. Silt, who must have sent tales of him to your aunt. It's you who've turned him out of Cadover. It's you who've ordered him to be ruined to-day. Mrs. Elliot, I beg your pardon.'

Now Herbert arose. 'Out of my sight, sir! But have it from me first that Rickie and his aunt have both behaved most generously. No, no, Agnes, I will not be interrupted. Garbled versions must not get about. If the Wonham man is not satisfied now, he must be insatiable. He cannot levy blackmail on us for ever. Sir, I give you two minutes; then you will be expelled by force.'

'Two minutes!' sang Ansell. 'I can say a great deal in that.' He put one foot on a chair and held

his arms over the quivering room. He seemed transfigured into a Hebrew prophet passionate for satire
and the truth. 'Oh, keep quiet for two minutes,' he
cried, 'and I'll tell you something you'll be glad to
hear. You're a little afraid Stephen may come back.
Don't be afraid. I bring good news. You'll never see
him nor any one like him again. I must speak very
plainly, for you are all three fools. I don't want
you to say afterwards, "Poor Mr. Ansell tried to be
clever." Generally I don't mind, but I should mind
to-day. Please listen. Stephen is a bully; he drinks;
he knocks one down; but he would sooner die than
take money from people he did not love. Perhaps
he will die, for he has nothing but a few pence that
the poor gave him and some tobacco which, to my
eternal glory, he accepted from me. Please listen
again. Why did he come here? Because he thought
you would love him, and was ready to love you. But
I tell you, don't be afraid. He would sooner die now
than say you were his brother. Perhaps he will die,
for he has nothing but a few pence that the poor
gave him and some tobacco which, to my eternal
glory, he accepted from me. Please listen again——'

'Now, Stewart, don't go on like that,' said Rickie
bitterly. 'It's easy enough to preach when you are
an outsider. You would be more charitable if such
a thing had happened to yourself. Easy enough to
be unconventional when you haven't suffered and
know nothing of the facts. You love anything out of
the way, anything queer, that doesn't often happen,
and so you get excited over this. It's useless, my
dear man; you have hurt me, but you will never
upset me. As soon as you stop this ridiculous scene
we will finish our dinner. Spread this scandal; add
to it. I'm too old to mind such nonsense. I cannot
help my father's disgrace, on the one hand; nor, on

the other, will I have anything to do with his black-guard of a son.'

So the secret was given to the world. Agnes might colour at his speech; Herbert might calculate the effect of it on the entries for Dunwood House; but he cared for none of these things. Thank God! he was withered up at last.

'Please listen again,' resumed Ansell. 'Please correct two slight mistakes: firstly, Stephen is one of the greatest people I have ever met; secondly, he's not your father's son. He's the son of your mother.'

It was Rickie, not Ansell, who was carried from the hall, and it was Herbert who pronounced the blessing—

Benedicto benedicatur.

A profound stillness succeeded the storm, and the boys, slipping away from their meal, told the news to the rest of the school, or put it in the letters they were writing home.

XXVIII

The soul has her own currency. She mints her spiritual coinage and stamps it with the image of some beloved face. With it she pays her debts, with it she reckons, saying, 'This man has worth, this man is worthless.' And in time she forgets its origin; it seems to her to be a thing unalterable, divine. But the soul can also have her bankruptcies.

Perhaps she will be the richer in the end. In her agony she learns to reckon clearly. Fair as the coin may have been, it was not accurate; and though she knew it not, there were treasures that it could not buy. The face, however beloved, was mortal, and as liable as the soul herself to err. We do but shift responsibility by making a standard of the dead.

There is, indeed, another coinage that bears on it not man's image but God's. It is incorruptible, and the soul may trust it safely; it will serve her beyond the stars. But it cannot give us friends, or the embrace of a lover, or the touch of children, for with our fellow-mortals it has no concern. It cannot even give the joys we call trivial—fine weather, the pleasures of meat and drink, bathing and the hot sand afterwards, running, dreamless sleep. Have we learnt the true discipline of a bank-ruptcy if we turn to such coinage as this? Will it really profit us so much if we save our souls and lose the whole world?

PART THREE

WILTSHIRE

◆

XXIX

Robert——there is no occasion to mention his surname: he was a young farmer of some education who tried to coax the aged soil of Wiltshire scientifically——came to Cadover on business and fell in love with Mrs. Elliot. She was there on her bridal visit, and he, an obscure nobody, was received by Mrs. Failing into the house and treated as her social equal. He was good-looking in a bucolic way, and people sometimes mistook him for a gentleman until they saw his hands. He discovered this, and one of the slow, gentle jokes he played on society was to talk upon some cultured subject with his hands behind his back and then suddenly reveal them. 'Do you go in for boating?' the lady would ask; and then he explained that those particular weals are made by the handles of the plough. Upon which she became extremely interested, but found an early opportunity of talking to some one else.

He played this joke on Mrs. Elliot the first evening, not knowing that she observed him as he entered the room. He walked heavily, lifting his feet as if the carpet was furrowed, and he had no evening clothes. Every one tried to put him at his ease, but she rather suspected that he was there already, and envied him. They were introduced, and spoke of Byron, who was still fashionable. Out came his hands—the only rough hands in the drawing-room, the only hands that had ever worked. She was filled with some strange approval, and liked him.

After dinner they met again, to speak not of Byron but of manure. The other people were so clever and so amusing that it relieved her to listen to a man who told her three times not to buy artificial manure ready made, but, if she would use it, to make it herself at the last moment. Because the ammonia evaporated. Here were two packets of powder. Did they smell? No. Mix them together and pour some coffee—— An appalling smell at once burst forth, and every one began to cough and cry. This was good for the earth when she felt sour, for he knew when the earth was ill. He knew, too, when she was hungry: he spoke of her tantrums— the strange unscientific element in her that will baffle the scientist to the end of time. 'Study away, Mrs. Elliot,' he told her; 'read all the books you can get hold of; but when it comes to the point, stroll out with a pipe in your mouth and do a bit of guessing.' As he talked, the earth became a living being —or rather a being with a living skin,—and manure no longer dirty stuff, but a symbol of regeneration and of the birth of life from life. 'So it goes on for ever!' she cried excitedly. He replied: 'Not for ever. In time the fire at the centre will cool, and nothing can go on then.'

He advanced into love with open eyes, slowly, heavily, just as he had advanced across the drawing-room carpet. But this time the bride did not observe his tread. She was listening to her husband, and trying not to be stupid. When he was close to her—so close that it was difficult not to take her in his arms—he spoke to Mr. Failing, and was at once turned out of Cadover.

'I'm sorry,' said Mr. Failing, as he walked down the drive with his hand on his guest's shoulder, 'I had no notion you were that sort. Any one who behaves like that has to stop at the farm.'

'Any one?'

'Any one.' He sighed heavily, not for any personal grievance, but because he saw how unruly, how barbaric, is the soul of man. After all, this man was more civilized than most.

'Are you angry with me, sir?' He called him 'sir', not because he was richer or cleverer or smarter, not because he had helped to educate him and had lent him money, but for a reason more profound—for the reason that there are gradations in heaven.

'I did think of you—that a man like you wouldn't risk making people unhappy. My sister-in-law—I don't say this to stop you loving her; something else must do that—my sister-in-law, as far as I know, doesn't care for you one little bit. If you had said anything, if she had guessed that a chance person was in this fearful state, you would simply have opened hell. A woman of her sort would have lost all——'

'I knew that.'

Mr. Failing removed his hand. He was displeased.

'But something here,' said Robert incoherently. 'This here.' He struck himself heavily on the heart. 'This here, doing something so unusual, makes it not matter what she loses—I——' After a silence, he asked, 'Have I quite followed you, sir, in that business of the brotherhood of man?'

'How do you mean?'

'I thought love was to bring it about.'

'Love of another man's wife? Sensual love? You have understood nothing—nothing.' Then he was ashamed, and cried, 'I understand nothing myself.' For he remembered that sensual and spiritual are not easy words to use; that there are, perhaps, not two Aphrodites, but one Aphrodite with a Janus face. 'I only understand that you must try to forget her.'

'I will not try.'

'Promise me just this, then—not to do anything crooked.'

'I'm straight. No boasting, but I couldn't do a crooked thing—no, not if I tried.'

And so appallingly straight was he in after years, that Mr. Failing wished that he had phrased the promise differently.

Robert simply waited. He told himself that it was hopeless; but something deeper than himself declared that there was hope. He gave up drink, and kept himself in all ways clean, for he wanted to be worthy of her when the time came. Women seemed fond of him, and caused him to reflect with pleasure, 'They do run after me. There must be something in me. Good. I'd be done for if there wasn't.' For six years he turned up the earth of Wiltshire, and read books for the sake of his mind, and talked to gentlemen for the sake of their patois, and each year he rode to Cadover to take off his hat to Mrs. Elliot, and, perhaps, to speak to her about the crops. Mr. Failing was generally present, and it struck neither man that those dull little visits were so many words out of which a lonely woman might build sentences. Then Robert went to London on business. He chanced to see Mr. Elliot with a strange lady. The time had come.

He became diplomatic, and called at Mr. Elliot's rooms to find things out. For if Mrs. Elliot was happier than he could ever make her, he would withdraw, and love her in renunciation. But if he could make her happier, he would love her in fulfilment. Mr. Elliot admitted him as a friend of his brother-in-law's, and felt very broadminded as he did so. Robert, however, was a success. The youngish men there found him interesting, and liked to shock him with tales of naughty London and naughtier Paris. They spoke of 'experience' and 'sensations' and 'seeing life', and when a smile ploughed over his face, concluded that his prudery was vanquished. He saw that they were much less vicious than they supposed: one boy had obviously read his sensations in a book. But he could pardon vice. What he could not pardon was triviality, and he hoped that no decent woman would pardon it either. There grew up in him a cold, steady anger against these silly people who thought it advanced to be shocking, and who described, as something particularly choice and educational, things that he had understood and fought against for years. He inquired after Mrs. Elliot, and a boy tittered. It seemed that she 'did not know' that she lived in a remote suburb, taking care of a skinny baby. 'I shall call some time or other,' said Robert. 'Do,' said Mr. Elliot, smiling. And next time he saw his wife he congratulated her on her rustic admirer.

She had suffered terribly. She had asked for bread, and had been given not even a stone. People talk of hungering for the ideal, but there is another hunger, quite as divine, for facts. She had asked for facts and had been given 'views', 'emotional standpoints', 'attitudes towards life'. To a woman who believed that facts are beautiful, that the living world is beautiful beyond the laws of beauty, that manure is neither gross nor ludicrous, that a fire, not eternal, glows at the heart of the earth, it was intolerable to be put off with what the Elliots called 'philosophy', and, if she refused, to be told that she had no sense of humour. 'Marrying into the Elliot family.' It had sounded so splendid, for she was a penniless child with nothing to offer, and the Elliots held their heads high. For what reason? What had they ever done, except say sarcastic things, and limp, and be refined? Mr. Failing suffered too, but she suffered more, inasmuch as Frederick was more impossible than Emily. He did not like her, he practically lived apart, he was not even faithful or polite. These were grave faults, but they were human ones: she could even imagine them in a man she loved. What she could never love was a dilettante.

Robert brought her an armful of sweet-peas. He laid it on the table, put his hands behind his back, and kept them there till the end of the visit. She knew quite well why he had come, and though she also knew that he would fail, she loved him too much to snub him or to stare in virtuous indignation. 'Why have you come?' she asked gravely, 'and why have you brought me so many flowers?'

'My garden is full of them,' he answered. 'Sweet-peas need picking down. And, generally speaking, flowers are plentiful in July.'

She broke his present into bunches—so much for the drawing-room, so much for the nursery, so much for the kitchen and her husband's room: he would be down for the night. The most beautiful she would keep for herself. Presently he said, 'Your husband is no good. I've watched him for a week. I'm thirty, and not what you call hasty, as I used to

be, or thinking that nothing matters like the French.
No. I'm a plain Britisher, yet—I—— I've begun
wrong end, Mrs. Elliot; I should have said that I've
thought chiefly of you for six years, and that though
I talk here so respectfully, if I once unhooked my
hands——'

There was a pause. Then she said with great
sweetness, 'Thank you; I am glad you love me,' and
rang the bell.

'What have you done that for?' he cried.

'Because you must now leave the house, and
never enter it again.'

'I don't go alone,' and he began to get furious.

Her voice was still sweet, but strength lay in it
too, as she said. 'You either go now with my thanks
and my blessing, or else you go with the police. I
am Mrs. Elliot. We need not discuss Mr. Elliot.
I am Mrs. Elliot, and if you make one step towards
me I give you in charge.'

But the maid answered the bell not of the drawing-room, but of the front door. They were joined
by Mr. Elliot, who held out his hand with much
urbanity. It was not taken. He looked quickly at his
wife, and said, 'Am I *de trop*?' There was a long
silence. At last she said, 'Frederick, turn this man
out.'

'My love, why?'

Robert said that he loved her.

'Then I am *de trop*,' said Mr. Elliot, smoothing
out his gloves. He would give these sodden bar-
barians a lesson. 'My hansom is waiting at the door.
Pray make use of it.'

'Don't!' she cried, almost affectionately. 'Dear
Frederick, it isn't a play. Just tell this man to go, or
send for the police.'

'On the contrary; it is French comedy of the best

type. Don't you agree, sir, that the police would be an inartistic error?' He was perfectly calm and collected, whereas they were in a pitiable state.

'Turn him out at once!' she cried. 'He has insulted your wife. Save me, save me!' She clung to her husband and wept. 'He was going—I had managed him—he would never have known——' Mr. Elliot repulsed her.

'If you don't feel inclined to start at once,' he said, with easy civility, 'let us have a little tea. My dear sir, do forgive me for not shooting you. *Nous avons changé tout cela.* Please don't look so nervous. Please do unclasp your hands——'

He was alone.

'That's all right,' he exclaimed, and strolled to the door. The hansom was disappearing round the corner. 'That's all right,' he repeated in more quavering tones as he returned to the drawing-room and saw that it was littered with sweet-peas. Their colour got on his nerves—magenta, crimson; magenta, crimson. He tried to pick them up, and they escaped. He trod them underfoot, and they multiplied and danced in the triumph of summer like a thousand butterflies. The train had left when he got to the station. He followed on to London, and there he lost all traces. At midnight he began to realize that his wife could never belong to him again.

Mr. Failing had a letter from Stockholm. It was never known what impulse sent him there. 'I am sorry about it all, but it was the only way.' The letter censured the law of England, 'which obliges us to behave like this, or else we should never get married. I shall come back to face things: she will not come back till she is my wife. He must bring an action soon, or else we shall try one against him. It

seems all very unconventional, but it is not really.
It is only a difficult start. We are not like you or
your wife: we want to be just ordinary people, and
make the farm pay, and not be noticed all our lives.'

And they were capable of living as they wanted.
The class difference, which so intrigued Mrs. Failing, meant very little to them. It was there, but so
were other things. They both cared for work and
living in the open, and for not speaking unless they
had got something to say. Their love of beauty, like
their love for each other, was not dependent on
detail: it grew not from the nerves but from the
soul.

I believe a leaf of grass is no less than the journey
     work of the stars,
And the pismire is equally perfect, and a grain of sand,
     and the egg of the wren,
And the tree toad is a chef-d'œuvre for the highest,
And the running blackberry would adorn the parlours
     of heaven.

They had never read these lines, and would have
thought them nonsense if they had. They did not
dissect—indeed they could not. But she, at all
events, divined that more than perfect health and
perfect weather, more than personal love, had gone
to the making of those seventeen days.

'Ordinary people!' cried Mrs. Failing on hearing
the letter. At that time she was young and daring.
'Why, they're divine! They're forces of Nature!
They're as ordinary as volcanoes. We all knew
my brother was disgusting, and wanted him to be
blown to pieces, but we never thought it would
happen. Do look at the thing bravely, and say, as
I do, that they are guiltless in the sight of God.'

'I think they are,' replied her husband. 'But they
are not guiltless in the sight of man.'

'You conventional!' she exclaimed in disgust.

'What they have done means misery not only for themselves but for others. For your brother, though you will not think of him. For the little boy—did you think of him? And perhaps for another child, who will have the whole world against him if it knows. They have sinned against society, and you do not diminish the misery by proving that society is bad or foolish. It is the saddest truth I have yet perceived that the Beloved Republic'—here she took up a book—'of which Swinburne speaks'—she put the book down—'will not be brought about by love alone. It will approach with no flourish of trumpets, and have no declaration of independence. Self-sacrifice and—worse still—self-mutilation are the things that sometimes help it most, and that is why we should start for Stockholm this evening.' He waited for her indignation to subside, and then continued. 'I don't know whether it can be hushed up. I don't yet know whether it ought to be hushed up. But we ought to provide the opportunity. There is no scandal yet. If we go, it is just possible there never will be any. We must talk over the whole thing and——'

'—And lie!' interrupted Mrs. Failing, who hated travel.

'—And see how to avoid the greatest unhappiness.'

There was to be no scandal. By the time they arrived Robert had been drowned. Mrs. Elliot described how they had gone swimming, and how, 'since he always lived inland,' the great waves had tired him. They had raced for the open sea.

'What are your plans?' he asked. 'I bring you a message from Frederick.'

'I heard him call,' she continued, 'but I thought

he was laughing. When I turned, it was too late. He put his hands behind his back and sank. For he would only have drowned me with him. I should have done the same.'

Mrs. Failing was thrilled, and kissed her. But Mr. Failing knew that life does not continue heroic for long, and he gave her the message from her husband: Would she come back to him?

To his intense astonishment—at first to his regret —she replied, 'I will think about it. If I loved him the very least bit I should say no. If I had anything to do with my life I should say no. But it is simply a question of beating time till I die. Nothing that is coming matters. I may as well sit in his drawing-room and dust his furniture, since he has suggested it.'

And Mr. Elliot, though he made certain stipulations, was positively glad to see her. People had begun to laugh at him, and to say that his wife had run away. She had not. She had been with his sister in Sweden. In a half-miraculous way the matter was hushed up. Even the Silts only scented 'something strange'. When Stephen was born, it was abroad. When he came to England, it was as the child of a friend of Mr. Failing's. Mrs. Elliot returned unsuspected to her husband.

But though things can be hushed up, there is no such thing as beating time; and as the years passed she realized her terrible mistake. When her lover sank, eluding her last embrace, she thought, as Agnes was to think after her, that her soul had sunk with him, and that never again should she be capable of earthly love. Nothing mattered. She might as well go and be useful to her husband and to the little boy who looked exactly like him, and who, she thought, was exactly like him in disposition. Then Stephen was born, and altered her life. She could still love people passionately; she still drew strength from the heroic past. Yet, to keep to her bond, she must see this son only as a stranger. She was protected by the conventions, and must pay them their fee. And a curious thing happened. Her second child drew her towards her first. She began to love Rickie also, to be more than useful to him. And as her love revived, so did her capacity for suffering. Life, more important, grew more bitter. She minded her husband more, not less; and when at last he died, and she saw a glorious autumn, beautiful with the voices of boys who should call her mother, the end came for her as well, before she could remember the grave in the alien north and the dust that would never return to the dear fields that had given it.

XXX

Stephen, the son of these people, had one instinct that troubled him. At night—especially out of doors—it seemed rather strange that he was alive. The dry grass pricked his cheek, the fields were invisible and mute, and here was he, throwing stones at the darkness or smoking a pipe. The stones vanished, the pipe would burn out. But he would be here in the morning when the sun rose, and he would bathe, and run in the mist. He was proud of his good circulation, and in the morning it seemed quite natural. But at night, why should there be this difference between him and the acres of land that cooled all round him until the sun returned? What lucky chance had heated him up, and sent him, warm and lovable, into a passive world? He had other instincts, but these gave him no trouble.

He simply gratified each as it occurred, provided he could do so without grave injury to his fellows. But the instinct to wonder at the night was not to be thus appeased.

At first he had lived under the care of Mr. Failing—the only person to whom his mother spoke freely, the only person who had treated her neither as a criminal nor as a pioneer. In their rare but intimate conversations she had asked him to educate her son. 'I will teach him Latin,' he answered. 'The rest such a boy must remember.' Latin, at all events, was a failure: who could attend to Virgil when the sound of the thresher arose, and you knew that the stack was decreasing and that rats rushed more plentifully each moment to their doom. But he was fond of Mr. Failing, and cried when he died. Mrs. Elliot, a pleasant woman, died soon after.

There was something fatal in the order of these deaths. Mr. Failing had made no provision for the boy in his will: his wife had promised to see to this. Then came Mr. Elliot's death, and, before the new home was created, the sudden death of Mrs. Elliot. She also left Stephen no money: she had none to leave. Chance threw him into the power of Mrs. Failing. 'Let things go on as they are,' she thought. 'I will take care of this pretty little boy, and the ugly little boy can live with the Silts. After my death, well, the papers will be found after my death, and they can meet them. I like the idea of their mutual ignorance. It is amusing.'

He was then twelve. With a few brief intervals of school, he lived in Wiltshire until he was driven out. Life had two distinct sides—the drawing-room and the other. In the drawing-room people talked a good deal, laughing as they talked. Being clever, they did not care for animals: one man had never seen a hedgehog. In the other life people talked and laughed separately, or even did neither. On the whole, in spite of the wet and gamekeepers, this life was preferable. He knew where he was. He glanced at the boy, or later at the man, and behaved accordingly. There was no law—the policeman was negligible. Nothing bound him but his own word, and he gave that sparingly.

It is impossible to be romantic when you have your heart's desire, and such a boy disappointed Mrs. Failing greatly. His parents had met for one brief embrace, had found one little interval between the power of the rulers of this world and the power of death. He was the child of poetry and of rebellion, and poetry should run in his veins. But he lived too near to the things he loved to seem poetical. Parted from them, he might yet satisfy her, and stretch out his hands with a pagan's yearning. As it was, he only rode her horses, and trespassed, and bathed, and worked, for no obvious reason, upon her fields. Affection she did not believe in, and made no attempt to mould him; and he, for his part, was very content to harden untouched into a man. His parents had given him excellent gifts—health, sturdy limbs, and a face not ugly,—gifts that his habits confirmed. They had also given him a cloudless spirit—the spirit of the seventeen days in which he was created. But they had not given him the spirit of their six years of waiting, and love for one person was never to be the greatest thing he knew.

'Philosophy' had postponed the quarrel between them. Incurious about his personal origin, he had a certain interest in our eternal problems. The interest never became a passion: it sprang out of his physical growth, and was soon merged in it again. Or, as he put it himself, 'I must get fixed up before starting.' He was soon fixed up as a materialist. Then he tore up the sixpenny reprints, and never amused Mrs. Failing so much again.

About the time he fixed himself up, he took to drink. He knew of no reason against it. The instinct was in him, and it hurt nobody. Here, as elsewhere, his motions were decided, and he passed at once from roaring jollity to silence. For those who live on the fuddled borderland, who crawl home by the railings and maunder repentance in the morning, he had a biting contempt. A man must take his tumble and his headache. He was, in fact, as little disgusting as is conceivable; and hitherto he had not strained his constitution or his will. Nor did he get drunk as often as Agnes suggested. The real quarrel gathered elsewhere.

Presentable people have run wild in their youth. But the hour comes when they turn from their boorish company to higher things. This hour never came for Stephen. Somewhat a bully by nature, he kept where his powers would tell, and continued to quarrel and play with the men he had known as boys. He prolonged their youth unduly. 'They won't settle down,' said Mr. Wilbraham to his wife. 'They're wanting things. It's the germ of a Trades Union. I shall get rid of a few of the worst.' Then Stephen rushed up to Mrs. Failing and worried her. 'It wasn't fair. So-and-so was a good sort. He did his work. Keen about it? No. Why should he be? Why should he be keen about somebody else's land? But keen enough. And very keen on football.' She laughed, and said a word about So-and-so to Mr. Wilbraham. Mr. Wilbraham blazed up. 'How could the farm go on without discipline? How could there be discipline if Mr. Stephen interfered?

Mr. Stephen liked power. He spoke to the men like one of themselves, and pretended it was all equality, but he took care to come out top. Natural, of course, that, being a gentleman he should. But not natural for a gentleman to loiter all day with poor people and learn their work, and put wrong notions into their heads, and carry their new-fangled grievances to Mrs. Failing. Which partly accounted for the deficit on the past year.' She rebuked Stephen. Then he lost his temper, was rude to her, and insulted Mr. Wilbraham.

The worst days of Mr. Failing's rule seemed to be returning. And Stephen had a practical experience, and also a taste for battle, that her husband had never possessed. He drew up a list of grievances, some absurd, others fundamental. No newspapers in the reading-room, you could put a plate under the Thompsons' door, no level cricket-pitch, no allotments, and no time to work in them, Mrs. Wilbraham's knife-boy underpaid. 'Aren't you a little unwise?' she asked coldly. 'I am more bored than you think over the farm.' She was wanting to correct the proofs of the book and re-write the prefatory memoir. In her irritation she wrote to Agnes. Agnes replied sympathetically, and Mrs. Failing, clever as she was, fell into the power of the younger woman. They discussed him at first as a wretch of a boy; then he got drunk and somehow it seemed more criminal. All that she needed now was a personal grievance, which Agnes casually supplied. Though vindictive, she was determined to treat him well, and thought with satisfaction of our distant colonies. But he burst into an odd passion: he would sooner starve than leave England. 'Why?' she asked. 'Are you in love?' He picked up a lump of the chalk—they were by the arbour—

and made no answer. The vicar murmured, 'It is not like going abroad—Greater Britain—blood is thicker than water——' A lump of chalk broke her drawing-room window on the Saturday.

Thus Stephen left Wiltshire, half-blackguard, half-martyr. Do not brand him as a socialist. He had no quarrel with society, nor any particular belief in people because they are poor. He only held the creed of 'here am I and there are you', and therefore class distinctions were trivial things to him, and life no decorous scheme, but a personal combat or a personal truce. For the same reason ancestry also was trivial, and a man not the dearer because the same woman was mother to them both. Yet it seemed worth while to go to Sawston with the news. Perhaps nothing would come of it; perhaps friendly intercourse, and a home while he looked around.

When they wronged him he walked quietly away. He never thought of allotting the blame nor of appealing to Ansell, who still sat brooding in the side-garden. He only knew that educated people could be horrible, and that a clean liver must never enter Dunwood House again. The air seemed stuffy. He spat in the gutter. Was it yesterday he had lain in the rifle-butts over Salisbury? Slightly aggrieved, he wondered why he was not back there now. 'I ought to have written first,' he reflected. 'Here is my money gone. I cannot move. The Elliotts have, as it were, practically robbed me.' That was the only grudge he retained against them. Their suspicions and insults were to him as the curses of a tramp whom he passed by the wayside. They were dirty people, not his sort. He summed up the complicated tragedy as a 'take in'.

While Rickie was being carried upstairs, and

while Ansell (had he known it) was dashing about the streets for him, he lay under a railway arch trying to settle his plans. He must pay back the friends who had given him shillings and clothes. He thought of Flea, whose Sundays he was spoiling— poor Flea, who ought to be in them now, shining before his girl. 'I daresay he'll be ashamed and not go to see her, and then she'll take the other man.' He was also very hungry. That worm Mrs. Elliot would be through her lunch by now. Tying his braces round him and tearing up those old wet documents, he stepped forth to make money. A villainous young brute he looked: his clothes were dirty, and he had lost the spring of the morning. Touching the walls, frowning, talking to himself at times, he slouched disconsolately northwards; no wonder that some tawdry girls screamed at him, or that matrons averted their eyes as they hurried to afternoon church. He wandered from one suburb to another, till he was among people more villainous than himself, who bought his tobacco from him and sold him food. Again the neighbourhood 'went up', and families, instead of sitting on their doorsteps, would sit behind thick muslin curtains. Again it would 'go down' into a more avowed despair. Far into the night he wandered, until he came to a solemn river majestic as a stream in hell. Therein were gathered the waters of Central England— those that flow off Hindhead, off the Chilterns, off Wiltshire north of the Plain. Therein they were made intolerable ere they reached the sea. But the waters he had known escaped. Their course lay southward into the Avon by forests and beautiful fields, even swift, even pure, until they mirrored the tower of Christchurch and greeted the ramparts of the Isle of Wight. Of these he thought for a

moment as he crossed the black river and entered
the heart of the modern world.

Here he found employment. He was not ham-
pered by genteel traditions, and, as it was near
quarter-day, managed to get taken on at a furniture warehouse. He moved people from the suburbs to London, from London to the suburbs, from
one suburb to another. His companions were hurried and querulous. In particular, he loathed the
foreman, a pious humbug who allowed no swear-
ing, but indulged in something far more degraded
—the Cockney repartee. The London intellect, so
pert and shallow, like a stream that never reaches
the ocean, disgusted him almost as much as the
London physique, which for all its dexterity is not
permanent, and seldom continues into the third
generation. His father, had he known it, had felt
the same; for between Mr. Elliot and the foreman
the gulf was social, not spiritual: both spent their
lives in trying to be clever. And Tony Failing had
once put the thing into words: 'There's no such
thing as a Londoner. He's only a country man on
the road to sterility.'

At the end of ten days he had saved scarcely anything. Once he passed the bank where a hundred
pounds lay ready for him, but it was still inconvenient for him to take them. Then duty sent him
to a suburb not very far from Sawston. In the evening a man who was driving a trap asked him to hold
it, and by mistake tipped him a sovereign. Stephen
called after him; but the man had a woman with
him and wanted to show off, and though he had
meant to tip a shilling, and could not afford that,
he shouted back that his sovereign was as good as
any one's, and that if Stephen did not think so he
could do various things and go to various places.

On the action of this man much depends. Stephen changed the sovereign into a postal order, and sent it off to the people at Cadford. It did not pay them back, but it paid them something, and he felt that his soul was free.

A few shillings remained in his pocket. They would have paid his fare towards Wiltshire, a good county; but what should he do there? Who would employ him? To-day the journey did not seem worth while. 'To-morrow, perhaps,' he thought, and determined to spend the money on pleasure of another kind. Twopence went for a ride on an electric tram. From the top he saw the sun descend —a disc with a dark red edge. The same sun was descending over Salisbury intolerably bright. Out of the golden haze the spire would be piercing, like a purple needle; then mists arose from the Avon and the other streams. Lamps flickered, but in the outer purity the villages were already slumbering. Salisbury is only a Gothic upstart beside these. For generations they have come down to her to buy or to worship, and have found in her the reasonable crisis of their lives; but generations before she was built they were clinging to the soil, and renewing it with sheep and dogs and men, who found the crisis of their lives upon Stonehenge. The blood of these men ran in Stephen; the vigour they had won for him was as yet untarnished; out on those downs they had united with rough women to make the thing he spoke of as 'himself'; the last of them had rescued a woman of a different kind from streets and houses such as these. As the sun descended he got off the tram with a smile of expectation. A public-house lay opposite, and a boy in a dirty uniform was already lighting its enormous lamp. His lips parted, and he went in.

Two hours later, when Rickie and Herbert were going the rounds, a brick came crashing at the study window. Herbert peered into the garden, and a hooligan slipped by him into the house, wrecked the hall, lurched up the stairs, fell against the banisters, balanced for a moment on his spine, and slid over. Herbert called for the police. Rickie, who was upon the landing, caught the man by the knees and saved his life.

'What is it?' cried Agnes, emerging.

'It's Stephen come back,' was the answer. 'Hullo, Stephen!'

XXXI

Hither had Rickie moved in ten days—from disgust to penitence, from penitence to longing, from a life of horror to a new life, in which he still surprised himself by unexpected words. Hullo, Stephen! For the son of his mother had come back, to forgive him, as she would have done, to live with him, as she had planned.

'He's drunk this time,' said Agnes wearily. She too had altered: the scandal was ageing her, and Ansell came to the house daily.

'Hullo, Stephen!'

But Stephen was now insensible.

'Stephen, you live here——'

'Good gracious me!' interposed Herbert. 'My advice is, that we all go to bed. The less said the better while our nerves are in this state. Very well, Rickie. Of course, Wonham sleeps the night if you wish.' They carried the drunken mass into the spare room. A mass of scandal it seemed to one of them, a symbol of redemption to the other. Neither acknowledged it a man, who would answer them back after a few hours' rest.

'Ansell thought he would never forgive me,' said Rickie. 'For once he's wrong.'

'Come to bed now, I think.' And as Rickie laid his hand on the sleeper's hair, he added, 'You won't do anything foolish, will you? You are still in a morbid state. Your poor mother—— Pardon me, dear boy; it is my turn to speak out. You thought it was your father, and minded. It is your mother. Surely you ought to mind more?'

'I have been too far back,' said Rickie gently. 'Ansell took me a journey that was even new to him. We got behind right and wrong, to a place where only one thing matters—that the Beloved should rise from the dead.'

'But you won't do anything rash?'

'Why should I?'

'Remember poor Agnes,' he stammered. 'I—I am the first to acknowledge that we might have pursued a different policy. But we are committed to it now. It makes no difference whose son he is. I mean, he is the same person. You and I and my sister stand or fall together. It was our agreement from the first. I hope—No more of these distressing scenes with her, there's a dear fellow. I assure you they make my heart bleed.'

'Things will quiet down now.'

'To bed now; I insist upon that much.'

'Very well,' said Rickie, and when they were in the passage, locked the door from the outside. 'We want no more muddles,' he explained.

Mr. Pembroke was left examining the hall. The bust of Hermes was broken. So was the pot of the palm. He could not go to bed without once more sounding Rickie. 'You'll do nothing rash,' he called.

'The notion of him living here was, of course, a passing impulse. We three have adopted a common policy.'

'Now, you go away!' called a voice that was almost flippant. 'I never did belong to that great sect whose doctrine is that each one should select —at least, I'm not going to belong to it any longer. Go away to bed.'

'A good night's rest is what you need,' threatened Herbert, and retired, not to find one for himself.

But Rickie slept. The guilt of months and the remorse of the last ten days had alike departed. He had thought that his life was poisoned, and lo! it was purified. He had cursed his mother, and Ansell had replied, 'You may be right, but you stand too near to settle. Step backwards. Pretend that it happened to me. Do you want me to curse my mother? Now, step forward and see whether anything has changed.' Something had changed. He had journeyed—as on rare occasions a man must—till he stood behind right and wrong. On the banks of the grey torrent of life, love is the only flower. A little way up the stream and a little way down had Rickie glanced, and he knew that she whom he loved had risen from the dead, and might rise again. 'Come away—let them die out—let them die out.' Surely that dream was a vision! To-night also he hurried to the window—to remember, with a smile, that Orion is not among the stars of June.

'Let me die out. She will continue,' he murmured, and in making plans for Stephen's happiness, fell asleep.

Next morning after breakfast he announced that his brother must live at Dunwood House. They were awed by the very moderation of his tone.

'There's nothing else to be done. Cadover's hopeless, and a boy of those tendencies can't go drifting. There is also the question of a profession for him, and his allowance.'

'We have to thank Mr. Ansell for this,' was all that Agnes could say; and 'I foresee disaster,' was the contribution of Herbert.

'There's plenty of money about,' Rickie continued. 'Quite a man's-worth too much. It has been one of our absurdities. Don't look so sad, Herbert. I'm sorry for you people, but he's sure to let us down easy.' For his experience of drunkards and of Stephen was small. He supposed that he had come without malice to renew the offer of ten days ago.

'It is the end of Dunwood House.'

Rickie nodded, and hoped not. Agnes, who was not looking well, began to cry. 'Oh, it is too bad,' she complained, 'when I've saved you from him all these years.' But he could not pity her, nor even sympathize with her wounded delicacy. The time for such nonsense was over. He would take his share of the blame: it was cant to assume it all.

Perhaps he was over-hard. He did not realize how large his share was, nor how his very virtues were to blame for her deterioration. 'If I had a girl, I'd keep her in line,' is not the remark of a fool nor of a cad. Rickie had not kept his wife in line. He had shown her all the workings of his soul, mistaking this for love; and in consequence she was the worse woman after two years of marriage, and he, on this morning of freedom, was harder upon her than he need have been.

The spare room bell rang. Herbert had a painful struggle between curiosity and duty, for the bell for chapel was ringing also, and he must go through the drizzle to school. He promised to come up in the interval. Rickie, who had rapped his head that Sunday on the edge of the table, was still forbidden to work. Before him a quiet morning lay. Secure of his victory, he took the portrait of their mother in his hand and walked leisurely upstairs. The bell continued to ring.

'See about his breakfast,' he called to Agnes, who replied, 'Very well.' The handle of the spare room door was moving slowly. 'I'm coming,' he cried. The handle was still. He unlocked and entered, his heart full of charity. But within stood a man who probably owned the world.

Rickie scarcely knew him; last night he had seemed so colourless, so negligible. In a few hours he had recaptured motion and passion and the imprint of the sunlight and the wind. He stood, not consciously heroic, with arms that dangled from broad stooping shoulders, and feet that played with a hassock on the carpet. But his hair was beautiful against the grey sky, and his eyes, recalling the sky unclouded, shot past the intruder as if to some worthier vision. So intent was their gaze that Rickie himself glanced backwards, only to see the neat passage and the banisters at the top of the stairs. Then the lips beat together twice, and out burst a torrent of amazing words.

'Add it all up, and let me know how much. I'd sooner have died. It never took me that way before. I must have broken pounds' worth. If you'll not tell the police, I promise you shan't lose, Mr. Elliot, I swear. But it may be months before I send it. Everything is to be new. You've not to be a penny out of pocket, do you see? Do let me go, this once again.'

'What's the trouble?' asked Rickie, as if they had been friends for years. 'My dear man, we've other things to talk about. Gracious me, what a fuss! If you'd smashed the whole house I wouldn't mind, so long as you came back.'

'I'd sooner have died,' gulped Stephen.

'You did nearly! It was I who caught you. Never mind yesterday's rag. What can you manage for breakfast?'

The face grew more angry and more puzzled. 'Yesterday wasn't a rag,' he said without focusing his eyes. 'I was drunk, but naturally meant it.'

'Meant what?'

'To smash you. Bad liquor did what Mrs. Elliot couldn't. I've put myself in the wrong. You've got me.'

It was a poor beginning.

'As I have got you,' said Rickie, controlling himself, 'I want to have a talk with you. There has been a ghastly mistake.'

But Stephen, with a countryman's persistency, continued on his own line. He meant to be civil, but Rickie went cold round the mouth. For he had not even been angry with them. Until he was drunk, they had been dirty people—not his sort. Then the trivial injury recurred, and he had reeled to smash them as he passed. 'And I will pay for everything,' was his refrain, with which the sighing of raindrops mingled. 'You shan't lose a penny, if only you let me free.'

'You'll pay for my coffin if you talk like that any longer! Will you, one, forgive my frightful behaviour; two, live with me?' For his only hope was in a cheerful precision.

Stephen grew more agitated. He thought it was some trick.

'I was saying I made an unspeakable mistake. Ansell put me right, but it was too late to find you.

Don't think I got off easily. Ansell doesn't spare one.
And you've got to forgive me, to share my life, to
share my money.—I've brought you this photograph—I want it to be the first thing you accept
from me—you have the greater right—I know all
the story now. You know who it is?'

'Oh yes; but I don't want to drag all that in.'

'It is only her wish if we live together. She was
planning it when she died.'

'I can't follow—because—to share your life?
Did you know I called here last Sunday week?'

'Yes. But then I only knew half. I thought you
were my father's son.'

Stephen's anger and bewilderment were increasing. He stuttered. 'What—what's the odds if you
did?'

'I hated my father,' said Rickie. 'I loved my
mother.' And never had the phrases seemed so
destitute of meaning.

'Last Sunday week,' interrupted Stephen, his
voice suddenly rising, 'I came to call on you. Not
as this or that's son. Not to fall on your neck. Nor
to live here. Nor—damn your dirty little mind!
I mean to say I didn't come for money. Sorry.
Sorry. I simply came as I was, and I haven't altered
since.'

'Yes—yet our mother—for me she has risen
from the dead since then—I know I was wrong——'

'And where do I come in?' He kicked the hassock.
'*I* haven't risen from the dead. *I* haven't altered
since last Sunday week. I'm——' He stuttered again.
He could not quite explain what it was. 'The man
towards Andover—after all, he was having principles. But you've——' His voice broke. 'I mind it
—I'm—*I* don't alter—blackguard one week—live
here the next—I keep to one or the other—you've

hurt something most badly in me that I didn't know was there.'

'Don't let us talk,' said Rickie. 'It gets worse every minute. Simply say you forgive me; shake hands, and have done with it.'

'That I won't. That I couldn't. In fact, I don't know what you mean.'

Then Rickie began a new appeal—not to pity, for now he was in no mood to whimper. For all its pathos, there was something heroic in this meeting. 'I warn you to stop here with me, Stephen. No one else in the world will look after you. As far as I know, you have never been really unhappy yet or suffered, as you should do, from your faults. Last night you nearly killed yourself with drink. Never mind why I'm willing to cure you. I am willing, and I warn you to give me the chance. Forgive me or not, as you choose. I care for other things more.'

Stephen looked at him at last, faintly approving. The offer was ridiculous, but it did treat him as a man.

'Let me tell you of a fault of mine, and how I was punished for it,' continued Rickie. 'Two years ago I behaved badly to you, up at the Rings. No, even a few days before that. We went for a ride, and I thought too much of other matters, and did not try to understand you. Then came the Rings, and in the evening, when you called up to me most kindly, I never answered. But the ride was the beginning. Ever since then I have taken the world at second-hand. I have bothered less and less to look it in the face—until not only you, but every one else has turned unreal. Never Ansell: he kept away, and somehow saved himself. But every one else. Do you remember in one of Tony Failing's books, "Cast bitter bread upon the waters, and after many days it really does come back to you"? This has been true of my life; it will be equally true of a drunkard's, and I warn you to stop with me.'

'I can't stop after that cheque,' said Stephen more gently. 'But I do remember the ride. I was a bit bored myself.'

Agnes, who had not been seeing to the breakfast, chose this moment to call from the passage. 'Of course he can't stop,' she exclaimed. 'For better or worse, it's settled. We've none of us altered since last Sunday week.'

'There you're right, Mrs. Elliot!' he shouted, starting out of the temperate past. 'We haven't altered.' With a rare flash of insight he turned on Rickie. 'I see your game. You don't care about *me* drinking, or to shake *my* hand. It's some one else you want to cure—as it were, that old photograph. You talk to me, but all the time you look at the photograph.' He snatched it up. 'I've my own idea of good manners, and to look friends between the eyes is one of them; and this'—he tore the photograph across—'and this'—he tore it again—'and these——' He flung the pieces at the man, who had sunk into a chair. 'For my part, I'm off.'

Then Rickie was heroic no longer. Turning round in his chair, he covered his face. The man was right. He did not love him, even as he had never hated him. In either passion he had degraded him to be a symbol for the vanished past. The man was right, and would have been lovable. He longed to be back riding over those windy fields, to be back in those mystic circles, beneath pure sky. Then they could have watched and helped and taught each other, until the word was a reality, and the past not a torn photograph, but Demeter the goddess rejoicing in the spring. Ah, if he had seized those high opportunities! For they led to the highest of all, the symbolic moment, which, if a man accepts, he has accepted life.

The voice of Agnes, which had lured him then ('For my sake,' she had whispered), pealed over him now in triumph. Abruptly it broke into sobs that had the effect of rain. He started up. The anger had died out of Stephen's face, not for a subtle reason but because here was a woman, near him, and unhappy.

She tried to apologize, and brought on a fresh burst of tears. Something had upset her. They heard her locking the door of her room. From that moment their intercourse was changed.

'Why does she keep crying to-day?' mused Rickie, as if he spoke to some mutual friend.

'I can make a guess,' said Stephen, and his heavy face flushed.

'Did you insult her?' he asked feebly.

'But who's Gerald?'

Rickie raised his hand to his mouth.

'She looked at me as if she knew me, and then gasps "Gerald", and started crying.'

'Gerald is the name of some one she once knew.'

'So I thought.' There was a long silence, in which they could hear a piteous gulping cough. 'Where is he now?' asked Stephen.

'Dead.'

'And then you——?'

Rickie nodded.

'Bad, this sort of thing.'

'I didn't know of this particular thing. She acted as if she had forgotten him. Perhaps she had, and you woke him up. There are queer tricks in the world. She is overstrained. She has probably been plotting ever since you burst in last night.'

'Against me?'

'Yes.'

Stephen stood irresolute. 'I suppose you and she pulled together?' he said at last.

'Get away from us, man! I mind losing you. Yet it's as well you don't stop.'

'Oh, *that's* out of the question,' said Stephen, brushing his cap.

'If you've guessed anything, I'd be obliged if you didn't mention it. I've no right to ask, but I'd be obliged.'

He nodded and walked slowly along the landing and down the stairs. Rickie accompanied him, and even opened the front door. It was as if Agnes had absorbed the passion out of both of them. The suburb was now wrapped in a cloud, not of its own making. Sigh after sigh passed along its streets to break against dripping walls. The school, the houses were hidden, and all civilization seemed in abeyance. Only the simplest sounds, the simplest desires emerged. They agreed that this weather was strange after such a sunset.

'That's a collie,' said Stephen, listening.

'I wish you'd have some breakfast before starting.'

'No food, thanks. But you know——' He paused. 'It's all been a muddle, and I've no objection to your coming along with me.'

The cloud descended lower.

'Come with me as a man,' said Stephen, already out in the mist. 'Not as a brother; who cares what people did years back? We're alive together, and the rest is cant. Here am I, Rickie, and there are you, a fair wreck. They've no use for you here,— never had any, if the truth was known,—and they've only made you beastly. This house, so to

speak, has the rot. It's common sense that you
should come.'

'Stephen, wait a minute. What do you mean?'

'Wait's what we won't do,' said Stephen at the
gate.

'I must ask——'

He did wait for a minute, and sobs were heard,
faint, hopeless, vindictive. Then he trudged away,
and Rickie soon lost his colour and his form. But
a voice persisted, saying, 'Come, I do mean it.
Come; I will take care of you, I can manage you.'

The words were kind; yet it was not for their sake
that Rickie plunged into the impalpable cloud. In
the voice he had found a surer guarantee. Habits
and sex may change with the new generation, features may alter with the play of a private passion,
but a voice is apart from these. It lies nearer to the
racial essence and perhaps to the divine; it can, at
all events, overleap one grave.

XXXII

Mr. Pembroke did not receive a clear account of
what had happened when he returned for the interval. His sister—he told her frankly—was concealing something from him. She could make no reply.
Had she gone mad, she wondered. Hitherto she had
pretended to love her husband. Why choose such
a moment for the truth?

'But I understand Rickie's position,' he told her.
'It is an unbalanced position, yet I understand it;
I noted its approach while he was ill. He imagines
himself his brother's keeper. Therefore we must
make concessions. We must negotiate.' The negotiations were still progressing in November, the
month during which this story draws to its close.

'I understand his position,' he then told her. 'It is both weak and defiant. He is still with those Ansells. Read this letter, which thanks me for his little stories. We sent them last month, you remember— such of them as we could find. It seems that he fills up his time by writing: he has already written a book.'

She only gave him half her attention, for a beautiful wreath had just arrived from the florist's. She was taking it up to the cemetery: to-day her child had been dead a year.

'On the other hand, he has altered his will. Fortunately, he cannot alter much. But I fear that what is not settled on you, will go. Should I read what I wrote on this point, and also my minutes of the interview with old Mr. Ansell, and the copy of my correspondence with Stephen Wonham?'

But her fly was announced. While he put the wreath in for her, she ran for a moment upstairs. A few tears had come to her eyes. A scandalous divorce would have been more bearable than this withdrawal. People asked, 'Why did her husband leave her?' and the answer came, 'Oh, nothing particular; he only couldn't stand her; she lied and taught him to lie; she kept him from the work that suited him, from his friends, from his brother,—in a word, she tried to run him, which a man won't pardon.' A few tears; not many. To her, life never showed itself as a classic drama, in which, by trying to advance our fortunes, we shatter them. She had turned Stephen out of Wiltshire, and he fell like a thunderbolt on Sawston and on herself. In trying to gain Mrs. Failing's money she had probably lost money which would have been her own. But irony is a subtle teacher, and she was not the woman to learn from such lessons as these. Her suffering was more direct. Three men had wronged her; therefore she hated them, and, if she could, would do them harm.

'These negotiations are quite useless,' she told Herbert when she came downstairs. 'We had much better bide our time. Tell me just about Stephen Wonham, though.'

He drew her into the study again. 'Wonham is or was in Scotland, learning to farm with connections of the Ansells: I believe the money is to go towards setting him up. Apparently he is a hard worker. He also drinks!'

She nodded and smiled. 'More than he did?'

'My informant, Mr. Tilliard—oh, I ought not to have mentioned him. He is one of the better sort of Rickie's Cambridge friends, and has been dreadfully grieved at the collapse, but he does not want to be mixed up in it. This autumn he was up in the Lowlands, close by, and very kindly made a few unobtrusive inquiries for me. The man is becoming an habitual drunkard.'

She smiled again. Stephen had evoked her secret, and she hated him more for that than for anything else that he had done. The poise of his shoulders that morning—it was no more—had recalled Gerald. If only she had not been so tired! He had reminded her of the greatest thing she had known, and to her cloudy mind this seemed degradation. She had turned to him as to her lover; with a look, which a man of his type understood, she had asked for his pity; for one terrible moment she had desired to be held in his arms. Even Herbert was surprised when she said, 'I'm glad he drinks. I hope he'll kill himself. A man like that ought never to have been born.'

'Perhaps the sins of the parents are visited on the

children,' said Herbert, taking her to the carriage.
'Yet it is not for us to decide.'

'I feel sure he will be punished. What right has
he——' She broke off. What right had he to our
common humanity? It was a hard lesson for any
one to learn. For Agnes it was impossible. Stephen
was illicit, abnormal, worse than a man diseased.
Yet she had turned to him: he had drawn out the
truth.

'My dear, don't cry,' said her brother, drawing up
the windows. 'I have great hopes of Mr. Tilliard—
the Silts have written—Mrs. Failing will do what
she can——'

As she drove to the cemetery, her bitterness
turned against Ansell, who had kept her husband
alive in the days after Stephen's expulsion. If he
had not been there, Rickie would have renounced
his mother and his brother and all the outer world,
troubling no one. The mystic, inherent in him,
would have prevailed. So Ansell himself had told
her. And Ansell, too, had sheltered the fugitives
and given them money, and saved them from the
ludicrous checks that so often stop young men. But
when she reached the cemetery, and stood beside
the tiny grave, all her bitterness, all her hatred were
turned against Rickie.

'But he'll come back in the end,' she thought.
'A wife has only to wait. What are his friends beside
me? They too will marry. I have only to wait. His
book, like all that he has done, will fail. His brother
is drinking himself away. Poor aimless Rickie! I
have only to keep civil. He will come back in the
end.'

She had moved, and found herself close to the
grave of Gerald. The flowers she had planted after
his death were dead, and she had not liked to renew

them. There lay the athlete, and his dust was as the little child's whom she had brought into the world with such hope, with such pain.

XXXIII

That same day Rickie, feeling neither poor nor aimless, left the Ansells' for a night's visit to Cadover. His aunt had invited him—why, he could not think, nor could he think why he should refuse the invitation. She could not annoy him now, and he was not vindictive. In the dell near Madingley he had cried, 'I hate no one,' in his ignorance. Now, with full knowledge, he hated no one again. The weather was pleasant, the country attractive, and he was ready for a little change.

Maud and Stewart saw him off. Stephen, who was down for a holiday, had been left with his chin on the luncheon-table. He had wanted to come to Cadover also. Rickie pointed out that you cannot visit where you have broken the windows. There was an argument—there generally was—and now the young man had turned sulky.

'Let him do what he likes,' said Ansell. 'He knows more than we do. He knows everything.'

'Is he to get drunk?' Rickie asked.

'Most certainly.'

'And to go where he isn't asked?'

Maud, though liking a little spirit in a man, declared this to be impossible.

'Well, I wish you joy!' Rickie called, as the train moved away. 'He means mischief this evening. He told me piously that he felt it beating up. Good-bye!'

'But we'll wait for you to pass,' they cried. For

the Salisbury train always backed out of the
station and then returned, and the Ansell family,
including Stewart, took an incredible pleasure in
seeing it do this.

The carriage was empty. Rickie settled himself
down for his little journey. First he looked at the
coloured photographs. Then he read the directions
for obtaining luncheon-baskets, and felt the texture
of the cushions. Through the windows a signal-box
interested him. Then he saw the ugly little town
that was now his home, and up its chief street the
Ansells' memorable façade. The spirit of a genial
comedy dwelt there. It was so absurd, so kindly.
The house was divided against itself and yet stood.
Metaphysics, commerce, social aspirations—all
lived together in harmony. Mr. Ansell had done
much, but one was tempted to believe in a more
capricious power—the power that abstains from
'nipping'. 'One nips or is nipped, and never knows
beforehand,' quoted Rickie, and opened the poems
of Shelley, a man less foolish than you supposed.
How pleasant it was to read! If business worried
him, if Stephen was noisy or Ansell perverse there
still remained this paradise of books. It seemed as
if he had read nothing for two years.

Then the train stopped for the shunting, and he
heard protests from minor officials who were working on the line. They complained that some one
who didn't ought to, had mounted on the footboard
of the carriage. Stephen's face appeared, convulsed
with laughter. With the action of a swimmer he
dived in through the open window, and fell comfortably on Rickie's luggage and Rickie. He declared it was the finest joke ever known. Rickie was
not so sure. 'You'll be run over next,' he said. 'What
did you do that for?'

'I'm coming with you,' he giggled, rolling all that he could on to the dusty floor.

'Now, Stephen, this is too bad. Get up. We went into the whole question yesterday.'

'I know; and I settled we wouldn't go into it again, spoiling my holiday.'

'Well, it's execrable taste.'

Now he was waving to the Ansells, and showing them a piece of soap: it was all his luggage, and even that he abandoned, for he flung it at Stewart's lofty brow.

'I can't think what you've done it for. You know how strongly I felt.'

Stephen replied that he should stop in the village; meet Rickie at the lodge gates; that kind of thing.

'It's execrable taste,' he repeated, trying to keep grave.

'Well, you did all you could,' he exclaimed with sudden sympathy. 'Leaving me talking to old Ansell, you might have thought you'd got your way. I've as much taste as most chaps, but, hang it! your aunt isn't the German Emperor. She doesn't own Wiltshire.'

'You ass!' sputtered Rickie, who had taken to laugh at nonsense again.

'No, she isn't,' he repeated, blowing a kiss out of the window to maidens. 'Why, we started for Wiltshire on the wet morning!'

'When Stewart found us at Sawston railway station?' He smiled happily. 'I never thought we should pull through.'

'Well, we *didn't*. We never did what we meant. It's nonsense that I couldn't have managed you alone. I've a notion. Slip out after your dinner this evening, and we'll get thundering tight together.'

'I've a notion I won't.'

'It'd do you no end of good. You'll get to know people—shepherds, carters—' He waved his arms vaguely, indicating democracy. 'Then you'll sing.'

'And then?'

'Plop.'

'Precisely.'

'But I'll catch you,' promised Stephen. 'We shall carry you up the hill to bed. In the morning you wake, have your row with old Em'ly, she kicks you out, we meet—we'll meet at the Rings!' He danced up and down the carriage. Some one in the next carriage punched at the partition, and when this happens, all lads of mettle know that they must punch the partition back.

'Thank you. I've a notion I won't,' said Rickie when the noise subsided—subsided for a moment only, for the following conversation took place to an accompaniment of dust and bangs. 'Except as regards the Rings. We will meet there.'

'Then I'll get tight by myself.'

'No, you won't.'

'Yes, I will. I swore to do something special this evening. I feel like it.'

'In that case, I get out at the next station.' He was laughing, but quite determined. Stephen had grown too dictatorial of late. The Ansells spoilt him. 'It's bad enough having you there at all. Having you there drunk is impossible. I'd sooner not visit my aunt than think, when I sat with her, that you're down in the village teaching her labourers to be as beastly as yourself. Go if you will. But not with me.'

'Why shouldn't I have a good time while I'm young, if I don't harm any one?' said Stephen defiantly.

'Need we discuss it again? Because you harm yourself.'

'Oh, I can stop myself any minute I choose. I just say "I won't" to you or any other fool, and I don't.'

Rickie knew that the boast was true. He continued, 'There is also a thing called Morality. You may learn in the Bible, and also from the Greeks, that your body is a temple.'

'So you said in your longest letter.'

'Probably I wrote like a prig, for the reason that I have never been tempted in this way; but surely it is wrong that your body should escape you.'

'I don't follow,' he retorted, punching.

'It isn't right, even for a little time, to forget that you exist.'

'I suppose you've never been tempted to go to sleep?'

Just then the train passed through a coppice in which the grey undergrowth looked no more alive than firewood. Yet every twig in it was waiting for the spring. Rickie knew that the analogy was false, but argument confused him, and he gave up this line of attack also.

'Do be more careful over life. If your body escapes you in one thing, why not in more? A man will have other temptations.'

'You mean women,' said Stephen quietly, pausing for a moment in his game. 'But that's absolutely different. That would be harming some one else.'

'Is that the only thing that keeps you straight?'

'What else should?' And he looked not into Rickie, but past him, with the wondering eyes of a child. Rickie nodded, and referred himself to the window.

He observed that the country was smoother and

more plastic. The woods had gone, and under a
pale-blue sky long contours of earth were flowing,
merging, rising a little to bear some coronal of
beeches, parting a little to disclose some green
valley, where cottages stood under elms or beside
translucent waters. It was Wiltshire at last. The
train had entered the chalk. At last it slackened at
a wayside platform. Without speaking he opened
the door.

'What's that for?'

'To go back.'

Stephen had forgotten the threat. He said that
this was not playing the game.

'Surely!'

'I can't have you going back.'

'Promise to behave decently then.'

He was seized and pulled away from the door.

'We change at Salisbury,' he remarked. 'There is
an hour to wait. You will find me troublesome.'

'It isn't fair,' exploded Stephen. 'It's a low-down
trick. How can I let you go back?'

'Promise, then.'

'Oh, yes, yes, yes, yes. Y.M.C.A. But for this occasion
only.'

'No, no. For the rest of your holiday.'

'Yes, yes. Very well. I promise.'

'For the rest of your life?'

Somehow it pleased him that Stephen should
bang him crossly with his elbow and say, 'No. Get
out. You've gone too far.' So had the train. The
porter at the end of the wayside platform slammed
the door, and they proceeded towards Salisbury
through the slowly modulating downs. Rickie pretended to read. Over the book he watched his
brother's face, and wondered how bad temper
could be consistent with a mind so radiant. In spite

of his obstinacy and conceit, Stephen was an easy person to live with. He never fidgeted or nursed hidden grievances, or indulged in a shoddy pride. Though he spent Rickie's money as slowly as he could, he asked for it without apology: 'You must put it down against me,' he would say. In time—it was still very vague—he would rent or purchase a farm. There is no formula in which we may sum up decent people. So Ansell had preached, and had of course proceeded to offer a formula: 'They must be serious, they must be truthful.' Serious not in the sense of glum; but they must be convinced that our life is a state of some importance, and our earth not a place to beat time on. Of so much Stephen was convinced: he showed it in his work, in his play, in his self-respect, and above all—though the fact is hard to face—in his sacred passion for alcohol. Drink, to-day, is an unlovely thing. Between us and the heights of Cithæron the river of sin now flows. Yet the cries still call from the mountain, and granted a man has responded to them, it is better to respond with the candour of the Greek.

'I shall stop at the Thompsons' now,' said the disappointed reveller. 'Prayers.'

Rickie did not press his triumph, but it was a happy moment, partly because of the triumph, partly because he was sure that his brother must care for him. Stephen was too selfish to give up any pleasure without grave reasons. He was certain that he had been right to disentangle himself from Sawston, and to ignore the threats and tears that still tempted him to return. Here there was real work for him to do. Moreover, though he sought no reward, it had come. His health was better, his brain sound, his life washed clean, not by the waters of sentiment, but by the efforts of a fellow-man.

Stephen was man first, brother afterwards. Herein lay his brutality and also his virtue. 'Look me in the face. Don't hang on me clothes that don't belong— as you did on your wife, giving her saint's robes, whereas she was simply a woman of her own sort, who needed careful watching. Tear up the photographs. Here am I, and there are you. The rest is cant.' The rest was not cant, and perhaps Stephen would confess as much in time. But Rickie needed a tonic, and a man, not a brother, must hold it to his lips.

'I see the old spire,' he called, and then added, 'I don't mind seeing it again.'

'No one does, as far as I know. People have come from the other side of the world to see it again.'

'Pious people. But I don't hold with bishops.' He was young enough to be uneasy. The cathedral, a fount of superstition, must find no place in his life. At the age of twenty he had settled things. 'I've got my own philosophy,' he once told Ansell, 'and I don't care a straw about yours.' Ansell's mirth had annoyed him not a little. And it was strange that one so settled should feel his heart leap up at the sight of an old spire. 'I regard it as a public building,' he told Rickie, who agreed. 'It's useful, too, as a landmark.' His attitude to-day was defensive. It was part of a subtle change that Rickie had noted in him since his return from Scotland. His face gave hints of a new maturity. 'You can see the old spire from the Ridgeway,' he said, suddenly laying a hand on Rickie's knee, 'before rain as clearly as any telegraph post.'

'How far is the Ridgeway?'

'Seventeen miles.'

'Which direction?'

'North, naturally. North again from that you see Devizes, the vale of Pewsey, and the other towns. Also towards Bath. It is something of a view. You ought to get on the Ridgeway.'

'I shouldn't have time for that.'

'Or Beacon Hill. Or let's do Stonehenge.'

'If it's fine, I suggest the Rings.'

'It will be fine.' Then he murmured the names of villages.

'I wish you could live here,' said Rickie kindly. 'I believe you love these particular acres more than the whole world.'

Stephen replied that this was not the case: he was only used to them. He wished they were driving out, instead of waiting for the Cadchurch train.

They had advanced into Salisbury, and the cathedral, a public building, was grey against a tender sky. Rickie suggested that, while waiting for the train, they should visit it. He spoke of the incomparable north porch.

'I've never been inside it, and I never will. Sorry to shock you, Rickie, but I must tell you plainly. I'm an atheist. I don't believe in anything.'

'I do,' said Rickie.

'When a man dies, it's as if he's never been,' he asserted. The train drew up in Salisbury station. Here a little incident took place which caused them to alter their plans.

They found outside the station a trap driven by a small boy, who had come in from Cadford to fetch some wire-netting. 'That'll do us,' said Stephen, and called to the boy, 'If I pay your railway-ticket back, and if I give you sixpence as well, will you let us drive back in the trap?' The boy said no. 'It will be all right,' said Rickie. 'I am Mrs.

Failing's nephew.' The boy shook his head. 'And you know Mr. Wonham?' The boy couldn't say he didn't. 'Then what's your objection? Why? What is it? Why not?' But Stephen leant against the time-tables and spoke of other matters.

Presently the boy said, 'Did you say you'd pay my railway-ticket back, Mr. Wonham?'

'Yes,' said a bystander. 'Didn't you hear him?'

'I heard him right enough.'

Now Stephen laid his hand on the splash-board, saying, 'What I want, though, is this trap here of yours, see, to drive in back myself'; and as he spoke the bystander followed him in canon, 'What he wants, though, is that there trap of yours, see, to drive hisself back in.'

'I've no objection,' said the boy, as if deeply offended. For a time he sat motionless, and then got down, remarking, 'I won't rob you of your sixpence.'

'Silly little fool,' snapped Rickie, as they drove through the town.

Stephen looked surprised. 'What's wrong with the boy? He had to think it over. No one had asked him to do such a thing before. Next time he'd let us have the trap quick enough.'

'Not if he had driven in for a cabbage instead of wire-netting.'

'He never would drive in for a cabbage.'

Rickie shuffled his feet. But his irritation passed. He saw that the little incident had been a quiet challenge to the civilization that he had known. 'Organize', 'Systematize', 'Fill up every moment', 'Induce *esprit de corps*'. He reviewed the watch-words of the last two years, and found that they ignored personal contest, personal truces, personal love. By following them Sawston School had lost its quiet usefulness and become a frothy sea, wherein plunged Dunwood House, that unnecessary ship. Humbled, he turned to Stephen and said, 'No, you're right. Nothing is wrong with the boy. He was honestly thinking it out.' But Stephen had forgotten the incident, or else he was not inclined to talk about it. His assertive fit was over.

The direct road from Salisbury to Cadover is extremely dull. The city—which God intended to keep by the river; did she not move there, being thirsty, in the reign of William Rufus?—the city has strayed out of her own plain, climbed up her slopes, and tumbled over them in ugly cataracts of brick. The cataracts are still short, and doubtless they meet or create some commercial need. But instead of looking towards the cathedral, as all the city should, they look outwards at a pagan entrenchment, as the city should not. They neglect the poise of the earth, and the sentiments she has decreed. They are the modern spirit.

Through them the road descends into an unobtrusive country where, nevertheless, the power of the earth grows stronger. Streams do divide. Distances do still exist. It is easier to know the men in your valley than those who live in the next, across a waste of down. It is easier to know men well. The country is not paradise, and can show the vices that grieve a good man everywhere. But there is room in it, and leisure.

'I suppose,' said Rickie as the twilight fell, 'this kind of thing is going on all over England.' Perhaps he meant that towns are after all excrescences, grey fluxions, where men, hurrying to find one another, have lost themselves. But he got no response, and expected none. Turning round in his seat, he watched the winter sun slide out of a quiet sky.

The horizon was primrose, and the earth against it gave momentary hints of purple. All faded: no pageant would conclude the gracious day, and when he turned eastward the night was already established.

'Those verlands——' said Stephen, scarcely above his breath.

'What are verlands?'

He pointed at the dusk, and said, 'Our name for a kind of field.' Then he drove his whip into its socket, and seemed to swallow something. Rickie, straining his eyes for verlands, could only see a tumbling wilderness of brown.

'Are there many local words?'

'There have been.'

'I suppose they die out.'

The conversation turned curiously. In the tone of one who replies, he said, 'I expect that some time or other I shall marry.'

'I expect you will,' said Rickie, and wondered a little why the reply seemed not abrupt. 'Would we see the Rings in the daytime from here?'

'(We do see them.) But Mrs. Failing once said no decent woman would have me.'

'Did you agree to that?'

'Drive a little, will you?'

The horse went slowly forward into the wilderness, that turned from brown to black. Then a luminous glimmer surrounded them, and the air grew cooler: the road was descending between parapets of chalk.

'But, Rickie, mightn't I find a girl—naturally not refined—and be happy with her in my own way? I would tell her straight I was nothing much—faithful, of course, but that she should never have all my thoughts. Out of no disrespect to her, but because all one's thoughts can't belong to any single person.'

While he spoke even the road vanished, and invisible water came gurgling through the wheel-spokes. The horse had chosen the ford.

'You can't own people. At least a fellow can't. It may be different for a poet. (Let the horse drink.) And I want to marry some one, and don't yet know who she is, which a poet again will tell you is disgusting. Does it disgust you? Being nothing much, surely I'd better go gently. For it's something rather outside that makes one marry, if you follow me: not exactly oneself. (Don't hurry the horse.) We want to marry, and yet—I can't explain. I fancy I'll go wading: this is our stream.'

Romantic love is greater than this. There are men and women—we know it from history—who have been born into the world for each other, and for no one else, who have accomplished the longest journey locked in each other's arms. But romantic love is also the code of modern morals, and, for this reason, popular. Eternal union, eternal ownership—these are tempting baits for the average man. He swallows them, will not confess his mistake, and—perhaps to cover it—cries 'dirty cynic' at such a man as Stephen.

Rickie watched the black earth unite to the black sky. But the sky overhead grew clearer, and in it twinkled the Plough and the central stars. He thought of his brother's future and of his own past, and of how much truth might lie in that antithesis of Ansell's: 'A man wants to love mankind, a woman wants to love one man.' At all events, he and his wife had illustrated it, and perhaps the conflict, so tragic in their own case, was elsewhere the salt of the world. Meanwhile Stephen called from the water for matches: there was some trick with paper which Mr. Failing had showed him, and which he would show Rickie now, instead of talking non-sense. Bending down, he illumined the dimpled surface of the ford, 'Quite a current,' he said, and his face flickered out in the darkness. 'Yes, give me the loose paper, quick! Crumple it into a ball.'

Rickie obeyed, though intent on the transfigured face. He believed that a new spirit dwelt there, expelling the crudities of youth. He saw steadier eyes, and the sign of manhood set like a bar of gold upon steadier lips. Some faces are knit by beauty, or by intellect, or by a great passion: had Stephen's waited for the touch of the years?

But they played as boys who continued the non-sense of the railway carriage. The paper caught fire from the match, and spread into a rose of flame. 'Now gently with me,' said Stephen, and they laid it flower-like on the stream. Gravel and tremulous weeds leapt into sight, and then the flower sailed into deep water, and up leapt the two arches of a bridge. 'It'll strike!' they cried; 'no, it won't; it's chosen the left,' and one arch became a fairy tunnel, dropping diamonds. Then it vanished for Rickie; but Stephen, who knelt in the water, declared that it was still afloat, far through the arch, burning as if it would burn for ever.

XXXIV

The carriage that Mrs. Failing had sent to meet her nephew returned from Cadchurch station empty. She was preparing for a solitary dinner when he somehow arrived, full of apologies, but more sedate than she had expected. She cut his explanations short. 'Never mind how you got here. You are here, and I am quite pleased to see you.' He changed his clothes and they proceeded to the dining-room.

There was a bright fire, but the curtains were not drawn. Mr. Failing had believed that windows with the night behind are more beautiful than any pictures, and his widow had kept to the custom. It was brave of her to persevere, lumps of chalk having come out of the night last June. For some obscure reason—not so obscure to Rickie—she had preserved them as mementoes of an episode. Seeing them in a row on the mantelpiece, he expected that their first topic would be Stephen. But they never mentioned him, though he was latent in all that they said.

It was of Mr. Failing that they spoke. The Essays had been a success. She was really pleased. The book was brought in at her request, and between the courses she read it aloud to her nephew, in her soft yet unsympathetic voice. Then she sent for the Press notices—after all no one despises them—and read their comments on her introduction. She wielded a graceful pen, was apt, adequate, suggestive, indispensable, unnecessary. So the meal passed pleasantly away, for no one could so well combine the formal with the unconventional, and it only seemed charming when papers littered her stately table.

'My man wrote very nicely,' she observed. 'Now, you read me something out of him that you like. Read "The True Patriot".'

He took the book and found: 'Let us love one another. Let our children, physical and spiritual, love one another. It is all that we can do. Perhaps the earth will neglect our love. Perhaps she will confirm it, and suffer some rallying-point, spire, mound, for the new generations to cherish.'

'He wrote that when he was young. Later on he doubted whether we had better love one another, or whether the earth will confirm anything. He died a most unhappy man.'

He could not help saying, 'Not knowing that the earth had confirmed him.'

'Has she? It is quite possible. We meet so seldom in these days, she and I. Do you see much of the earth?'

'A little.'

'Do you expect that she will confirm you?'

'It is quite possible.'

'Beware of her, Rickie, I think.'

'I think not.'

'Beware of her, surely. Going back to her really is going back—throwing away the artificiality which (though you young people won't confess it) is the only good thing in life. Don't pretend you are simple. Once I pretended. Don't pretend that you care for anything but for clever talk such as this, and for books.'

'The talk,' said Leighton afterwards, 'certainly was clever. But it meant something all the same.' He heard no more, for his mistress told him to retire.

'And my nephew, this being so, make up your quarrel with your wife.' She stretched out her hand to him with real feeling. 'It is easier now than it will be later. Poor lady, she has written to me foolishly and often, but, on the whole, I side with her against you. She would grant you all that you fought for— all the people, all the theories. I have it, in her writing, that she will never interfere with your life again.'

'She cannot help interfering,' said Rickie, with his eyes on the black windows. 'She despises me. Besides, I do not love her.'

'I know, my dear. Nor she you. I am not being sentimental. I say once more, beware of the earth. We are conventional people, and conventions—if you will but see it—are majestic in their way, and will claim us in the end. We do not live for great passions or for great memories or for anything great.'

He threw up his head. 'We do.'

'Now listen to me. I am serious and friendly to-night, as you must have observed. I have asked you here partly to amuse myself—you belong to my March Past—but also to give you good advice. There has been a volcano—a phenomenon which I too once greatly admired. The eruption is over. Let the conventions do their work now, and clear the rubbish away. My age is fifty-nine, and I tell you solemnly that the important things in life are little things, and that people are not important at all. Go back to your wife.'

He looked at her, and was filled with pity. He knew that he would never be frightened of her again. Only because she was serious and friendly did he trouble himself to reply. 'There is one little fact I should like to tell you, as confuting your theory. The idea of a story—a long story—had been in my head for a year. As a dream to amuse myself—the kind of amusement you would recommend for the future. I should have had time to write it, but the people round me coloured my life, and so it never seemed worth while. For the story is not likely to pay. Then came the volcano. A few days after it was over I lay in bed looking out upon the world of rubbish. Two men I know—one intel-

lectual, the other very much the reverse—burst
into the room. They said, "What happened to your
short stories? They weren't good, but where are
they? Why have you stopped writing? Why haven't
you been to Italy? You *must* write. You *must* go.
Because to write, to go, is you." Well, I have written, and yesterday we sent the long story out on
its rounds. The men do not like it, for different
reasons. But it mattered very much to them that
I should write it, and so it got written. As I told you,
this is only one fact; other facts, I trust, have happened in the last five months. But I mention it to
prove that people are important, and therefore,
however much it inconveniences my wife, I will
not go back to her.'

'And Italy?' asked Mrs. Failing.

This question he avoided. Italy must wait. Now
that he had the time, he had not the money.

'Or what is the long story about, then?'

'About a man and a woman who meet and are
happy.'

'Somewhat of a *tour de force*, I conclude.'

He frowned. 'In literature we needn't intrude
our own limitations. I'm not so silly as to think that
all marriages turn out like mine. My character is to
blame for our catastrophe, not marriage.'

'My dear, I too have married; marriage is to
blame.'

But here again he seemed to know better.

'Well,' she said, leaving the table and moving
with her dessert to the mantelpiece, 'so you are
abandoning marriage and taking to literature. And
are you happy?'

'Yes.'

'Why?'

'Because, as we used to say at Cambridge, the

cow is there. The world is real again. This is a room, that a window, outside is the night——'

'Go on.'

He pointed to the floor. 'The day is straight below, shining through other windows into other rooms.'

'You are very odd,' she said after a pause, 'and I do not like you at all. There you sit, eating my biscuits, and all the time you know that the earth is round. Who taught you? I am going to bed now, and all the night, you tell me, you and I and the biscuits go plunging eastwards, until we reach the sun. But breakfast will be at nine as usual. Good night.'

She rang the bell twice, and her maid came with her candle and her walking-stick: it was her habit of late to go to her room as soon as dinner was over, for she had no one to sit up with. Rickie was impressed by her loneliness, and also by the mixture in her of insight and obtuseness. She was so quick, so clear-headed, so imaginative even. But all the same, she had forgotten what people were like. Finding life dull, she had dropped lies into it, as a chemist drops a new element into a solution, hoping that life would thereby sparkle or turn some beautiful colour. She loved to mislead others, and in the end her private view of false and true was obscured, and she misled herself. How she must have enjoyed their errors over Stephen! But her own error had been greater, inasmuch as it was spiritual entirely.

Leighton came in with some coffee. Feeling it unnecessary to light the drawing-room lamp for one small young man, he persuaded Rickie to say he preferred the dining-room. So Rickie sat down by the fire playing with one of the lumps of chalk.

His thoughts went back to the ford, from which they had scarcely wandered. Still he heard the horse in the dark drinking, still he saw the mystic rose, and the tunnel dropping diamonds. He had driven away alone, believing the earth had confirmed him. He stood behind things at last, and knew that conventions are not majestic, and that they will not claim us in the end.

As he mused, the chalk slipped from his fingers, and fell on the coffee-cup, which broke. The china, said Leighton, was expensive. He believed it was impossible to match it now. Each cup was different. It was a harlequin set. The saucer, without the cup, was therefore useless. Would Mr. Elliot please explain to Mrs. Failing how it happened.

Rickie promised he would explain.

He had left Stephen preparing to bathe, and had heard him working up-stream like an animal, splashing in the shallows, breathing heavily as he swam the pools; at times reeds snapped, or clods of earth were pulled in. By the fire he remembered it was again November. 'Should you like a walk?' he asked Leighton, and told him who stopped in the village to-night. Leighton was pleased. At nine o'clock the two young men left the house, under a sky that was still only bright in the zenith. 'It will rain to-morrow,' Leighton said.

'My brother says, fine to-morrow.'

'Fine to-morrow,' Leighton echoed.

'Now which do you mean?' asked Rickie, laughing.

Since the plumes of the fir-trees touched over the drive, only a very little light penetrated. It was clearer outside the lodge gate, and bubbles of air, which seemed to have travelled from an immense distance, broke gently and separately on his face.

They paused on the bridge. He asked whether the little fish and the bright green weeds were here now as well as in the summer. The footman had not noticed. Over the bridge they came to the crossroads, of which one led to Salisbury and the other up through the string of villages to the railway station. The road in front was only the Roman road, the one that went on to the downs. Turning to the left, they were in Cadover.

'He will be with the Thompsons,' said Rickie, looking up at dark eaves. 'Perhaps he's in bed already.'

'Perhaps he will be at The Antelope.'

'No. To-night he is with the Thompsons.'

'With the Thompsons.' After a dozen paces he said, 'The Thompsons have gone away.'

'Where? Why?'

'They were turned out by Mr. Wilbraham on account of our broken windows.'

'Are you sure?'

'Five families were turned out.'

'That's bad for Stephen,' said Rickie, after a pause. 'He was looking forward—oh, it's monstrous in any case!'

'But the Thompsons have gone to London,' said Leighton. 'Why, that family—they say it's been in the valley hundreds of years, and never got beyond shepherding. To various parts of London.'

'Let us try The Antelope then.'

'Let us try The Antelope.'

The inn lay up in the village. Rickie hastened his pace. This tyranny was monstrous. Some men of the age of undergraduates had broken windows, and therefore they and their families were to be ruined. The fools who govern us find it easier to be severe. It saves them trouble to say, 'The innocent must suffer with the guilty.' It even gives them a thrill of pride. Against all this wicked nonsense, against the Wilbrahams and Pembrokes who try to rule our world Stephen would fight till he died. Stephen was a hero. He was a law to himself, and rightly. He was great enough to despise our small moralities. He was attaining love. This evening Rickie caught Ansell's enthusiasm, and felt it worth while to sacrifice everything for such a man.

'The Antelope,' said Leighton. 'Those lights under the greatest elm.'

'Would you please ask if he's there, and if he'd come for a turn with me. I don't think I'll go in.'

Leighton opened the door. They saw a little room, blue with tobacco-smoke. Flanking the fire were deep settles, hiding all but the legs of the men who lounged in them. Between the settles stood a table, covered with mugs and glasses. The scene was picturesque—fairer than the cut-glass palaces of the town.

'Oh yes, he's there,' he called, and after a moment's hesitation came out.

'Would he come?'

'No. I shouldn't say so,' replied Leighton, with a furtive glance. He knew that Rickie was a milksop. 'First night, you know, sir, among old friends.'

'Yes, I know,' said Rickie. 'But he might like a turn down the village. It looks stuffy inside there, and poor fun probably to watch others drinking.'

Leighton shut the door.

'What was that he called after you?'

'Oh, nothing. A man when he's drunk—he says the worst he's ever heard. At least, so they say.'

'A man when he's drunk?'

'Yes, sir.'

'But Stephen isn't drinking?'

'No, no.'

'He couldn't be. If he broke a promise—I don't pretend he's a saint. I don't want him one. But it isn't in him to break a promise.'

'Yes, sir; I understand.'

'In the train he promised me not to drink—nothing theatrical: just a promise for these few days.'

'No, sir.'

'"No, sir,"' stamped Rickie. '"Yes! no! yes!" Can't you speak out? Is he drunk or isn't he?'

Leighton justly exasperated cried, 'He can't stand, and I've told you so again and again.'

'Stephen!' shouted Rickie, darting up the steps. Heat and the smell of beer awaited him, and he spoke more furiously than he had intended. 'Is there any one here who's sober?' he cried. The landlord looked over the bar angrily, and asked him what he meant. He pointed to the deep settles. 'Inside there he's drunk. Tell him he's broken his word, and I will not go with him to the Rings.'

'Very well. You won't go with him to the Rings,' said the landlord, stepping forward and slamming the door in his face.

In the room he was only angry, but out in the cool air he remembered that Stephen was a law to himself. He had chosen to break his word, and would break it again. Nothing else bound him. To yield to temptation is not fatal for most of us. But it was the end of everything for a hero.

'He's suddenly ruined!' he cried, not yet remembering himself. For a little he stood by the elm-tree, clutching the ridges of its bark. Even so would he wrestle to-morrow, and Stephen, imperturbable, reply, 'My body is my own.' Or worse still, he might wrestle with a pliant Stephen who promised him glibly again. While he prayed for a miracle to convert his brother, it struck him that he must pray for himself. For he, too, was ruined.

'Why, what's the matter?' asked Leighton. 'Stephen's only being with friends. Mr. Elliot, sir, don't break down. Nothing's happened bad. No one's died yet, or even hurt themselves.' Ever kind, he took hold of Rickie's arm, and, pitying such a nervous fellow, set out with him for home. The shoulders of Orion rose behind them over the top-most boughs of the elm. From the bridge the whole constellation was visible and Rickie said, 'May God receive me and pardon me for trusting the earth.'

'But, Mr. Elliot, what have you done that's wrong?'

'Gone bankrupt, Leighton, for the second time. Pretended again that people were real. May God have mercy on me!'

Leighton dropped his arm. Though he did not understand, a chill of disgust passed over him, and he said, 'I will go back to The Antelope. I will help them put Stephen to bed.'

'Do. I will wait for you here.' Then he leant against the parapet and prayed passionately, for he knew that the conventions would claim him soon. God was beyond them, but ah, how far beyond, and to be reached after what degradation! At the end of this childish detour his wife awaited him, not less surely because she was only his wife in name. He was too weak. Books and friends were not enough. Little by little she would claim him and corrupt him and make him what he had been; and the woman he loved would die out, in drunkenness, in debauchery, and her strength would be dissipated by a man, her beauty defiled in a man. She would not continue. That mystic rose and the face it illumined meant nothing. The stream—he was above it now—meant nothing, though it burst from the pure turf and ran for ever to the sea. The bather, the shoulders of Orion—they all meant nothing, and were going nowhere. The whole affair was a ridiculous dream.

Leighton returned, saying, 'Haven't you seen Stephen? They say he followed us: he can still walk: I told you he wasn't so bad.'

'I don't think he passed me. Ought one to look?' He wandered a little along the Roman road. Again nothing mattered. At the level-crossing he leant on the gate to watch a slow goods train pass. In the glare of the engine he saw that his brother had come this way, perhaps through some sodden memory of the Rings, and now lay drunk over the rails. Wearily he did a man's duty. There was time to raise him up and push him into safety. It is also a man's duty to save his own life, and therefore he tried. The train went over his knees. He died up in Cadover, whispering, 'You have been right,' to Mrs. Failing.

She wrote of him to Mrs. Lewin afterwards as 'one who has failed in all he undertook; one of the thousands whose dust returns to the dust, accomplishing nothing in the interval. Agnes and I buried him to the sound of our cracked bell, and pretended that he had once been alive. The other, who was always honest, kept away.'

XXXV

From the window they looked over a sober valley, whose sides were not too sloping to be ploughed, and whose trend was followed by a grass-grown track. It was late on Saturday afternoon, and the valley was deserted except for one labourer, who was coasting slowly downward on a rusty bicycle. The air was very quiet. A jay screamed up in the woods behind, but the ring-doves, who roost early, were already silent. Since the window opened westward, the room was flooded with light, and Stephen, finding it hot, was working in his shirt-sleeves.

'You guarantee they'll sell?' he asked, with a pen between his teeth. He was tidying up a pile of manuscripts.

'I guarantee that the world will be the gainer,' said Mr. Pembroke, now a clergyman, who sat beside him at the table with an expression of refined disapproval on his face.

'I'd got the idea that the long story had its points, but that these shorter things didn't—what's the word?'

'"Convince" is probably the word you want. But that type of criticism is quite a thing of the past. Have you seen the illustrated American edition?'

'I don't remember.'

'Might I send you a copy? I think you ought to possess one.'

'Thank you.' His eye wandered. The bicycle had disappeared into some trees, and thither, through a cloudless sky, the sun was also descending.

'Is all quite plain?' said Mr. Pembroke. 'Submit these ten stories to the magazines, and make your own terms with the editors. Then—I have your word for it—you will join forces with me; and the four stories in my possession, together with yours, should make up a volume, which we might well call "Pan Pipes".'

'Are you sure "Pan Pipes" haven't been used up already?'

Mr. Pembroke clenched his teeth. He had been bearing with this sort of thing for nearly an hour. 'If that is the case, we can select another. A title is easy to come by. But that is the idea it must suggest. The stories, as I have twice explained to you, all centre round a Nature theme. Pan, being the god of——'

'I know that,' said Stephen impatiently.

'——Being the god of——'

'All right. Let's get furrard. I've learnt that.'

It was years since the schoolmaster had been interrupted, and he could not stand it. 'Very well,' he said. 'I bow to your superior knowledge of the classics. Let us proceed.'

'Oh yes—the introduction. There must be one. It was the introduction with all those wrong details that sold the other book.'

'You overwhelm me. I never penned the memoir with that intention.'

'If you won't do one, Mrs. Keynes must!'

'My sister leads a busy life. I could not ask her. I will do it myself since you insist.'

'And the binding?'

'The binding,' said Mr. Pembroke coldly, 'must really be left to the discretion of the publisher. We cannot be concerned with such details. Our task is purely literary.' His attention wandered. He began to fidget, and finally bent down and looked under the table. 'What have we here?' he asked.

Stephen looked also, and for a moment they smiled at each other over the prostrate figure of a child, who was cuddling Mr. Pembroke's boots. 'She's after the blacking,' he explained. 'If we left her there, she'd lick them brown.'

'Indeed. Is that so very safe?'

'It never did me any harm. Come up! Your tongue's dirty.'

'Can I——' She was understood to ask whether she could clean her tongue on a lollie.

'No, no!' said Mr. Pembroke. 'Lollipops don't clean little girls' tongues.'

'Yes, they do,' he retorted. 'But she won't get one.' He lifted her on his knee, and rasped her tongue with his handkerchief.

'Dear little thing,' said the visitor perfunctorily. The child began to squall, and kicked her father in the stomach. Stephen regarded her quietly. 'You tried to hurt me,' he said. 'Hurting doesn't count. Trying to hurt counts. Go and clean your tongue yourself. Get off my knee.' Tears of another sort came into her eyes, but she obeyed him. 'How's the great Bertie?' he asked.

'Thank you. My nephew is perfectly well. How came you to hear of his existence?'

'Through the Silts, of course. It isn't five miles to Cadover.'

Mr. Pembroke raised his eyes mournfully. 'I cannot conceive how the poor Silts go on in that great house. Whatever she intended, it could not have been that. The house, the farm, the money,—everything down to the personal articles that belong to Mr. Failing, and should have reverted to his family——!'

'It's legal. Intestate succession.'

'I do not dispute it. But it is a lesson to one to make a will. Mrs. Keynes and myself were electrified.'

'They'll do there. They offered me the agency, but——' He looked down the cultivated slopes. His manners were growing rough, for he saw few gentlemen now, and he was either incoherent or else alarmingly direct. 'However, if Lawrie Silt's a Cockney like his father, and if my next is a boy and like me——' A shy beautiful look came into his eyes, and passed unnoticed. 'They'll do,' he repeated. 'They've turned out Wilbraham and built new cottages, and bridged the railway, and made other necessary alterations.' There was a moment's silence.

Mr. Pembroke took out his watch. 'I wonder if I might have the trap? I mustn't miss my train, must I? It is good of you to have granted me an interview. It is all quite plain?'

'Yes.'

'A case of half and half—division of profits.'

'Half and half?' said the young farmer slowly. 'What do you take me for? Half and half when I provide ten of the stories and you only four?'

'I—I——' stammered Mr. Pembroke.

'I consider you did me over the long story, and I'm damned if you do me over the short ones!'

'Hush! if you please, hush!—if only for your little girl's sake.' He lifted a clerical palm.

'You did me,' his voice drove, 'and all the Thirty-nine Articles won't stop me saying so. That long story was meant to be mine. I got it written. You've done me out of every penny it fetched. It's dedicated to me—flat out—and you even crossed out the dedication and tidied me out of the introduction. Listen to me, Pembroke. You've done people all your life—I think without knowing it, but that won't comfort us. A wretched devil at your school once wrote to me, and he'd been done. Sham food, sham religion, sham straight talks—and when he broke down, you said it was the world in miniature.' He snatched at him roughly. 'But I'll show you the world.' He twisted him round like a baby, and through the open door they saw only the quiet valley, but in it a rivulet that would in time bring its waters to the sea. 'Look even at that—and up behind where the Plain begins and you get on the solid chalk—think of us riding some night when you're ordering your hot bottle—that's the world, and there's no miniature world. There's one world, Pembroke, and you can't tidy men out of it. They answer you back—do you hear?—they answer back if you do them. If you tell a man this way that four sheep equal ten, he answers back you're a liar.'

Mr. Pembroke was speechless, and—such is human nature—he chiefly resented the allusion to the hot bottle; an unmanly luxury in which he never indulged; contenting himself with night-socks. 'Enough—there is no witness present—as you had doubtless observed.' But there was. For a little voice cried, 'Oh, mummy, they're fighting—such fun——' and feet went pattering up the stairs. 'Enough. You talk of "doing", but what about the money out of which you "did" my sister? What about this picture'—he pointed to a faded photograph of Stockholm—'which you caused to be filched from the walls of my house? What about—enough! Let us conclude this disheartening scene. You object to my terms. Name yours. I shall accept them. It is futile to reason with one who is the worse for drink.'

Stephen was quiet at once. 'Steady on!' he said gently. 'Steady on in that direction. Take one-third for your four stories and the introduction, and I will keep two-thirds for myself.' Then he went to harness the horse, while Mr. Pembroke, watching his broad back, desired to bury a knife in it. The desire passed, partly because it was unclerical, partly because he had no knife, and partly because he soon blurred over what had happened. To him all criticism was 'rudeness': he never heeded it, for he never needed it: he was never wrong. All his life he had ordered little human beings about, and now he was equally magisterial to big ones: Stephen was a fifth-form lout whom, owing to some flaw in the regulations, he could not send up to the headmaster to be caned.

This attitude makes for tranquillity. Before long he felt merely an injured martyr. His brain cleared. He stood deep in thought before the only other picture that the bare room boasted—the Demeter of Cnidus. Outside the sun was sinking, and its last rays fell upon the immortal features and the shattered knees. Sweet-peas offered their fragrance, and with it there entered those more mysterious scents that come from no one flower or clod of earth, but from the whole bosom of evening. He tried not to be cynical. But in his heart he could not regret that tragedy, already half-forgotten, conventionalized, indistinct. Of course death is a terrible thing. Yet death is merciful when it weeds out a failure. If we look deep enough it is all for the best. He stared at the picture and nodded.

Stephen, who had met his visitor at the station, had intended to drive him back there. But after their spurt of temper he sent him with the boy. He remained in the doorway, glad that he was going to make money, glad that he had been angry; while the glow of the clear sky deepened and the silence was perfected, and the scents of the night grew stronger. Old vagrancies awoke, and he resolved that, dearly as he loved his house, he would not enter it again till dawn. 'Good night!' he called, and then the child came running, and he whispered, 'Quick, then! Bring me a rug. Good night,' he repeated, and a pleasant voice called through an upper window, 'Why good night?' He did not answer till the child was wrapped up in his arms.

'It is time that she learnt to sleep out,' he cried. 'If you want me, we're out on the hillside, where I used to be.'

The voice protested, saying this and that.

'Stewart's in the house,' said the man, 'and it cannot matter, and I am going anyway.'

'Stephen, I wish you wouldn't. I wish you wouldn't take her. Promise you won't say foolish things to her. Don't—I wish you'd come up for a minute——'

The child, whose face was laid against his, felt the muscles in it harden.

'Don't tell her foolish things about yourself— things that aren't any longer true. Don't worry her with old dead dreadfulnesses. To please me— don't.'

'Just to-night I won't, then.'

'Stevie, dear, please me more—don't take her with you.'

At this he laughed impertinently. 'I suppose I'm being kept in line,' she called, and, though he could not see her, she stretched her arms towards him. For a time he stood motionless, under her window, musing on his happy tangible life. Then his breath quickened, and he wondered why he was here, and why he should hold a warm child in his arms. 'It's time we were starting,' he whispered, and showed the sky, whose orange was already fading into green. 'Wish everything good night.'

'Good night, dear mummy,' she said sleepily. 'Good night, dear house. Good night, you pictures —long picture—stone lady. I see you through the window—your faces are pink.'

The twilight descended. He rested his lips on her hair, and carried her, without speaking, until he reached the open down. He had often slept there himself, alone, and on his wedding-night, and he knew that the turf was dry, and that if you laid your face to it you would smell the thyme. For a moment the earth aroused her, and she began to chatter. 'My prayers——' she said anxiously. He gave her one hand, and she was asleep before her fingers had nestled in its palm. Their touch made him pensive, and again he marvelled why he, the accident, was here. He was alive and had created life. By whose authority? Though he could not phrase it, he believed that he guided the future of our race, and that, century after century, his thoughts and his passions would triumph in England. The dead who had evoked him, the unborn whom he would evoke—he governed the paths between them. By whose authority?

Out in the west lay Cadover and the fields of his earlier youth, and over them descended the crescent moon. His eyes followed her decline, and against her final radiance he saw, or thought he saw, the outline of the Rings. He had always been grateful, as people who understood him knew. But this evening his gratitude seemed a gift of small account. The ear was deaf, and what thanks of his could reach it? The body was dust, and in what ecstasy of his could it share? The spirit had fled, in agony and loneliness, never to know that it bequeathed him salvation.

He filled his pipe, and then sat pressing the unlit tobacco with his thumb. 'What am I to do?' he thought. 'Can he notice the things he gave me? A parson would know. But what's a man like me to do, who works all his life out of doors?' As he wondered, the silence of the night was broken. The whistle of Mr. Pembroke's train came faintly, and a lurid spot passed over the land—passed, and the silence returned. One thing remained that a man of his sort might do. He bent down reverently and saluted the child; to whom he had given the name of their mother.

PRINTED IN GREAT BRITAIN
AT THE UNIVERSITY PRESS, OXFORD
BY VIVIAN RIDLER
PRINTER TO THE UNIVERSITY